HEIRS OF FLAME AND FROST

A "GAME OF GODS" NOVEL

E. M. LEANDER

For my family

1. The Arena
2. Tavern
3. Dorms
4. Stables
5. School
6. Earth Mages
7. Water Mages
8. Fire Mages
9. Wind Mages
10. Temple
11. Main Gate
    inscription 'LUCEAT LUX VESTRA'
    ('Let your light shine')
12. Library
13. Baths
14. Dining Hall

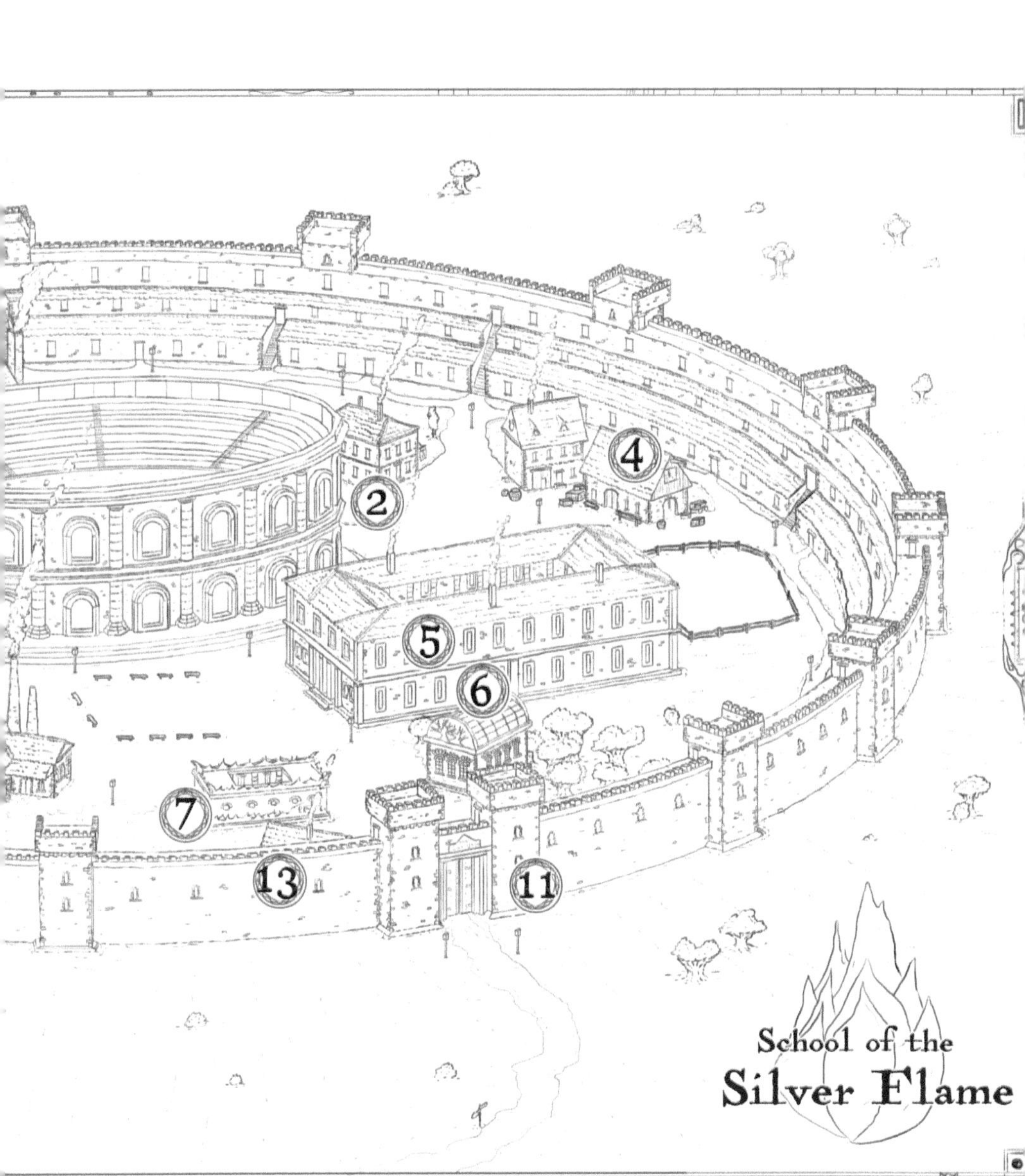
2
4
5
6
7
13
11
School of the
Silver Flame

Polar Ice
The Vault
Abelon Wastes
Abelon City
N
W
S
The Broken Sea
Crescent Islands
Basti
As commissioned by His Majesty
King Leonidas II

Temple of Aenon
The Iron Needle
Soltaire
Chanet Forest
Roallac
Raverra
The Black Strait
Ocron
Estana
Golmere River
School of the Silver Flame
The Isles
Aclimes
Spit

N
W
E
S
Roallac
Estana
School of the
Silver Flame
The Isles
Aclimes
Spit
As commissioned by His Royal Highness
King Leonidas II

First edition

ISBN Hardback: 979-8-9904666-1-6
ISBN Paperback: 979-8-9904666-3-0
ISBN E-book: 979-8-9904666-2-3

Editing by Ben Gibson and Leonora Stewart

Dust jacket artwork and chapter headings by Lizbe Coetzee

Cover designs by E. M. Leander

Map Illustration by Foreign Worlds Cartography
(https://foreignworlds.net/)

TRIGGER WARNINGS

Self-harm, attempted sexual assault, violence (sword fights, wounds), gaslighting, PTSD, cursing, closed-door sexual scenes

PROLOGUE

"You're up late," Aris says, breaking Wren's concentration. She lets the letter she's reading fall forward onto her lap and rolls out the kinks that have accumulated in her neck.

"Night Mage," she reminds him with a tired smile. "I thought you were going to bed."

"I had a little visitor," he says, a crooked smile on his handsome face. "She insisted on another bedtime story. She wanted to hear about Caelus and his golden swords again."

Aris circles the small library in the Temple of the God of Night, Caladrius, their home since the Battle of Soltaire. It's a cozy room, lined with books and lit by a magic fire that never burns out. Aris moves behind Wren's chair, lifting her long braid out of the way so he can massage her shoulders. The white streak runs through it like a ribbon; where it meets the skin at her temple, a black scar branches out across her cheek. External marks of the toll that magic has taken on her body.

"Mmm," she says, leaning back into his calloused hands. Here in the temple, the two of them have healed physically and emotionally after the battle with the genocidal god of water. While Wren's marks are easily visible, Aris's are more subtle and don't mar the sculpted physique he prides himself on. She can still see his pain, though, in the long moments when he stares into the distance, when his nightmares steal his rest, when he scowls at his gladiuses like he wants to throw them off the mountain.

Aris clears his throat and leans forward to see what Wren was reading.

"Another letter from Ismini?" he asks.

Wren's eyes flutter open, and she manages an "mm-hmm" of agreement.

"Anything new?" Aris asks.

Wren sighs and unrolls the letter from her first teacher, her surrogate mother, her friend.

Dear Wren,

The situation is becoming more dire. The Water Mages have determined that Aenon's interference has done something to the tides, changed the cool water off our eastern coast and brought up a warm current from the south. With it, I'm afraid, come waves of the insects that carry the plague. While we've been able to identify the vector, we are no closer to a cure. Victims continue to mount. Some of the smaller towns, especially along the coast, have nearly been wiped out. We've dispatched every healer we can spare, but it's not enough.

I've never seen King Leonidas so worn out, not even when he first came back from Soltaire. Queen Orothea does what she can, of course, but she's been preoccupied with the triplets (who remain blessedly healthy).

I spend what time I can between the library and the greenhouse. I'm convinced we can find a cure for this plague, one that doesn't depend on burning out our healers. We have to.

I know you still hear from Caladrius in your dreams—can you see if he can talk to Cephus? The god of earth may know of a way we can beat this sickness. I've tried every combination of healing herbs and plants that I can think of. If the king hadn't been so quick to hide the Books of Bronze, Silver, and Gold away after Soltaire, I'd ask Cephus myself. We may even have to consult Aenon, as he's the patron god of healers; let us exhaust all other options first. I can't imagine he'll be in a forgiving or generous mood after Soltaire.

I pray that you and that Shield of yours remain healthy. Give him Aleka's love, and send any updates as soon as you can. The realm may depend on it.

All my love,
Ismini

CHAPTER 1

"Hi! I'm Koralia Remidi, but you can call me Kora—and in two years, you're going to choose me in the games."

I blink, for a moment stunned at the audacity of the girl who's standing in my way. She's extended her hand, and when I finally take it, she shakes it firmly, as if sealing our fates.

"I'm Delphine," I say.

"I know," Kora says, falling into step beside me. She's even shorter than me, with long strawberry-blond hair and a heart-shaped face. She is already wearing a tan Mage robe with a red stripe at the cuffs and hem. Fire Mage, then. She's the only one who's dared to approach me, so I am begrudgingly impressed.

I look past her, glancing about the gray stone courtyard. I see the Earth Mages with their green stripes, yellow for Wind Mages, and blue for Water Mages. The Mages who have already graduated wear a solid-color robe—like Wren, in her black robe. The rest of the new Shield and Mage students in the courtyard turn to look at us as we pass, but no one says anything, so I don't either. I keep my focus on my horse, and on Kora as she tells me about her family—all strong Fire Mages, apparently. The other students who rode with me from

Estana have already moved on, glad to be away from me. Well, good riddance. I didn't bother to learn their names, anyway.

It's hard to believe I'm finally here, that I finally get to start my Shield training in earnest. For the past four years, I've had one-on-one tutelage from Aris Valorius, the mightiest Shield of our generation—according to him, and, fine, a lot of other people too. It's time to put what I've learned to the test, to prove to the whole world I'm as good as he says I am. To prove I'm more than just a symbol of errant magic, that I'm more than just my shifted form.

"Come on," Kora says, nodding toward what looks to be the stables. "Let's put up your horse, and I'll help you take your things to your room."

"I can do it myself, thanks," I say, but she comes along anyway.

"I know you can," she says cheerily. "Shields are strong. We all know that. Doesn't mean you have to do it alone, and what kind of friend would I be if I let you wander around by yourself on your first day?"

I arch an eyebrow. She just nods, like the decision has been made.

"We're going to be best friends. I can already tell. For now, I'll settle for tour guide. Come on!"

"Best friends?" I ask, struggling to keep up with her chirpy conversation.

"Yep," she says, and she grabs my horse's reins from my hand. She heads toward the stables—not quite walking, more like bouncing along. "Come on, bestie!"

I've never had a best friend before—or any friends, really. Not unless I count Uncle Tekton, and now Wren, Aris, and a few others. Who, honestly, are more like family. But finding people my own age to talk to when I was growing up?

It was rarer than being a dragon shifter.

We stable the horse I borrowed in Estana and unload my bags. I don't have much—just some clothes and small weapons. Kora grabs one of the bags before I can protest—she's pushy, but she's growing on me. Especially when everyone else so far either whispers when I pass or shrinks away from me, like they're afraid I'm going to breathe fire at them.

Whatever. Despite what Kora thinks, I'm not here to make friends. I'm here to prove to everyone that *I'm* the best Shield, dragon shifter or not, and when I win the Shield games in two years, the whole world will know it.

"I don't want to sound like I'm bragging, but I'll be the strongest Fire Mage in our year. I'm a Fire Mage; you're a dragon—we'd make sense, don't you think?"

"Sure," I say, hoisting my bag of weapons over my back. I follow her on a path between a long two-story building of gray stone and the arena to my right.

The School of the Silver Flame is not pretty. The building on my left has no adornments other than structural fluted columns and a small, plain pediment over the entrance.

To my right is a massive coliseum, with arched openings between pillars bigger around than I am tall. As we pass an entrance, I look down the long stone corridor and catch a glimpse of the sandy arena. I'll become intimately acquainted with the arena—and probably the sandy floor too—over the next two years of my training. Shields are forged in that arena. Lives are changed. The games are held there at the beginning of every fall, after the new classes come in, and I can't wait to see them.

There's a murmur of voices and a clamor up ahead. Kora and I exchange a glance and head around the end of the academic building to the main courtyard. The courtyard was quiet when I entered—who could possibly warrant more attention than *me*?

Entering through the massive gate of the school are five horses with riders. At the head of the small group is a Shield I don't recognize, on one of Ocron's prized warhorses, a massive beast with white feathering on his feet.

The Shield rides past us, straight to the stables without stopping, like he's glad to be away from his charges.

The other four riders seem much less sure of themselves and

cluster together, to the point where their fine horses are jostling against each other and tossing their heads. They don't have much luggage, and their clothing is plain.

"Black Water Witches," one of the ungifted groundskeepers behind me says, spitting on the ground after, like the words leave a bad taste in his mouth.

I've heard rumors that some of the Water Mages from Roallac—well, the island formerly known as Roallac, as I guess we're calling it all Ocron now—would be coming to the school. King Leonidas has been true to his word and is doing his best to integrate our cultures.

After two years, I'll graduate and compete in the Shield games to earn the right to claim a Mage, in a binding magical contract that will strengthen us both, a tradition as old as time, but Roallacan Water Mages don't have Shields. They claim they are strong enough without the bond, but we all know that really, Rigrasil's magic doesn't extend to their continent, and they just don't have any Shields in the first place. It's one of the things their Snake Queen was pissed about, when I rescued Aunt Wren from her clutches. Then Wren went a little mad too, when the god of night funneled his magic into her across the veil between the realms—and then Wren killed the Roallacan queen. My teenage years have been a little atypical, to say the least. Since then, Roallac has been a part of Ocron, though not everyone in Ocron is happy about it.

Judging from the looks on the Roallacan Mages' faces, they aren't too pleased about it either.

And judging from the looks on the faces of the rest of the people in the courtyard, neither is anyone else here.

I look over the four students, all Water Mages around my own age of eighteen. There are two men and two women, and I'm sure we're all memorizing their faces so we can actively avoid them for the next two years. One of the men is tall and pale as moonstone, with black hair, and the one pressed closest to him is shorter, with round glasses. He has dark hair too, though his is messier, and he's a little more tan, like he's slithered out into the sun once or twice in his life. The two women might be twins—both with long dark hair, dark eyes, and olive-toned skin. They're pretty, but look ... cold. Frigid even. In fact, none of the Roallacan students are smiling. They could all be carved from stone or ice, for all the expression they show.

"Welcome!" a voice booms across the courtyard.

I turn to see Iraklis, Head Mage of Ocron and headmaster of the School of the Silver Flame, coming from the academic building, which we've just passed, his arms outstretched, green robe flapping. He's sun-browned and freckled, with a smile as wide as the sky, in harsh contrast to the solemn, black-clad students before us.

The tall boy nods to the other three, and they dismount in unison. The others follow him to Iraklis, who firmly shakes their hands. The crowd forms a rough ring around them, Kora and I included.

"We're so pleased to have you with us," Iraklis says, his voice warm and welcoming. "Come, we'll stable your horses, and I'll show you around."

"That won't be necessary," another man says, pushing through the crowd. He's tall too, and thin, and wearing the solid blue robe of a full Water Mage, not the tan one of a student.

"He's one of the Water Mage teachers," Kora whispers to me.

"Head Mage," the man says formally, giving Iraklis a small bow. "I'd be honored to show my countrymen around."

Iraklis looks back at the tall student, who nods almost imperceptibly.

"Very well, Mage Caius. Once you're done, please bring them to my office. I'd like to speak to them personally before classes start."

"Of course, Head Mage," the man says. His dark hair is very long and slicked back, like he just got done swimming, though no water drips from it.

Then he does the strangest thing—he turns to the tall, moonstone-pale student and bows at the waist, significantly farther than he did to Iraklis.

The difference is not lost on anyone watching—and there are a lot of us now crowded into the main courtyard to gawk.

"Your Highness," Caius says.

An audible gasp goes up from the crowd. Kora nudges me with her elbow.

"*That's* Prince Reyn? The heir of Roallac?" she says, looking the pale man over. "He's better looking than I thought."

He might be easy on the eye, with a face as beautiful—and expressive—as if it were sculpted from marble, but my heart plummets to my feet at hearing his name.

Prince Reyn stiffens at the affectation, and his companions shuffle awkwardly.

"Just 'Reyn' now," he says, so quietly I almost don't hear it.

I cross my arms. I've heard we might have Roallacan magic students, but *royal* ones? Well, formerly royal, anyway. *Ugh.* We stole his legacy, his crown, his country—and judging by the look of him, stern and serious, he's not the forgiving type. This should make the next two years interesting.

Not that I care what he thinks. His queen imprisoned and tortured Aris, Wren, Rafael, Remiel, and King Leonidas ... and he was her heir? I bet he is just as cruel. My hands clench at the thought.

"My mistake," Caius says, though judging by his tone, I'd say it was absolutely deliberate.

I roll my eyes. *Great. Let's stir up trouble. I'm ready for it.*

Caius signals one of the ungifted grooms to take Reyn's horse and then gestures for the Roallacan students to follow them to the stables.

Kora grips my elbow tightly, bouncing on the balls of her feet, eager to get a look at them as they pass by. The motion attracts the attention of the fallen prince, and he looks sharply at her. Then he stops, his breath halting.

And he turns to look at me with eyes as dark as obsidian.

Caius stops too, uncertain, looking between us.

"I'm sorry. Do you know this girl, Prince Reyn?"

"Just 'Reyn,'" he says again, absently, not looking at the Mage. His eyes are fixed on me instead, unblinking, his face a carefully composed mask—so I glare right back. I have nothing to say to him.

Dragons do not deal with snakes.

"The Dragon Girl of Ocron," Reyn says, the sound like acid dripping from his tongue as he stares at me.

"The Fallen Prince of Roallac," I spit back to mask my anxiety, in a tone just as acerbic.

This close, I can see that his eyes aren't black, like his hair, but rather green, dark at the edges and nearly emerald in the center.

He snorts at my reply, but keeps staring at me. I wonder how he was able to identify me—was it the disdain dripping from my every pore? The murderous gleam in my eyes? Or had he been told to look for me, to look out for me? I'm nothing remarkable to look at, with no discerning features to give me away—brown eyes, straight brown hair, fair skin, small-boned. Average in every way but one.

"I thought you would be ... more impressive in person," he says, looking me over, clearly finding me wanting.

I'm aware of the many eyes in the courtyard, all fixed on us, like our interaction will define the way we all view these Roallacan intruders for the next two years, and the way everyone views me as well.

So I shuck off my jacket—and unfurl my wings.

Partial shifting is something not every Shield can do. Uncle Aris likes to shift either his tiger fangs or claws, which came in handy when he was captured in Roallac. Remiel can shift just his fox ears, which, for a spy, is pretty helpful. He can shift just his bushy tail too, a trick that always makes me laugh.

Partial-shifting wings on a hawk shifter would be laughable—tiny bird wings on their back? Cute, maybe, but useless. Some shifters can scale them up or down a little, but not enough to fly with them.

Not like mine.

Mine are glorious, each over ten feet long and covered in long, glossy black-and-red feathers. I extend them out to their full length, knocking someone over behind me—I don't know who, and I don't bother to look—and messing up Kora's hair. There's an audible gasp from the crowd, and my chest puffs out a bit.

"Better?" I ask, taunting this enemy prince.

His eyes don't leave mine, don't stare in awe at the wings on my back, don't show any reaction at all.

He just turns away and walks toward the stables, silent as a ghost. I'm left feeling a little silly, actually, to be ignored like that. I don't like it.

"Wow," Kora breathes when the other Roallacan students have passed us. "That was *awesome*!"

The chatter in the courtyard resumes. I fold my wings, and they shrink back into my human shoulder blades.

"Come on," Kora says, grabbing the bag I dropped. "You're going to be swamped with questions after that display. Let's get you settled before they all have a chance to catch their breath."

CHAPTER 2

Kora had the forethought to reserve an empty room next to hers for me. The girl doesn't take no for an answer, and I'm beginning to warm up to her. She picked two rooms for us on the third floor of the outer wall before even meeting me—exactly what I would have picked for myself.

"The only thing above us is sky," Kora crows, flinging the window in my room open.

It's a small room, smaller even than my room back home, but it's neat and clean. I don't plan on spending much time here, anyway. The view is spectacular, at least—green plains and a wide, lazy river winding east until it reaches the sea. We're on the top of a hill in a lush valley, and I can't wait to fly over it.

I love flying. It gives me perspective, and peace, in a way that almost nothing else does. From the air, the river will look like a ribbon; the school, smaller than a child's toy. I'll bet I can even see the great sea—that much empty water has always fascinated me. I've never been on a ship, but I love hearing Wren's stories of them, and of growing up with the sea, the way I had the mountains.

I didn't have much of a chance to take in the sights the last time I flew up the eastern coast.

"Hello, ladies," a voice drawls from the door, shaking me from my daydream.

I turn, arching an eyebrow at the intruder. It's a muscular Shield student with golden hair that curls and crystal-blue eyes. He looks like he could have been the inspiration behind many of the sculptures of Rigrasil back in Estana, with a strongly arched nose and full lips.

The dragon in me rejoices—there's a visceral part of me that just loves pretty or shiny things.

"Athanasios Mineas," he says, strolling into the room and extending a hand to me with a wink. "But *you* can call me Athan."

"I'm Delphine," I say, shaking his hand.

He doesn't let mine go, just looks at me with a charming grin on his face.

"And I'm Kora!" Kora calls from behind me.

She comes around and assesses him, arms crossed. This amuses him. He doesn't take his eyes off me, though, just slowly drags those blue eyes over my tight leather travel clothing.

I'm equally frank in my assessment. He's toned and practically bulging with muscles, not to mention *gorgeous*. I'd grown tired of the boys back in Aeturnus. After being an outcast, a forsaken, for most of my life, I'd found some of the perks of being a hero quite enjoyable. Maybe Athan could break my dry spell.

"Do I pass inspection?" Athan asks, raising an eyebrow.

I give him a sly smile and a wink.

"So far," Kora answers for me. "Say, do you have any friends?"

Athan walks with us to the dining hall. The sun is setting, and the school has this crazy rule about not being out after nightfall unless we're with a full-fledged Mage or Shield. It's supposed to keep us out of trouble.

It doesn't, to hear Uncle Aris talk.

Dinner is a noisy affair. The dining hall is a squat building over past the library, with a partially hidden kitchen at the back and rows of long tables in the middle. It, like most of the school, was built for functionality, not beauty. There are fires roaring in the fireplaces at either end of the hall, kept burning with magic instead of fuel, and banners overhead with the red-and-gold flag of Ocron, and smaller ones for the individual cities, like Raverra. At either end are huge white flags with a silver flame emblazoned on them—the emblem of the school.

There is no Roallacan flag, though—no banner with a snake eating its own tail, coiled in a circle.

The Shields grab platters of starchy vegetarian food and water mixed with the ashes of burned plants, meant to keep our energy up and replace the sweat we lose training. The Mages, like Kora, get a little more variety in their meals. We're quickly surrounded by a crowd of new students, all of whom want to hear more about the Battle of Soltaire. I do my best to answer their questions, but after a while my answers get shorter and shorter. I grow tired of their unending tide of questions.

And I don't want to admit to them that I still hear the screaming of the people I killed in my dreams.

The Roallacan students are keeping to themselves, eating quietly in a corner. No one talks to them. I catch Reyn looking at me twice. The second time, I give him a rude hand gesture and turn my attention back to handsome Athan.

Shields don't have to sleep as often as Mages. We're also stronger and have more endurance.

Three features I put to good use that evening, before kicking Athan out of my room around midnight.

"So, what was it like, training with Aris?" Athan asks.

We're on about the eighth mile of our ten-mile warm-up. Vassilis —our instructor—sets a brutal pace. I'm sure it's to weed out the weaker Shields. Athan and I hold our own, right behind him. We've been carrying on a conversation as we run, mostly to try and psych each other out. I have to work hard not to pant while I talk—I don't dare show weakness, not today, when everyone's trying to figure out the pecking order. We're all wearing Shield training clothing for the first time too, which means the men are bare-chested, and my head swivels when I pass them. It's very distracting, and it takes me a moment to figure out how to respond to Athan.

What was it like training with Aris every day for the past four years? It started off as a kind of hero worship, honestly. I did everything he asked, without question, desperate to earn his approval. He was the first Shield to take an interest in teaching me, and I was eager to learn it all.

And after a while? I'd started calling him "Uncle Aris" as kind of a joke—and then I kept at it, and then I kind of meant it. He and Wren became as close to me as my real family, Tekton.

Then they had Rosie. I fell in love with her instantly. She is by far the cutest thing I've ever seen, with soft black hair and big jade-green eyes. She's fairer than Wren and Aris, probably because she spends most of her time inside the temple in Aeturnus. She's a precocious little girl, just over two now, and has them chasing her all over. She shifted early, too—most Shields don't shift until they're at least toddlers. I didn't shift until I was almost ten.

We'd placed bets on whether Rosie would be a Mage or a Shield —Aris, of course, had never been in doubt. Dimitra Rose Valorius sneezed—*sneezed*—and shifted into a snow leopard before she turned one. Wren rolls her eyes at both Aris and Rosie a lot now, and mutters half-hearted prayers to Caladrius for patience.

Gods, I miss them.

But do I tell Athan all this? Of course not.

"It was great," I say, keeping my sentence short so I don't lose face by panting.

Just keep going, one foot in front of the other. Aris had me running up and down the mountain stairs at the temple every day. This gently rolling stroll through the countryside? Easy by comparison. Or so I tell myself.

"I was the same year as Aris, for his first games," Vassilis calls over his shoulder. His red hair is dark with sweat, but he's barely winded. "Good Shield. One of the greatest. Always in trouble, though."

"Sounds about right," I say, grinning.

Aris spoke highly of Vassilis, so I'm eager to impress him. As we round the final mile back toward the school, I shoot a sly look at Athan and then put on a burst of speed.

He whoops and takes off after me, and the two of us sprint the final mile back to the arena.

By the time the others catch up, we've had a moment to catch our breath and pretend we aren't dying.

"Pace yourselves," Vassilis warns. "Don't burn yourself out on the first day."

I snort. Shields don't burn out, at least not usually by themselves. "Going gray" is the other term we use for it—it's what happens when a magically gifted person, a Shield or a Mage, pushes themselves too far, uses too much magic. They end up a husk, a washed-out shadow of the person they were. Most die within a few days after turning gray. Some live and end up being put to work doing menial tasks, no better than a dumb beast of burden. Sometimes I wake up at night in a cold sweat, thinking about it.

Mages, though, are much more likely to burn out. A Shield can at the same time, if they're bonded to a Mage, in the way we claim a Mage at the Shield games. Both are made stronger by the bond—but each is the other's weakness too.

At the Battle of Soltaire, Caelus gave up his own life to turn his vile Mage gray. He saved us all. His tomb in Estana is practically a shrine now, with its Rigrasil-blessed golden weapons. It eases the sting of missing him a little, knowing that Rigrasil himself was proud of Caelus's choice.

I heard his Mage, Mariana, didn't last the week after she went gray. She'd been cold when she'd come to the Temple of Caladrius with the others, but I'd never imagined she could betray them all the way she did. She'd been a traitor the whole time, a Black Water Witch hiding among the Ocronian Mages, waiting to strike like a snake hiding in the grass. I wonder about Reyn and the other Roallacan Mages—I'll have to be on guard at all times against them.

Mariana, at least, got what was coming to her. But I do miss Caelus. And Tekton really enjoyed having another academic around.

Vassilis puts us through round after round of exercises the first day. It's easy to see who the strongest Shields are—there are twelve of us in total, a moderate-sized class. Athan, who's a wolf shifter, turns out to be even better with a gladius than he was in bed. I'm sweating heavily by the end, but I manage to keep up with Vassilis's grueling instructions. Thank Rigrasil for revealing Shield clothing—simple red cloth undergarments, with a skirt of reinforced pleated leather. I also keep my favorite knife strapped to my waist. The women also get a leather band to wrap over the red cloth for our chests. This allows for mobility and, more importantly, keeps us cool. Gods, I hate the heat here. It's like the summer is determined to stick around for as long as possible. I long for the cool of my mountain home. And wearing sandals instead of boots is going to take some getting used to. I don't like having sand rubbing against my toes.

At the end of the run while we're stretching, Vassilis makes us introduce ourselves, having everyone say where they're from, what their shift is. When he gets to me, I shrug.

"You all know who I am," I say.

He rolls his eyes so hard I think he might strain something. "Humor me," he says.

I sigh. "Delphine Kalla. Aeturnus. Dragon," I say, and inhale. A tongue of flame shoots from my mouth for several feet, making the small girl beside me flinch and back away. It's a trick that took me ages to master—first as a dragon and then as a girl. Usually a dragon's fire, once lit, burns and burns until the accelerant pouches in its throat are empty.

It's a fact I was made brutally aware of the first time I shifted.

"Show off," the girl beside me mutters.

I shrug. Learning to control that was something I ended up writing letters to Rafael about for months—if anyone knew control, it was him. And I'm not some dumb beast. I am a *Shield*—and I'll be damned if my own body does *anything* except what I tell it to do.

"Just wanted to establish who the dominant predator is here," I say, not looking at her.

"Careful," Athan whispers at my other side. "That one might slip a knife between your ribs one night."

"I'd like to see her try," I say back, not bothering to lower my voice.

The small girl raises an eyebrow at me, then states her own name.

"Lyssa Khabrias. Raverra. Wolf," she says, baring her teeth—woefully human-sized—at me.

I snort, looking back at Vassilis like I wasn't even looking at her. I'm slight for a Shield—I've always assumed it's because as a dragon, I need to stay light, or I won't get airborne—but Lyssa is even smaller than me, not an ounce of spare flesh on her tiny frame. She is solid muscle, though, with an attitude to match. I'd be stupid to dismiss her just because of her size.

"I've got two years to get into your head, Delphine," Lyssa hisses.

"Because you can't beat me in a fair match in the arena?" I ask, crossing my arms. I'm already getting tired of her posturing.

She comes closer, jabbing a finger into my shoulder. I swat her away, like the insect she is.

"I'm saying that when the time comes, I won't have to. I'll have won before we even step over that red chalk line."

"Well, aren't you a little ray of sunshine," Athan says. He's got a small towel wrapped around his neck, and he yanks it off to snap it at her like a whip. "Go on. Go pester someone else."

If I didn't know Lyssa's shift form was a wolf, I'd be tempted to think she was a snake. And I can't stand snakes.

There are several wolves in our group, though—not surprising. It seems there have been more lately. I wonder if Caelus had anything to do with that. I like to think so. There are also two bears, a panther, an eagle, and a hawk, those last both destined for the King's Messengers.

That leaves nine for me to beat at the Shield games in two years, since the messengers wouldn't compete. A few usually drop out—or, more rarely, are killed—and sometimes Shields from older classes join in, like Aris, when his first Mage died, or Caelus, when his first Mage decided to devote himself to Rigrasil's temple.

I know one of the Mages has an older brother who plans to claim her at this year's games. So that leaves eleven Mages for me to sort through in our year, and maybe—like with Aris—another dozen or so in the class below us, if I choose to wait. Kora said she was the strongest Fire Mage of our year—pretty bold statement, considering classes haven't even started yet. Still, I appreciate her boldness, staking a claim for me right as I walked in through the gates. I'll definitely have to take that into account. After all, a claim is for life. And a good Mage makes a Shield even stronger, and vice versa. It's not something to be taken lightly.

The rest of the afternoon goes pretty much as I expect. Vassilis puts us through a series of drills but never lets us fight each other, never lets us wield a real weapon. We run an obstacle course through the arena, one where we're forced to climb vertical walls, leap on rolling logs over a pit, and duck through a maze of sharpened spikes. A few students get minor injuries. For the most part, it's bloodied lips and a few scrapes, ones that our magic heals within minutes. I emerge unscathed. One Shield lands on his ankle awkwardly after the vertical wall climb, and I can hear the bone snap. He crumples but doesn't cry—well, good for him, anyway—and Vassilis jogs over to help him set it.

"Next month, you'll be spending mornings with the healers after your runs," he tells us.

"Why?" Athan asks, running a hand through his golden hair, flexing his arm muscles as he does so, making sure I'm watching. Like most of the men, he trains shirtless, wearing only a leather skirt and wrapped sandals. And like most Shields, he is gorgeous, his chest a wide golden expanse of sculpted muscle, the dips between his abdominals serving to funnel the sweat down his stomach. I force myself to drag my gaze back to his face and find him smirking at me.

"Because ..." Vassilis says, setting the ankle with a snap. The boy whimpers but then bites his lip. Within seconds, the swelling and bruising have diminished. Vassilis pats the boy on the shoulder. "If we *didn't* set that break immediately, it would have healed wrong, and Herondas here would either be limping the rest of his life or have to endure having it rebroken and set by a healer," he says, eyeing us one by one to make sure his lesson sinks in. "In the midst of a battle, knowing how to set your own bones, and bind your wounds, can make the difference between life and death. Rigrasil's blessing will only carry you so far."

We grumble as he dismisses us for the day. It isn't until we head to the baths, to wash the sweat of the day off, that I glance at the Water Mages' building, the home of the healers. Not all Water Mages have healing abilities, but most have at least some. Kora said that Caius could practically bring someone back from the edge of death itself—for a non-Shield, it sounded pretty impressive.

The Water Mage building is an ugly rectangular building made of the same gray stone as the rest of the school. Its only adornments are columns at the corners and a pattern of waves carved into the stone around the top. By design, it's near the baths. I've heard they also have a pool for swimming. I'm not overly fond of swimming. I'm a beast of fire and air, after all.

The sun is on its way down, and soon we'll be under curfew and herded back to our dorms. The Water Mages' class is ending too, and five of them funnel out of the building—one in front, clutching a book to her chest and hurrying toward the library, and the other four stuck together like they have been glued that way.

The Roallacan Water Mages. *Ugh.*

And that's when it hits me.

When we have classes on healing, it'll be with the Water Mage students.

Next month, I'll be having classes with the Prince of Snakes himself.

Dinner is a more subdued affair than it was last night. It seems reality is setting in for most of the students, like Herondas—who is walking fine now. He regales us with tales of his home, on the coast down by what was formerly Aclines. It's one of the places the plague is starting to pop up again in, and he says his family writes updates to him daily.

"Estana's dispatching healers up and down the coast, they say," he tells us around mouthfuls of barley, his leg bobbing up and down and up and down under the table.

I like Herondas, I decide. I don't want to sleep with him, but I like him in the way some people like puppies. He's cute, and his energy is infectious, even at the end of a long day. He's got wide brown eyes and wildly curly hair. I kind of want to pet him.

Kora brings a large book with her to our table—the table we've already claimed, one in the middle of the room—and sets it down with a loud whump, a look of doom on her face.

"My aunt Laelia is one of the fire instructors," she explains. "She won't settle for me being anything less than the best. My three older brothers 'set quite the precedent,' she says, and sighs. "At least you don't have to worry about that. You're the *dragon*. The heroine of Soltaire. Death on Feathered Wings. You're perfect without even trying."

I look down at the barley in my bowl, let it run off the back of my spoon. My stomach clenches, but I can't force myself to eat it.

"I mean, she trained for *four years* with Aris Valorius as her personal tutor—of course she's the best," Athan cheers, putting an arm around my shoulders and giving me a squeeze.

I shrug him off, though it doesn't seem to upset him. Around us, the other students vie for my attention, to be a part of our select group, and start complimenting me too.

It's hard to measure up when your story is legendary. I'm already on a pedestal, and everyone is just waiting to see when I'll fall.

I feel hollow inside, the competing voices threatening to overwhelm me, like an avalanche. Sweat breaks out on the small of my back despite the cool late-summer evening. Suddenly it's hard to get enough air.

"I'm ... tired," I say, disentangling myself and standing abruptly.

Kora and Athan exchange glances.

"Want some company later?" Athan says, giving me a very charming smile.

It's tempting, but I need a different kind of distraction this evening.

"Not tonight," I say, and I feign a yawn.

His face droops, though he tries to hide it.

"See you for drills in the morning," I say, and leave. I drop my plate off to be washed—the food untouched—and leave the dining hall. My fists are clenched, my pulse pounding. I need to *do* something. The pressure to be the best feels like a giant weight on my chest, and I need to release it before I explode.

Then the back of my neck prickles, and I look over my shoulder just as I reach the door.

There, on the opposite side of the room, sit the Roallacan Water Mages.

And staring right at me is the Fallen Prince himself, with eyes as dark as all the hells.

I glare at him for a moment before leaving the hall. I slam the door behind me, which does little to alleviate the squeezing sensation in my chest.

I get back to my room and remove my knife from its sheath on my hip. Frostbite has been my constant companion recently, and as I drag its razor-sharp edge over and over across my forearms—not deep enough to scar, only deep enough that my Shield healing can erase it in just a few minutes—I finally begin to breathe a little easier.

I focus on the pain until the squeezing in my chest finally fades away along with the cuts on my skin.

CHAPTER 3

The Shield games take place a week into our semester. I don't know any of the Shields involved, but that doesn't matter. It's the biggest social event of the season, a chance to check out what *we* will be doing in two years. The Mages get their Winter Festival, and we get the games.

When we all got back to Estana after the Battle of Soltaire, we were a tired, bedraggled mess. Wren was the worst—she looked like a strong wind might blow her over. Aris decided to take her west, for privacy, while she healed. I didn't want to stay in Estana without them and Tekton, so I ended up back in Aeturnus too.

When Aris and Tekton got permission to build the school, simply called the Aeturnus School (thank the gods, and not "The School of the Obsidian Labyrinth," like Tekton had wanted), I made Aris regale me for days with stories of his games. We had practically miles of subterranean tunnels and halls, but no arena to start with. The snowy mountains are fun but not really conducive to aboveground buildings in the wintertime. So some Earth Mages from the Prasinos Mine came over, including Aris's asshole brother Spyridon and his Mage, Stathis—Aris was on edge the whole time they were there—

and helped us expand. Stathis and his friends designed an arena that was the grandest thing I'd ever seen, an indoor obsidian-sand pit with rows and rows of seating. It was definitely bigger than the one Wren destroyed in Soltaire. Aris and I spent countless hours there over the past few years.

Gods, I miss him.

One of my favorite stories was about the games where Aris claimed Wren. He battled Caelus there too and said he was one of the smartest fighters he'd ever met. Zale, the giant Shield he fought for the last round, was a big, brutal Shield. He died in Soltaire too, as part of King Leonidas's entourage. Being a Shield isn't without its risks, I guess, no matter our strength and healing abilities.

And now I am going to my first games. Kora is practically vibrating with excitement. The school's tavern manager, Kemp, has a cart well stocked with ale and wine for the spectators. He pretends not to notice that we swipe a few bottles when his back is turned.

The arena is packed. Aleka and Ismini have come from Estana and give me proud hugs before joining their fellow alumni. They're all excited to see who claims who and have bets going on for their choices. Aleka hopes to recruit some of them to the capital, though Shield Commander Markos is also here and jokes with her about poaching his best candidates. At his side is Lukas Valorius, who I haven't met before but couldn't miss. He looks exactly like his brother Aris, just a little taller, and his eyes are nearly black instead of blue. He follows Commander Markos like a hulking shadow.

"I heard one of the second-years say that Commander Markos is going to retire soon," Kora says, jostling her shoulder against mine. She's drunk, her face flushed, and she giggles at every little thing.

I carefully take the wine bottle from her hands before she can spill it, and take a deep drink myself. We're sitting at the very top level on the side opposite the teachers, and we have a good view of everything. There's a tense feeling to the air, a charge, like lightning about to strike. It's as intoxicating as the wine.

"Think Lukas will take his place?" Athan asks, stealing the bottle from me.

"Hey, gimme that back!" Kora says.

"At least *one* of the Valorius Shields has some honor," Lyssa says. She's chosen to sit right in front of me so I can hear every stupid remark she makes.

I flush red—Aris killed Caelus, a fellow Shield and his friend, in Soltaire. Never mind that Caelus *asked* him to. Never mind that Aris turned the tide of that battle, single-handedly turning Mariana gray *and* sending Aenon back to the immortal realm.

Never mind that Aris *still* has nightmares about it.

Aris broke the third law of the Shields: *Your fellow Shields shall be closer to you than your own flesh and blood. Any evil committed against them is made against Rigrasil himself.*

For killing a fellow Shield, Aris could have been sentenced to death himself. Instead, the Council of Shields found the only possible penalty even more severe – Aris was expelled from our order. The title and honor that had meant most to him, stripped away. He says often that it doesn't bother him, but we all know he's lying.

"Aris is still the best Valorius fighter," Athan insists. "I bet he could take us all on with one hand tied behind his back."

"Yeah, and he's taken down a kraken, a dragon, *and* a three-headed hydra! Lukas never did *any* of that," Kora says in support. The stories are practically legends already.

"Four," I add quietly. "The hydra had four heads when he killed it."

"*Four* heads! You hear that Lyssa?" Athan cheers. "That's why he's in charge of the Shields at the new school."

"Ah, yes," Lyssa says, unimpressed. "The *other* school. Founded by an outcast and a forsaken. I can't believe *anyone* would want to go to that place."

My fists clench, and I reach for the dagger at my hip. My uncle Tekton was born a Shield, with strength and healing, but without a shifted form. It doesn't happen often, but often enough that there is a name for it. *Forsaken.* Like his god found him unworthy of a shift. There is no more offensive term in all of Ocron, not to a Shield.

Lyssa gives me an unconcerned glance, flipping her short braid over her shoulder as she turns her attention back to the games.

Kora puts a hand on my arm, looking up at me with warning in her wide eyes.

"Later," she says, darting a glance to where Aleka and the rest of the teachers are sitting.

I feel like a kettle, boiling, ready to scream—but she's right. I don't want to start a fight here, not with everyone watching. Not at the games.

I straighten my shoulders and focus instead on the sand of the arena, on which the newly graduated Shields are warming up. Here's my chance to learn what the games are all about, and I intend to pay attention to every last detail, though it's hard to put Lyssa's comment from my mind.

There's an urgency to the fights. Friend turns on friend, each striving to be first, to gain the honor that comes with it as well as first pick of the Mages. We discuss the choice of weapons—most Shields fight with a gladius and a shield, whereas some, like Aris, choose two swords. One of the Shields actually uses a trident—the favored weapon of those from the Isles. I've already decided that I'm going to use two swords for my games. *Dimachaerus*, we call it. A dual wielder.

After several rounds, the winner is declared—a bear shifter named Alphenor. He's a huge man, six and a half feet tall and covered in black hair. He's an honorable Shield, a prime example of what we should strive for, according to Commander Markos's congratulatory speech. Could I take down a Shield like that someday? No one in my class has his size, but some of them might still be growing. Athan, maybe.

I grasp Frostbite at my hip—I *will* win my games. Shifting isn't allowed during the games, so I'll have to prove that I'm just as deadly in my human form, that I don't rely on my dragon form to win. And I will. I have to.

My skin tingles with the thought, itches for Frostbite's touch.

When the last Shield has chosen his Mage, we make our way back to the dining hall with the crowd of spectators. Kora and I are singing a vulgar song off-key with our arms linked around each other when I hear my name called.

"Delphine!"

It's a deep voice, and the authority in it cuts through the crowd. I turn and see Lukas Valorius, standing a head taller than most, beckoning me with one hand, like I'm a dog to be summoned.

I have half a mind to turn around and ignore him, but Commander Markos is standing next to him, and he's *also* looking at me. The Shield Commander is not a man I want to cross, not when my entire postschool future depends on him—and, gods, *fine*, it probably depends on Lukas too.

"I'll catch up with you guys in a bit," I say, disentangling myself from Kora.

She's flushed from the wine, but her brow still furrows with concern.

"I can wait with you," she offers. She glances toward Lukas and back at me.

"I'm good," I tell her. "Go on. I'll meet you later, all right?"

Kora gives me a quick hug. "Good," she whispers. "Because I have another bottle of wine smuggled under this robe!"

I giggle, an unfortunately undignified effect of the alcohol, and walk toward Lukas and the Commander.

I do my best to straighten my posture and rumpled clothes as I approach. Lukas looks like a scarier version of Aris, even bigger and with eyes as black as coal. He wears his hair long too, pulled back into a neat tail. The Commander I've met before, and he's intimidating but also ... I don't know. He kind of reminds me of someone's doting grandfather. He knows the name of every Shield who stops to say hello to him, and though his own Mage retired long ago, he continues—at least for now—to lead our armies with honor and strength. He radiates charisma, the kind of man who people just automatically respect.

Lukas, not so much.

"Delphine," the Commander says warmly, offering a one-armed hug. He's a massive man, barrel-chested, with iron-gray hair. "Did you enjoy your first games?"

"I look forward to my own," I tell him, raising my chin.

Lukas snorts.

"Lukas and I have somewhat ... differing ideas about your future," Commander Markos tells me with an indulgent grin. "I say you need two years' training, like the rest of your class. He thinks your time at the school is ..."

"Wasted, I believe, is the term he used," Vassilis says, coming up unexpectedly at my back. He gives Lukas a terse smile.

"My intent was only to convey that Delphine is already a fearsome weapon, as we all well know," Lukas says smoothly. "We could utilize her much better by letting her fight *now*."

"You want me to fight ... now?" I ask. I'm not proud of how my voice cracks on that last word, and I clear my throat. I didn't even think that was a possibility. Surely, they couldn't ... they wouldn't ...

I reach again for Frostbite at my hip. The very thought of fighting —of *killing*—and my throat has gone bone-dry. I know it's in my future, but it's always been ... nebulous. Distant. I kind of assumed I'd get used to the idea over time.

"You are going to save a lot of lives," Lukas says, like he's offering me a prize, like he wants me to help convince Commander Markos of it. "You are a gift from Rigrasil himself. You really want to wait two more years? I would have thought, after four years with my dear brother Aris, that you would feel more than sufficiently ready."

But I don't. Gods, I don't.

I can't answer him, not without admitting that not even Aris's training makes me feel ready.

Vassilis puts his hand on my shoulder. "She is not a weapon to be wielded. She is a Shield, and as such, the Law of Shields requires that she undergo two years of training *and* the chance to claim her Mage before her peers. Or do you intend to challenge the Council of Shields?" he asks, cocking an eyebrow.

I keep quiet. Lukas looks surprised, like he thought I'd agree with *him*, but I stay next to Vassilis. I feel nauseated—too much wine, no doubt.

"Peace, Vassilis," Commander Markos says, raising a hand with a little laugh, defusing the tension. "No one is going to take your star pupil away today. But"—he looks at me—"I think I speak for us all when I say that we are quite invested in your future."

Like I didn't already know that. Like I didn't already feel the pressure of everyone's expectations, every hour of every day. So now the Shield Commander wants me to know he's personally keeping track of me. *Great.*

"Thank you," I mutter, not really sure what else to say. I have never wanted to shift and fly away from a conversation so badly in my life.

"It'll be curfew soon," Vassilis says.

I look up—it's nowhere near time, but he catches my eye and nods toward the dining hall. "Go with your friends."

I look at Commander Markos, who nods his dismissal and turns to whisper something to Lukas. I give a grateful nod to Vassilis and make my escape.

Lukas, meanwhile, never takes his black eyes off me. I can feel them boring into my back until I reach the dining hall and close the door behind me.

It takes me a few days after the games, but eventually I catch Lyssa alone.

And now I'm a mess.

We get one day off training each week—most students sleep in or stay otherwise occupied in their beds. The sun is barely up today, though, and I'm already covered in blood. She's broken my nose, and it has gushed down my shirt like a fountain. There's a good reason Shields usually wear black when we're not wearing our leathers.

But I'd stuffed her mouth full of sand for saying those things about my family, so it was worth it.

It's promising to be another hot, sticky morning, but not even that can put a damper on my good mood. This early there's no one up, so I reason there's no one to see me as I head directly to the baths, one hand pinching the bridge of my nose to stem the bleeding as I wait for my magic to heal it.

And of course, who do I run into leaving the Water Mage building just as I approach?

The Prince of Snakes himself.

He catches my eye—but if he's startled to see me, or the blood, he doesn't show it.

"Early-morning studies, Prince?" I ask. My voice still sounds nasal and thick, my nose struggling to heal back into its proper position. I sniff and nearly choke on a blood clot. I spit it out at the prince's feet.

"On my way to the library," he says, not appearing to notice the spit. His voice is tinged with suspicion. "You?"

"Same," I say. He snorts—and then does the last thing I expect.

He comes over to me. He's quite a bit taller than I am, but I'll be damned if I let a Black Water snake intimidate me. I fight the urge to incinerate him on the spot. He's confident, this prince, and difficult to read. His face remains a mask.

"What happened to you?" he asks, tilting his head down and studying my face.

I can only imagine what I look like—nose crooked, blood all over me, hair stuck up where Lyssa yanked on it. I give him a grin, aware that one of my teeth is loose. I probably look deranged. *Good.*

"Fell down the stairs," I say.

Every one of my muscles is tensed, ready to shift or fight if needed. I don't like being alone with the Snake Prince, even if it's in the middle of the courtyard. For all I know, he's got a knife up his sleeve, ready to sink into me as soon as my back is turned.

Then again, I've got a knife up my sleeve too. Or on my hip. Whatever.

We stare each other down for a few moments, his dark green eyes steady. He studies my face like he might study a page of notes. Then he raises his hand, like he wants to touch the wounds, and I flinch.

He freezes, and his hand falls to his side again, fingers flexing slightly.

He turns and leaves, showing his back to me, either not caring that he's presenting me with an easy target or not feeling that I'm a threat. He's confusing, this snake, and his reaction unsettles me more than I care to admit.

But then I finally make it to the baths, and as I soak in the warm water and my body heals itself, as I enjoy this rare moment of peace and solitude—and, fine, feeling a little victorious too—all thoughts of the Fallen Prince fade away.

CHAPTER 4

A month passes in the blink of an eye. Aris was a fantastic tutor, but he's just one Shield—here I have to compare myself to every single Shield in my year, and sometimes those in the second-year class as well. It becomes my obsession, ranking my abilities. Athan is faster than I am at a sprint, though I have more endurance. Lyssa is better at strategy—map reading, history, the academic stuff. Surprisingly, Herondas, the guy who broke his ankle the first day, is really good at partial shifting. We make a game of calling out different body parts to him, and he shifts in an instant. Nose. Ears. Tail ... and other things.

And in all categories, I have to be first. There is no alternative. I train obsessively. When the others go to Kemp's for a drink, or to Athan's room for some cards, I train more. I read everything I can find. And I obsess.

Kora, at least, is good company. She's just as determined not to let her family down, to prove she's the best Fire Mage of our year. Sometimes I sneak into her room at night, and we read together until she falls asleep. Sometimes she talks to Calix, an Earth Mage; he spends half of his free time in the greenhouse, and the rest with Kora. Usually they just study together, two silent bookworms—and Calix's pet squirrel. I think Calix wants more, but Kora is so focused on her studies that she doesn't want any distractions.

I welcome any distraction, or sometimes two, as often as I can.

Relations between Roallacan and Ocronian students remain ... uneasy. There's rarely overt cruelty one way or the other; the Roallacan students are more like a fog, putting a damper on everything but not really causing any major problems. Mostly I just try to stay out of their way. Seeing them reminds me too much of the Battle of Soltaire, and that's not something I enjoy reliving. I get enough of that in my dreams.

Athan, however, has the misfortune to come back from training one afternoon and find his entire room encased in ice. His bed, his weapons, everything is set in blocks of ice. The Roallacan students are to blame, of course, but we can't prove it.

We laugh at first. Kora offers to melt it for him and help him dry everything. Nothing is ruined, but it is a giant pain in the ass. I don't dare unleash my dragon fire in his room—I want to thaw things, not incinerate them—but I can help a little.

It takes hours, and the next day we are all tired. Athan and I are nearly stumbling on our run. It's the day of our first class with the Black Water Mages, and I can't help but think this little attack was personal. A way to knock us off-balance before our first class together.

As we leave the arena and head toward the Water Mage building, I scan the brass plaques adorning the walls of the tunnel beneath the stands. The oldest are on the outside, the newest toward the arena. Five plaque columns back, I find Aris, his name atop the list of Shields for that year. A few more, and I find his name again. The only Shield to win the games twice. To do any less than come out on top would be an insult to the time and effort he has invested in me. I reach for the knife on my hip, feeling reassured by its presence.

I've reached for it more and more lately.

We reach the squat Water Mage building and, on entering, are immediately hit with a wave of humidity. Even my pin-straight hair begins to curl a little, the mist instantly cooling my heated face.

At odds with the austere outside of the building, the inside is like a giant bathhouse. The floors and walls are tiled in white and blue, and fountains burble in every nook and cranny. Down the main hall, which is lined with beautiful marble columns and archways decorated with mosaics, we reach a classroom with tiered seating, a large gray stone at the front, and a pool of water forming something like a moat between the instructor and the students. There's a large slate on the wall behind the podium, with a very detailed chalk drawing of a naked man. Some of the Shields elbow each other and snicker as we file in.

The girl I noticed the other day—the only non-Roallacan Water Mage this year—is already seated, studiously writing in a notebook and ignoring us and the naked picture. Her coiled black hair is pulled back in a series of complex braids, her fingernails painted bright blue.

"That's Aletheia," Athan says beside me. He gazes at her with a softness he doesn't usually show. "Must be hard, being the only real Water Mage in her year."

"Why don't you go comfort her, then?" I ask, arching an eyebrow.

He grins.

We haven't shared a bed since that first lapse in judgment, but that doesn't mean I dislike him. In fact, he might be the only friend I have here besides Kora. I just don't want to sleep with him again. He shoots me a very wolfish grin and goes to sit by the quiet girl. I don't know her well, but they strike up a conversation easily, thoroughly leaving me out.

The other Shields file into the empty seats, leaving me standing by myself.

"Lonely at the top?" Lyssa says, bumping her shoulder roughly against mine as she passes.

I sneer at her and pretend to be busy stretching. If there was one thing Aris always insisted on after exercise, it was stretching.

I am so busy pretending to be busy that I nearly miss Caius entering the room, along with the Roallacan Mages. He's chattering away at Reyn, who doesn't appear to be listening. Reyn's eyes find mine immediately—and then he turns away from a still-talking Caius to take a seat at the end of the room farthest from me. His entourage follows, casting suspicious glances at me over their shoulders, especially the twins. His quiet shadow, Silas, offers me a timid smile.

Assholes, the lot of them. I can't believe Iraklis agreed to let them in.

I sit down, finding myself in the middle of the room—the Shields to the far left of me with Aletheia, and the Roallacan Mages to the far right. And me, alone. My fingers go reflexively to the knife hilt at my hip, and the pressure in my chest eases, feeling the familiar grip, tracing the designs.

"Welcome, Shields!" Caius says, clapping his hands together. His hair is slicked back, like always, and he wears a spotless blue robe over fine clothing, his boots polished to shining. "We'll start with some basics of human anatomy this year, as well as an introduction to healing in the field, both Shields and non-Shields. Next year, we'll cover anatomy of your shifted forms, as well as more advanced splinting and suturing techniques."

One of the Roallacan twins, Eugenia or Isadora—I can't really tell them apart—raises a hand. Caius nods at her.

"So, we'll be expected to heal *her* too?" she asks, looking pointedly at me.

I fight down the rush of heat that threatens to spread to my face, and look straight ahead.

"Yes," Caius says, patient but a little exasperated. "As a healer of Ocron, you will be expected to give aid to anyone who needs it, magical or nonmagical."

"Even to someone who burned down our home?" the other twin

says, her voice sharp enough to cut glass. *That's a stupid exaggeration,* I think. I only burned part of the arena. I stare straight ahead at the podium, wrapping my fingers around the knife hilt until my knuckles ache.

Caius sighs and folds his hands on top of his stand. Athan whispers something to Aletheia, who blushes but keeps her eyes focused.

"We are all citizens of Ocron now, aren't we?" Caius asks.

Aletheia nods, but no one else really moves.

"I myself was a citizen of Soltaire during the ... during the end of Queen Evanthia's reign," he says carefully. "And here I am, one of the first Roallacan graduates of the School of the Silver Flame, and the first Roallacan teacher. To put it bluntly, Delphine was following orders, the same as we were." He stares at the twins.

One of them crosses her arms.

"You do not blame the sword that is wielded by your opponent, do you?" Caius asks.

The twin huffs, but neither of them speaks again.

"Good," he says. "Now, we're going to start with the skeletal structure ..."

I don't pay attention during most of Caius's first lecture. I'm stuck reliving the Battle of Soltaire—the panic attack I had before shifting, my breath coming so fast that Adriana, Aris's hawk-shifting sister, was worried I'd pass out. The sounds of people screaming as my flames reached them. The way I vomited for hours once I landed and shifted back. There is still a small scar on the back of my right shoulder where an icy spear punched through my wing—I don't even remember feeling the pain at all. I was too numbed by the experience.

And the stupidest part was that I'd insisted on going. When I heard Wren had been captured, and Aris too, there was no way I could just stand by and do nothing. I might have only been fourteen, but I was still a dragon, with scales most mortal weapons couldn't pierce, and flame that would melt rock and bone alike. And I would do it again, even knowing the price I'd pay.

I am a creature made for death.

And I'll have to kill again someday.

My hand is clenched so tight around Frostbite that my fingers are nearly numb. Relief is only a cut away.

I'm the first one to exit the classroom when Caius is done.

CHAPTER 5

It's another fucking hot day. The heat has me on edge—my dragon fire keeps me hot enough, but add in the stifling sunshine, with not even a merciful cloud in the scalding blue sky? I *hate* the weather here. I hate the way the sweat makes the sand in the arena stick to my skin, to my sandals, and, well, to *everywhere*. I hate how the leather of my fighting gear chafes under my arms when it's wet, and the blisters forming on my feet, even though my Shield healing will have taken care of them by tomorrow.

And I'm so focused on how much I hate, hate, *hate* the heat that I completely miss Athan's counterjab until his fist knocks me under the chin, clattering my teeth together with a jarring clack and sending me sprawling onto my back.

"*Fuck*, Del. Are you all right?" he asks, eyes wide, probably as surprised as me that he landed that hit. He probably expected me to block it, or I doubt he would have swung so hard. I put a hand to my jaw, probing gingerly at the knot already forming there. My eyes are watering from the blow, which throbs and is swelling more every moment.

Athan offers me a hand up, and I take it.

"Aw, need him to hold your hand, princess?" Lyssa sneers.

Her pack howls, jostling each other as they follow her lead with commentary of their own.

I try to ignore them.

"Wolves are better than dragons!"

Athan is a wolf, but I never hold that against him. He does cringe at this comment, though.

"Not so tough now, are you, Dragon Girl?"

"Oh, look! Something shiny! Why don't you go play with it and leave the fighting to the real Shields?"

I snarl and leap for the nearest—Lucius, a real idiot—but Athan stops me with a thick arm around my waist.

"Vassilis is watching," he murmurs, steering me toward the water bench. "Don't let them get to you."

I shrug Athan's arm off and give him a push for good measure. "I don't need you telling me how to act, Athan!"

He blinks and puts his hands out, palms up. "Hey, I'm not the enemy here. You were distracted, and I took advantage of it. It happens. I'm on *your* side."

I shove past him, eyes still watering—*From pain, damn it, that's all!*—and grab a mug of water, which I splash over my head to cool me off. The water is warm but still better than the hot, sticky air.

"*I* don't get distracted," I growl. Then I grab his arm and lead him back to the practice circle we were in. "Come on. Let's go again."

We go again. And again. And again. Eventually, Vassilis calls off our practice and tells us we're done for the evening. Athan and the rest of Shields head off to the dining hall or the baths—but I stay. I stay, and I do the same moves on the practice dummies, over and over, until my knuckles are split and bleeding.

At night, on the rare nights I'm alone, I don't sleep much. I lie down and stare at the ceiling, counting cracks in the ancient stones—and I think. As a Shield, it's a somewhat novel experience. Brawn over brains, as they say.

I miss Uncle Tekton. It's not fair how he was made only half a Shield. He has the strength and healing of a Shield, but no shift. It's humiliating for him. No wonder he shut himself away in the Temple of the God of Night, literally spitting in the face of the god of day, who was supposed to give him a shift. He's made some peace with it, or at least he pretends to have when I'm around.

For a long time, I think he was secretly happy that I hadn't manifested a shift either. Most Shields do as toddlers or young children. I never did. My parents were so disappointed in me—they foisted me off to my grandfather as often as they could, which was basically all the time. They were always gone on Shield missions, things that as a child I'd mimic in the backyard of our little cabin, fighting off imaginary trolls. My grandfather always smiled at me indulgently when I came back in at the end of the day, covered in dirt. I healed like a Shield—but then, so did Tekton. So when my fifth birthday came and went, then my sixth, and seventh, my parents took me to a priest of Rigrasil to see if anything was wrong with me. There wasn't anything wrong, he said, but what did he know? my mother said. He was a thousand years old and smelled like incense and spoiled eggs.

I went to healers too, a lot of them. Again, there was nothing wrong with me—nothing other than my parents' disappointment. *They* were real Shields. My mother shifted at age three, a black bear. My father shifted by age four, a huge wolf. I remember him licking my cheeks when I cried.

The theory was that since magic was fading from the world, getting all crazy with the plague and Tekton and all, fewer Shields were being born. And when I didn't manifest a shift, well ... I caught my mother crying once. She was sitting on their bed, crying into my father's shoulder, wailing about how such a thing could happen to *them*. They were *good* Shields. They obeyed their king and commander and served with honor. How could Rigrasil do such a thing to *them*?

It's a hard thing for a child to hear, that they don't live up to their parents' expectations. I resolved that night—I must have been seven or eight—that I'd train as hard as I could to be the best, strongest Shield they'd ever seen. They'd be so impressed when I won my games at the school that they'd smile and hug me and tell me what a *blessing* from Rigrasil I was. So I trained, and I tried anything and everything I could imagine to trigger a shift. My parents tried too—my father telling me not to worry, as it would come when it was ready, whereas my mother had a more aggressive approach, inflicting fear or pain to waken it. None of it worked.

And then they died.

I try not to think about it too much.

My grandfather was long dead by that point; Tekton was really the only family I had left. *Forsaken*, they called us. People whose god had abandoned them. He lived just down the road from us, but my parents didn't like me spending a lot of time with him, like he was contagious or something.

He stayed with me, though, when my parents were away on missions, and Tekton was the one who told me that they had died. He was surprised by the lack of tears, the lack of any kind of emotion, he told me later. I just stood there, silent as a statue.

And when an unsuspecting neighbor came by later that day, asking merely whether I could return the book my father had borrowed a few weeks back—I finally shifted.

And I burned that poor man, and the house I had grown up in, to ash.

Tekton was burned too, but he healed quickly. He never lost his calm, just talked to me and petted me like I was a skittish horse, until I stopped flaming, and I could follow his instruction to shift back. He wrapped me in his jacket, carried me into town, hired a pair of horses, and we left my hometown without so much as a backward glance.

I can barely remember what it all looked like, can barely remember what my mother or father looked like.

Aeturnus and the temple are my home now. Tekton and Aris and Wren and Rosie are my family. Tekton is twice my age, and I worry sometimes he's jealous that I ended up shifting and he didn't, but he's never said so. He is the most patient, steadfast, kind, generous person I've ever met. For *years* I prayed to Rigrasil, every night, to grant Tekton a shift. It could be anything, a bird or a badger or whatever, but *something* to prove to him that there was nothing wrong with him, that he wasn't unworthy or forsaken or defective.

I don't pray anymore. I asked King Leonidas if I could use the books to talk to Rigrasil myself, that surely, he'd grant such a good person this one tiny thing—the king smiled and told me that the books were too well hidden for me or anyone else to access. I bit my tongue to prevent myself from screaming at him, before I turned and ran away, digging my nails into my palms to keep from crying.

It was Tekton who spent long, patient hours helping me learn to control my shift, back and forth; who taught me to fly, after we had spent weeks studying how the birds flew in the mountains; who taught me how to cook using the mushrooms and plants that grew on our mountain; who questioned every King's Messenger who ever came to the temple about flying—not that there were many—since they were all bird shifters. He hoped to learn something from them, but he never got far before they got suspicious of his questions. And then it was Tekton who made me a harness, so we could fly together, and I could get stronger.

Gods, I miss him. With Tekton, it was always about being the best I could be, not comparing myself to anyone else, because there *was* no one else.

But here, at the school? All those old wounds from childhood, when I worried I wasn't good enough, have resurfaced. It wasn't as bad in Aeturnus after the Battle of Soltaire; Aris tried to help each of us recognize and hone our own strengths, to run our own race, as he said.

But here? Without my family? Here is where Frostbite and I have become more intimately acquainted. The small dagger I always wear is a constant, soothing presence, a reminder that I can always find a way to relieve some of the pressure, to mask my emotional pain with physical pain.

For a little while, anyway.

CHAPTER 6

As Shields, we get hurt. A lot. It's part of the deal. We heal quickly, so that's nice, but we get used to pain. Some Shields—like Aris's father and my mother—believe that pain is as essential to training as physical conditioning and rest. You have to get used to being in pain and doing what needs to be done anyway.

Aris, thankfully, is not in favor of that particular training ideology, and neither is Vassilis. Sure, broken bones and cuts and things happen, but pain isn't meted out just for fun.

We still get sent to the healers a lot, mostly so the healers can practice with our injuries, and only incidentally so we can actually get healed.

One morning, Lyssa and I "fall down the stairs" again. That happens a lot. The first-year students on healing duty always seem surprised how many students fall down the stairs. One even suggested that we should have the Head Mage take a look, see if anything can be done to make the stairs safer for us. The more senior healers just roll their eyes, accept the lie, and set our broken noses and things.

Lyssa gets called in first this time, which she acknowledges with a triumphant smile in my direction, like she's won something or bested me somehow by being more beat up than me and getting first priority from the healers. *Whatever.*

I get called in a second later, and when I reach the little curtain partition where I sit to be evaluated, the healer is already waiting for me.

"No," I say immediately. "Anyone but you."

Prince Reyn regards me calmly, his robe hanging neatly over plain black clothing. Not a hair is out of place on his stupid princely head.

"I'm perfectly capable of healing you," he says, gesturing for me to take a seat.

"How can you say that? You don't even know what's wrong with me yet," I say, frowning.

He gives me a slow, head-to-toe assessing look, noting the blood on my shirt, the way my wrist is swollen and bent, the tear in my earlobe, the dislocation of my shoulder. Even so, I bet I could kill him a dozen different ways.

"Sit," he says softly, in that practiced soothing tone of a healer. "It will only take a moment of your precious time."

"On second thought, I'm fine. I don't need a healer," I say, struggling to control my wince as I turn to leave.

"You do if you want to keep using that arm," he says firmly.

I look at my shoulder—it throbs, the pain setting me on edge, but it's nothing I can't deal with. It should be fine on its own. Eventually. I can probably have Athan relocate it. And the swelling in my wrist is already improving.

"Just let me help you, Dragon Girl, and we can both be on our way," Reyn says in mild exasperation.

I put my hand on Frostbite.

"You're as likely to kill me as help me," I say. "I want a different healer."

He rolls his eyes and lets out a frustrated breath.

"At least let me help with the pain, which is so obviously clouding your judgment," he says, extending a hand. Blue light shimmers at his fingertips.

I raise Frostbite, ugly memories starting to surface.

"Pain is part of being a Shield," I snarl. "You should know that. Did you offer Aris your 'healing' when you had him caged in Soltaire? When your soldiers were beating him?"

Evanthia—Reyn's queen, the one he would have succeeded as ruler of Ocron—trapped Uncle Aris for days in her cells, forcing him to fight for her amusement. He'd never tell me the full extent of what was done to him. I should kill Reyn for having been a part of Aris's torture.

The volume of my voice is rising, and the curtains are drawn back sharply by one of the senior healers, a blond woman in a blue robe with an irritated expression on her pinched face.

"*I* was too busy taking care of burn victims," Reyn spits back, ignoring the other healer. He still has his hand extended to me, though it's beginning to tremble with restrained fury. "You should know, dragon fire is incredibly hard to heal."

How dare he? *How* fucking *dare he!*

I yell and lunge at him, hoping the impact of my fist on his smug face won't shatter my injured wrist.

Or I try to, but the senior healer has frozen my feet to the floor, and instead, I just kind of topple forward. My feet are already going numb, and I level a string of muttered curses at the healer as I try to use my bad arm to steady myself on the nearby cot.

"Reyn, I'll take this one. Please see Tereos for your next assignment," the woman says, her thin lips pursed.

He drops his hand and leaves without another word.

Fine. Anyone but Reyn.

The woman frees my feet from their icy shackles. She heals me in a moment, relocating my shoulder and banishing the other minor injuries.

She makes no effort to dull the pain from her ministrations, though, and I nearly crack a tooth from gritting my teeth so hard. I refuse to cry out, but soon I'm covered in sweat and shaking. Still, I don't give her the satisfaction. At least the Snake Prince didn't get his hands on me.

By the time she's done, all the fight has gone out of me. I skulk out of the infirmary and back to Shield practice.

It's early one foggy morning, and the Shields have just returned from our usual ten-mile run. Vassilis has picked up the pace recently, and a few Shields lag behind, coming into the courtyard at last, red-faced and panting. They're embarrassed, trying not to show how tired they are. Vassilis claps a hand on their backs as he passes, probably saying something encouraging.

I got back several minutes ago. Athan and I are sitting on some barrels at the side of the stables, sharing an easy silence as we recover. The school is just waking up, the sun barely breaking over the walls. For a moment, it's beautiful, the fog all lit up like a golden haze.

I see Silas emerge from the dormitories, his arms full of books. His tan robe hangs on him awkwardly, a little too long for him. His hair is messy, like always, though he looks more tired than usual. I look around—I don't see Reyn or the twins anywhere. It's rare for the Roallacan Mages to go anywhere alone, which honestly is smart of them.

As soon as the thought enters my head, I see two of the slow-running Shields approach him, cackling and egging each other on. "Fucking snake," they call him. "Black Water bitch."

Silas ducks his head and walks faster, heading toward the library—but the Shields keep up, glad of someone to distract them from their own inadequacies. Athan takes a big bite of an apple he's conjured up from somewhere, watching the scene with interest.

"I'll bet you two silvers he cries," Athan says around bites.

The Shields realize Silas is ignoring their taunts, so they move on to something physical. First just pushing him to get his attention, then knocking the books from his arms. When he stoops to get them, one of them plants a foot on Silas's back, sending him flying, prostrate, across the courtyard. He hits his face, hard, on the cobblestones. I can see blood trickling from his upper lip.

He stops, and I realize he's taking slow, deep breaths to control himself.

"Rumor is that if the Roallacan Mages get so much as a single disciplinary action against them, they'll *all* be banished from the school," Athan says, enjoying the spectacle. "It'd be worth getting water-whipped by Silas if it meant we got rid of them."

I want to see it as Athan does, without emotion, like he's watching a cat toy with a mouse and not a person being humiliated. I fidget on the barrel for a moment, chewing my lip. But Aris didn't train me to stand by when someone was being hurt. Even if that person was a Black Water snake.

Silas goes to get up, and the Shields knock him down again.

"Come on, you idiots. He's not worth it," I call. It's a calculated jab—it makes it look like I'm calling Silas the weak one, when he's got more self-control than those two knuckleheads. Plus, it doesn't make me look like I'm protecting a snake.

The Shields freeze when they realize I'm watching them. Athan startles too, nearly dropping his apple. Silas looks up at me, dirt and blood smeared on his face. I can't stand the hollow look in his eyes, so I look away.

"Yeah, if you want a fight, pick on someone your own size!" one of the second-years chimes in from across the courtyard.

There's a rumble of agreement from the students starting to gather. The Shields who've been pestering Silas grumble, spitting on him as they pass—but they otherwise leave him alone.

Silas gets to his feet, collecting his books calmly, though his hands are shaking. I get up from my barrel to join the other Shields headed toward class—but Silas steps in front of me, blocking my way. It looks like he's tried to wipe his face with his sleeve—all it has done is smear the blood around.

"You'll want to see a healer about that lip," I tell him.

He grins, and I see that his teeth are bloodied too. Hells, maybe he bit his tongue.

"Thank you," he says.

Yep, his voice sounds muffled. Definitely bit his tongue.

"Don't mention it," I say, shouldering past him.

He puts a hand out, grabbing my shoulder, and I'm so stunned that I actually do stop and look at him.

"I mean it," he says, holding my eyes. There's an earnestness to his broad face that makes my chest hurt.

"So do I," I say, shrugging off his hand. "I've got a reputation to uphold."

He nods and gets out of my way. When I look back over my shoulder at him a few steps later, he gives me a small smile.

And across the courtyard, I see Prince Reyn watching from the shadows, as still as ice.

CHAPTER 7

The rest of the first semester follows pretty much the same pattern. Run in the morning, classes until lunch, then exercise all afternoon. Vassilis *still* won't let us use actual weapons—we're "not ready," he says. We have classes on healing but also history, battle tactics, weapon and armor crafting with Tulliano at the forge—one of my favorites—and survival training. This last one is the most boring for me. Aris has taught me most of it already, how to identify safe plants to eat, where to find fresh water, how to navigate using the stars—though Wren helped with that last one. I spend most of that class doodling weapons in the margins of my notebook pages or staring out the window at the courtyard. Sometimes I see the Roallacan Water Mages, and most often they're accompanied by Caius, who is still nauseatingly deferential to Reyn.

I'm not sure if Caius sticks with them for their protection or his own sycophantic need for attention. Reyn looks down at the man like Caius is a bug he is considering squashing. I kind of wish he would—then maybe I wouldn't have to endure healing class. Since that first day, the class has remained split—Shields and Aletheia on one side, Roallacan Mages on the other. I think briefly about joining the Shields but figure it would make me look weak, pandering for acceptance. Instead, I remain sitting alone in the middle of the room. Always alone.

"Bet he'd kiss his boots if he asked him," Athan whispers beside me, catching me watching Reyn and Caius outside.

I snort, getting the attention of the teacher, who purses her lips at me. I give her a forced smile and go back to doodling.

Announcements for the Winter Festival sweep through the school like wildfire. A date has been set, the date of our last exams for the semester. Kora is practically bursting with glee when she tells me—she's been planning her outfit for *years*, she says. It's a chance for students to mingle for an evening in the courtyard, after curfew. Aris said it was a good excuse to get drunk after exams; Wren, of course, never made it past her first few weeks.

We're walking across the courtyard to the dining hall when a slim hawk dives from the sky. Kora laughs and ducks as it chucks an envelope at us before wheeling away.

"Grumpy, wasn't he?" she says, watching the messenger fly off.

"Mmm," I mumble, grabbing the letter. It's addressed to me, in neat handwriting I know well.

Delphine,

I hope you've settled in well and that you are working hard in all of your classes.

. . .

I take a quick break to roll my eyes here.

I wanted to let you know that I'll be coming down for the Winter Festival—Ismini has some business with Head Mage Iraklis, about the plague popping up again in the Isles, and I thought I'd use it as an excuse to spend some time with you. Hope you've been keeping up with your training—I'd love to see you knock Aris on his arrogant ass next time you see him. I have no doubt you'll be even greater than he ever was (but don't tell him I said that).

Aleka

"Oh, a letter? From who?" Athan says, bounding up beside us, Aletheia his quiet shadow. Today she has bright blue paint above her eyes, and blue and white bracelets clattering on each arm.

"Aleka," I say, grinning.

"Aleka? Like captain of the city guard Aleka Relloti?" Athan asks, his blue eyes wide.

"Just ... Aunt Aleka," I say, grinning wider.

I've missed her. From the very moment we met, she's taken me under her wing—and when Estana fell under attack from the Black Water Witches, she stayed at my side, protecting me as fiercely as a mother bear defending her cub. Watching her and Ismini fight, side by side—they were amazing. Ismini literally rearranged the stone walls of the palace to trap the Roallacan soldiers, and those she couldn't catch, Aleka cut down with unerring efficiency.

I can only hope to have that kind of bond with someone, someday. Could I have it with Kora? I look over at the bubbly head of coppery hair beside me. Maybe. She *is* the strongest Fire Mage in our year, as it turns out—probably better than half the second-years too.

She works tirelessly, never wanting to be left in her brothers' shadows. It's a drive we both share.

Athan whistles, and I laugh, drawing the attention of a few other students in the courtyard, including Reyn and his court, as we've come to call them. A few of the students—Shields and Mages both—have tried to befriend them, but the four always seemed to move together, sit together, eat together. Like a flock of ducks or something.

"I bet they all sleep together too," Athan whispers, following my gaze, and I snort out a laugh.

"Aleka's coming down for the Winter Festival," I tell him, shoving the letter into a pocket.

"Speaking of," Athan says, taking Aletheia's hand. A red flush stains her dark cheeks. "This festival is a big deal, apparently. Some of the second-years are getting their outfits handmade and brought in from Estana."

"The caravans will be here soon," Aletheia says softly. "They're supposed to have all kinds of clothes and things. It should be nice."

"Better than nice," Kora says, bouncing on the balls of her feet. "You all get the Shield games. This is a chance for the *Mages* to show off a little, to get the attention of the Shields for a change."

"We all know whose attention you're after," Athan says, rolling his eyes. "So you don't have to worry. Right, Del?"

"Mm-hmm," I agree.

"Actually, that's not entirely true—it's a masked ball this year!" Kora says, clutching the printed announcement to her chest. "What if you don't recognize me?"

I look pointedly at her hair, which is shining brightly in the afternoon sun.

"Maybe I'll change it," she says, twirling a long strand around her fingers. "Won't that be fun? But of course, I *will* have the most flammable, flamboyant outfit of all!"

"Yeah," Athan says, rolling his eyes.

Kora punches him in the arm.

"Do Shields dress up too?" I ask Kora.

She nods enthusiastically, and I sigh. *Great.*

"The caravans should be coming in next week," Kora says. "They are supposed to bring some good stuff before the festival. They know we'll buy up all the clothes and frills they have, so it's supposed to be a good time to shop. I'll go with you! We'll pick you out an outfit to match mine!" She claps her hands excitedly.

I have to smile at her now. Seeing her so excited is making me—begrudgingly—more curious.

"The ball isn't usually masked," Aletheia says quietly, studying the announcement with a slight frown. "I wonder why they changed it this year."

I look across the courtyard, to where the four Roallacan Water Mages are huddled, talking quietly among themselves. Reyn stiffens, like he can feel me looking at him. His eyes find me across the courtyard like a magnet, probably plotting my imminent demise.

"I can think of four reasons," I say, not turning away until he does.

Classes are boring. I understand that it's important for me to learn about the great battles of Ocron's history, but we're spending a lot of time discussing the Battle of Soltaire and basically how badly we all got bogged down in the ... well, bog. So now we're studying how to use terrain to our advantage or work around it.

Boring.

I'd rather be doing literally anything else, even playing discus with Lyssa and her pack in the courtyard—they're awful cheats. The teachers, especially Philandra, a wolf Shield whose Mage has retired, likes to point me out and ask me specifics. "What was it *like* there?"

she often asks. Philandra fought in Roallac with Commander Markos, but they arrived after I'd razed the arena—and after Wren's magic had decimated the city. I usually shrug when she asks me, or offer some noncommittal answer.

The truth is, I don't want to remember. I was cocky and sure of myself when Adriana reported back to Commander Markos that Wren was caged in starsteel—and dragon fire was the only way they could think of to destroy it. We were pretty sure her robe would protect her—Rafael and I had trained together, after all, and I'd never harmed him during our practices.

But as I flew down through the clouds, heading straight toward a ten-foot-tall, blue-skinned water god and an arena full of angry Water Mages, I wanted to vomit in fear. Fortunately, as a dragon, that involved fire, so I could pretend it was my plan all along. I spewed my flames across the sand, melting big chunks of it into glass where the Water Mages couldn't protect it—and melting the cage Wren was locked in.

I don't dare imagine what would have happened if her robe had been taken away. We knew my dragon fire wouldn't melt Rafael's robe, after all the testing we had done, but still. The protective spells on her Mage robe might be different. Maybe Rafael's, being a Fire Mage, was more immune to fire. And even though her robe *was* fireproof, what if she hadn't been able to cover herself with it in time? I could have *killed* her.

I still wake in a cold sweat several times a week, dreaming about it.

The highlights of my days are, well, any time I'm not in class—even the Shield training. I like exercise, but I feel my heart start to race just thinking about how I'm going to keep up with Athan on the run, or whether Lyssa is going to try and literally stab me in the back during sparring—accidentally, of course. I'm constantly being watched, either by Sinon, one of the predatory second-years who keeps trying to get into my pants, or by literally everyone else in my year who knows that I'm going to be the one to beat come our own games. Every time I stumble or bleed or do anything that is less than perfect, Lyssa and her pack are the first to howl and laugh.

Some evenings, though, after dinner, Tulliano lets me join him in the forge. He must be the oldest person at the school, and even though he's not a Shield, he's practically as big and strong as one. He lets me practice my flames once all the students have cleared out for the day. The Fire Mage building is as bland as the rest of the school, but it does have a really big chimney, and all the forges are spelled to withstand the brutal temperatures of Fire Mages practicing their abilities. So it's the safest place for me to practice too. Dragon fire can melt anything—even starsteel—but after Kora's aunt reinforced the spells here, I can do little real damage, as long as I keep my flame where it's supposed to go.

Which, usually, I do. And when I don't, that's why Tulliano's there, redirecting my flames away from anything that might be charred, including him. He's got layers of waxy burn scars on his burly arms, any arm hair long since singed away. Part of being a Fire Mage, I guess. He's got a bulbous nose and hands as big as my head, but he's the kindest, quietest Mage I've worked with yet, and I find a kind of peace working with him. He also doesn't ask me stupid questions. I like that.

Besides being a Fire Mage, Tulliano is a master blacksmith. I like to watch him craft the helmets and swords that are his specialty. He was the one who made Dimitra's dagger out of the tooth of the dragon that killed her. The fact that he can make such beautiful things with his massive hands is fascinating to me. Apparently, he also made Aris a really nice helmet, but he lost it, twice. And when I'm a second-year, I'll have class with Tulliano every week, learning the basics of weapon crafting and maintenance. It's an easy thing to lose myself in the work, forgetting that everyone else in my class wants to see me fail, that I am held to a standard that feels impossible to maintain.

At least anytime Tulliano works with broken crystals or has bits of tempered metal he can't use, he lets me have them, if I did a good job in my lessons. Sometimes I'm in charge of keeping his fire going at exactly the right temperature—and as a reward, I get sparkly things. I think I'll wire them all together and hang them up, so they catch the light and reflect it all around my room. It's a pretty good incentive for a dragon to do her best.

CHAPTER 8

"Here, I made you something!" Kora says, bouncing on the balls of her feet as she digs in her satchel. The movement makes her hair swing; she has to use one hand to hold back the coppery veil as she keeps looking for ... whatever it is. She finally pulls out a paper-wrapped item with a little crow of triumph and hands it to me.

"What is it?" I ask, holding it gingerly by its string binding. I move to the side of the corridor, near the stairwell in the dorms—it's been a long day, and I could really use a bath. I've been daydreaming about soaking in the water all afternoon during lessons—who'd have thought a dragon enjoyed baths? But I do enjoy them. I really do.

"It's a birthday gift!" Kora blurts out excitedly. "You mentioned your birthday was near the winter solstice. I couldn't figure out how to ask you for the exact date without seeming suspicious, so ... I just kind of picked today for you." Her cheeks are turning pink.

I haven't celebrated a birthday since my parents were alive. We used to celebrate, just the three of us. As I was a forsaken then, they didn't like being seen with me in public. In private, though, they were kind enough. After they died ... well, Tekton and I agreed it didn't feel right, celebrating without them. So I just sort of ... stopped.

"That's ... so thoughtful," I say, choking down the lump in my throat. *I will not cry. Dragons do not cry.*

"Don't say that until you open it," she teases, but the pink on her cheeks deepens.

I untangle the string—tied in an expert bow that thwarts me for a moment—and peel back the paper. Inside is a sturdy silver chain, with a smoky quartz crystal pendant. The pendant is wrapped in wire in a style that I instantly recognize as Tulliano's.

The glowing flame *inside*, though, is all Kora. I bring it up to my face and turn it around and around—it's like the fire is embedded in the crystal somehow.

"How did you ...?" I ask.

Kora laughs at the confusion on my face. "Put it on," she says.

The chain is long, so I'm able to just loop it over my head.

When I touch the crystal again, it starts to glow.

I drop it immediately. It goes dark, bouncing softly against my jacket.

"I charmed it!" she squeals, clapping her hands together. "Like we do with the heatless candles and lanterns! When you touch it while wearing it, you'll have light! Not, like, a lot, but it should be about four or five candles' worth. I may have to redo the spell in a year or so."

"That's brilliant!" I say, touching it again. It glows, lighting up the dark stairwell, but there's no heat. I've never heard of anything like it. "How did you do this?"

"Oh, I went to Tulliano for the metalwork," she says, grinning widely. "The charm I figured out myself. What do you think?"

"I think there's going to be a high demand for these once word gets out," I say.

She claps her hands excitedly.

"Seriously," I continue. "Do you know how handy something like this would be in Aeturnus or in the mountain tunnels out west?"

And Kora just "figured it out"? She claims she wants to be a battle Mage, but sometimes I wonder.

"Thank you," I say, letting the pendant go dark again.

Kora flings her arms wide and gives me a huge hug. "Happy birthday to my best friend!" she cheers. Then she grabs my hand and drags me toward the stairs. "Come on. I made cookies too!"

"I know we're supposed to stick to our Shield diet and all, but *damn* Kora," Athan says, eating his fifth or sixth almond cookie.

She preens and hands him another.

I've lost track of how many I've consumed, but there are a *lot* of crumbs on my bed now.

"I like to bake," she admits shyly. "I know I should be focusing on throwing fireballs and things, but baking ... calms me. You know?"

I think of Frostbite; the cookie suddenly sticks in my throat, and I cough for a moment.

"I'm cutting you off," Athan says, grabbing the plate of cookies and plopping it in his lap.

"These are seriously good," I tell her. "Better than anything they serve here."

"Hey! You should make some for the Winter Festival!" Athan says.

Kora freezes. "Oh, no, I couldn't ..."

"Sure you can! We'll help, won't we?" Athan says, nudging me with his foot. "And if you want to practice some more recipes, I'll help with that too!"

"I do have a few ideas ..." Kora starts shyly, glancing for a moment at the pendant at my neck. "I thought ... if I can put fire magic in charms and things, why not food?"

It's Athan's turn to sputter, and crumbs go everywhere.

"I've been working on a cookie that will keep you warm for hours after eating it. It'd be nice to have in the winter. I've been fiddling with the recipe, but it's not quite right yet. The ingredients have to mesh with the magic, not fight it. Cinnamon, of course, and cloves, which are just so hard to come by. I had to get them imported from the Isles—" She stops as she realizes she's rambling.

"Keep going!" Athan says through a mouthful of cookie.

"It's just a stupid hobby," she says, looking down at a cookie in her own hands.

I realize she hasn't eaten a single one. It occurs to me then that she's echoing something someone has told her before. An ache settles in my chest.

"It's all right if you do things for fun," I say, grabbing her hand and squeezing it. "You don't have to be a battle Mage all the time. And if you ever wanted to, seriously, you'd put the cooks here out of business."

"Really?" she says, looking up at us through her lashes.

Athan nods emphatically. "Oh, I bet we could get your Earth Mage friend to help us with the cloves—they can grow anything in that greenhouse of theirs!" he says, caught up in the moment. "How about candies that make you breathe fire when you chew them?" He sets the empty plate aside. "I'd love that!"

I snort. "Just don't swallow those candies," I say.

Kora sputters, then starts giggling.

And she can't stop. It's like she's let out her secret; the relief is just pouring off her in waves.

Soon we're all laughing, and Athan is pretending he's farting flames, and I realize that this might be the best birthday I've ever had.

CHAPTER 9

"If that dress was cut any lower, your ass would be on display."

"You'd like that, wouldn't you?" I say, punching Athan on the arm.

He's cleaned up well too, wearing a blue shirt and mask that sets off his eyes—and, conveniently, exactly matches the color of Aletheia's magic. The boy is tripping over himself for her, and I'm a little surprised at the pang in my chest. I certainly don't want Athan, so I rub the center of my chest until the strange feeling eases.

"I'm just saying, the only decent thing you're wearing is that necklace," he says.

"And you still smell like a wet dog," I retort.

He grins.

"Come on. Let's get drunk," he says, gallantly offering me his arm.

I take it, and we head into the courtyard, where Kora is causing a stir.

It seems that she's been underselling her outfit after all—she's wearing a tall black crown with burning embers, like rubies, on top of her curled rose-gold hair. Her dress is black too, to match mine, but where mine is sleek and simple, hers is artfully charred, the puffy, layered edges smoldering but not burning, not producing much heat. It takes a lot of effort to keep that kind of spell up. I'm impressed and tell her so. She blushes, though it's hard to tell under her ornate lacy black mask, and she is pleased to see I'm wearing her pendant. I have a mask too, a plain black silk one to match my dress. Like anyone will be able to mistake who I am.

The courtyard is alight with Mages and Shields of both years, plus some teachers and alumni. Strings of spelled lights in all colors span the courtyard, making the usual austere architecture seem festive. It's cold, but the Wind Mages have at least cleared the sky of clouds today, and my dragon fire keeps me warm enough.

There's food and drinks at every turn. Some of the second-year Mages are having little contests to see who can make their outfit more incredible, vying to attract a strong Shield when the games come around. It's like birds putting on a display for a mate. The thought makes me giggle into my wine.

One of the Earth Mages wears a ball gown entirely made of leaves—two of them strategically over her breasts—with big pink flowers blooming on the hem of the skirt. Her mask is made of delicate vines twining through her hair.

Another wears a dress made of sand. It must weigh a ton, but it shifts and moves with her like it is made of silk. Gaius, one of the second-year Fire Mages, wears a fine black suit fit for the halls of Estana—but flames lick up the cuffs, not consuming but rather decorating it. He wears a small, simple red mask with flames glowing on the edges. My eyes feel dazzled by all the finery, my inner dragon reveling in the opulence.

Then Athan grabs me around the waist, pulling me over to where Aletheia and some of the other Mages of our year are standing. Aletheia wears a dress that looks like water is cascading down her body, with jewels of ice, like diamonds, scattered in the coiled braids of her hair. Her mask is a thin, delicate thing sculpted from ice, contrasting beautifully against her dark skin. She's breathtaking.

But she's the only Water Mage of our year I see. I finally spy Silas with one of the twins, over on the periphery. They're both wearing their usual black, with their Mage training robes. Neither looks happy to be there, and no one approaches them either. They're not even wearing masks.

"They could have at least made an effort," Kora grumbles. Sparks dance in coils around her wrists; the effect is mesmerizing.

I go back to ignoring the snakes and try to enjoy myself. I'm just grateful no one cares—much—what the Shields wear to these events. I like dressing up as much as the next girl, but I'm not the one here to impress everyone, for a change.

"They don't get claimed by Shields, so I guess they don't feel the need to impress anyone," Aletheia says quietly, still looking at the Roallacan Mages. "Not to mention, designing an outfit made of water is really hard."

"No, wind has got to be way harder than water to design an outfit around," I argue. "No offense," I tell Aletheia.

She shrugs. "Do you understand how hard it is to keep this water flowing over me like this? It'll take me a week to recover my magic," she says, grinning and gesturing at her gown.

I gesture to one of the Wind Mages. He wears his normal clothes but is walking a foot above the ground, an impressive display of his flying talent.

"Look at him," I say, gesturing with my head. "That's different."

"It's not that impressive," Kora scoffs, the embers of her dress flaring.

One of the second-years—Batten, another Wind Mage—picks that moment to show up naked and tries to convince the teachers that he is "clothed in air." Athan laughs so hard that ale comes out his nose.

"Finally," he wheezes. "Someone gets straight to the point."

I'll admit, it is funny—but Batten's sent away wrapped in a tablecloth, to our dismay.

Aleka and Ismini arrive just as the party is getting underway. They dismount at the gate; there are a few others with them, notably two Water Mages in blue robes, but I don't pay too much attention. I've been waiting for them, watching the gate every second, and when I see them, I race over to hug them both tightly. They smell of horses and leather, and *I will not start crying, damn it.* Aleka wears black Shield gear, along with a golden sun emblem on her chest, designating her as the captain of Estana's guard. She has cropped white-blond hair, and though she is nearly as small as I am, she walks with the bearing of pride that she's earned over the years.

Ismini is the opposite side of Aleka's gruff coin—she's everything soft, with her fluffy red hair and green robe and kind smile. She smells like spicy geraniums and dirt and sunshine. If I hadn't seen her single-handedly rearrange the walls of an entire palace to trap Roallacan soldiers with my own eyes, I'm not sure I'd have believed it.

The last member of their group is a wizened old man riding in a cart laden with plants and cuttings of all shapes and colors. It's being pulled by a mare with white hairs peppering her nose.

Ismini gestures toward the cart. "I've brought a few things along that Head Mage Iraklis wanted to try," she explains. "Our healers are stretched too thin, and our usual remedies don't seem to have much effect on the plague. I have a theory that combining them with the leaves from the Century Tree here will enhance their properties."

Her mouth is pressed tight, fine lines gathering at the corners. The plague has her worried. I guess we've been more insulated from it here than I realized.

Soon there's a small crowd around us—the two Water Mages with them are healers, apparently. They've come with Ismini to address the plague that's now popping up on the eastern coast.

"Are they ... Roallacan Mages?" I ask, eyeing them.

Aleka shakes her head. "Ocronian. Those other two over there are their Shields," she says, nodding toward the other two men, still on horseback. They're tall, strong-looking, and eyeing the whole courtyard like they expect to be attacked at any moment.

"Gods, girl, aren't they feeding you here?" Ismini laments, pinching my bare arm. With all the workouts we've been doing, there isn't a scrap of fat on me.

I shrug, not sure I trust my voice not to wobble.

"Hi! I'm Kora!" Kora says, coming over and extending her hand to Ismini. "Del's told me all about you."

"Ah, this is your Fire Mage?" Aleka asks, crossing her arms and sizing Kora up.

Kora's smile wavers for a second, the flaming edges of her gown sputtering—Aleka is fucking intimidating, after all—but she holds her ground. Eventually, Aleka claps her on the shoulder.

"I know your brothers well. If you're half the Mage they are, you'll do just fine."

"I'm *twice* the Mage they are," Kora says, lifting her chin.

Aleka grins. She approves.

"Oh, I like her," Ismini whispers to me. "Good choice."

We're soon swarmed by teachers who know them. I see Aleka and Ismini for only a few short minutes before Head Mage Iraklis steals them away—but at least, for a moment, it was nice to have family with me. Ismini admires my dress, tells me to eat more again, and Aleka tells me to behave. Typical auntie behavior. I hug them tightly when they go.

The evening otherwise passes in a haze of drink and talk. Before too long, I find myself in a courtyard full of people—and yet somehow I am completely abandoned. Kora's off in some dark corner with her Earth Mage boy, and Athan and Aletheia have been missing for some time now.

As I stand there, in the simple black dress I've worn specifically to make a statement, at odds with the elaborate finery around me, I'm all alone. I feel ... out of place. Like a stone in a raging river, people talking and swirling all around me as I fight the current. My skin itches, and my pulse starts racing. A trickle of sweat runs down my back despite the chill in the air. Suddenly I feel the walls of the school closing in around me, and my breath feels thick, inadequate. I have to go somewhere I can breathe.

No one even notices when I slip down the alleyway between two of the buildings and make my way back to the dorms. No one stops me. No one asks if I'm all right, because I'm always all right. I am the Dragon Girl. I am put on a podium by myself, and it feels suddenly, overwhelmingly *lonely*. I wish that Aleka or Ismini would reappear, but of course, they have more important things to do. Everyone does.

I consider going back to my room, but I couldn't sleep even if I wanted to. I'm too amped up, too much pressure inside me, like a teapot about to scream. *I am the Dragon Girl*—I do not run away from anything, let alone a party. I tell myself that I am too intimidating, and that's why people avoided me tonight. And Kora couldn't stay by me the whole time, not when she was eyeing Calix the whole time. I'm alone because I *choose* to be. I could have practically anybody in my bed right now if I wanted to.

So I rip my mask off and go up to the rooftop, the top of the wall above my room, where I can look down on the noise and laughter in the courtyard below—and I make my way around to the other side of the wall, the far side, back behind the stables, where it's quiet, and when I look out over the valley, all I can see is the river, a silver ribbon, winding across the dark grassy plains to the horizon. I catch a brief glimpse of old Geoff, the cat who spends his days sunning himself on the stone wall and his nights keeping the guards company in exchange for treats and pets.

But even he leaves me.

Up here, at least, the air is fresh and sweet, no sickly smells of spilled wine and sweat and too much perfume. The pressure in my chest lightens, just enough so that I can take a single deep breath.

It's not enough.

I put my foot on a crenel of the outer wall and lift my skirt so I can take out the blade I have strapped to my thigh. The silk, which felt as light as moonlight against my skin, now feels heavy and itchy. It's a cool evening, but I'm never cold. Even now I feel hot, too hot, like my dragon fire will explode right out of my skin if I let it. I run my finger over the edge of my knife, sighing with relief as the fine edge draws a drop of blood.

There's a sound behind me, a single sharp inhalation.

I whirl, flipping the knife point out and flaring my wings out in the next heartbeat. No one should *dare* sneak up on a dragon.

A trickle of blood runs from my finger to my palm, making the knife handle slick.

And sitting there in the dark, nearly hidden by the crenellation of the wall, is the Fallen Prince himself.

He unfolds himself from the darkness to stand before me, a crushed black mask in one hand. He's dressed in his usual plain black clothes, without his Mage robe. Even with a mask, it would have been easy to identify him from his bearing—proud, like an eagle. With the dark hair he's let grow since he's been here, and those black-rimmed green eyes, there's no disguising him. I'd be able to pick him out anywhere.

"You weren't at the party," I say. I can feel the rapid flutter of my heartbeat pulsing in my neck and will it to slow. I am *not* afraid of this man. He simply startled me.

He smirks, giving a little huff of a laugh as he looks down at the mask in his hand.

"No," he says, and he turns from me, cocks his arm back, and throws the mask over the wall. We watch it flutter down, until it gets lost in the long grasses below.

"You don't like having fun?" I ask, folding my wings back, until they shrink into my shoulder blades. I keep holding my knife—the last thing I want is to give him an eyeful as I sheathe it on my thigh, though I have to wonder exactly how much he saw when I removed it. I'm as concerned about that as whether he guessed my secret. Shields get comfortable with nudity—but somehow, lifting my skirt in front of him feels much more intimate than simply being naked after shifting.

"The winter solstice is the anniversary of the Battle of Soltaire," he reminds me.

I wince. Yeah, that's a terrible coincidence. I bet he lost some friends that day, maybe family too. I wonder if he had any part of the event—he would have been fourteen or so at the time, like me. I wonder if he watched as Wren took down his queen, as Aris banished his god.

As I burned down his whole world.

"I just wanted to clear my head," he says, shrugging, leaning on the outer wall. "You?"

"Same," I say.

It's more words than I've heard him say to me all semester.

He nods, then takes a slow step closer to me, and another. I glare up at him and consider stabbing him with my knife if he takes one more step, Prince of Snakes or not.

He looks down at my hand, his black hair shadowing his face, and takes it between his. His hands are as cool as ice, the fingers long and firm where they reach out and grip mine, and I'm momentarily too shocked to withdraw.

He pulls the knife from my hand—I resist at first, but he fixes me with those emerald eyes, dark brows furrowed, and I release my grip at his silent request. I feel like a mouse mesmerized by a snake, but his touch is gentle, steady. For a moment, I think he might try something with my knife, but he just places it on the wall, holding my fingers captive in his own. *I could stop him*, I think. *I* should *stop him.* Then he touches the cut on my finger with one of his, whispers a soft word, and a cool blue glow transfers from his hand to mine, healing the wound instantly.

I inhale sharply, snatching my hand back from him, and swipe my knife from the wall.

"It would have healed on its own in a few moments," I say, clutching the hand to my chest and pointing my knife at him again.

My hand still feels cold, like the kind of frostburn you could get from spending time in the mountains in winter.

"I would have thought a Shield of your ... renown," he says, looking me over, a knowing smile on his stupid handsome face, "would be more careful with her weapons."

He knows. Fuck it, *he knows.*

He looks steadily at me, waiting for me to say something, to deny it, to rage. I bet he can't wait to hold this over my head. I can deny it, of course, but it won't matter. The Dragon Girl is a cutter. She can't handle the pressure, says the heir of Roallac. Word will spread faster than dragon fire, my reputation forever tarnished, ending me more effectively than if he'd just stuck the knife in my chest. Shields don't show weakness. We don't *have* weaknesses. We handle anything that comes our way, no matter what. Especially the Dragon Girl.

I swallow, my mouth suddenly bone-dry, and stare right back at him.

"You know nothing about me," I say. I meant my voice to sound strong, but it comes out as barely a whisper. So I push past him, heading for the stairs.

I pause for just a moment, looking back over my shoulder, to see if he's going to be stupid enough to try to follow, the knife in my hand ready to stab him if so—but he's just leaning with his back against the outer wall, hands in his pockets, watching.

I race back to my room. Once there—with the door bolted—I look at my knife in the spelled lantern light. My blood has dried into the decorative grooves in the handle, which will be a bitch to clean.

And the tightness in my chest is worse than ever, a screaming, raging presence that begs for release.

I look at the knife, remembering the look in Reyn's eyes when he saw my hand—*Was it really concern, or pity? Why did I let him take my hand?*—and throw the knife across the room, letting it clatter to the floor under the desk. I've given my enemy an opening. All I can do is wait for him to tell someone—which I'm sure he'll do at the worst possible opportunity.

I throw my face down into the pillow on my bed and scream until I'm hoarse and my cheeks are sticky with salt water.

I dream that night of a giant black snake with emeralds for eyes, coiling around me tighter, and tighter, squeezing the air from my lungs—and when I wake up, I'm covered in sweat and panting for breath.

CHAPTER 10

The next morning, with Frostbite tucked firmly back into its sheath at my hip—and all traces of blood thoroughly scourged from the handle—I go looking for the Snake Prince. I have to find some way to convince him to keep my secret—I can't think of any compelling reason offhand, other than I'll pummel him if he does, but I can worry about that after I've found him. I'll teach him.

You fuck around with a dragon; you get burned. Or eaten. The point is you die an excruciating death. Which is exactly what I wish on the Snake Prince at the moment, if he lets anyone know my secret.

The school has, mercifully, given us all day after the Winter Festival off to sleep off the late night and alcohol.

And I'm up at dawn, stalking the halls like a wildcat, looking for Reyn.

I can't find him anywhere, which only makes my heart race faster. I reach for Frostbite several times, wanting to feel the sting of pain grounding me—but each time, I let my hand fall without drawing it.

I check the dormitory halls. I pass his room once, twice, before getting up the courage to knock. There's no answer, so I try the handle—locked. *Shit.* Well, I half hoped I'd find him in some compromising position that I could hold over his head so he wouldn't tell my secret. Maybe sleeping with a Shield or something. Maybe Lyssa—she seems obsessed with him lately. Too bad.

I cover the school all morning. I check the dining hall, the baths—I even peek into the men's chambers, much to the amusement of a few early-morning bathers. He's nowhere to be found. I check the Water Mage building and Caius's office—I have to pick the lock, which isn't hard with dragon claws. No one there, though it's hard to tell through all the clutter. Hastily labeled jars of water, from all over, line one shelf, some books scattered across his desk and even piled on the floor. Other jars, of opaque brown glass, lie stashed beside the skeleton of a viper, meticulously put together with wires. Small silvery spikes are strewn across his desk from a toppled box, a half-eaten meal forgotten beside them. I wrinkle my nose at the smell—garlic—and leave the building, my breath starting to come fast.

"What's got you up so early?" Vassilis asks, yawning widely.

I nearly jump out of my skin when I hear his voice boom behind me.

He rolls his shoulders and starts stretching for one of those early-morning runs he's so fond of.

"Oh, um," I say, my eyes widening as they fall on the library. "Thought I'd use the time off to ... study."

Vassilis raises an eyebrow but doesn't comment further, so I rush off in the direction of the library. If I were an evil snake prince with a secret that would ruin my enemy's life, where would I hide?

Well, Shields don't generally use the library. We're the muscle; Mages are the brains. So I head there next. I imagine myself throwing Reyn into the stacks of books, and that makes the nervous energy in my blood settle down a little.

I open the door with a bang and wince. I want to catch him unawares, not announce my presence. I creep down each row on the upper floor before taking the stairs at the rear to the lower levels.

One of the benefits of having Earth Mages here is that they turned the hill of the school into a warren of tunnels and rooms—the lower levels of the library descend deep into the earth, and I go down each and every row of musty old books with not even a candle to light my way. I move like Aris taught me, heel first, silent and swift.

I'm at the end of the third lower level when I finally see a flickering light at the end of a row of books. *Aha!*

I sneak down the row of books, barely breathing. One of the tables is occupied, a pair of spelled candles lighting the space—candles that burn and produce plenty of light but no heat. Handy for a library.

And sitting in the space is Reyn, a look of intense concentration on his face.

But he's not reading.

He's ... sculpting something. Out of ice.

His hands swirl over his desk, next to the forgotten book in front of him, and a form coalesces from the sparkling blue magic. It's indistinct at first, but as he whispers, it takes shape. It's a beautiful sight, his face serious as he concentrates, lips pulled to one side, the blue light gliding over the angular planes of his face, the high cheekbones and the hollows beneath them, as the magic slowly takes shape before him.

It's a girl, dress blown tight against her body, arms outstretched, long hair unadorned.

And a pair of huge feathered wings sprouting from her back.

I inhale sharply—Reyn's eyes snap to mine, finding me lurking there in the dark, much the way he was spying on me last night.

I step from the shadows, intent on confronting him.

Instead, I find myself flung backward into the nearest shelf without a warning, my wrists shackled by bolts of ice to the wood. I tug and then pull, but they don't move. Reyn gets up from his chair slowly, fingers still outstretched toward my wrists. I narrow my eyes.

When he's close enough, I hang from my wrists and curl at the waist to lash my feet outward, catching him in the ribs as he tries to step back. He growls, holding his side, and with another word, my feet are bound to the floor by more ice.

"Since you're just hanging there, mind telling me why you're haunting the library at this hour?" he asks. His breathing is a little labored, and I grin as he winces.

"Studying," I say.

He snorts.

"What are *you* doing?"

I look at the statue on his desk, a sculpture of ice so clear it could be diamond. The facets catch the flickering light of the candles. It's the most beautiful thing I've ever seen.

And it is, undeniably, me.

He frowns, and the statue turns into a puff of mist that disperses in the dry library air. I cry out, my inner dragon upset at seeing something so pretty destroyed. He raises his eyebrows, intrigued or amused, and then the shackles on my wrists and ankles vanish too. I rub my wrists—though they are cold, they are not hurt. Not like his side. I smirk. I could have melted his stupid manacles, but I'd have burned myself and probably half the library in the process. I could have shifted and broken them ... and again, destroyed the library in the process. I *was* prepared to do one or the other if he hadn't freed me himself.

"What do you want?" Reyn asks, one hand hovering over his side. A curl of blue magic makes its way from his palm to his ribs, where it sinks into him. He stretches, breathing deeply as his magic heals him. Then he crosses his arms and glares at me.

"I want a deal," I say, mimicking his pose.

"About what?" he asks.

About what? He cannot possibly be that dense.

"About ... last night. On the wall."

"What, you don't want anyone knowing we spoke? Me neither," he says, sitting back at his desk and ignoring me.

"I don't want anyone knowing ... the other thing," I say, my hand straying to Frostbite at my hip.

"It's ... done," he says, watching my hand.

I leave my knife where it is. His eyes flick back to mine—I cannot trust him to keep his word. I need leverage.

"Look, what I do with my body is my business," I snap. "As a healer, you should respect that."

"I do. I've told you, twice now. I won't tell anyone," he says. "But you should."

He turns his back to me and sits back down at his table. He flips a page in his book, pretending to ignore me.

Heat flashes through me. I stomp over to him and see he's not reading a book; he's writing in a notebook. Neatly inked lines in the language of the gods fill the pages.

Tēcum lūdere sīcut ipsa possem,
et trīstīs animī levāre cūrās!

He slams the notebook shut, keeping his hands firmly on the cover, like he's worried I'm going to snatch it from him. I roll my eyes—I couldn't care less about his bad poetry.

"This isn't about ... Look. You tell anyone about what you saw—*anyone*—and I'll tell them what you do in the dark down here when you think of me."

His eyes flash to mine. I smirk—there's a definite flush creeping up the back of his pale neck. I've got him. I lean over the desk, putting my palms on it and staring him down.

"Mark my words, *snake*," I say. "I *will* be the end of you."

"No one will believe you," he says, but there's a definite catch in his voice.

"No one will believe *you*," I counter. "I'm the Dragon Girl, remember? God-blessed. Savior of Ocron." The nicknames come out sounding sarcastic, even to my own ears. *I'm the "lucky one,"* I think. *"God-blessed." So why does it always feel so much like drowning?*

"I won't ... Look, I just sculpt things sometimes. It relaxes me. I don't care who knows," he says.

"Do you always so prominently feature the nipples in your other sculptures?" I ask archly. "I mean, they *are* rather nice. And it was a little chilly last night." I look down at my chest.

He runs his hands into his hair. I've frustrated him or embarrassed him—*Good.* Reyn lets out a long breath as he considers his options.

"All right, I accept your deal," he says after a moment. "Not a word, then. From either of us."

"Not a word. I swear." I grin. I've won.

We glare at each other for a moment, the air between us charged with something more than just dust and icy mist. A muscle feathers in his jaw as he clenches his teeth. I can't pretend I've tamed this snake, just put a leash on him. *Wait, do you leash a captured snake? Caged him, then. Maybe. Whatever.*

"Well. Back to your studies, then, Prince."

He turns from me, brows drawn tight, and glares at the book in front of him until I see frost start curling up the cover.

I turn and leave the library. My panic has ebbed; my battle has been won. Still, I feel troubled. I grab Frostbite's handle as I climb the stairs, one thought resounding in my mind.

Why was *the Snake Prince making a sculpture of* me?

CHAPTER 11

"Today we continue our study on terrain," Philandra says, pacing the room.

All twelve of the Shields in my class are fixated on her. Most of us are wearing black Shield clothing, our informal uniform for when we're not in the arena. Lyssa prefers the short leather skirt and leather breast band that shows off her ... well, everything. I wear the black shirt, pants, and boots like the rest, but with the shirt untucked and mostly unbuttoned, so everyone knows I don't care about it too much. It's a calculated thing.

Philandra, our instructor, is an older Shield, and an accomplished one. She fought with Aleka years ago and won battles all over the continent and the Isles. Her lessons are always peppered with little stories from her years of service, and we hang on her every word.

Battle strategy is taught in one of the first-floor classrooms of the academic building. It's plain gray stone, like everything else, with benched tables lined up in neat rows. At the front is a large map of the world, from Abelon to Roallac.

Philandra strides to the front, one finger—gnarled from being broken many times—pointing to the marshy area in the western peninsula of what was once Aclines—and then she points to the swamps of Roallac.

“Aclines and Roallac. Two wars waged in our lifetimes, two countries conquered. The terrain in each was used by our opponents to their advantage, more successfully in Roallac. Aclines with their marsh, Roallac with their swamps. Similar terrain. So why was Roallac so hard to penetrate?”

The word *penetrate* gets a snicker from Athan.

“I’m sure Delphine can tell us,” Lyssa says sweetly. Today she’s wearing her shoulder-length brown hair in twin braids, plaited tight against her scalp. There’s not a hint of softness about her, no matter what honeyed words she spills. She knows I hate talking about Soltaire.

“If you don’t know the answer, you don’t deserve to be here,” I retort.

Philandra crosses her arms, the sinewy muscles crisscrossed with scars that she wears like badges of honor.

“Delphine, tell us,” Philandra says, frowning.

I sigh. She *always* calls on me. It’s one class I can’t daydream in. I finger Frostbite’s hilt, cool and reassuring on my thigh.

“Magic,” I say simply.

Philandra rolls her eyes. “Elaborate,” she prompts.

I shoot a glare at Lyssa. “Aclines has—had no Mages, no magic,” I say. Well, not before Wren, anyway. I feel clammy, thinking about that day in Soltaire. “Evanthia turned the water of Roallac against us. Our Water Mages couldn’t combat it, at least not quickly. They knew their terrain well. Between the poisonous fogs of swamp gas, flooding our camp, and pushing our boats around, the campaign took much longer than Aclines.”

“You are so *lucky*, oh Slayer of Soltaire, to have been there,” Lyssa continues. “Remind me, how long were you in the battle? Five minutes?”

"What can I say? I'm efficient," I say, studying a peeling callus on my hand.

Lyssa mutters something under her breath.

"If only Lyssa had been there to save us from the Black Water Witches with her sharp tongue," Athan barks. He is the only wolf Shield who isn't part of her little pack, and his comment gets a round of murmured agreement from the other non-wolfy Shields.

"For your assignment today," Philandra continues, eyeing us and handing us each a sheet of paper with a map of Roallac on it. My stomach clenches. "You will each evaluate the terrain of Roallac. Knowing that they had many strong Water Mages on their side, you will write a plan of attack on the city of Soltaire. I expect your completed plan in two days. I want detailed accounts of troop movements, supplies—everything Commander Markos would have needed to consider."

I snort.

Philandra continues on for a while about the mountains in the west, and how the trolls like to ambush travelers there. I mostly tune her out. Instead, I take the piece of paper and write a single sentence on it.

It's not that I'm not proud of what I did. I am. I saved Wren, and probably a whole lot of other people too. I brought that battle to a swift end. But at what price? Aris had wanted to keep me out of there, and I hate to admit it, but he was probably right. I hadn't gotten good control of my fire yet, and once I started flaming, I couldn't stop.

I'd intended to scare a bunch of those Water Mages into attacking me, paying attention to *me* so that Wren and Aris could get away.

But one of the bastards on the wall shot a spear of ice at me, and it punched right through my wing. My tightly controlled stream of flame flared, spewing out of control as I roared from the pain. I shook my head before I could think through the pain, before I could make myself keep the flame directed at the sandy arena floor.

I don't know how many Roallacan lives that lapse cost me. More than three, probably less than ten. Obliterated in an instant, nothing left of those soldiers but piles of melted metal and ash.

And Ocron calls me a hero.

Was it worth it?

Commander Markos and Lukas think so. King Leonidas thinks so. So it *must* be worth it. It has to be. Or those souls will be weighed against mine on the immortal scales when my time comes to stand before Rigrasil.

At the end of class, I hand in my paper.

Plan of attack on Soltaire:
Fly in and burn it to the ground.

I'm exhausted. Tulliano is an exacting tutor. I've learned so much from him, but I'm tired and covered in soot and sweat, and all I want to do is sleep—but at least I've also earned some treasures tonight. In my pocket, a handful of shiny metal pieces and a faceted crystal jingle softly. The crystal has a flaw, Tulliano said, pointing out the dust speck inside. The sword he was making was a ceremonial weapon for a visiting dignitary from the Isles, and he couldn't afford it to have any blemishes. I think he was making it up, but I appreciate the trinket anyway. It's a fine jewel and will make the finishing touch for the suncatcher I've been working on. It's a crude thing, a private thing, but when the morning light hits it, the sparkles and shimmers light up my whole room. No dragon's hoard in history could have sparkled more.

I push open the door to my room, anticipating the delight at adding this crystal to my collection—and I freeze, instantly aware that something is terribly wrong.

My room is usually messy. But this ... the bed has been overturned, the bookshelf knocked over. My clothes have all been thrown into a corner. I heave the bookshelf upright and search for my treasures before anything else—my pendant from Wren is there, unbroken; the handful of obsidian beads are scattered, but they are all there. I place them back carefully, then find the crystal from Estana's chandelier in the pile of clothes in the corner. There's a chip in one of the rounded pieces, but otherwise, it's intact. The books and other things I shove onto the bottom shelf haphazardly.

I turn my bed over with a grunt and go through the bedding piece by piece.

I finally find my suncatcher twisted in the sheets. Someone has taken the delicate wires and broken them, twisted them together into a mess. The bits of reflective metal are bent, the glass broken. The crystals Tulliano has gifted me—shattered.

I roar into the night, not caring who I wake. Someone has dared violate my hoard, my room, and ruined something that is *mine.* Thank Rigrasil I'm wearing Kora's necklace—it makes her happy to see me wear it, so I rarely take it off anymore. I'd have been crushed if it had been ruined.

I straighten my room a little and consider the suspects. The twins, of course, and Lyssa. I doubt Silas would have done it, unless the twins goaded him into it somehow. Sinon might be an idiot, but he wants to get *into* my bed, not destroy it. The rest of the students might not like me, but I doubt they are stupid enough to do something that would incur my wrath like this. Reyn? He hates me enough to do something like this, but he isn't stupid either.

So that leaves Eugenia, Isadora, and Lyssa. They hate me enough, and they're definitely stupid enough.

I stay awake the rest of the night, plotting my interrogations.

"The plague is spreading from the Isles," Kora says to me over lunch in the dining hall. "Now it's in Aclines. Worst outbreak the country's seen in years."

"Where are the healers?" I ask. I touch the chain around my neck, avoiding activating the charm. I twist the chain around my fingers. I'm no closer to figuring out who wrecked my room, and I touch the necklace frequently to make sure it is still there. I haven't told anyone about it. Admitting someone dared come after me like that? Not good for my reputation.

"In the cities, mostly," she says. "Raverra's been hit really hard. The king is telling people to leave the rural parts of Aclines especially and get to the cities for treatment."

"We call it Ocron now," Aletheia supplies helpfully, nodding at the banners swinging overhead. "Aclines. It's Ocron now. Just like Roallac."

"Ah, yes. King Leonidas the Conqueror," Athan says, downing his glass of ash water. "What next? The stars? The immortal realm?"

"The point is," Kora says, flicking a pea at him, "with all those roads the king made, the new ports, he's made it even easier for people to travel, and the plague to spread. It'll be here before next semester; you can bet on it."

"How do you know all this?" I ask.

"Calix told me," she says, her cheeks flushing pink.

Her on-again, off-again Earth Mage lover. I find him about as interesting as a rock, but he does seem to balance out some of Kora's bubbliness.

"With Aenon trying to get back into the mortal realm and all the disruption to magic? We've got nowhere near the healers we need to combat this plague, and the local herbalists aren't having any luck with natural remedies," Aletheia explains, like we don't already know all that.

Today she's got her hair done up in two little buns, like ears or horns, and her nails are painted black. She's gotten Kora to make her a pair of crystal-flame earrings that glow when she touches them, so they look like little stars. A Water Mage wearing Fire Mage jewelry. She's a combination of cute and strange that I don't really understand, but I have to admire her for it—she doesn't care what anyone else thinks about her. That must be nice.

I stick my knife into the wood of the table, breaking off splinters as my mind spins.

"Head Mage Iraklis and King Leonidas have been trying to grow stronger strains of oregano and lemon balm to combat it," Kora says. "Calix says a lot of his classes have been about using herbs and plants for treatments lately."

"Without enough healers, they must be getting desperate," Athan says. "I mean, how effective are these ... magic lemon oregano plants? Sounds like we're fighting the plague with a strong cup of tea."

"*Disgusting* tea," Aletheia adds.

"They are pretty desperate," Kora says, toying with the cuffs of her robe.

I nod in agreement, frowning. I don't like it. The plague isn't a foe I can fight or crush with my claws.

"Funny how it's not affecting Roallac, isn't it?" Athan says, taking a big bite out of an apple.

"We call that Ocron now too," Aletheia reminds him, poking him in the ribs.

My heart squeezes. Aclines is where Wren is from, before it was absorbed by Ocron a few years back.

"Where in Aclines is affected, do you know?" I ask her, stirring the barley in my bowl.

"I don't know. Just the outer edges, I think. The outmost parts," Kora says.

Fuck.

That evening, Vassilis asks to talk to me after another round of weapons-free exercises. I'm not sure what he wants, but being singled out makes me anxious and makes my skin itch. I palm Frostbite as I wave Athan and the others off. I wipe the sweat from my face with the back of my hand and stand straight, hoping to project the cockiness and confidence I don't feel.

"You've been doing well," Vassilis starts.

I raise an eyebrow—if he's leading with a compliment, it must mean he wants something. After all, he has Head Mage Iraklis's ear, and Commander Markos's. Has Lukas convinced him to send me to the front after all? My heart rate doubles, and sweat runs down my back, which has nothing to do with the workout we just finished.

"I need to ask you something, Delphine—a favor. From the king," he says. He runs a hand through his sweaty red hair, a movement that reminds me so much of Aris that for a moment I feel it like a dagger to my heart, and it hurts to breathe.

He takes my silence for encouragement to continue.

"Healers are being dispatched all over the continent. We're sending them by horse, by boat—but it's not enough. There are barely enough healers, and we can't get them where they're needed most."

"I've heard," I say, nodding, beginning to suspect what Vassilis wants to ask me.

It doesn't sound like Lukas got to him, not if Vassilis is talking about healers. Lukas doesn't care about healers; he cares about battles. I think—I hope—that if and when the plague comes to the school, the healers here will be enough to fight it off.

"The king wants you to take one of his healers south, to Aclines. To Spit specifically," he says, eyes scanning my face.

Spit. Wren's old home. Kora mentioned the area, vaguely, but to name the town directly ... my chest clenches. How many people can one healer take care of? I'm not sure. We have a number of students who have some healing ability, and Caius, along with the healers assigned to the school. We'll be safe here. At least as a Shield, with my healing abilities, I'm largely immune to infections like the plague. I've never even had a cold. But Spit? Aclines doesn't have magic, or not much. The plague will rip through the southern part of our continent like a fox through a henhouse.

"Can't he take a boat?" I ask.

"Too slow," Vassilis says, frowning. "I don't like it either, but the fact is that you're much faster. It would take two weeks by horse, at least a week or ten days by boat. You can do it in three days."

"To Spit? Maybe two," I say. It's not bragging if it's true.

Vassilis nods. "The healer will be arriving tomorrow. King's Messengers are already alerting the town and inns on the way south, so they'll be expecting a dragon."

He assumes I'm going to agree to this. Well, he's not wrong. A chance to get away from the school for a few days, to really stretch my wings? To help Wren's old home? To prove I'm worth the training Aris gave me, able to take on an assignment before the end of my first year? Of course I'm going.

"We're going to see some changes around here," Vassilis continues, his gaze unfocused. "The Earth Mages are growing healing herbs. The Water Mages are learning more and more healing techniques. Wind Mages are being deployed to the navy by the score. It's not an enemy that most Shields can fight—but you can."

I straighten up. I *can*, and I *will*.

"I'm ready to go," I say.

Vassilis nods, a relieved smile on his face. He claps my shoulder with one calloused hand.

"I knew you'd want to help," he says. "Just like Aris."

It's the highest compliment he's ever given me. I try not to show it, but I'm sure I'm grinning like a fool.

The healer never arrives.

I've got a bag packed, waiting with Vassilis in the courtyard, near the stables. The weather should be clear. Unless the healer is a totally incompetent rider and falls off, the trip should be easy. Caius stops by at one point and chats with Vassilis for a while. He seems genuinely concerned about the state of the Ocronian healers, and their lack of numbers. He laments the good Water Mages that were lost in the Battle of Soltaire. I tune him out after a while.

But the healer still doesn't show.

By noon I'm beyond irritable. I offer to fly out and see if I can meet the healer, but Vassilis makes me stay put. I flip Frostbite end over end instead. We get some curious looks from the students as they pass us between classes, but no one approaches me.

Midafternoon a hawk swoops into the school and beelines to the Wind Mage tower and into the turret. A minute later, a disheveled-looking King's Messenger makes his way out of the building. Vassilis and I exchange a glance and go meet him.

The healer has been dispatched to Basti and then the Crescent Islands instead. I start to protest, but Vassilis puts a hand on my shoulder.

"Sometimes it's a numbers game, Del. Fact is that there are more people in Basti and the coast there than down in Spit."

I think back to my sleep-inducing lessons—I don't envy the decisions the king must be making, to make the best use of a scant resource to serve the most people possible.

Still. There has to be *someone* they can send to Spit. The messenger shrugs, holding one of the school's spare robes around his thin shoulders.

"There's no one left," he says. His face looks hollow, his cheeks practically concave.

It's not just the healers who are stretched thin, I realize.

"Well, you might as well go for a run or something, get some use out of this wasted day," Vassilis says. He gives me a smile, but I see it fall from his face as soon as he turns away from me.

A run does sound like a good idea—but it'll have to wait. I refuse to admit defeat.

I head to the library. I want time alone, and I need to check something. I wonder if Reyn is still there, still making sculptures, but I don't look for him. I only need a map, and those are near the entrance.

I pass Kemp's tavern and the dining hall. I pass Kora's friend/lover, Calix, with a wheelbarrow full of plants that he's moving somewhere, and a squirrel with a stubby tail perched on his shoulder. He gives me a friendly nod—Calix, not the squirrel. A lot of the Mages' classes seem to have been suspended for the day as the teachers orchestrate efforts to help plague victims. I've never seen the school so ... green. Even the grassy area between the dining hall and the library is now roped off, lemon balm taller than I am growing in massive clusters. The evening air smells amazing with the mix of herby green growth, and I breathe it in deeply.

The library is a blocky building like the rest, with a well-curated atrium that gets progressively less organized and more dusty the deeper you go. They'll only let visitors take spelled candles in for light, and in the depths, it is pretty dismal. And it definitely doesn't smell like lemon balm. Just dust and stale air. Each bookshelf is stamped with a giant silver flame emblem, with the contents of the shelf listed below.

Fortunately, what I need is pretty simple. It won't take long. I grab what I need from the shelves and spread the paper over an empty table. This time of night, most people are in the dining hall, so I've got the room to myself.

Good thing, too. I use the candle to anchor down one corner of the rolling paper and my hand to smooth the opposite side. There, sticking out like an afterthought, is a squiggly little bit of land in the far southeast corner of Ocron, in what was formerly known as Aclines.

And at the tip of that peninsula, a small, insignificant town named Spit.

I groan, letting my head fall forward and smack against the table. Two days. I could definitely have had that healer there in two days. I guess they'd expect us to stay a few days, maybe, and then two days back. A week total, maybe. They couldn't spare the king's healer for a *week* before sending him to stinking Basti?

Maybe I could fly north and kidnap him. That would be fun.

I think back to what Wren's told me of her childhood. It was lonely—honestly, fairly similar to mine. She grew up isolated, working with her father in a lighthouse until the plague killed him. She ran the lighthouse for years until her strange magic started manifesting, freaking out the superstitious idiots in her town, and she was brought to the School of the Silver Flame for training.

But would she really want her town to just die? It's a small town. It wouldn't take much. How would I feel if there was a plague in Aeturnus? I'd definitely kidnap whoever I needed to, to keep it safe.

Gods, I wish there was something I could do. I feel useless, trapped here at this school while something like this is going on. A plague isn't an enemy for a dragon to conquer.

I sit up, blinking, staring at the old wooden rafters of the ceiling as I think.

A noise breaks my concentration, a pair of hushed voices coming up from the stacks below. I roll the map up and hurriedly stuff it back on the shelves just as two men rise from the lower levels.

Two very familiar faces—Reyn and his shadow, Silas. Silas is nice enough. We could have been friends, maybe, if he wasn't a snake. He's quiet and shy and takes his studies seriously. Aletheia says he's kind and funny. She likes him more than the other Roallacan Water Mages.

Reyn, on the other hand, I'm certain I'd still want to strangle even if he wasn't a Roallacan prince.

"What are you doing here?" we ask each other at the exact same time.

"Studying," Reyn replies, raising an eyebrow. "You?"

"Studying," I say sarcastically, my heart pounding for some reason. "Shields *can* read, you know."

"I guess so," he says with a shrug. Then he continues walking.

Silas is silent, holding a stack of books.

"You make him carry your books, Highness?" I ask after him—probably just anxious, a little embarrassed, and wanting him to feel as awkward as I do. I don't know why I feel so tongue-tied around him. I can't possibly be afraid of him. Silas turns to me, though, smiling a little.

"Reyn tutors me in healing after classes most days," Silas explains, shifting the books in his arms. "I'm hopeless."

"You're getting better every day," Reyn says without turning, though he does stop.

"Only because of you," Silas says, with a self-deprecating smile. "You won't find a more gifted healer in all of Ocron, not even Caius. I'll bet you a gold coin."

Reyn starts walking, shaking his head, and Silas scurries after him.

The wheels in my head, rusty though they may be, start turning.

There are no healers left in the realm to go to Spit, none to heal the town where Wren grew up, where her father and grandfather and great-grandfather spent their lives, where her own parents died of the plague years ago.

But, I realize, my chest turning to lead—or ice, maybe—there *is* a student gifted at healing who may be able to help.

CHAPTER 12

Like all the hells am I going to ask *Reyn* for help. Like *all the fucking hells*. He's as likely to kill the people of Spit out of spite as he is to help.

Instead, I ask the second-year Water Mages. There are six of them, only one from Roallac. I like my chances.

But they all turn me down.

I can't ask Silas or the twins. Eugenia and Isadora would probably stab me in the back, and I still don't know for sure that they weren't the ones who destroyed my suncatcher. Silas doesn't have the necessary depth of magic; he's said as much himself. Aletheia turns red and can barely answer me when I ask her—Athan glares at me and won't talk to me the rest of the day after. She is better with tides and waves than healing, she says. And Athan wouldn't dream of letting her go anywhere without him.

I flip Frostbite end over end, frowning as I walk the halls. I still can't believe there's *no one* King Leonidas can send. Maybe I'll write to Ismini. She'll know what to do.

And then, as if summoned from my worst nightmares, I turn a bend and see Reyn talking to Silas. Reyn somehow always manages to look … royal. Even with his hair growing long, brushing his ears. He is always poised, always composed. I, on the other hand, look like shit. I've just come from training, and I've been too busy agonizing over the Spit situation to bother going to the baths. I'm sweaty and covered in sand, and I stink.

Reyn and Silas both freeze when they see me. Reyn stiffens, his easy smile freezing into a hard mask of indifference as he eyes me.

Well, Rigrasil, I'm going to take this as a sign. I take a deep breath.

"Can we talk?" I spit out, looking at Reyn.

His brows furrow. "All right," he says, a tinge of suspicion in his voice.

Silas clutches his books to his chest like he's afraid I'm going to throw my knife at him. I belatedly realize I'm still holding it and sheathe it at my hip.

"Alone?" I ask, nodding at his ever-present shadow.

Silas gives Reyn a grin and heads into what must be his room.

"Let me remind you that killing a healer is harder than you think," Reyn says, crossing his arms.

I roll my eyes. "If I wanted to kill you, you'd be dead already," I say.

He snorts.

"I … need your help."

His eyebrows nearly touch his hairline.

I tell him briefly what I want him to do, each word feeling like spikes in my chest. *Gods, is there really* no one *else?*

Reyn considers my request silently, the moment stretching, long and awkward, between us, like a thread about to snap.

I throw my hands up. "I don't know why I thought you'd go along with this," I mutter.

"Me neither," he says, one eyebrow raised.

He turns and walks off, his tan robe flaring behind him down the corridor. I grit my teeth, sending another silent prayer to Rigrasil, and follow.

"There's no one else the king can spare, not even Caius," I

explain, chasing after him. He's taller, but I'm fast, and I have no problem keeping up with his long-legged gait.

"That's not my problem," he says.

I grab his arm, whirling him around.

"It *is* your problem," I say, glaring at him.

He pointedly looks at my hand—the hand that dared to touch him, that *still* touches him, tight on his arm, preventing him from leaving.

"The plague will spread north from Spit. It could even be here in a few weeks. Will it be your problem then? What about when it spreads to Roallac? You want to be a healer? Well, now's your chance!"

"Why do you care?" he asks after a moment. His eyes look between each of mine, like he's searching for something.

"Because ... someone needs to, and no one else will!"

"So is this a god complex, then, some desperate need to be a hero again?" he asks.

I clench my fists at my sides. "I'm no hero," I mumble.

At least he's stopped walking for a minute. I take a deep breath and go for it.

"Someone ... someone important to me is from there," I say.

Do I tell him it's Wren? She killed his queen and caused the downfall of his country, so ... probably not. But I can't just stand by and do *nothing* when I know I can do *something*.

I blame Aris's bad influence.

Reyn watches me, waiting for me to laugh, to tell him it was all joke, maybe, or to change my mind. I do neither. This seems to confuse the Snake Prince, who otherwise lives to irritate me. He clearly can't believe I'm serious about this plan.

"Ask me nicely," Reyn says after a moment, eyes glittering, a smirk curving his lips. "Ask me nicely, and maybe I'll consider it."

Shit. Why did I ever think this was a good idea?

Because there's literally no one else *you can ask*, I tell myself. Again.

"It'll make you a hero," I say, appealing to a different side of him.

"The Fallen Prince, offering to heal the king's subjects. I know you and your friends aren't ... accepted here," I say. "This will go a long way toward ... gaining approval."

"I don't think so," he says, and he wrenches his arm from my hand. "I said, ask me nicely."

I frown, not clear on what exactly he's asking.

"I'm not going to kiss your shoes, or anything else, if that's what you're asking," I say archly, looking him over.

"Nice, but not what I was referring to," Reyn says. He leans over me, crowding me back against the stone wall of the corridor, until I can feel the coolness of his breath against my face. "Say please. *Beg* me for my help. Preferably on your knees."

Something flutters in my stomach—probably revulsion. I hope I'm about to vomit on him.

"Never," I say, staring right back at him, our faces mere inches apart.

He regards me for a long moment, like he's waiting for me to change my mind. I purse my lips tighter. He snorts and stands up tall again.

"Pity," he says, and he turns away.

"Wait!" I say.

He stops but doesn't turn back.

I clench my hands at my sides—but the word still won't leave my mouth.

For Wren, I tell myself. I lick my lips. *Like all the hells will I beg. But ... I can do* this. *I can be polite to my enemy for one moment in time if it gets me what I want.*

"Please," I whisper.

Reyn doesn't turn, doesn't give any indication that he heard me for a minute. Then I hear him let out a long breath.

"If I do this, you'll help Silas and the twins integrate into the school," he says. "You'll sit with them at mealtimes, every day. You'll say hello when you see them in the halls. You'll include them in any social activities. You're the Dragon Girl, after all. If you befriend them, then everyone else will too."

I grit my teeth so hard I worry they'll fracture. I notice he doesn't include himself in his request—either he doesn't want my help, or he doesn't think he needs it. Which is fine, because I'd sooner cut off my own foot than pretend to be *his* friend in public.

"I agree," I say.

I never used to be a religious person. We all kind of pray to Rigrasil, or swear on his name, but that's really it. My family didn't celebrate the summer solstice, and we never visited his temples.

But back then I didn't really believe in the gods. They might have existed, once, but they were gone. Like my parents. Even though Tekton and I lived in the Temple of the God of Night, I wouldn't say we were particularly devout. We never prayed to him or anything; we just kind of kept up the place.

When I saw a ten-foot-tall, blue-skinned, angry water god throw a tidal wave's worth of water at me, though, my mind changed really fast.

Which is why, probably, after talking to Reyn, I find myself seeking out the temple in the western part of the school. The school is really more like a town, with the big circular wall around it. There's a thin coating of snow and ice on most of the stone these days, and smoke billows up from the Fire Mage forge. And like every good town, the school has a stable, a tavern, and all that stuff.

It also has a temple. It's as austere as the rest of the place, but not dedicated to any particular god, which is unusual. There was some effort made to make the building look respectable, though—columns around the outside, a wide marble pediment with the school's motto carved in deep relief: LUCEAT LUX VESTRA. *Let your light shine.*

Inside it's quiet as a tomb. It's one big rectangular room, with some benches on either side of a main walkway. At the front is a big stone altar, with symbols of the gods carved on it. A sun. A moon. Dirt, with a little sprout. Windy swirls. A flame. A wave. But no golden altars, like at Rigrasil's temple in Estana. No stained-glass windows that are so beautiful they make my draconic heart ache. Still, there's a presence here. A feeling of ... something. Reverence, maybe.

I sit. I'm not really sure what I want to ask of Rigrasil. Not like he's ever listened to me before, but ... I could use some guidance, and there's no one here I can turn to. My family are an entire continent away. Kora and Athan would *definitely* try to talk me out of it. Vassilis wants me to go, but with Reyn? I'm not sure. Am I even doing the right thing? Am I really seeking glory, the chance to be the first Shield recruit sent on a real assignment, or do I actually want to help?

Is this some way for me to try to atone for what happened at the Battle of Soltaire? I'm not even sure how many I killed. I'm sure the stories have blown it out of proportion—and I'll probably never know, since my fire is so hot they just ... disappeared. Maybe I even killed Reyn's family. Or Silas's. Or the twins'. It's not like I've bothered to ask them. And isn't that why Rigrasil made me, anyway? To be his weapon? Or am I a mistake, a product of errant magic, like Uncle Tekton?

I bury my head in my hands, threading my fingers into my hair. I keep it braided mostly, like Wren does—once Rosie's gets long enough, I bet she'll have braids too. Gods, I miss them so much it hurts. Would Wren approve of me going to Spit? Probably not, even if I'm doing it because of her.

Aris would, though.

CHAPTER 13

"I thought I might find you up here." Reyn's voice drifts to me in the fading afternoon light.

"Fuck off," I say, sheathing my dagger, curling my bleeding palms closed.

I turn my face from him. I'm sitting on the wall, on the side that overlooks the shallow valley and the long, winding river. Snow dusts the stone wall and covers the world below in a smooth white blanket. Drops of blood glitter like rubies, falling, sparkling through the air until they meet the ground below.

"Can you fly?"

I blink.

"What?" I ask him. *I'm a dragon, you idiot. Of course I can fly.*

He stands at the top of the stairs, watching me with his head tilted.

"When you flare your wings out. Can you fly, or is it just for show?" he asks.

"Are you planning on pushing me off the wall or something, Prince?" I spit back.

My feet dangle over the edge, nothing but air beneath them. I'm in no danger of falling, though—even if I did, a fall from this height might hurt, but I'd heal. Probably wouldn't even scar. The cuts on my hands are already sealed, already fading away.

I feel numb, but not from the cold. It's like I can't even *feel* properly. The only thing I do feel is guilt—every time I think of Soltaire, every time I dream of Soltaire, I hear the screams. I can smell the skin and flesh burning as I razed that arena to free Wren. I have prayed to Rigrasil a thousand times over—not for forgiveness, exactly. But peace. I'd settle for some peace. *You don't blame the sword wielded by your enemy,* Caius said. He's an oily man, but that phrase has stuck with me and has given me some small measure of comfort.

Then asking Reyn for help and thinking about the friends and family he must have lost—I can't bear it anymore. I can't keep that pain inside, where it eats away at me like a parasite. And the rage at finding my room invaded, my suncatcher ruined. Between rage and shame, my feelings are so mixed up I don't know where one starts and the others end. *Gods, I shouldn't even have these feelings at all. I am the Dragon Girl. Dragons aren't tormented by their feelings.*

I found no peace in the temple today. I find it now, as the day ends, the only way I know how.

Reyn comes and leans against the wall, one merlon over, close enough to be inconvenient and yet far enough away for our proximity to be coincidental, almost. Maybe he just likes walking the walls in the afternoon, particularly if he gets the chance to gloat.

"It must be nice, being able to just fly away from it all, whenever you want," he muses.

I wipe the dried blood off my hands—there are no scars, no traces that I was ever injured. Only the lingering pain there, grounding me.

"Yeah," I say, swinging my legs, staring out at the river as it makes its lazy way across the plains. "But you have to come back down eventually."

He considers this for a moment. I can't imagine that he just came up to make small talk, so I grit my teeth—and consider punching his

—as I wait for him to make up his mind about whatever he wants to say.

"I spoke to Caius about your plan," he says after an interminable silence. He's got his back against the wall, studying something in the courtyard below, carefully avoiding looking at me.

I whirl on him, forgetting the pain in my palm and gripping the stone tightly. My heart leaps in my chest.

"You did?" I ask, breathless. Is he seriously considering my offer after all?

He looks at me then, his emerald eyes carefully blank. "I wanted to make sure you weren't luring me into some sort of twisted trap," he says. "Getting me on my own, away from Caius and the other Water Mages—it would be easy for me to have an accident and fall to my death from your back, don't you think?"

I blink. Well, that's fair.

"Look, I do hate you," I admit.

He snorts. "Not helping."

"But," I say, unable to look him in the eye, "I *need* you to make this plan work. We can be there and back in a few days, with minimal interruption to our studies. And it's a waste of both our talents to be stuck here when there are people *dying* out there." I swing one hand out over the landscape beyond us.

He's watching me carefully, probably unsure if my vehemence is more from my hatred of him or my feeling of responsibility for the people of Spit. I'm not really sure either.

"Caius agrees with you," he says.

"He does?" I ask, blinking again. "Really?"

Gods, I wish I'd been there to see that. I bet it caused him physical pain to actually agree with me on anything.

"He says we should leave tomorrow. He's even got Head Mage Iraklis to approve the plan. Just the same as it would have been with the king's healer, but with me instead."

"I ..." I start, but I don't really know what I want to say.

"You're welcome," he says anyway.

I sigh. Well, isn't this what I wanted? Not necessarily to be flying the Prince of Snakes to a place nearly as sacred to me as Rigrasil's own temple, but to be helping people? Isn't that what Shields and Mages are for?

That was something Aris always taught me—that, and that a Shield *never* stands by when help is needed. As a dragon, I can't fight the plague—but I can get Reyn there, in a fraction of the time it would take Mages on horseback or on ships.

I take a deep breath. "I *can* fly. When I partially shift my wings. Just in case you're having second thoughts about shoving me off this wall," I tell him.

A ghost of a smile creeps over his features before vanishing.

"*Alis volat propriis*," he whispers, as if to himself.

I snort. *She flies with her own wings.* Well, yeah. Obviously. What am I going to do? Borrow someone else's? *Poetic idiot.*

"I hope you're a better healer than a poet," I whisper, though it doesn't come out sounding as harsh as I intended. It's practically a prayer to Rigrasil as much as a comment to Reyn.

He looks out over the courtyard, gaze unfixed, his mind somewhere else. "Me too."

CHAPTER 14

I haven't thought this through.

Vassilis drills me on the route down to Spit for hours, until I feel like I've memorized every pebble between the school and Wren's old home. He's packed me a bag and given me some coins to pay for inns on the way, and he has me memorize specifically where each one is.

"The towns already know to expect you," Vassilis reminds me.

"I *know*. I'll be fine," I assure him.

The bag I've packed isn't heavy—some extra clothes, a pair of dented practice gladiuses, and that's about it—and I swing it down from my shoulders. I roll my neck and stretch my arms. I haven't flown for so long in ages, and I'm looking forward to it. It's the most glorious feeling, with the wind in my wings, the world below fading away, until even great palaces are as small as children's toys. I'm really looking forward to that part.

Caius and Reyn come out of one of the stairwells of the outer wall and meet us in the courtyard. Reyn's face is as guarded as ever, Caius's too. Vassilis told me that Caius has been drilling Reyn in the ways to fight the plague while conserving as much of his magic as he can, to do the most good for the most people. To avoid going gray. To be a beacon of good faith from Roallac to the people of Ocron. It's a lot of pressure on him, but he seems grimly determined to see it through. That, at least, I can respect.

"And you're sure you can do this?" Caius asks me for the tenth time, pursing his lips. "It's ..."

"A long way. I *know*," I say, hands on my hips. "But not half as far as from Estana to Soltaire. And I did *that* four years ago."

Vassilis rolls his eyes skyward, muttering a prayer to Rigrasil. Caius blanches but doesn't say anything else.

"Ready, Prince?" I ask.

Reyn wears his tan-and-blue student robe over black traveling clothes, a bag thrown over his shoulder. There's nothing about him that speaks of his royal background, except maybe the lack of dirt on him. Come to think of it, I've never seen *any* ornamentation on his clothes—no jewels, no fancy embroidery. None of the pretentious gem-encrusted sandals or arm coils or cloth-of-gold tunics that are so common in our capital. In fact, he never wears anything that might set him apart from his fellow Roallacan Mages. I suspect it has to be intentional, and I wonder why that might be.

Reyn nods.

I shift, my own clothes falling to the sandy ground. I flare my wings out and arch my neck, stretching proudly in the cool morning air. I can tell I'm growing—with my tail, I've got to be close to fifty feet long now. *Gods, being a dragon never gets old.* All the people in the courtyard stop to watch me, so I strut a little as Caius and Reyn watch.

Vassilis stuffs my discarded things into the bag and then slings my steel-reinforced brace around my shoulders. I have to lie down for him to do this, my shining black scales scuffing the dirt.

Caius keeps his distance, like he doesn't trust me not to eat him —which is fair—but Reyn is unafraid. He approaches me, looking me over like I'm a horse or something equally as ordinary, for all the emotion he shows. He walks around me as he inspects me, and I swear I can feel his gaze like an icy wind on my scales. I lift my feathered wings and snake my head around to watch him complete his circle. Vassilis gives one last yank on my harness and then jumps off my back.

"Up you go, then," he says, gesturing to Reyn.

Oh, I *really* have not thought this through.

The prince trails his cold fingers around my chest as he walks. He takes a moment, studying things, and then reaches up, grabs one of the spines at the base of my neck, and steps up lightly from my shoulder. He swings a long leg over my back and settles himself down. I feel the muscles of his thighs clench against my back—there are no footholds for him, but as long as he holds on to the harness, he should be fine. I've never had anyone fall off. Well, other than Tekton that one time, but that was years ago. I let out a long snort of air, smoke mixing with the dust that rises from the courtyard stones.

Reyn loops our bags through the straps on my neck, one to either side. I shudder as he moves, unused to having passengers lately, and he lays a hand on my neck, like I'm a nervous horse he's trying to soothe.

It works. Either that, or the casual touch startles me so much that I freeze.

"Straight south to Alora and the Shark Tooth Inn," Vassilis reminds me.

I snort again, smoke curling from my nostrils. I have the pleasure of seeing Caius blanch again, and think with some satisfaction that he might just faint. I bare my teeth at him in a dragony grin for good measure. I have more teeth in this form, and they're a *lot* bigger and sharper. Vassilis rolls his eyes again, patting my shoulder as he gets out of my way.

Reyn sits easily on my back, moving as I move, not stiff-backed like Wren was the first time she rode. I bet he's an accomplished horseman.

And, well, the way his hips are rocking against my back is

distracting, honestly. *Gods, it's been a while since I've been ridden. Fuck! I mean, had a passenger. As a dragon. Calm down, Del. Gods.*

I flare out my wings, stretch my neck up to the sky—and launch, my wings pushing air aside in great gusts as we climb up and up and up, the joy of flying pushing any other thoughts away.

Take that, *Prince. I bet no noble steed of yours ever* flew.

I half expect Reyn to slide off. I don't make it easy for him, this first flight, don't make any attempt to fly smoothly—and I definitely don't expect him to laugh, a *real* laugh, crowing as we circle the school and then turn south. I crane my head around to look at him—I've never seen him look like he is genuinely having *fun* before. He arches an eyebrow at me, his mask restored, the laughter gone.

I frown, as much as I can in this form, and fly on.

We land outside the town of Alora, and Reyn slides off effortlessly. He undoes the straps of my harness and keeps his back to me for a few minutes while I shift and dress. His pale face is tinged pink—whether from the wind and sun or something else, it's hard to say. I fold up my harness as best I can and sling it over my shoulder. It's kind of a pain to travel with this. It's bulky and noisy when I'm in Shield form. When I'm shifted, I barely even feel it.

The Shark Tooth Inn is easy to find, at least, with an oversized pair of wooden shark jaws on top of the sign, and the innkeeper is indeed expecting us. We're shown to a decent room upstairs with a pair of beds, and we're promised that food will be ready soon.

"You're faster than they think," Reyn says, claiming one of the beds.

I snort—it's barely early afternoon. Vassilis thought I wouldn't get here until dark.

"Well, they figured you might fall off a few times. That's probably why Caius told me to fly over the water when I could," I retort.

Reyn laughs, just a little, and lies back on the bed, one arm draped over his eyes. He's long and lean, barely fitting on the bed; his dark hair is wind-blasted. Despite the fact we're alone, he has no fear of me.

"Aren't you worried I'm going to stab you in your sleep or something?" I ask, frustrated. He *should* be afraid of me, prince or not.

He doesn't even uncover his eyes. "If you must, make it quick, will you?"

I huff and head downstairs to see if they have any ale.

"Does nothing frighten you, Prince?" I ask.

Away from the school, I can almost pretend we're not who we are. Almost. Like we're just two people taking a trip instead of two enemies momentarily united by a common goal. And I have so many questions that have been burning in my mind since I first laid eyes on the Prince of Snakes.

"Why?" He regards me over the table, long fingers curled around a cup. There isn't ale, but they do have wine, and I have no hesitation spending Vassilis's coin on it.

"You could have fallen today. I had a hundred opportunities to kill you," I say, exasperated.

"Thank you for *not* doing that," he says easily, taking a sip of his wine. "I figured you wouldn't try, anyway, until after we've healed that town." He states this simply, like his life is not in my hands.

It's like the man has no sense of self-preservation. I'll have to watch him extra carefully just to make sure nothing unintentionally happens to him on my watch. It wouldn't bode well for my future as a Shield if I "accidentally" murdered the Roallacan heir.

"Aren't you afraid of *anything*?" I ask again. The wine is making me pensive, which isn't usually my thing. But Reyn just has me so confused—no awe when I shifted, no fear of falling. No emotion at all, really. A heart of ice, with just that momentary glimpse of joy.

He looks down, turning his cup in his hand, studying the way the wine swirls. We could be talking about the weather, for all the emotion he shows.

"You want the real answer, or the one I'm supposed to say?" he asks.

I blink in surprise.

"Real one," I say, and I refill both our cups.

It's late now, and we're the only patrons still sitting in the inn's dining room. The fireplace is comfortably warm; my stomach is full of food and wine, and I'm feeling bold. Well, bolder than usual.

"I've been afraid my whole life," he says, not looking at me. "It's easier to be ... cold. Numb."

I let out a low whistle and take a long drink.

"Easier, but not much fun," I say.

Sure, he might not feel fear, but what about exhilaration? Joy? I know he could feel that, at least for a heartbeat when we started flying, even if he tried to mask it.

"My relatives are mostly dead or imprisoned," he says softly. "My country, my culture has been obliterated. I wanted a quiet life spent healing, helping people—now I'm seen as, at best, an emissary to a foreign country where Caius warns me about plots against my life daily. My life will never be my own."

Gods, I'm an idiot sometimes. I might have momentarily forgotten who we were, but Reyn clearly hasn't.

"Having fun, finding joy—it feels like a betrayal, you know?" he continues, looking up. Then he downs his wine in a single long gulp.

"Were you ... close to her? Evanthia?" I ask.

"We were barely related," he says, touching a finger to his empty tin plate. From the contact, a delicate spiral of frost spreads, forming swirls like that of a shell Tekton showed me once. They branch and twist across the metal, around the crumbs of bread and cheese and the apple core from our simple meal. It's shockingly pretty.

"King Leonidas's crown will pass to his son," he continues, answering my unspoken question, not looking at me, his voice flat like he's reading the words from a boring book. "To the oldest of his children. In Roallac, the crown passes to the strongest of the ruler's heirs. Anyone of royal blood can compete for it, no matter how distantly related they are."

"Compete? How?" I ask.

"Murder, generally," he says nonchalantly, lifting his finger from the completed design on the plate.

I raise an eyebrow—as heir, how many people did Reyn have to murder? Perhaps I've been vastly underestimating him.

"So how were you named heir, then?" I ask quietly, into the silence stretching between us.

He fixes me with his hypnotic gaze. "My older brother, Michail, was the heir. He systematically murdered everyone in the family he thought could be a threat. He couldn't do it directly, or the court would have revolted. So he tried to poison me twice, and once my horse slipped on a patch of ice and threw me. I broke my neck that time. Assassins came for me on my twelfth birthday, and another half a dozen other times. But like I said, it's hard to kill a healer."

Oh, shit. I lick my lips, and his gaze follows briefly before returning to my eyes. He listed off Michail's attempts to kill him like he was reciting one of Philandra's boring texts—flatly, without emotion.

"Not that it's any of your business, and I certainly don't care what you think—but then he challenged a friend of mine, someone he knew was weaker than him," he says, not meeting my eyes, looking instead at the frost on the plate. "Our challenges take ... took place in the arena, before the entire kingdom. He said she'd done something to offend him, and to restore his honor, he challenged her to a duel. Really, she'd rejected him, and he was upset because she preferred my friendship to his. I knew she'd die if she faced Michail, so I took her place, which is what he intended all along." In a single movement, he touches the plate again, and the ice melts, little rivulets collecting in the dented center.

He looks at me then, looking for validation, or understanding, maybe. I'm not sure what he sees, but he lowers his eyes again and gets up from the table without another word. He heads toward the dark stairs, and our little shared room.

So the rumor of the Fallen Prince killing his brother for the throne is true, though in a slightly different way than I assumed. If, in fact, I believe him at all.

But I find myself wondering about this "friend" whose place he took, and how important she must have been to him, for him to risk his life to protect hers. To perhaps risk something even greater, risk taking on a mantle that he never wanted, just to make sure she was safe.

And now he's here.

"Wait," I say, calling after the shadows. I don't see anything, but I hear a faint rustling, as if he's paused, perhaps turned around. I wish I could partial-shift my eyes. Dragon eyes are fantastic at seeing in the dark, better than cats' eyes—but of course, I'd only learned to shift the showy stuff, wings and fangs and fire, not the practical stuff.

"What happened to her? This friend of yours?" I ask.

"She died." His voice drifts to me from the darkness. "At the Battle of Soltaire."

I don't sleep at all that night, instead lying on the bed next to Reyn's, listening to his slow, steady breathing. Did I kill this "friend" of his? This girl who was so important to him? I've never heard him talk so freely. I've never bothered to listen, anyway. I wonder if it was the wine, making him feel brave enough to tell me.

Probably, because when he wakes, he's quiet again. Guarded. Frozen.

The morning, at least, is glorious. I soar high on the warmer currents over the sea, loving the way it flows through my feathers, caresses my scales. I look back over my shoulder to make sure Reyn is paying attention—he raises an eyebrow at me in question, before I bare my teeth in a dragony grin.

And drop from the sky.

I fold my wings tightly against my back, only flaring them out again when I'm just a few feet from the water. My claws dip into the salty waves before I use the momentum of the dive to push me back up and up into a loop. The force of my speed keeps Reyn stuck tightly to my back as we turn upside down, his long legs clamped against my shoulders—and when I level out again, he whoops, laughing long and loud, with nobody but me to hear it.

I'm not really sure why I did that. I like flying, and I like showing off.

And I realize, as cool fingers stroke the scales of my neck, that I like his laugh too.

CHAPTER 15

Despite my efforts to engage Reyn in conversation, he remains aloof the following night and goes to sleep immediately after we land at the next inn. He can't possibly be *that* tired, so I can only assume it's so he won't have to talk to me.

We land in Spit a few hours after sunrise the next day. It's a desolate place, all sharp gray rocks and scrawny pine trees. The town itself isn't much better off—just a collection of low buildings made of stone with straw-thatched roofs. I can see a curl of land where Wren's lighthouse must have stood—it looks like a mound of rubble now, though I can see a few people walking toward it. Maybe to pay their respects. Or maybe just to haul away the stone, erasing generations of her family's history.

I veer west to avoid having to face the remnants of Wren's past any longer, hoping that Reyn didn't notice the rubble, or the flicker of sadness I felt when I saw it. I glide over the town. As a dragon, I can smell the wood fires, the loaves of bread baking, the horses in the stables—and over all of it is the clean smell of salt water. It doesn't smell like a town full of sickness.

I dive for the cobblestone courtyard in the center of town, flaring my wings up at the last minute and landing in a gust of wind that knocks a few people down.

I think a few even faint.

I shift almost immediately. Reyn's already gotten used to me shifting out from under him and lands neatly on his feet. He slings my cloak around my shoulders, and I stand, barefoot but at least somewhat covered. I don't really care about modesty—most Shields don't, as it's a luxury we can't really afford—but I don't need to shock these backward folk any more than I already have.

Turns out, they don't care about me *at all*. Once they've gotten over the shock of seeing me, they rush Reyn, hands clawing at him, screams and pleas for help tearing from their throats. They were expecting a healer days ago—a full healer, not a student—and now they're desperate. He is pushed back by the mob, his hands outstretched to try to placate them. I scramble into my pants and a loose shirt and grab the pair of gladiuses from my pack. They're old, but they'll do.

I roar, letting my throat fill with accelerant and spewing out a tongue of flame into the air.

That gets their attention.

So do the dented swords I draw, the early-morning sunlight reflecting off their blades.

"Now," I say, keeping my voice soft, my tone as deadly as my weapons. I step in between Reyn and the crowd. He looks amused, a small smile on his lips as the people back away from me. "We are here to help you—which we cannot do if you trample my Mage. Now someone tell me who the fuck is in charge here."

A round middle-aged man with no hair on his head and plenty on his burly forearms raises his hand and pushes to the front of the mob. Many of the people before us appear pale, sweaty, their bodies ravaged by the plague. Worst of all are the children, as thin as bundles of sticks, their coughs rattling their chests.

"Please," the man says, gesturing toward a slightly larger hovel at the side of the square. "We've been waiting for you. Veniamin runs the inn, there. We've gathered everything you might need, and you can stay there too, for as long as you like. Filia's our herbalist—she's also at your disposal." He shoves forward a round young woman who must be his daughter. Her apron is stuffed full of what looks like oregano, mountain tea, and lemon balm. I've gotten pretty good at identifying those lately, thanks to the efforts at the school.

"Right," Reyn says, taking in the situation.

A horde of hopeful people turns to him, but they eye my swords warily and don't dare approach. Reyn thinks for a moment, his mouth twisted a little to the side as he takes stock of the situation.

"Right," he repeats, taking charge and standing up straight. "Line up at the door, then. Filia—can you triage them for me? Sickest first."

The girl blushes as red as a tomato but nods.

"Thank you," he says, smiling at her.

She then turns positively purple at his acknowledgment and won't meet his eyes.

"We'll go set up. Give me a few minutes, and I'll start bringing people in. One at a time, understand? Delphine is my Shield, and she'll make sure everyone behaves."

I grin at the crowd, flashing my teeth. They seem as enraptured by Reyn as they are terrified of me, which is pretty much what I wanted.

He's efficient; I'll give him that. He has the common room of the inn cleaned out in minutes, a treatment area with a cot and a few chairs set up by the fire. The innkeeper, Veni for short, brings out food and mugs of water for us, and with that, we get to work.

The first few people are terrible. If we hadn't arrived, I'm not sure they'd have lasted the day. Reyn doesn't rush, doesn't look shocked, just listens patiently to the crying parents, to the devastated husbands, to the moans of the sick. He whispers as he goes, his fingers trailing lightly over sweaty brows and wheezing chests. Everywhere he touches, a glow of blue, like a swirl of smoke, trails behind his fingers, sometimes settling into the person like a drop of ink dispersing in water.

And everywhere he touches, he brings relief. Cooling where there is heat, comfort where there is pain. The lines on faces ease within minutes, and soon I am as entranced as the people of Spit.

Filia does her part too, making sure the sickest are brought in first, and that no one tries to cut the line. No one asks about Reyn—who he is, where he's from. They have accepted him gratefully, without question. Regardless, I keep my hands on my weapons.

The villagers don't ask about me either. A few brave young men eye me, appreciating my curves in my black Shield leathers, but a few rude hand gestures—and once a threat of castration—soon have them leaving me alone. I hold the line at the door, keeping the families from overwhelming Reyn, and force him to take a break every few hours.

It's well after midnight when I call the whole thing off. The last few patients Reyn saw were mildly ill at best, and he's been looking more frail by the minute, like he is made of ice himself and might shatter at any moment.

"That's it. We're done for today," I say, ushering the last patient out the door—and slamming it against his back.

"*Thank you!*" the patient's voice echoes through the wood anyway.

I roll my eyes.

Reyn chuckles. He's seated by the fire, hands dangling between his knees, his neck seemingly too tired to hold his head up anymore.

I force him to take a few bites of the fish stew the innkeeper has offered—I'm grateful for once to be a vegetarian, as I hate fish—and then push him up the stairs. He doesn't protest much.

The room the innkeeper shows us is spacious, if rustic, with large glass windows.

And a single large bed.

Fuck.

Reyn, meanwhile, is practically asleep on his feet, leaning heavily on me.

"Is this the only room you have available?" I growl through clenched teeth.

"Why? Is there something wrong with it?" Veni asks, a nervous sweat breaking out on his brow.

"It's perfect, thank you," Reyn says, and he begins to stumble toward the bed.

I curse under my breath, locking the door against Veni and catching Reyn as he begins to fall. Well, like all the hells am I letting him sleep alone, where I can't keep an eye on him.

"What do you need?" I ask him, hauling him over to the bed.

He grips the edge as he sits, like he's trying hard not to just keel over.

I roll my eyes again and reach for his boots.

"Sleep with me," he says.

I freeze, my fingers still on the laces of his boot.

"What?" I say. Clearly, the man is delirious.

"It's a big bed. You need to rest. If you can promise not to seduce me," he says. He's trying to be serious, maybe even flirtatious, but he's so tired he just looks a little silly.

I yank on his boot, nearly pulling him off the bed.

"No chance in all the hells, Prince," I say, going for his other boot. "Besides, I'm a Shield. I can go days without sleep."

"Still. It would be nice ..." he starts.

"What?" I say, setting his boots by the end of the bed.

But when I turn, I find his eyes closed, his body swaying. He's fallen asleep sitting upright.

"Come on," I say, pushing his shoulder, forcing him to lie down.

I grab his feet and swing his long legs into the bed, then cover him with a blanket. I watch him for a moment, watch the way his chest rises and falls. He looks different when he's asleep. Less princely.

I sit in the chair by the fire, taking off my own boots and

stretching my legs out. I grab a book from the shelf—*The Pirate King and the Maid*, an unsurprisingly very dirty novel—and settle myself in for a vigil, of whatever short time is left of this night.

I don't make it too far into the book; instead, I replay the day over in my head. At first I consider it a miracle that no one today died. Then I realize that the sickest probably already *have* while they waited for us to come. I wonder if I could have made the flight in one day. If I'd flown through the night, I might have made it here yesterday. Reyn could have slept on my back. That time I spent drinking wine with him at the Shark Tooth Inn might have cost Spit lives. It's an uncomfortable realization, and I try—unsuccessfully—to focus on the book, and the improbable positions the pirate and his lover enjoy.

I'm not sure when I drift off, but I wake shortly after dawn, the light beginning to trail in through the windows.

The blanket I put on Reyn is now draped carefully over me, tucked neatly around my shoulders. I'm ashamed I didn't wake. Aris would have had my hide.

It takes me a moment to realize that if Reyn's blanket is on me, then there is no more blanket on Reyn.

I sit up, looking around—and realize there *is* no Reyn.

I leap out of the armchair, grab the hilts of my swords where they lean against the chair, and draw them as I race from the room, my Shield magic roaring through me, ready to fight this entire damned town to find him.

I take the stairs two at a time, landing with a thud of my bare feet against the inn floor.

Three sets of eyes look up at me.

The innkeeper's, startled by my sudden and aggressive appearance, no doubt.

Then a young man's, glassy brown eyes in a too-pale face.

And then Reyn's, across from the young man, his emerald eyes glittering with amusement.

"Sleep well?" Reyn asks me.

I lower my swords, breathing a sigh of relief.

"I thought ... You should have woken me!"

"I told you, you needed to rest," he says, frowning and putting his thumb on his patient's forehead, between his eyes.

The man groans and closes his eyes, shivering as a blue glow washes over him like a pail of water.

"I'm not your patient," I grumble.

Reyn smirks but otherwise ignores me and focuses on his *actual* patient.

"There you go," Reyn mutters, drawing his hand back.

The man's eyes open, now clear and alert. He blinks a few times, like he's waking from a dream.

"Take it easy for a few days," Reyn tells him.

The man leaps from the chair and shakes Reyn's hand enthusiastically, stuttering, unable to voice his thanks. Reyn gives him a tired smile and a pat on the shoulder, then waves for the next person to come in.

I go and get my damned boots and try to ignore the smile curving Reyn's lips.

I make him stop a few times during the day for breaks. The people today are less sick, but they just keep coming. Filia has an assistant today, a pretty girl with long blond curls who bats her eyes at Reyn. She is soft and delicate, in a blue dress that she swishes when she walks. The kind of girl a prince would like. I catch Reyn watching her too.

Ugh.

By the end of the day, I have a problem. Reyn and the girl, Kaiti, talk quietly in the corner—she giggles and touches his arm. I grind my teeth together to keep from yelling at her.

"I thought you two were together," the innkeeper's wife, a stout lady named Danai, says. She's cleaning a mug at the bar, where I sit, trying not to glare at the pair.

I slipped before, calling Reyn *my Mage*—it seemed so natural. He was my partner for this venture, though we didn't share a claim. And he called me *my Shield*. I don't fool myself for a moment that *those* words came out easily, not for a Roallacan prince. I'm not sure what I thought it meant, but it certainly doesn't mean whatever Danai thinks.

"No," I say, taking a sip.

Danai isn't familiar with Shields—Aclines hasn't been a part of Ocron for long, and Rigrasil's original blessing doesn't seem to extend to here—but when Reyn requested ash water for me, she was happy to try to make it. It's not bad, actually.

Danai smooths a stray red curl back behind her ear. She wears her hair in a long braid—most of the women here do, including Kaiti. It reminds me so sharply of Wren suddenly that it's hard to breathe.

"Then try not to break my mug," Danai says softly, giving me a wink when I look up. "Go get some rest. She only lives next door. He'll be fine."

I mumble something into my mug as I drain it, and then I head up the stairs without looking back.

The idiot has been expending his energy *all day* helping the people of this town—he should be sleeping, not ... well, I have an idea about how exactly Kaiti plans on repaying him for his help, and I do *not* approve.

I slam a few things around in our room before grabbing my dirty pirate-romance novel and sitting back down by the fire, but I'm too agitated to read. I'm supposed to be *protecting* Reyn—but if he wants to burn himself out just because he'd rather get laid, well then, that's on him.

I stare at the page for a few minutes and consider hurling it into the fire, but then the door behind me squeaks open.

I leap to my feet, dagger drawn—but it's just Reyn.

Alone.

"Easy," he says, putting his hands up.

"Sorry," I mumble. "I thought you were ... um, someone else."

"Expecting someone?" he asks, raising a brow.

He locks the door behind him and sits on the bed, running a tired hand through his hair. The obsidian strands seem darker next to the pallor of his face, the purple circles smudged under his eyes.

"No. Just ... figured you'd be sleeping somewhere else tonight. Or not sleeping—it's not my business," I mumble.

I sit back down in my chair and open my book, reading the same paragraph a few times because my brain won't focus.

"Kaiti? Gods, no," he says, chuckling. "She's not my type. I was just trying to be polite."

Oh.

"Well then," I say, still looking at my book.

"Not all of us are casual with our bed partners," he says.

I think he means it to be a lighthearted comment, but I'm so keyed up that all I hear is an insult. I'm free to sleep with whoever I want, just as he is.

"Sure, you have standards. So do I. Anyone that's not a snake," I say, flipping the page, though I'm not actually reading a thing anymore.

He doesn't say anything. I hear him moving behind me, shedding his robe and climbing into the bed. I want him to say something—I want him to yell at me. I want to pick a fight.

But the bastard goes to sleep, leaving me with my raging emotions and no outlet.

No outlet except my blade, which is still clenched in my fist.

CHAPTER 16

The last patient of the next day—and hopefully of this whole trip—is a girl about six or seven years old named Shanna. Her parents stand behind me—it is my job to control the loved ones, essentially, to keep them out of the way as Reyn works. These two at least are calm, though they are wringing their hands, their faces drawn. They had the sickness weeks ago, they say—she's never shown any symptoms until just a few days ago, and her breathing keeps getting worse despite the potions from the local herbalist. The girl is panting, and scared. She keeps looking to her parents, not trusting the strange man in the strange robe before her.

"Did you know that in Roallac, the snake is a symbol of healing?" Reyn asks as he takes the girl's hand.

Her face is pale, sweaty, her eyes glassy, but she fixates on Reyn's smooth voice like she's hypnotized.

I narrow my eyes, waiting to see how exactly he plans to spin this.

"Really?" the little girl asks.

"Really," he says, smoothing a hand over her brow and whispering.

A trickle of his blue healing magic drifts over her face like smoke before disappearing. I can literally see the pink color coming back into her cheeks, her eyes brightening as I watch.

"Snakes shed their skin as they grow. It is a symbol of rebirth. That it's never too late to change who you are, into who you want to be," he says, setting his thumb at the notch at the top of her breastbone. The spot glows blue, a faint sweat breaking out at his temples, and the girl takes a deep breath. "That's a nice thought, isn't it?"

"I like that," the girl says, her breathing now free of wheezing and coughing. She beams at him. "I want to be like that when I grow up. Can I be a snake, too?"

He smiles at that, but it's a tired expression, his eyes as dark as coal.

"I want to be as brave as you when *I* grow up," he says. He stands, stretching, his hands high overhead as he works out the kinks in his back from sitting for so long.

I watch from the shadows, and a thought occurs to me that sends my mind reeling.

What a king he would have made.

I realize I'm staring at him, and he's looking back at me with his head tilted, like he's puzzled by something. I shake my head, surreptitiously wiping at my cheek to make sure I didn't have oatmeal or something stuck to it.

"Done? I'm exhausted," I lie, ushering the family out of the inn. The father's holding Shanna tightly, and her mother is sobbing happy tears as they walk.

I close the door and turn to find Reyn gripping the back of the chair he's been sitting on tightly, his fair skin as pale as marble. He wobbles slightly, his eyes beginning to roll back. A trickle of blood drips from his nose.

"Oh no you don't," I say, rushing to him.

I jam myself against his side and throw his long arm over my shoulders. He barely protests. He's taller than I am, but he's lean, and I'm gifted with Shield strength. I might even be able to throw him over my shoulder and carry him if I wanted, though his long arms would drag on the floor.

"You overdid it," I chastise him, locking one arm around his waist and placing my other hand flat against his chest. I can feel his heart hammering behind his ribs—and he doesn't answer me.

"Don't you go gray on me," I mumble, maneuvering him toward the stairs.

He's able to muster the strength to lift his feet up the stairs, one by one, but it's a chore. By the time I get him to our room, he's leaning on me more than standing. I don't like it. Not at all. Gods, there will be hell to pay if he goes gray on my watch. I was so taken with watching him that I forgot my primary objective—to watch *over* him, to prevent him from overextending. First rule of being a Shield.

"Just ... need rest," he pants. "You talk ... too much."

He collapses into the bed with a groan, and I swear he's asleep before I even have the door closed, sprawled on his back, his black hair spilling like silk over the pillow. I roll my eyes and grab a blanket from a chair in the corner.

As I wipe the nosebleed from his face and pull the blanket over him, the neckline of his fine shirt pulls to the side, revealing the edge of a tattoo on the right side of his chest. It looks large, done in finely detailed black ink.

All I can see is scales.

I hold my breath—but he's breathing easily, deeply, his pale chest rising and falling in steady rhythm.

His marble-smooth skin is a sharp contrast to the harsh black ink, and it's got my curiosity piqued.

I reach over him and shift the edge of his shirt a few inches farther, revealing the tattoo.

It's a large snake forming a circle, biting its own tail, in extremely fine detail. And it's done entirely in black ink. Some of the lines are as fine as a hair, but I swear it glitters in the candlelight.

The symbol of Roallac, tattooed across the whole of his right pectoral.

If I was ever in doubt as to his loyalty, well, there it is, literally inked onto his own skin. He's a healer—if he'd wanted, he could have erased it.

I inhale sharply at the realization—no matter how Reyn pretends he's all right with being a citizen of Ocron, he doesn't really believe it. No matter the rubbish he spouts about shedding skin.

His eyes fly open at the sound of my breath, black with emerald centers, his dark eyebrows slashing downward. His hand flies to mine, where it still rests on the lapel of his shirt, grabbing my wrist and pulling a knife from somewhere with the other hand.

In the same heartbeat, my nails extend, growing into claws sharp as any sword. They punch holes in the shirt where I'm holding him.

We stare at each other, locked in an impasse—he still has a knife pointed at my chest, and I still have my claws on his.

He blinks, then lowers his knife.

"You startled me," he says, yawning, his breath cool against my face, seemingly not caring that I'm standing over him with dragon claws extended. "Has something happened?" He tucks the knife back into a holder at his hip—one that I'm ashamed I didn't notice until now.

My gaze strays back to his tattoo, glittering black, a stain on his skin that is otherwise pale and unblemished.

I swear that his eyes darken further, nearly black in their entirety. I can't get the words out, but it seems I don't have to. As usual, his unblinking gaze misses nothing and pulls the question right out of me.

"The ink is mixed with starsteel dust," he says, pulling his shirt over the tattoo. The fabric is ripped from my claws, but he seems too tired to care. "Impervious to magical healing, or any other manipulation."

If I chose to believe the Prince of Snakes, that would mean that he'd carry this mark the rest of his life.

His eyes close, and then he rolls onto his side, presenting his back to me, pulling the blanket up and over his shoulders.

"Thanks for the blanket," he murmurs.

Thanking Rigrasil I'm a Shield, I spend the rest of the night in the chair in the corner, watching him, waiting for ... well, anything. He clearly doesn't feel that I'm a threat. He breathes evenly, fast asleep—so either he's faking being asleep, waiting for me to make a move and stab him, or he's so exhausted he doesn't even care that he's sleeping next to his enemy. I can't believe I nearly forgot who he is, who we both are.

Even if I'd wanted to, I couldn't have slept.

He rises just before dawn—I expect out of force of habit, as he doesn't look particularly well rested. His hair is disheveled, his face paler than normal, his emerald eyes lacking their usual glitter.

"You look like shit," I say.

He snorts and runs a hand through his hair. "Thanks," he grumbles, and he slips on his boots.

I consider what I'm about to say carefully, which isn't my usual habit.

"I could cut it off for you, you know," I say.

His fingers still on his laces, and he looks at me with confusion. "What part of my anatomy, exactly, are you planning to cut off?"

"Your snake. The tattoo, I mean," I blurt out. My face feels hot. "You could heal it as I go. I'd stay above the muscle. You probably wouldn't even scar. It would hurt, but I bet you could take something beforehand to dull the pain."

He sits up, hands on his knees, and regards me for a minute.

"You'd do that for me?" he asks.

My throat is dry, so I just nod and swallow, trying to get some moisture back.

"If you wanted," I mumble, rubbing the back of my neck. "It's not a big deal. I might just stab you through the heart while I'm at it."

"My heart's on the other side, Del," he says, tapping the left side of his chest with a crooked grin. "I appreciate the offer. But ... it's also my history, you know? So thank you, my bloodthirsty Shield, but no. I'll keep it for now."

He stretches and grabs his tan Mage robe from the edge of the bed.

"Any more fall ill last night?" he asks, shrugging into it. The hood catches on his hair and messes it, and he combs it absently with his fingers.

My bloodthirsty Shield. My Shield. He's committed to the roles we're playing here, at least, even if he won't give up his tattoo.

"Doesn't matter. You're in no shape to take care of them," I say, crossing my arms.

He looks at me, surprised, then sighs. "You're probably right," he says. "Anyway, let's go get something to eat. I'm starving."

The innkeeper tells us that there have been no new cases of the plague—for which I send up a silent prayer to Rigrasil. Reyn couldn't heal a sick mouse right now, much less a person.

"We'll head out today, then," I decide.

Reyn raises an eyebrow. "Will we?" he asks.

"We're not needed anymore. You heard him," I say. "And you need rest. You can sleep all day if you need to while I fly."

"I hate to tell you this, but your back is *not* a comfortable place to sleep," he mutters, shoving a huge spoonful of oatmeal into his mouth. "You're so bony."

"You think I *like* having *your* scrawny ass on my back for hours at a time?" I ask, face flushing. Suddenly all I can think about is the pressure of his strong legs around me, his cool hands tracing the scales down my spine. I clear my throat.

"Let me get a few blankets for you," the innkeeper's wife calls, a smug look on her face. "Problem solved. Now eat up, both of you!"

I shift in the town square. Most of the town has turned out to see Reyn off, to thank him profusely for his help. No one thanks *me*. It was only my idea, only my dragon shift that got him here so quickly.

I snort, and curls of hot smoke rise from my snout. Reyn pats my nose absently, like he's calming a horse. The casualness in his touch shocks me—I wonder if, as a dragon, I remind him of his precious snakes.

Yuck.

Kaiti, the pretty girl who threw herself at him so flagrantly, stands at the back, making eyes at him still. He doesn't seem to notice. Dragons don't gloat—but I do arch my neck, letting the sunlight sparkle over my fine black-and-red scales.

Reyn settles the extra blankets from Danai over my back. I have to lay my belly down in the dirt so he can reach, and awkwardly extend one wing so he can get around, my glossy feathers stirring up dust. He climbs up from my bent knee to my back with his usual grace, and I'll admit that the blankets do make it a lot more comfortable.

I *won't* admit, not even to myself, that I liked it better before.

The town cheers as he waves. I rear up, extending my wings out as far as they'll go and shooting a bit of flame into the sky.

"Show-off," Reyn says softly, but I can feel the smile in his words, almost as strongly as I can feel the coolness of his hand stroking my spine.

I shake my head, wishing I could make some snarky retort.

Instead, I crouch and launch into the sky, blasting the town square with a gust of wind that knocks off several hats. The children squeal in delight, so I circle the square a few times for good measure before taking off, due north.

Reyn has lashed himself to my back, and after I level off, he lays himself down, pillowing his arms on a blanket at the base of my neck. I can feel his chest rise and fall against me as he falls asleep, mere minutes into the flight. He's completely exhausted, the fool—he gave too much. Cared too much.

I fly as smoothly as I can for the rest of the day.

CHAPTER 17

I decide to skirt the mountains on the eastern side of the continent, which means a long stretch flying over the sea. I don't mind—it glitters below me like a bed of sapphires, and the winds are with us. The coast glistens with white cliffs and rocky beaches. There are scattered fishing villages hugging the shore too, with white buildings and blue roofs. We pass several fishing boats and some larger ships—people scream as we pass, and I make a game of seeing how closely I can fly to their masts without hitting them. I don't think they like it much, but it passes the time. Reyn doesn't even notice. He wakes up at one point, pats my back, and then goes back to sleep. Gods, he is exhausted.

It's just before dusk, and I'm starting to veer back to the land to find the inn we're to stay at tonight.

Then there's a loud sound, like a tree branch snapping, and a sharp pain seizes my wing. I crumple, spiraling in a free fall with a wing that won't open.

Fuck!

I do my best to stay level and upright, but I'm losing altitude fast, my one good wing unable to keep us aloft.

Something cold shoots down my injured wing, and I crane my head to see Reyn, his hand on my wing joint, sending another blast of healing magic down my wing. His face is calm, collected, and desperately pale.

The wing snaps open, halting our fall, though it still hurts like all hells. I roar, trying to see what is going on—

And there's a fucking javelin stuck in my wing.

Behind me, a ship flying a blue flag I don't recognize lets loose the string of some kind of giant mechanical bow, and another javelin flies toward us.

Probably shouldn't have toyed with that one.

"They don't know you're a Shield!" Reyn shouts from my back.

No shit. I roar in acknowledgment. I try to veer west, toward land, but my wing nearly crumples again.

"Hang on," he says, and I feel him shifting around on my back. "I've got to get the spear out, or I can't heal you."

I look back under my shoulder—the last two javelins the ship loosed have fallen harmlessly into the waves below me, but the ship is catching up. I can't outrun them with an injured wing, and I somehow doubt they'll allow me to shift and explain things.

"Fly steady," Reyn says, one cool hand on my spines.

Wait ... what in all the hells is he doing?

I roar, but Reyn has already unstrapped himself from my back and leans precariously over my right wing, his fingers reaching for the shaft of the javelin. Fire burns in my throat—*What is he thinking? A fall from this height could kill him!*

"Steady," he whispers as a current of air buffets me.

I snort a ring of smoke, my tail whipping through the air. I am more displeased at him risking himself than I am at the assholes gaining on us. They launch another javelin, and I'm forced to swerve, to dive.

For a moment, I can't feel Reyn on my back anymore. I roar, spewing flames in my distress—but then he's there again, his weight reassuring against my back. Relief floods through me like a tidal wave.

Right as he rips the javelin out of my wing and tosses it into the ocean below.

My wing screams in pain, the air tearing across the exposed nerves like a thousand daggers.

And then it stops. The pain is muffled, wrapped in the chill that I recognize as Reyn's healing magic. In the span of a few heartbeats, the pain stops. I flap the wing gently, testing the muscles. It's still bleeding, but the pain is gone. I roar again, now intent on burning down the idiots who dared attack me—

But then I feel Reyn slip, his fingers trailing down my side, as he tumbles off and into the waves.

CHAPTER 18

It's nearly midnight by the time Reyn wakes. His hair has dried, sticking out in all directions, and his clothes are stained with salt. He opens his eyes blearily, blinking a few times and rubbing the salt crystals from his face before sitting up.

"What happened?" he asks, looking around.

"You mean, after I scooped your unconscious princely self from the ocean?" I say, relieved he's awake and looking relatively unharmed.

It took me a minute to find him. When I finally spotted his tan robe floating around him in the water, my heart seized, and I flew as fast as I could, the ship with the blue flag forgotten, until I got to the shore and a convenient copse of trees. It would have to do to hide us while I figured things out.

"Yeah, after that," he says, frowning. "The ship ... did you ...?"

"Relax, Prince. I didn't burn it," I say, rolling my eyes, trying to outwardly portray a confidence and serenity that I most certainly did not feel. His anxious posture relaxes somewhat, so I can't help adding, "Even if they did deserve it."

"They couldn't have known you were a Shield," Reyn says. Then he coughs, his voice scratchy.

I pass him a waterskin, and he downs it in one go, the column of his throat bobbing as he swallows.

Gods, I was terrified when we landed. I'd never admit it, especially to the Snake Prince, but I was in a full panic, so worried I'd fucked up and killed him that I vomited—twice—and was so torn between getting him somewhere with an actual bed and a healer and being too afraid of whoever had shot at us to risk it that I swear my heart nearly tore from my chest.

"Probably thought I was some fiend of Ignatius's, out to destroy them," I say wryly, then wince. "Probably didn't help that I'd made a game out of skimming their masts as I passed."

"You did what?" Reyn asks, and a chuckle escapes him before he can help it.

I grin. A little color is coming back into his pale cheeks—that means he'll be fine, I think.

"I was bored, so I tried to see how close I could get without actually touching them," I admit.

He runs a tired hand over his face, still chuckling.

I sigh in relief, the movement making my shoulder yank on the tender area from the javelin injury. "In my defense, I *was* left unsupervised."

"I shall endeavor not to do so again," he says gravely.

Silence stretches between us, as taut as a bowstring.

"You shouldn't have put yourself at risk like that," I scold him after a moment, frowning.

He raises an eyebrow, regarding me over the small campfire I made.

"You were injured," he says simply, stretching his arms, rolling his neck.

I feel heat surge up my neck, embarrassed that my boredom caused him to overextend what little energy he'd regained.

"I would have been fine!" I protest with a growl.

Reyn clearly disagrees, but he doesn't say anything, just shakes his head and then puts his hands to the fire, warming them.

An uncomfortable feeling builds in my chest. Shame. If it hadn't been for me and my games, Reyn would never have fallen. Gods, he could have injured his head or drowned.

"Thank you," he says, his eyes on the flames. "For saving me."

I swallow hard.

"You saved me first," I admit.

He looks up at me, surprised, a smile quirking one side of his lips.

"That doesn't mean I approve of what you did!" I say.

"Noted," he says, still smiling. "We'll call it even, then."

"Agreed," I say.

Gods, I'm so relieved he's all right. When we landed, he was practically blue with cold. I could barely feel him breathing. I shifted and covered him with blankets before getting a roaring fire started. I considered removing his wet clothing, so he'd warm faster, but I paused with my hand at his throat, where his pulse fluttered rapidly in his neck, and decided to just bundle him up instead. I remember the idea with another rush of heat to my face.

"Are you all right, then? Nothing broken?" I ask.

"It's pretty hard to kill a healer," Reyn reminds me, and he has the audacity to wink at me.

I roll my eyes.

He gets up, stretching again, working out whatever kinks his sleeping body has worked itself into. "How's the arm? Or does a wing injury affect your shoulder blade when you shift back?"

I shrug, hiding a wince. "It's fine," I lie.

He comes over to me and sits at my side. He stares at me so intently that I can't look at him.

"Let me take a look," he says gently.

Somehow he always knows when I'm lying. I don't know why my face feels so hot. I don't answer him, just stare at the fire and grit my teeth.

Cool, firm fingers reach for the edge of my jacket and slide it down along my arm to the elbow.

I feel the sharp exhalation of his breath like an icy wind across my bare arm, and I can't suppress a shudder.

"How long was I asleep?" he asks quietly, removing the bandage I hastily wrapped around my shoulder.

I feel the cloth yanking on the wound, no matter that he is trying to be gentle.

"A few hours," I manage to say, clenching my hands into fists to keep from groaning in pain.

"You should have healed by now," he says.

I feel his cool touch on the tender skin and can't fight back a wince.

"I know," I say, looking over at him.

I can feel perspiration on my upper lip as I try to keep from shaking. I *should* have healed by now. Instead, there's still a fist-sized wound in my shoulder trying to heal, the edges of the muscle still bleeding, the muscle fibers twitching in response to the cool breath washing across them. Gods, why isn't it healing? I've tried not to think about what that might mean. Infection? What if my healing ability is gone forever? What if ...?

"The javelin must have been coated with starsteel pins," Reyn says, frowning, studying the wound.

"How do you know that?" I ask, instantly suspicious.

"It's something we were working on in Roallac, to incapacitate the Ocronian invaders," he says absently as he probes the area.

Gods, it hurts.

"Stop touching it," I snarl, swatting his hand away.

He grabs my hand in one of his, gently, and his thumb absently traces circles on the back of it as he considers my wound. The casualness of his touch, the way he uses the contact to try to reassure me, calm me, is as unfathomable to me as this enemy prince.

"There's a spike still embedded here. It broke off to prevent you from healing. I've seen it before," he says.

Reyn lets go of my hand and, in a sudden, sharp lance of pain, rips something from my shoulder. I shout, clasping a hand over the wound, and he holds the metal out to me, a little pin with a backward-facing barb to lock it in place.

"I suppose I should be grateful," I say after a moment, after the sudden pain in my shoulder eases.

I feel relief as my body begins to heal as it should. Fuck, I was afraid there was something wrong with me, like whatever Shield magic I had was now gone. Like I was forsaken again. A shaky breath escapes me. Reyn's other hand is still on my shoulder, and I focus on that, on the cool, reassuring touch, instead of the pain as I heal.

"You're welcome," he says, staring at the little barb. "Starsteel is rare, and expensive. So how did a ship in the middle of the sea know to have it on board? In Roallac, we tipped arrows, but never something as large as spears."

"You think they were looking for me?" I ask. I assumed they were just pissed that I had rattled their masts, or scared because, well, I'm a dragon.

"Someone knew you'd be there," he says, meeting my eyes.

He realizes then that he's still touching me and removes his hand as if he's been singed. He slips the metal barb into a pocket of his jacket. "Someone wants you dead."

"Someone other than you, you mean," I grumble.

Sure, I'm cocky and a pain in the ass, but who else could I have pissed off so much that they'd go out of their way to hurt me like this?

"I don't want you dead," he says after a moment. It's more a whisper, like it's a secret he doesn't want to admit.

For a moment, our eyes lock, the firelight dancing along his pale skin, tangling itself in the dark hair curling behind his ear. Time seems to slow, the fire even seems to pause its flickering, as if the whole world was suddenly holding its breath.

Then a log on the fire pops and settles, the moment broken.

"Besides," Reyn says, clearing his throat and standing, "I don't want to have to walk all the way back to the school. Do you need me to heal your shoulder, or do you think your own magic can take it from here?"

"I can do it," I say stubbornly, feeling suddenly colder as he moves away. I don't need him using up whatever small amount of magic he's recovered just to heal me. If he goes gray trying to heal me just because I'm too vain and don't want a scar, I'll never forgive myself.

"You've had enough practice, I suppose," he says, and I fight a flare of indignation.

"Are you seriously going to bring that up right now?" I ask.

He looks back at me and shrugs. "Seems as good a time as any." He seems more comfortable now that we're quarreling again. "There's no one around to hear. Tell me. Why do you cut yourself?"

"Fuck you," I spit. I can't believe I saved this bastard.

He doesn't react.

"It must be hard, being the Dragon Girl, the special one," he says.

I feel ice cracking in my chest.

"Cutting gives you something to control, a way to let out the pressure."

"You know nothing about me, Prince," I say. It comes out as a whisper. I fight the urge to punch him.

"No," he agrees.

"I don't need you to fix me," I say. "Leave it alone."

"I can't do that. I'm too invested, in too deep," he says, though he doesn't explain that further. And he's still so calm, so *frozen* that I want to scream at him. "But," he adds, cocking his head to the side, "maybe you should see a better healer. Caius, maybe. Or maybe we can find you a better outlet."

"If you're suggesting sex, Prince, I've tried that already," I say. Like all hells am I going to talk to Caius about my cutting. "Many, many different ways."

In the flickering firelight, an unmistakable flush crawls up Reyn's face, and I smirk.

"I was going to suggest meditation," he mumbles, rubbing the back of his neck.

"Gods, I should have let you drown," I say, shaking out my bedroll. My shoulder is feeling better by the second, though I don't tell Reyn that.

"Maybe," he whispers after a moment—and I can't help but notice the pain in his tone, some sorrow lurking beneath his unflappable marble surface.

"Good night, Prince," I say into the silence.

I keep my eyes closed. We're remote here, and I need a few hours of sleep. If anyone comes for us tonight, well, I'll tell Rigrasil I tried my best.

"Good night, Dragon Girl," he says.

Reyn is quiet the following morning, and paler than usual. I don't like it. But he moves steadily and even eats a little before I shift.

Once he gets onto my back, he straps himself in again and goes back to sleep.

I'm left alone with my thoughts all day as he rests. I find myself itching for Frostbite, wishing I was in my Shield form instead.

We land outside Alora. If the ship with the javelins knew I was coming, the Shark Tooth Inn might too. We decided not to risk it and make camp a little way out into the country, inside a run-down barn. We share some provisions that the people of Spit gave us—I'm a Shield, so I don't need to eat often, but Reyn refuses to unless I join him. I roll my eyes and take a bite out of a seed-coated roll, which finally appeases him.

He's quiet during our meal. I made us a small campfire, so I know he isn't cold. I wonder if his little ocean swim injured him more than he wants to admit. I don't like the silence stretching awkwardly between us. I take out Frostbite, flipping the dagger end over end.

"This is your first time camping," I say.

Reyn shrugs. "Does last night count?"

"You were unconscious for most of it, so ... I'd say not," I say.

He rubs the back of his neck.

"Yeah, well. Even as a child, I was watched pretty closely. Not allowed to do much that would put me at risk—and camping outside, without a thousand guards, definitely counts as risky. Although," he says, looking up at the holes in the roof overhead, where stars are twinkling already, "I'm starting to see the appeal. It's ... peaceful, not to have so many people around."

"Not missing your feather bed, then? Your silk pajamas?" I tease, taking another big bite of the roll.

One side of his mouth quirks upward in a grin. "No," he admits, something wicked flashing in his eyes. "I prefer to sleep naked."

The dry roll sticks in my throat, and for a moment I cough, choking. I pound my chest with my fist and take a swallow of water from our shared flask. His smirk grows, and it takes me a minute before my breathing settles. I try to glare at him, but he's so pleased with himself I can't keep it up and settle for just rolling my eyes instead.

"You know ... you're not at all what I expected," he says, watching me carefully.

"I know. I'm much better looking in person," I say.

There's a faint pink glow on his pale face, probably a trick of the firelight.

"Where I come from, Shields are monsters. Men and women ruled by their animal instincts. They're the stories we scare children with when we want them to behave. 'Don't stay out too late, or the Shields will get you,'" he says.

I frown. "I'm no monster," I say, but it comes out sounding like a question, a plea. Like I want him to agree with me.

He doesn't, and my chest tightens.

I clear my throat. "I mean, I love being a dragon. But I don't want to be a monster. I'm *not* a monster. But ... I think Rigrasil gave me teeth and claws and fire for a reason. I have to believe that."

"He also gave you wings," Reyn says, a hint of a smile on his lips.

I nod. Obviously, I have wings.

Once again it seems like he wants to say more, but he doesn't.

Now I'm thinking about a whole generation of little Roallacan kids being threatened that the Dragon Girl will snatch them up if they misbehave. Each of them looks like Rosie in my mind, and if I keep thinking about how I'd feel if Rosie were afraid of me, I'll unravel. I square my shoulders instead and change the subject.

"There's something *I* want to know," I say.

His eyes flash to mine, suspicious.

"You don't have to answer, but ... since we've saved each other's life on this trip, I figure we're not entirely enemies anymore, right?"

"Sure," Reyn says, which is not all that convincing.

He opens his mouth and licks a seed from the roll off his finger. I focus on it for a moment—*What, did I expect his tongue to be forked or something?*

"How does a healer become heir of Roallac?" I blurt out, clearing my throat. "I've never seen you use a weapon, other than that dagger you pulled on me the other night. You don't have the build of a fighter. You don't even like *looking* at my dagger. And I've heard Aris talk about your older brother—I don't understand ..."

"How someone as puny as I could take him down?" he asks archly.

"I didn't say you were puny," I argue, heat flaring in my cheeks. "But ... come on. My four-year-old cousin could knock you over with one hand tied behind her back."

He looks down at his hands. Dueling is something that our Mages practice, but it's considered unforgivable to use magic on each other outside of class and carries the penalty of expulsion.

"Did you know that when they're young, a viper's bite is more likely to be deadly?" Reyn asks.

I frown. "What's that got to do with anything?"

"I'm saying magic ... is like our venom. You can't judge someone's strength by their appearance."

I look him over. He's lean as a snake himself, his muscle definition highlighted by his lack of body fat. A thought occurs to me.

"How old were you?" I ask quietly.

He doesn't look at me. "Old enough. It was only a month before the Battle of Soltaire."

He was the same age I was when I razed his home. Events that have left their indelible marks on both of us.

"Michail ... was a lot like Evanthia. I never wanted to be a fighter—I wanted to be a healer from the time I could use magic. But," he says, staring into the flames, "there are things I learned about the body. Ways to ... use it against itself. Turns out there's a lot of water inside us."

I freeze, holding perfectly still. I've heard rumors of some Water Mages—like Mariana—drowning their victims on dry land, flooding their lungs. What kind of terrible thing did he do?

Reyn looks up, meeting my eyes unflinchingly.

"I froze the blood in his veins," he says, calmly. "He died instantly."

If I thought Reyn had no part of him that relished battle before, it is amplified a thousandfold now. He looks leached of color, like just the memory of what he did is enough to make him go gray.

"I swore to Aenon I'd never harm anyone again," he says, looking down at his hands, rubbing his fingertips together absently, like he can't feel his magic there now, his healing hands depleted for the moment.

I roll my eyes again at the mention of the perfidious god of water. Reyn's face falls, and a pang grips my chest.

"It's a reflex for me to cringe when you invoke your traitor god. I'm not judging you for killing your brother, or deciding to be a healer," I explain, shrugging back into my jacket. There's a bloodstain on the shoulder that's now dried and gross, but there's no way for me to clean it, and it's far too cold to do without.

I take a deep breath. "I think ... I think when you are forced to do something terrible, to protect the people you care about, I ... it changes you. Something breaks. And sometimes ... it can't be put back together."

"Maybe we're more alike than either of us wants to admit, Dragon Girl," he says quietly.

I swallow, the next words sticking in my throat like sand.

"Afterward ... you had your vow of healing. And I had Frostbite," I say, sheathing my dagger. "Does it ... does it keep the nightmares away, your vow?"

"Not always," he admits. "Does your dagger?"

"Not always," I echo quietly.

Reyn gets up and adds a few more dead sticks to the fire. He settles his long limbs back down on the ground, pulling his robe around him. He gazes into the fire for a long time, like he's trying to read answers there.

"Were you ever planning on telling me that we were going to the old home of the Night Mage?" he asks. There's a resigned tone in his voice, like he's disappointed in me for that, and that alone.

I sit up straighter. If I were in dragon form, the feathers around my face would be flaring, trying to make me look bigger than I am.

"What?" I ask.

He looks up at me then, the firelight dancing in his emerald eyes, and I squirm—a little—under the direct gaze.

"I'm a Roallacan prince, Delphine. You think I wouldn't recognize the name, wouldn't recognize the hometown of one of the most hated people in my country? That I wouldn't recognize her torn-down lighthouse?"

I bite my tongue. There's no answer I can give that would suffice.

"I don't know if it's worse that you didn't think I was smart enough to figure it out or that you thought I would refuse to heal those people if I knew the truth," he says, still looking at me.

I look away, at the fire, but I can still feel his eyes burning into me.

"You said it yourself—you're a Roallacan prince. Why would I expect anything else of you?" I ask.

The words drop like stones into a still pond, ripples spreading out.

Then he's falling to the side, and his eyes start to roll back. I'm fairly certain it's not a plot to get me to come closer, not with as pale as his face suddenly gets, and I'm painfully reminded that the man overextended his magic *and* nearly drowned yesterday. I leap forward, catch him under one arm, and lower him to lie flat on the ground.

"I'm fine," he says, and he wrenches his arm away from me—but I can see he's not, see the clamminess breaking out on his forehead.

"All right," I say anyway. "Tell me what you need. Water?"

"You talk too much," he says, but the corner of his mouth twitches as he says it. "I just need a moment to rest."

I'm crouched at his side, and when I move to stand, he grabs my wrist—not hard, his cool fingers gentle but firm against my skin. I could break away if I wanted to, but I don't.

"Have I ever given you reason to doubt me, Dragon Girl?" he asks.

His voice is low, soft, and I'm suddenly anxious. I don't reply. I wonder if he did hit his head when he fell after all. Or perhaps he's delirious from overextending his magic.

"You think I don't wish I was someone, anyone, else? If I wasn't the Prince of Snakes, if I'd grown up in Ocron, would you view me differently than you do now?"

"Of course I would," I reply, just as soft. The realization jolts me, like a bolt of lightning, straight through me. "But you are. And I am the Dragon Girl of Ocron."

And I realize it's true. I realize it like a javelin to my chest—he's never done anything other than try to protect his fellow Roallacan classmates, even agreed to come on this crazy mission with me because people need him. He knew who the people of Spit were, and he healed them anyway—and would have gone on healing them until it killed him, because *that's* the kind of person he is. A healer, my enemy—and a gods-damned better person than I am. My eyes flick from his eyes to his lips, which are parted as he pants slightly for breath.

I jerk my wrist back from him, and he doesn't fight me. I stand, massaging the skin there, which is tingling all over, and move back to my place on the other side of the fire.

I arrange some of our things to make a rough pillow and burrow under a blanket. I need a few hours of sleep before I can even think of flying again. I turn away from Reyn, from the fire, letting it warm my back. I don't think there are any predators here. I didn't see any tracks as I flew, nor any sign of people, so it's probably all right for me to go to sleep. Not that I have much choice—my eyes are flickering closed. But a thought nags me, and I feel if I don't voice it, I'll keep it bottled up inside until Frostbite releases it.

"You mentioned snakes are symbols of healing in Roallac," I say into the night. It's easier, not looking at him.

Reyn doesn't reply. Maybe he's already asleep.

I lick my lips and take a deep breath. "Dragons shed their skin too. I don't know if you knew that already, but I do. It's awful. And itchy. But ... maybe it is a kind of healing too. A chance for me to be someone better too."

Overhead, the pine trees sway in a gentle breeze, bringing the scent of the fire over me, and the warm, sticky smell of pine sap. A thousand stars twinkle above, and I watch them, and think of Wren, until my eyes grow heavy. Would she be proud of what I did? I'd like to think so.

I turn over, looking at the fire, and at Reyn's back.

"Reyn, are you awake?"

"Yes," comes his muffled reply.

"Do you think ... that maybe, if a Roallacan prince can become an Ocronian healer, maybe ..."

"What is it?" he asks, turning over to face me.

"Maybe I don't have to be a killer either," I whisper.

His breathing halts for the barest second before resuming, but otherwise, he makes no sound, no judgment. His emerald eyes sparkle in the dim firelight, holding mine, grounding me. Now that I've said it, the rest of the thoughts come tumbling from my lips, like an avalanche.

"It's just ... I don't want to do it. Again, I mean. And as a dragon, I'm the deadliest Shield that the king has, the deadliest in history. I can joke about burning down a ship, but the reality is that I *could* do it, and a thousand other terrible things, and never risk another Ocronian soldier again. I can ... save lives, by taking them. It made some kind of weird sense once, but now ... I don't want to." I finish the last bit so quietly the words barely leave my lips. "I didn't sleep for days after Soltaire," I confess to my enemy. "Sometimes, I still can't."

We watch the fire burn down, the smoke drifting up to the stars overhead. I wiggle in my blanket, unable to get comfortable, but I think it's got more to do with the fact that I want to keep talking than the fact that the ground is hard as rock.

"Dragons ... they aren't weak," I whisper. "They're not afraid of anything. They don't ... they don't get overwhelmed, or anxious. I think, sometimes ... maybe I'm not a very good dragon. Maybe Rigrasil picked the wrong girl."

Reyn thinks for a minute, holding my eyes across the embers of our fire. He looks like something conjured from a dream, or a nightmare, possibly, with the glow flickering across his pale skin, ringing his emerald eyes with gold.

He takes a deep breath. "You're one of a kind, Dragon Girl. There's never been anyone like you. A dragon Shield is whatever *you* say she is, not the other way around."

A warmth has begun to settle in my chest, and I don't know that it has anything to do with the campfire between us.

"And I think," Reyn continues thoughtfully, "I think that you're the only one who can decide what your future holds. Besides ..." A smile tugs at one side of his mouth. "I pity anyone who tries to force you to do *anything* you don't want to."

This gets a reluctant laugh out of me. We exchange sheepish

glances—he's right, though Tekton always had a less tactful way of telling me when I was being a stubborn ass. And if Kora's set on being a battle Mage, to make her mark, well—I'll have to talk with her when we get back, see what kind of future we can make together. One that involves less fighting and more cookies.

"You don't think I'm a coward?" I whisper.

"I think you're a lot of things, but a coward is not among them."

I don't reply. I wonder what other things he thinks about.

"Good night, Delphine."

His voice is a whisper, so quiet I think for a minute I imagined it.

Neither of us says anything else, but neither of us turns their back again either. I can't stop my eyes from closing as sleep claims us both.

CHAPTER 19

"Why did I have to hear about your little trip *with the Snake Prince* from *Vassilis?*" Kora asks, enraged. Smoke is literally rising from the top of her head—she's *pissed*. "I thought you were taking an Ocronian healer!"

"It's not a big deal," I say, pushing past her. I'm tired. I just want to get to my room. I landed in the courtyard just seconds ago—I *want* to go to my room, but Reyn and I have to talk to Head Mage Iraklis first. And tell him that someone is trying to kill me. Or tried to, anyway.

Kora, however, is ... incorrigible.

"You could have taken *me*," she hisses, specifically standing on my left, away from Reyn on my right.

If Reyn hears her, he pretends not to notice. He's been particularly quiet since we landed, like he's resuming the role he plays at the school now, his mask back in place.

"You're not a healer, Kora," I remind her.

She pouts anyway, crossing her arms and sticking out her lower lip. "I still could have helped! You've carried two people before!"

All right, that's true.

"Look, it was fine, all right?" I say. "We ... had a little trouble, but we handled it."

"Trouble? What kind of trouble?" She grabs my arm, and I'm forced to stop walking.

My gaze darts to Reyn. *Do I tell her?*

"Nothing your friend couldn't handle," Reyn says smoothly, stepping between us, looking down on our squabble with disdain. "Now, if you don't mind, I'd like to get our debriefing with the Head Mage over with so that I can take a bath. I *stink* of dragon."

My face heats, and suddenly Kora and I are once more reunited in our passionate hatred of the Snake Prince. It's as if I never left, as if any kind of tenuous ceasefire between Reyn and I had never been. He's happy to abandon the role he played. Well, fine. So am I. No more nice Dragon Girl.

And I do not *stink*!

"It's the fumes from the accelerants! I'm sorry it's too much for your delicate princely nose!" I retort, chasing after him. *He's never complained about it before.*

We reach the door to the academic building, where the Head Mage's office is. It's blissfully cool and dark inside, like a cave.

"Just ... tell me next time," Kora says, the hurt in her voice as sharp and cold as ice. She stays at the doorway. "I'm your best friend. We don't keep secrets, remember?"

"Right. No secrets," I agree automatically, watching Reyn's retreating figure.

"Come along, Dragon Girl!" he hollers, not bothering to turn back and look at us.

I'd stab the idiot, but I'm practically numb with fatigue. I turn to Kora instead.

"Look ... we have to talk to Head Mage Iraklis. I'll come find you after and tell you the whole thing, all right?"

She pouts, and glares at Reyn, smoke once again rising from her head, but she doesn't say anything else as I turn and leave her.

Reyn and I tell Iraklis and Caius about what happened—according to Reyn, the blue flag was representative of one of the island kingdoms.

"No doubt they heard of your attack at Soltaire and sought to arm themselves against a similar fate," Caius says sniffily.

I ball my hands into fists to keep from punching him.

"Nevertheless, this requires a thorough investigation. Thank you. We will get to work on this immediately and let you know if we discover anything. Now, both of you, to the healers."

"I *am* a healer," Reyn grumbles, which catches me a little off guard.

Iraklis smiles, though, amused. "Yes. The finest we've seen since Caius. But being a great healer means knowing your limitations and when to ask for help. For my own peace of mind, go get checked out."

I leave before Reyn does, still pissed about his earlier comment, and head directly to the healers' rooms without waiting for him. I have half a mind to shove him into the decorative pool in the Water Mage building for good measure. *Dragons do* not *stink!*

Days go by, and nothing happens. I pester Head Mage Iraklis until he threatens me, laughing, with detention mucking out stable stalls. But nothing turns up about the attack—or at least, nothing anyone will tell me about. My shoulder scars a little, though it does otherwise heal fine on its own. There is no limitation to it in terms of strength or range of motion.

Though I can't look at it without thinking about Reyn.

The rest of the winter and the early spring pass without incident. The plague continues, though it seems to ease as the weather warms.

Rebels in Roallac are causing a lot of problems along the new roads through the swamps, and a lot of our lessons involve hearing where the current Shields are deployed and what strategies they might use.

Reyn and his Roallacan Water Mages avoid me, though, so I avoid them, other than the agreed-upon mealtimes when I sit at their table. At first Silas is shocked, and the twins glare daggers at me, but after a few days, when they realize I'm not going to stop, they warm up—a little.

I tell Athan and Kora about our agreement, that I would help the Roallacan Mages "make friends," and they reluctantly decide to help as well. It causes a ripple in the dining hall at first, my friends and the snakes sharing a space, but over time, the other students get used to it, and we stop getting funny looks. Mostly.

"I'm just saying, it's *bright*," I complain, looking at Kora's hair and wincing. Her strawberry-blond hair is now a vibrant shade of rosy pink, falling down her back in effortless waves. "Effortless" meaning she spent only *half* the morning on them.

"I know!" Kora says, beaming.

I think she registered my grumbling for a compliment—though, honestly, she's so pleased with herself that I don't think anything could dull her sparkle today. I roll my eyes but can't stop the smile on my face.

We reach the Wind Mage tower and start the long climb up the spiral stairs to the top, where the King's Messengers are.

"I didn't intend for it to be quite so pink, of course—but Aletheia assures me it will fade a little with time," she says, twirling a strand around her fingers.

I groan. "I should have known Aletheia was behind it," I say, shoving my shoulder against Kora's playfully.

"Well, her and Calix, really," Kora says, two pink spots appearing on her cheeks. "He really knows his plants! He helped her make some green dye for Haris—remember him? That second-year Earth Mage? He's really more into rocks than plants like Calix, but his hair turned out *so good*!"

"I'm pretty sure you could see his hair from Roallac," I say. Haris's hair was a shade of green that definitely didn't exist in the plant world. "I bet he glows in the dark."

We laugh and climb, and climb, and climb. It's about a million steps up to the top of the Wind Mage tower, or at least it feels like it. And it's a big tower, with classrooms on each level.

The top, though, with its conical roof, is reserved for the King's Messengers. Why they can't have a headquarters on the ground is beyond me. *I* can take off just fine from ground level—surely they can as well.

We pass the door, and a long row of hooks holds long, plain robes, with clothes and shoes in various sizes neatly stacked on shelves, for the messengers. In the center of the room is a round table, around which two Shields are sitting. One, a small blond girl with thin features and a long nose, is wearing the extra clothing that the school supplies messengers with.

The other, a girl with shining black hair and sky-blue eyes, wears only a robe, which has slid up to reveal her long legs.

"Adriana!" I shout, throwing myself at her.

Adriana leaps up from the table and gives me a huge hug. She's shorter than I remember—we're almost the same height now. She realizes this at the same time I do and laughs. My eyes sting, and I blink them rapidly to clear them.

"I didn't know you were back on this coast!" I say, dropping my letters to Ismini and Tekton on the table.

"Just flew in today!" she says, and she proudly hands me a letter from Uncle Tekton. I'd recognize his careful penmanship on the scroll anywhere. "He sends his love."

"I bet," I say, looking askance at Adriana. I have a sneaking suspicion she'll be "Aunt Adriana" someday, but I don't pry.

Adriana pretends to inspect her fingernails.

The first time she met my quiet uncle, she was stark naked. It certainly left an impression. I caught Tekton staring off into the sky after she left each time, a wistful expression on his face.

"You're Adriana? I've heard so much about you!" Kora gushes.

"Oh. Kora, this is Adriana, Aris's little sister," I say. "Adriana, this is Kora."

"Fire Mage?" Adriana says, assessing Kora's robe and raising an eyebrow. "Not Nicolaos's sister?"

"You've heard of me?" Kora preens.

"Delphine wrote to us about you," Adriana says, giving Kora a smile.

We sit at the table and catch up for a while, until the sun begins to set and the shadows in the courtyard lengthen. The quiet blond messenger shifted into her hawk form and flew off soon after we arrived.

"Aris trained me, but Adriana's the *real* reason I wanted to be a true Shield," I tell Kora.

Adriana likes this and punches me fondly on the arm.

Kora frowns. "You want to be a King's Messenger?" she asks.

"No, no!" I say. "I fully intend to claim a Mage when I win my games."

Kora looks mollified for the moment.

"That can't possibly be true, anyway," Adriana says generously. "You've practically worshipped Aris since you first met him!"

"It's true!" I protest, laughing. "I was *hiding* in the Temple of the God of Night for *years*, and in flies Adriana! Strong, fierce, and *free*."

Kora eyes Adriana thoughtfully.

"Not to mention stunning. You forgot stunning," Adriana says, her bare feet propped up on the table.

"Who could ever forget that?" a cheery voice grumbles from the stairs.

Adriana sits up, spine straight, feet off the table, as Vassilis enters the room.

"They haven't fired you?" Adriana says, but she goes over to Vassilis for a hug.

"Not yet." He chuckles, ruffling her hair. "We leave clothes for you all for a reason, you know," he says, eyeing her robe, the tie of which is barely keeping her decent.

She shrugs. "I'm about to shift and leave anyway. You have something for me?"

"Another letter to Rafael, if you don't mind," Vassilis says, handing Adriana a neatly rolled scroll. "From Reyn. I sealed it myself."

"Why is Reyn writing to Rafael?" I ask before I can stop myself.

Rafael, my first Fire Mage teacher, and friend, has been helping set up a school for magical children in Roallac, to prepare them for the School of the Silver Flame when they are old enough.

"Gods, they write each other *novels* about every other week," Adriana complains, hefting the scroll in her hands. "Boring stuff about the school and the city, repairs and things. How their new school is going, how many students they have enrolled. And usually some equally boring things about the city's art. Snakes everywhere, of course."

"Probably secret messages to the Roallacan rebels," Kora grumbles. "Is that why you read his letters yourself?"

"And seal them, so there can be no question about the contents," Vassilis confirms.

I wonder if anyone reads *my* messages, but probably not. I'm not the enemy here. Still, it must rankle Reyn that he can't even have privacy in his letters. I don't know exactly how I feel about that revelation.

Adriana pouts. "Rafael lets me read them."

"I'll pretend I didn't hear that," Vassilis says, giving Adriana a little bow, his hand on his chest. "Tell Aris he still owes me a rematch."

"Will do," Adriana says. Then she looks out the window. The last of the sun's rays are fading.

"Come on," Vassilis says to Kora and me. "Curfew. Let's go."

I give Adriana one more squeeze, then watch her shift. She changes into a gorgeous cream-and-brown hawk. We've wrapped the messages in a tight bundle tied with string, and she wraps her talons around them with expert grace. A few flaps, and she's out the window. I race to watch her, waving as she turns a few circles around the tower.

I spend the rest of my first-year days training, and my evenings studying. After that, when the Mages need their sleep, well, we Shields stay up. Gambling is the most common after-hours activity, done clandestinely, of course, as it is strictly forbidden by the school. I'm not much of a gambler.

The other favorite nighttime activity involves significantly less clothing. Shields, as I've found out, are quite proud of their bodies, and I enjoy a certain level of celebrity being the Dragon Girl. I am never short of willing bedmates, and one second-year named Makhon seems to find his way to my room more often than most. He has the most beautiful copper eyes, and golden skin that practically glows.

But eventually I grow tired of him.

None of it means anything, of course. Some of the men, I hardly remember their names—but it is an enjoyable way to pass the time. None of them care for me beyond what it might mean for their own status to claim me as a conquest, and after a while, it begins to lose its appeal. I start spending my nights alone more often than not, with only my knife for company.

By summer the second-years are all getting ready for their Shield games, and the first-years are focused on passing their exams. I wouldn't say that the Roallacan Mages and the Ocronian students are friendly, but we tolerate each other, and no one bullies Silas anymore.

"They're afraid you'll bite their balls off if they try," Athan confides in me one day as we walk to class.

"Ew," I say, shoving his shoulder. Then I sigh, seeing a familiar bulky form waiting for me outside the door.

Sinon. His hovering is getting old—I mean, he's not bad-looking. He's tall, a block of solid muscle with biceps as big as my waist. He's got a high-arched nose, which somehow makes him look distinguished instead of silly—like he's grown into it. I bet as a kid, he got teased. He's got thick reddish-brown hair that he wears pulled back like Aris does, but the resemblance ends there. Aris is playful, and loyal to a fault. Sinon is neither. He stalks me every chance he gets.

I am a predator. I don't appreciate being prey.

"I can arrange for him to spill his ash water all over himself," Isadora says helpfully as she walks past.

"I can stab him in the eye. It's hard to properly heal an eyeball. If you want," Eugenia says, without a hint of sarcasm.

I can't tell the twins apart usually, but when one of them says something violent, I can bet that it's Eugenia.

"Thanks for the offer," I say, eyeing Eugenia. I'm not sure she's kidding. "I've got this."

Eugenia shrugs and walks off with Isadora, though both of them glare at Sinon as they pass. I shove Athan after the twins, and he reluctantly leaves me. Sinon doesn't appear to have heard Eugenia's comments. At least Isadora is warming up to me a little, I think. Eugenia, I'm sure, just likes violence.

"When are you going to come watch me in the arena?" Sinon asks, pushing off the wall he was leaning on and walking beside me.

I roll my eyes. "Watching you pummel your fellow second-years into the sand isn't my idea of foreplay," I say. I walk faster, wanting this to be over, but he keeps pace.

"Why don't you tell me what is, sweetheart?" he asks, baring sharp white teeth in what he must assume is a charming grin.

Ugh.

"It's not going to happen," I say. I can't be any more clear than that. *Get it through your thick skull.*

"Come on, when are you going to give me a chance?" he asks.

The other students mostly get out of the way when they see us coming—either because of Sinon's size or because of my temper.

"Are you going to follow me all the way into history class?" I stop before the door of the academic building, where most of our classes are held. It's also the one where the teachers have their offices, so it's pretty busy this time of day. Lots of witnesses to him being rejected. Sinon looks around—and finally gives in.

"I'll see you later, then," he calls, though his tone sounds more sinister than playful.

I turn my back on him while he's talking and head into the building without turning around. His low chuckle makes me cringe. I finger Frostbite's hilt, running my fingertip over the designs, and try to put him out of my mind.

CHAPTER 20

I've been wanting to do something for Kora, after she got so mad when I went to Spit with Reyn. That's what friends do, right? Granted, I'm new at this whole "best friends" thing she keeps talking about.

"I'm going to cook for you!" I announce proudly at dinner.

Athan drops his spoon into his empty bowl, where it clatters loudly. His jaw is open. Kora doesn't look as excited as I expected.

"Um, thanks, Del," she says, tilting her head. "I didn't know you could cook."

I frown. "Shields gotta eat," I remind her. "I already talked to the cooks; they're going to let me use one of the back ovens tomorrow afternoon. All I need you to do is to sweet-talk Calix into letting me shop the greenhouse tonight."

Kora shakes her head. "No way. I am *not* sneaking out after curfew with you—*again*. I appreciate the offer, but it's really not necessary."

"She's worried you'll poison her, she means," Athan says, ineffectively using his hand to hide the smile on his face.

I kick him under the table, and he yelps.

"Ow! Accidentally, I mean, of course."

"We're *going* to make the best mushroom stew you've ever tasted," I tell her. "Let's get you to eat something besides cookies."

She mumbles something under her breath that sounds like "But I *like* cookies."

"Why don't you just ask Mage Gavriil for the mushrooms?" Athan asks.

I smack my hand against my forehead. "Why didn't I think of that?" I exclaim dramatically. "Oh, wait, I did. He said no. Actually, what he specifically said was 'No way in a thousand hells am I going to let a dragon loose in my precious greenhouse.'"

I was still fuming over that—it's not like I was going to shift in there or breathe fire on his precious plants. I just needed some mushrooms from the lower levels of the Earth Mage building, but he threatened me with detention if I tried. It wasn't fair. The cooks get basically any fresh ingredient they want there, so why couldn't I for once?

"Won't the cooks be suspicious if you use a bunch of things from the greenhouse?" Kora says.

She's wavering, I can tell.

"I told them I picked a bunch of mushrooms when I went flying yesterday," I say with a shrug.

It is partially true—I looked all over the valley, but there were too many wheat fields and not enough fallen trees or caves where the really good mushrooms grow, like spotted touch-me-nots and bristly redhats. I'm convinced they taste better than anything else in all of Ocron, but you've got to cook them properly. And we have *tons* of them in Aeturnus. When Tekton and I arrived, they grew over everything—but once Hector, the baker down in the village, lit up when we brought him some to identify, we took to cultivating them ourselves. Uncle Tekton has quite a knack for it—in another life, he would have made an excellent Earth Mage. Gods, thinking of him hurts my chest.

Kora hasn't completely agreed, but I don't take no for an answer.

I track down Calix as we head back to the dorms. He's quiet, and honestly, he's dull, apart from the fact he has a pet squirrel that follows him around constantly, but when I ask him about what mushrooms grow in the greenhouse, his face lights up.

"Yeah, we've got touch-me-nots. Oh, and those Ignatius peppers you were asking me about? They're coming in great, should be ready to pick any day now."

The hot peppers Athan keeps threatening to sneak into Lyssa's food—gods, I can't wait.

"I'd love to see them," I say, taking his arm and batting my lashes.

He freezes. "Uh-uh. No way. Mage Gavriil's orders. No dragons in the greenhouse."

"That seems unfair," I say, pouting. "I've never even been in it! I just want to make a special surprise for my best friend in the whole wide world—and it would mean *so much* to Kora if you could help me. Say, tonight? Around midnight?"

His broad face flushes red.

Kora's caught up to us by now, narrowing her eyes and glancing between us.

"What are you up to?" she asks me accusingly.

I widen my eyes. "Nothing."

Calix coughs into his hand, his eyes, brown as dirt, fixed on the stones at his feet. "Uh, right," he says. "Tonight, then." He glances at Kora, turns even redder, and flees for the stairs.

Kora punches my arm. "Don't you get him in trouble," she warns me. It's cute. Like a kitten growling at a lion. "I mean it!"

"I would never," I promise.

"We're going to get into so much trouble," Calix whines.

"We won't get caught if you just shut up," I tell him. I'm flattened against the wall, at a point as close to the greenhouse as we can get. It's a full moon, nearly as bright as day, which means we're stupidly visible. There's a small grove of old oaks between us and the greenhouse—they'll provide good cover. I risk a glance overhead to look for guards, but I think they must be at the far end of the school, because I don't see them.

I'm just about to give Calix the signal to follow me and dash to the big trees when I spy Caius and the twins, Isadora and Eugenia, talking in the shadow of the Water Mage building. It's not unusual to see him talking to the Roallacan Water Mages, taking a special interest in their learning, but there's something ... furtive in the way they're speaking tonight. They're all tucked against the side wall, their heads bent close together. It's weird. One of the twins even has her hood up, but I know it's her. They never go anywhere alone—and to be out at this time of night, even with a full Mage? It's *really* weird.

So, like any good Shield when the threat of imminent discovery looms, I go check it out. I hear Calix fidget behind me—he's following me, his heavy footsteps loud.

"Shh," I warn him, glaring hard enough to make him blanch, and push him back against the wall. "Stay here. I'll be right back."

Caius and the twins are close to the corner of the Water Mage building. I sneak closer, straining my ears to find out what they're discussing.

"So, classes are going well, then?" Caius asks.

I fight the urge to roll my eyes. *Boring!*

"Well enough," one of the twins huffs. Probably Isadora, since she didn't say anything about stabbing anyone. "It's bad enough that we have to be in the same school as *her*. Do we really have to take classes with her too?"

It doesn't take a genius to figure out who the "her" she's referring to is. I consider revealing myself then, just to see the shock on their faces, but then Eugenia talks, her voice low and sibilant, like a snake's.

"It would have been better if they had both died," she says. I hear a sharp intake of breath—but no reproach. I frown. Did she mean Wren and me, at Soltaire? Or possibly Reyn and me, over the sea?

"A troublesome time, to be sure," Caius says lightly. "There have been no threats of violence against you?"

"Not unless you count the terrible food," Isadora says with a snort. "These Ocronians. They are no more threatening than a sparrow."

A sparrow who brought your capital to its knees, I think. *So much for thinking she was warming up to me.* I clench my fists at my sides.

"What about Reyn?" Eugenia hisses.

I stop my indignant inner monologue and strain my ears to listen.

"If the prince was injured, Roallac would surely revolt," Caius's voice says carefully.

A warning? Or ... a command? His voice is low, so it's hard for me to hear any inflection. *What in the hells?*

"Michail never would have rolled over so easily when Ocron invaded," Eugenia mutters.

Isadora agrees.

I clench my fists so hard that my nails cut into my palms. Reyn worked tirelessly for them—he still does. I'd like to see any of *them* do better.

A rustle of cloth, and then it's quiet for a moment.

"The walls have ears," Eugenia whispers.

Shit. I duck behind a tree before glancing over my shoulder—the twins and Caius drift in separate directions. I swear Eugenia's black eyes fix on me for a long moment before she, too, disappears into the dorms. I let out a breath and silently make my way over to Calix.

He's standing behind a tree, looking nervously at the greenhouse. When I put my hand on his shoulder, he yelps. I spin him around and clamp my hand over his mouth. He's bigger than me, but he's soft, and I'm a Shield. What Kora sees in him, I have no idea. I'm beginning to wish I asked one of his classmates instead. And I'm more than a little unsettled by having stumbled on Caius and the twins.

"It's just me," I hiss. "Come on. Let's do this."

The greenhouse is a two-story structure of metal and greenish glass. It's beautiful, really, and during the day, it sparkles in the sun like a gem. The metal supports are bent into arches that remind me of the windows back home—structurally at odds with the austerity of the rest of the school. We creep up to the main door, and Calix puts his palm against it. A green glow coalesces around his fingers, and the door pops open.

"Come on," he says, more comfortable in the Earth Mage building than outside it. "Let's get this over with. And make sure you tell Kora how much I helped you!"

"Sure," I say, and I follow him.

The greenhouse is silent. A warm humidity permeates the air, smelling of rich soil and herbs and flowers.

I cover my nose to keep from sneezing.

In the center of the greenhouse is the Century Tree, a wizened, gnarled old thing that's been pruned daily over its lifetime. Its trunk is like a bunch of twisted ropes, each one branching out overhead, adorned with golden leaves, and hung with glowing green orbs—Earth Mage lights.

"It's beautiful," I say, heading toward it. In the moonlight, its golden leaves glimmer like nothing I've ever seen before.

"No dragons allowed, *especially* near the Century Tree," Calix warns, stepping in my way.

I frown, but he doesn't budge.

"Come on," he continues. "The entrance to the lower levels is this way."

He leads me past sectioned-off areas with desks and others with benches and pots. Rather than partitions for individual classrooms, the greenhouse is just one really large room broken up by hedges and stone walls. The perimeter of the greenhouse is lined with flower beds, each one with a different plant, each one thriving. Calix heads to what looks like a small shed, but inside is a dark staircase lined with more of those glowing green orbs. It smells dark and musty below—perfect for mushrooms.

Calix doesn't let me explore, though. He guides me directly down one level and into a small cave on the right. It's damp and loamy, with smooth walls that tell me it isn't a natural cave but rather one that the Earth Mages created themselves.

And I've never seen so many mushrooms—redhats and touch-me-nots, but also dragon's breath, snowcaps, and henbane. Tall, skinny ones and short, fat ones and ones with wide caps and ones with something black oozing down from the gills—I leave these alone. I gleefully sort through them and take a handful—not enough so that anyone would notice—and we head back up.

"You'll make sure Kora knows I helped?" Calix asks again.

We head past the potting benches and class areas to the entrance. He breathes easily now that the worst part of our nocturnal adventure is over.

"Let me take a leaf from the Century Tree, and you'll have a deal," I say, eyeing the golden leaves as we pass.

But Calix, gods bless him, stands firm.

"No way. I've done what you asked," he protests, crossing his arms. "I'd do anything for Kora, but Mage Gavriil would know if I touched that tree, and then I'd be expelled."

I pout, but he only glares at me. Well, fine. I'm definitely not jealous that he's so infatuated with my best friend—Calix isn't really my type. But I'm grudgingly impressed at how he's standing up to me.

"All right," I agree, though I do spare one last glance at the Century Tree, its gold leaves sparkling in the moonlight.

We make it back to the dorms without encountering anyone, including Caius and the twins. Calix is sweating profusely but seems pleased with himself—and I have a sack full of mushrooms.

I spend the next afternoon, which is our one precious free day per week, in the sweltering kitchen. I miss my cool mountain home even more, but when I'm cleaning and slicing the mushrooms and cooking them with butter, like Tekton taught me, I swear I can nearly smell the snow, feel the cool winds under my wings.

"It's ... not bad," Athan says, eyes wide.

I spooned some of the mushrooms over the barley the kitchen staff prepared for our evening meal, and served my friends proudly. I devoured my own bowl in swift bites—gods, it was good. Hearty and rich and with so much more flavor than our usual mush.

"Not much to work with in Aeturnus, but this was always one of my favorites," I say.

Kora was a little suspicious of the variety before her—but I reassured her that Calix wouldn't have let me pick any mushrooms that might potentially hurt her, and she seemed placated.

"It's really good, Del," she says with a smile. "Maybe after the games, we can visit Aeturnus. I'd love to see your home. You make it sound so ... magical."

I grin. "Wren's been working on a way to communicate more easily with Caladrius. I think she has one of the gods' books, but she wouldn't tell me. She's trying to repair whatever rift in magic Aenon caused," I say with a shrug. Academic stuff. I'm not that interested, unless Caladrius is going to grant Tekton a shift, which he hasn't. "Aris and Tekton have got the school really running. It's smaller than this, but it's way more people than the temple has seen in ages. It's like ... the temple was always supposed to be a place with lots of people, not some isolated thing. It's come back to life."

"Can I come too?" Athan asks, using his fork to stab a last piece of mushroom and pop it into his mouth.

"Depends. How are your wolf paws on snow?" I ask.

He grins, holding up his hands, which are large and calloused, like mine.

"You just try to keep up," he says.

Something inside me warms. I've never had friends like this before, ones that would cross a continent just to visit me. Wren and Aris are family, really. They don't count. But the thought of my friends and my family under one roof? Getting to show Kora the deep caves, where the molten rock bubbles up, or the hot springs where the mushrooms grow, or showing Athan the underground obsidian arena Aris designed? Gods, they'd love it.

CHAPTER 21

For Shields, there are a number of physical exams at the end of the year, as well as the written ones. How fast we can cover ten miles. How adept we are at the drills Vassilis has practically branded into our skulls. How quickly we can lock our shields together in two rows and form the tortoise formation, in the event we're bombarded with projectiles from an enemy. We also practice fighting in our shifted forms. Lyssa, the white wolf, can tear the straw-stuffed practice dummy's arm off in a single move. Iason, the bear, and Eleni, the panther, are pretty evenly matched when they fight, though Athan can beat both of them when unshifted.

I'm excluded from these sessions, for obvious reasons, partly because straw is flammable and partly because I can knock over the rest of the Shields with a flick of my tail—which I remind Lyssa of frequently, even if I don't actually get to do it.

We are just now allowed to use wooden weapons during class, and I grudgingly have to admit that perhaps there is some wisdom in the delay. A number of Shields end up with broken bones and splinters and stab injuries to various parts of their anatomy. Herondas in particular—I swear to Rigrasil that boy is the clumsiest Shield I've ever met. We spend a lot of time in the healers' room, in the Water Mage building, as the summer reaches its peak.

"You're lucky this didn't go any deeper," Reyn says. He is crouched over Herondas—since I am the one who inflicted his injury, I got the honor of escorting him to the healers.

It isn't a terrible wound, honestly—but Vassilis insisted. The tip of my wooden practice sword caught below Herondas's left ear and scraped a gash along the side of his jaw. It bled furiously, but that's just how facial wounds are. They're dramatic like that.

"Am I going to have a scar?" Herondas asks. It isn't from fear or pain—he, like most of us, is vain.

Caius rolls his eyes.

"Then again, it might make me look dangerous," Herondas says. "You can leave the scar if you want."

"You won't scar," Reyn says, annoyed. He looks up at me briefly, his emerald eyes carefully blank. "A wound any deeper than this can scar, especially if it goes down to muscle. Shields can heal these superficial ones without a trace. Anything deeper than skin and fat, and you need a healer."

"Good to know," Herondas says, assuming Reyn is still addressing him.

I look away, but I can't fight the heat that's spreading up my neck, probably staining my cheeks. Like I didn't know that already. I know *exactly* how deep I can go without damaging anything. I know how quickly I can heal each cut too, down to the minute. I can't look at Reyn. I focus on the ungifted girl restocking the room, rolling gauze, handing out cups of water to the healers; on the other students compounding some kind of tincture; even on the scuff marks on the tiled floor. *Stupid Reyn and his stupid healing.*

"Are you done? I'm missing my turn sparring," I say, letting out a bored sigh.

Reyn frowns and looks back at Herondas's face. Caius leans over him, lips pursed, watching Reyn's magic carefully, but doesn't make any corrections. Eventually, he must get bored doing nothing too, because he leaves Herondas in the hands of his pupil and goes somewhere else.

Reyn makes one more pass of his long, pale fingers over the skin of Herondas's face, and a whisper of blue magic seeps into the skin. The incision isn't just healed; it's vanished completely.

"All done," Reyn says, reaching for the cup at his side to take a deep drink.

The building is crowded and hot—the healers on duty, the Shields needing their attention, some ungifted with minor complaints, and one Fire Mage with terrible burns down his leg, all of us stuffed into this room. Reyn wipes his hands on a rag. He stands stiffly.

"Careful chewing on that side for a few more hours," Reyn warns. "It's probably going to be a little numb for a while."

Herondas runs a hand over the unblemished skin of his cheek. His own fingers are still bloodstained from stanching the wound. "Thanks," he says, offering the hand to Reyn.

Reyn blinks a few times, shakes his head as if to clear it, and takes Herondas's hand.

"You're welcome," he says, but the words sound ... garbled, and my head snaps around to look at him.

When Herondas releases his hand, Reyn turns and stumbles, going down to his knees, pitching forward.

I don't stop to think. I reach out, grabbing him around the shoulders before he can slam face-first into the cot Herondas was lying on.

"Reyn!" I yell, turning him around.

But Reyn can't respond. His eyes are glassy and unfocused, his fair skin bone white. At the corners of his mouth, white foam begins to collect as he bucks, gasping for air, his fingers clawing at his throat. His eyes begin to roll back. This isn't like at Spit, when he overextended—and there's no way healing Herondas should have used that much magic.

"Get Caius!" I shout to Herondas.

He blanches but runs from the room, calling for the Water Mage.

"Let me see him," one of the second-years says, trying to push me aside. He's a little taller than me, with a sturdiness to him I expect more of an Earth Mage than a Water Mage. I don't give him an inch.

"Who the fuck are you?" I ask, ready to pull out my knife if *anyone* dares touch Reyn.

"Tereos. I'm from Roallac too. Let me see," he says, his voice level and quiet. Tereos. Ok. I vaguely remember him now.

I press my lips together firmly and look down at Reyn, shaking, in my arms. Gods, he's going to seize. His fingers spasm, curling around the edge of my shirt. His eyes stare, unseeing.

"If he dies, I'm going to kill you," I tell Tereos. I lay Reyn on the cot and stand back.

"Noted," Tereos says wryly, and he lays his hands over Reyn's heaving chest.

Every breath Reyn takes sounds like a rattle, and the spittle on his lips is taking on a bloody tinge. My chest feels tight, my skin itchy. My hand finds Frostbite's grip by instinct, finding reassurance in the weight of it.

"Hurry up," I say.

I have no idea what's going on in the rest of the room—it could be burning down, for all I care. All I can see is the man in front of me, struck suddenly ill from ... something. But what?

A thought strikes me. I grab the cup from beside the cot and look inside. It's just water, but as I swirl it, there seems to be a thin gloss on the inside, something oily that catches the light.

Tereos has his hands spread over Reyn's chest, and a blue glow has suffused into Reyn's skin, following the path of his blood vessels, lighting them up. Reyn is still gasping, his arms and legs cramping.

"Here," I say, thrusting the cup at Tereos. "Do you know what this is?"

He looks at the cup, unseeing, then does a double take.

"That film," he says, his dark brows furrowing in concentration.

Reyn suddenly bucks off the bed, a spasm seizing him, and a strangled cry escapes his mouth. Gods, I feel so useless.

"Fuck, it's winter's bane," Tereos says, his eyes widening. Sweat is beading on his forehead. By now, a second Mage—a full Mage, a blond woman I recognize as one of the senior healers—has arrived and joins her hands over Tereos's.

"What?" I ask.

"Poison," Tereos says, his jaw clenching.

The blond woman does something, and Reyn relaxes, as if suddenly asleep. Or dead.

"What happened?" I ask, leaping forward, grabbing Reyn's shoulder.

"Peace, Shield," the blond woman says. "I've merely put him into a healing sleep. Now go, and let us work."

I stand, my hands clenching at my sides as I helplessly watch these Mages perform their healing magic. In a few more minutes, Caius rushes in, his slick hair wild, his face pinched. He flies to Reyn's side, and soon there is so much healing magic that Reyn is glowing from head to foot. I think back to that conversation I overheard by the greenhouse, when Calix and I snuck in to get mushrooms. If Caius intends to hurt Reyn, he's putting on a convincing act.

Still, I watch him carefully, making a mental note of every word he says, every little move he makes. So far, nothing seems suspicious.

"This will take time," one of the ungifted assistants says in a kindly voice. He steers me, ungently, toward the door. "You can come check on him in a few hours."

A few hours, my ass. I pace back and forth before that stupid building until Athan warns me that I am going to wear a trench into the cobblestones.

"Why are you so worried, anyway? Don't you hate him?" Kora asks. She's sitting on a bench outside the Water Mage building, munching an apple and flipping through one of her fire magic books. Periodically she twirls her fingers, and little flames dance over them as she studies.

"Of course I do," I spit. "But I was *there*, Kora. Don't you see? If something happens to him, everyone's going to assume it was me!"

"So you're not worried about him, then?" she asks, raising an eyebrow.

"Don't be stupid," I say, looking at the door of the Water Mage building for the thousandth time, willing it to open. "If the Fallen Prince of Roallac *dies* here, while supposedly under the protection of the school—what do you think it will mean for Ocron? Roallacan supporters will make him a martyr. The rebels will use this as an excuse to continue their attacks." That's what Caius and the twins said, anyway.

"I'm not stupid," Kora mutters, looking down at her boots.

Shit. I want to kick myself.

"Kora, I didn't mean—"

"So, you think someone poisoned him?" Athan interrupts.

"Let me see if I can get any information." Aletheia lets go of his hand and gives him a quick peck on the cheek. She pushes through the door into the building, leaving us standing outside.

"Winter's bane, Tereos said. Have you heard of it?" I ask.

"No," Kora says, shaking her head. "We could go to the library and look it up. That might be more helpful to him than just sitting here."

"Who would be mad enough to try to kill him, especially here?" Athan says. "We all know what the presence of the Roallacan Mages means to the king—and we all hate the guy, but I can't think of anyone who'd actually want to kill him, you included." He nods toward me.

At that moment, the blond healer emerges from the building, looking tired. She seems surprised to see the three of us standing there.

"How is he?" I ask.

She blinks for a second. "Isn't it past curfew?" she asks, looking up at the darkening sky.

"Yes. You can write us all up for detention," I say, rolling my eyes.

"Hey!" Athan protests.

"How is Reyn?" I ask again, glaring at Athan.

He shuts up.

"Alive," the healer says, and I swear to Rigrasil that relief hits me like an avalanche. "He'll need rest for a few days, but there shouldn't be any permanent damage done."

"Where did the poison come from?" I ask.

She frowns. "You don't need to know ..."

"Either you can tell me, or I'll go straight to the library and look up winter's bane. But that will mean I'm out past curfew a lot later," I warn.

She sighs. I guess she's too tired to fight me.

"It's a venom, extracted from a very rare snake. It's difficult to store, as any exposure to sunlight will make it lose its potency, so it's not often used."

"Snake venom?" Kora gasps, her eyebrows nearly reaching her hairline.

"Fitting, for the Prince of Snakes," Athan says.

I nod, thinking.

"And where can this rare snake be found?" I ask.

The healer closes her eyes and mutters what sounds like a prayer. "Roallac. Only in Roallac," she says.

A chill runs down my spine. *Roallac.* Is someone trying to make an example of Reyn? Is this some twisted plot of the Roallacan rebels to make a martyr of him, like Caius said? Or—and my heart stutters for a moment—could it have been the twins?

My money's on Eugenia.

"Now, if you're done interrogating me, I need to speak with the Head Mage."

The healer walks on, and we part to let her pass. My head aches with all the thoughts running through it, the worst of which is wondering whether Reyn will be all right.

CHAPTER 22

Darius Hall is a Wind Mage of some renown, mostly because he claims he was the one who "discovered" Wren in Spit all those years ago. He likes to leave out the part where he put a manacle on her wrist, binding her magic, and cast an air gag spell on her when she dared question him, meaning she couldn't speak for *days*. She came to the School of the Silver Flame as a prisoner.

And this long-haired, long-bearded, long-*toothed* Wind Mage is the one that Iraklis wants to question me?

Over my dead body. Or his, preferably.

He settles his bony self into a cushy armchair in Head Mage Iraklis's office, his silent bear of a Shield, Lennox, standing guard behind him with his burly arms crossed. I stick my tongue out at him when I catch him glaring at me.

Fun thing about the interrogation spell Darius uses: I'm compelled to tell the truth if he asks me for it—but I'm not compelled to be nice about it.

So I drop a lot of curse words in, just so he knows that he's already pissed me off before we even get started.

"Look, if I was going to kill Reyn, I would have done it already. I could have thrown him off when I flew him to Spit, or on the way back, or let him drown—or honestly, I could have stabbed him at any time over the past year. Poison isn't really my style."

"Thanks," Reyn mutters. He's leaning back against Iraklis's desk, arms crossed.

"Lucky for you, neither is murder," I say, rolling my eyes. I'm relieved to see that though he looks tired, there's color back in his pale cheeks, alertness back in his eyes. *Thank the gods for healing magic.*

"Maybe you realized we knew that about you, and you used poison to throw us off," Caius says.

I throw my hands into the air. "You really think I'm that smart?"

Reyn smothers a laugh. There are dark circles under his eyes, made even more prominent by his fair skin. I don't recall the ridges at the back of his neck protruding so much—he must not be eating. Ismini would order him out of here and to the dining hall in a heartbeat.

"Answer the question, Shield," Lennox growls.

I give him a rude hand gesture.

"For what it's worth, I don't think she did it," Reyn says, surprising me. "She was never anywhere near my cup."

"I *didn't* do it," I say, still under Darius's sway.

"Kept a close eye on her, did you?" Caius asks, narrowing his eyes at his prince.

"I'm sure you've noticed how distracting she can be," Reyn says.

I stick my tongue out at him.

"I've lost track of how many times people have tried to kill me over the years," Reyn continues. "That doesn't mean I've stopped paying attention to what's going on around me."

Reyn considers me a threat. Good to know. I feel kind of smug about that, and kind of ... I don't know ... unsettled, maybe.

"I heard that the poison was from Roallac," I say, watching Caius.

Not so much as a flicker of anxiety on his face, just the careful mask of concern for his precious prince.

"Have you interrogated the twins?" I ask.

Iraklis raises one eyebrow. "We have interrogated all of the Roallacan students for this reason, of course," he says. "None of them is the culprit."

All right, then. I notice that he says "students," which means he hasn't necessarily questioned Caius. Interesting. I throw out another idea—maybe I should play up the "dumb Shield" act after all. I'm tired of their interrogations focusing on me.

"What about the girl, the ungifted one, restocking the room?" I ask.

Darius frowns, looking down his considerable nose at me. "What girl?"

"The one who brought the drinks, obviously," I say. "Blondish hair, maybe my age?"

"Do you remember anything else about her?" Darius asks.

"No. I was kind of preoccupied when Reyn started foaming at the mouth," I say.

Reyn frowns. "I don't remember seeing a girl there," he says.

So much for staying aware of his surroundings.

"You were focused on healing Herondas. Again," I say, rolling my eyes. "*I* was doing my job."

"Guarding Prince Reyn is *not* your job," Caius hisses from the corner. "As you well know, Roallacan Mages do not bond with Shields. *We* do not need them."

"And as *you* well know, a Shield's duty is to all. To her Mage first, but then to any who need her protection. And Reyn needs ... needed me. Then. At that time."

Caius raises an eyebrow. "Your protection, you mean?"

"Are we done yet?" I ask. "How is this relevant to your investigation?"

I feel Darius's magic slip away, like chains around me that have suddenly lifted.

"That will be all," he says, fluttering his hand at me.

I storm out, slamming the door behind me before Reyn or Caius can stop me.

"Remind me why we're breaking into the Water Mage building after curfew?" Kora hisses. She doesn't like being woken up in the middle of the night. Her usual cheerful smile has been replaced with a tired, grumpy frown.

"Because the healers knew *exactly* what kind of poison was used on Reyn immediately," I say. "The *Black Water* healers. If it's as rare and hard to find as Caius says, *someone* must have kept it inside the school."

The Water Mage student, Tereos, recognized it within seconds. Or was he in on some plot against Reyn? Tereos saves him and looks like a hero? But would he really be stupid enough to use a poison that he knew was tied to Roallac? Iraklis said the students weren't guilty. *Ugh*. My head aches.

We creep along the tiled hall of the Water Mage building. The magical lights on the wall cast everything in blue shadow, giving my pale skin an ethereal glow and turning Kora's pink hair a weird shade of purple.

"Surely they would have disposed of it by now," Kora says.

We come to the healers' room, the room Reyn and I were in when he was poisoned. The door creaks loudly in the quiet evening air.

"I doubt they've had the chance to," I counter. "This place was swamped with healers and school staff when it happened."

"Maybe he put it in his pocket, then," she grumbles. "Or threw it in the garbage. Do you want me to go through the garbage next? If so, you might need to find yourself a new best friend."

"Look, I just need to look for clues, all right?" I say. I'm starting to get frustrated. "I'm the one they're blaming, remember? I need to prove my innocence."

"Well, I don't know if I'd say you're innocent, but I know you didn't poison the prince," Kora says, finally granting me a sly smile.

I shrug.

The burbling fountains, which seem so calming during the day, sound as loud as rapids at night. We creep past the long, shallow pool in the center of the building. I'm not sure what I hope to find—some discarded poison bottle that everyone else missed? I head straight to the end of the hall.

"Why are we going to Mage Caius's office?" Kora whispers.

I try the handle—locked.

"He's practically in love with Reyn," Kora continues. "He'd be the last one who'd want to poison him."

"Indeed," a sly voice says behind us.

I wince. *Uh-oh.*

"While I understand your eagerness to clear your own name, please do not drag mine through the mud too."

Caius. *Shit.* He looks profoundly smug, his arms crossed across his skinny chest, his hair slicked back from his face. Kora's mouth drops open—she's never been in any kind of trouble with the teachers before, never earned a single reprimand. I'm a Shield, so I act first and save the thinking for later.

"Kora didn't want to come. I forced her to," I blurt out, shoving Kora behind me.

She grabs my arm tightly.

I have Frostbite out in a second, though I keep it close to my side. I have to see if I can talk my way out of this, but if Caius *did* poison Reyn, who he practically worships, then he'd have little remorse about taking us out too.

"That's not true," Kora says, standing on her tiptoes to see over my shoulder. "It was my idea."

"Noble attempts, both of you. But unnecessary," Caius drawls. "It is only by sheer chance that I was returning to my office tonight—in my haste with Prince Reyn's attempted murder earlier, I forgot the essays I was supposed to grade."

"Convenient," I mutter, thinking it is anything *but* convenient.

"In any case," Caius says, raising an eyebrow, "I believe we were too lenient on you two earlier for your breach of curfew—a kindness that you apparently do not deserve. Detention, both of you. I will be informing Head Mage Iraklis of your infraction and will let him decide your punishment."

"Why don't you grab those essays and then escort us back to our rooms so you can make sure we behave?" I say, putting my hands on my hips. *Come on, you oily snake. We both know there are no essays in your office.*

"And give you more time to snoop around? I think not," he huffs. He grabs each of us by the arm, his grip nearly tight enough to bruise.

Kora's face is turning red. She's ashamed. She's getting detention, and it's all my fault. I have no idea how I'll make it up to her—or how I'll figure out what Caius is up to.

But I'm the Dragon Girl. Failure is not in my nature.

It turns out that making amends for Kora's detention involves shoveling a literal ton of horse manure from the stables. One of the ungifted is visiting a family member who is sick with the plague, so the odious duty falls to me for a day. Iraklis laid out two options for us, and I accepted this one without hesitation.

Kora, meanwhile, gets to spend her detention reshelving scrolls and tomes in the library.

It isn't a terrible day, though. I like horses well enough. I am really looking forward to learning the horseback maneuvers Vassilis keeps promising to teach us. I didn't get to ride much growing up, so I spend the day shoveling stalls but also learning about each of the school's horses. One of the other ungifted, a really chatty boy a little younger than me, goes on and on and on. Which horse likes to toss inexperienced riders, which one responds best to a firm hand or a gentle one. Which ones are steady, which are temperamental. The one I like best is a fiery gray gelding named Granite. He nearly bites me half a dozen times while I try to get him out of his stall so I can clean it.

The worst part of the detention, though, isn't the smell.

It's watching the gray people work.

The chatty boy sees me watching them and introduces one to me.

"That's Gabbro," he says. "He was a Shield with the king's army until his Mage died a few years back. He's a wolf shifter, I think. He doesn't talk, or shift anymore, actually. But he works good enough."

Gabbro is a man barely forty, with long hair and a shaggy beard. He's got the height and build of a Shield, but he's stooped, his face without a trace of emotion. His skin sags on limbs that once likely swelled with muscle, and everything about him seems ... drained. His skin and eyes and hair, all leached of color and life. He moves, tossing hay bales easily up into the loft, and follows direction, but that's it. When he's done with a task, he simply stands still until someone gives him another command.

His body is alive, but his heart died with his Mage.

I shudder and look away. *This* is the fate that awaits me if something happens to Kora after I claim her in the games. Me, the Dragon Girl. The Slayer of Soltaire. Winged Vengeance. Death on Feathered Wings.

No more. I will be reduced to shoveling horse shit for the rest of my life, all but forgotten.

Rigrasil, if such a fate ever befalls me, please, please, *kill me quickly*, I pray.

Better to be dead than gray.

CHAPTER 23

Reyn stops by my room a few nights later. I have a book of battle strategy spread over my bed, and I'm lying on my stomach as I flip the pages absently. I practically have each memorized by now.

He enters without knocking.

"I might not be alone," I mumble, flipping another page. "Try knocking next time."

"You didn't lock your door," he says, unconcerned.

"Only a fool would try to surprise a dragon," I say. I look up at him.

He shifts from foot to foot, like he's deciding what to say. I'm relieved that he looks like his usual self, if a bit thinner.

"Apparently, Makhon found his room flooded the other night," I say.

The faintest twitch pulls at one corner of his mouth.

"You wouldn't happen to know anything about that, I suppose?"

"Not a thing," he says, though he can't entirely keep the laughter from his voice.

"Are you here to try something similar, Prince?" I sit up, crossing my arms. I'm not in the mood for pranks.

"Not really," he says, frowning. "Here. As thanks for helping me." He pulls a glass jar with a wide cork stopper from his bag.

I get up and cross to the door rather than invite him farther in, and accept his gift. It's heavy, and when I pull out the cork, it's full of some kind of thick ointment. I didn't help him, not really. Just caught him before he broke his nose against the cot. It feels a little awkward, that this fallen prince feels he owes me anything.

"What is this? Scar cream?" I ask, raising an eyebrow. Presumptuous of the bastard.

He shakes his head. "There's nothing wrong with your scars," he says gently. "I would never try to erase them. They're proof that you're stronger than whatever hurt you."

"So ...?" I ask, dipping one finger into it. It's oily and smells faintly of mint. I turn his words over in my head—I mean, *I* hurt me, so ... I'm stronger than myself? Gods, he makes me dizzy sometimes.

"Back home ... back in Roallac, there are these nettles that grow everywhere. One touch, and you're red and itchy for days. We use this to soothe the itch and protect the skin, so I went to the greenhouse and made some up for you."

"Thanks?" I say, not following.

He smiles, looking at the floor, and I realize he's excited and a little anxious about giving this, whatever it is, to me.

"Use it the next time you shed," he says quietly.

Heat floods my face—so he remembered when I mentioned shedding to him. Gods, how embarrassing. I mean, it *is* really uncomfortable, but so are monthly cycles, especially when taking the moonberries that prevent pregnancy, and I wasn't about to ask Reyn for help with *those*.

"It'll help," he says. He fidgets a little, moving his weight from one foot to the other again. "Anyway. Good night."

"I have to tell you something," I whisper. My heart is thumping painfully against my chest. I don't know *why* I have to tell him, but I do. For some reason, it's important to me that he knows.

"What is it?" He stops but doesn't turn, doesn't look at me, which again, like that night I told him about shedding, makes talking to him easier.

"In Soltaire. I was never supposed to hurt anyone. It was an accident. My fire got out of control, and I ... I'm sorry," I blurt out. *I'm sorry.* The most pathetically underwhelming apology in the history of the world.

He stiffens, keeping his eyes focused on the wooden door in front of him.

After a moment, he lets out a long breath.

"I have to tell you something too," he says, addressing the door.

I wait, silent, my heart pounding.

"I had no idea what Evanthia was planning. At least not until King Leonidas and his party were attacked. I visited him a few times while he was imprisoned, but I was ... The guards wouldn't let me past, and I was too afraid of Evanthia to keep trying. For that ... I'm sorry too."

He turns to leave, and instinctively I reach for his sleeve—and find myself gripping his fingers instead. They coil around mine immediately, cool and comforting, for a moment, before letting go.

"Thank you," I say, looking at the jar in my arms. My vision blurs, and I can't hide the sniffle that escapes me. *He tried. Gods, he tried to help. He was just a child against the Snake Queen, and still he tried to help his enemy. Because that's what healers do. That's what* Reyn *does.*

He pauses, then leaves, shutting the door softly behind him on the way out.

I'm on my way through the halls, rushing to get to history class on time, though it's my least favorite subject. Coming in late only attracts more attention to me, and for once that does not work out in my favor.

I am thinking about Aleka's latest letter to me, telling me about the plague affecting more of the southern coast now, and Ismini's latest attempts to make herbal remedies. I should really track down Calix and see what he knows, whether Head Mage Iraklis has made any progress in the Earth Mage greenhouse.

I round the bend to see Lyssa surreptitiously closing a door that is definitely *not* hers.

I know this because the door is Reyn's.

"Make a habit of breaking into people's rooms uninvited?" I say, crossing my arms. I have the pleasure of watching her flinch before she sneers at me.

"What makes you think I was uninvited?" she says, making a show of buttoning her jacket up over her breasts, rearranging her hair. "Haven't you ever wondered why they call him the Snake Prince? It's not because he's from Roallac, I can tell you."

"Can't say it's crossed my mind," I say airily, refusing to be baited. "Did you ransack his room too? Toss the furniture?"

Her pinched face pales a little. "A Shield shouldn't kiss and tell. You could learn something from me," she says, turning to go down the hall, bumping her shoulder hard against mine as she passes. "Though I doubt I'll waste any more time with him. For a prince, it turns out he's completely broke."

I grab her elbow, hard enough to bruise, yanking her to a stop. "I hear Kalliope is getting pretty good at the interrogation spell Darius likes to use," I snarl. I never have been able to pin the destruction of my suncatcher on Lyssa, but that doesn't mean I've given up. Kalliope is one of the first-year Wind Mages, and a big fan of mine.

Lyssa definitely flinches this time. "You'd get expelled, using magic against another student like that," she says, but she isn't convinced. Her pupils are dilating, her nostrils flared.

"I'm the Dragon Girl, remember, bitch?" I say, giving her a vicious smile. "I'm untouchable."

She huffs. "Please. If you were a regular Shield, no one would give a shit about you. You're nothing special."

"You want me to learn from you?" I hiss, leaning closer. "You learn from me first. Leave me, and my friends, alone."

"I didn't realize you and the Snake Prince were close," she says, raising an eyebrow.

She yanks her elbow from my grasp and flounces down the hall, her shrill voice echoing through the stone hall.

"Guess I did learn something after all."

I lie on my bed, flipping Frostbite end over end, thinking about the attempts on Reyn's life and definitely not about Lyssa coming out of his room—was she ransacking it or having a tryst? I couldn't bring myself to knock on his door and find out.

Instead, I focus on the facts I *do* know. I thought that time I got hit by a starsteel javelin coming back from Aclines was about *me*, but the more I think about it, the less sense that makes. No, someone was after *Reyn*, and they knew he'd be with me.

It has to be someone here at the school, no matter what Darius says. He and his Wind Mages have interrogated *everyone*, even Head Mage Iraklis, and not come up with anything. And then the poison in Reyn's cup? Again, when I was there? Someone was trying to kill him and get me to take the fall for it. But who, and why? I still suspect the twins, and Caius, no matter that Iraklis said they'd all been interrogated and cleared.

A knock on my door disrupts my knife toss, and Frostbite clatters to the floor.

"Am I interrupting anything?"

As if summoned directly from all the hells specifically to torment me, Reyn, the Fallen Prince himself, stands in my doorway, looking at the knife on the floor. His pale face is a little flushed, and he's gripping the doorframe like he's going to fall if he lets go.

"Isn't it past your bedtime, Prince?" I ask, stooping to retrieve my knife. I can tell he's looking for blood—my blood.

"I thought ... maybe we could try to meditate, if you didn't already have company," he says, coming in and closing the door behind him.

I raise an eyebrow. "Is that a clothing-on or -off thing?" I ask. He's shaken me, coming here again, and I don't mind lashing out in response.

"Clothing on," he says with a small smile. "It just ... clears the mind. I was planning on doing it tonight anyway and thought you could try."

"What has your agile mind tied in knots?" I ask, putting Frostbite back into its sheath on my hip and sitting cross-legged on my bed.

He arches an eyebrow at me.

Right. Someone just tried to kill him, again, and we have no idea who.

I scratch the back of my neck as he looks around.

"After dinner, when I returned to my room tonight—someone had been in there. My books were all on the floor, my bed turned over. Nothing was missing, but the chair was broken. And I'd locked the door before I left," he says, looking around my room.

My own room is a mess, I realize a little self-consciously. The blanket is *mostly* on the bed. Clothes are strewn on the desk and puddled at the bottom of the shelves, and the shelves, in turn, are strewn with my treasures.

"No one ransacked *my* room tonight, Prince," I tell him. "It's always like this. Though one night a while back, someone did. They broke my suncatcher and made it into a bigger mess than it already was."

"It happened to you too?" Reyn asks, eyebrows lifting slightly.

I nod. "I suspect Lyssa. I saw her coming out of your room earlier. She said she was there for, uh, other reasons," I say. He remains unreadable. *Shit. Do I want him to deny it?* Regardless, pounding Lyssa's face into the arena sand the next time I see her has just become my top priority.

Reyn takes it all in, no emotion present on his face, until he sees my shelves. How pathetic it must look to him. The polished bits of broken glass and metal gifted to me by Tulliano, the faceted crystal stolen from the shattered chandelier in Estana, the green pendant Wren gave me to match hers, a frayed leather bracelet with obsidian beads to match the one I made Aris, a partially completed—and damaged—suncatcher, a few shiny trinkets, displayed like priceless treasures. Reyn probably grew up with cloth-of-gold diapers, eating off silver plates. I'm embarrassed that he's seeing them, that he's getting this pathetic look inside my heart.

"What's all this?" he asks with a smile.

He reaches out to touch the beads—and without thinking, I draw and throw Frostbite in a single motion. The knife buries itself deep into the wood, a scant inch from his reaching fingers.

He doesn't startle, this curious prince—he just pauses, then withdraws.

"My apologies," he says. "I should have known better than to disturb a dragon's hoard."

"Get out," I say, flushing and rolling my eyes. "You shouldn't be here."

"Sit," he says, and he settles himself into the chair at my desk, lowering his leather satchel to the floor. "This will only take a few minutes, and it will help both of us."

"You're really not going to leave unless I do this, are you?" I say, straightening the blanket before sitting back down on my bed.

"No," he says, and he gives me a smile.

"I could throw you out, you know," I grumble.

He sits cross-legged in the chair, so I mimic him, placing my hands palms up on my knees.

"If you do, I'll tell everyone I was only here because you begged me to sleep with you," he says.

I blink—is he *teasing* me?

"You wouldn't dare," I say, narrowing my eyes at him. "Besides, no one would believe you. Everyone thinks I tried to kill you."

His smile falters a little. His gaze falls to his hands, resting on his knees.

"Right," he says, taking a deep breath. "We're going to start with a mantra. We each choose a word and focus on it, repeating it over and over in our heads as we breathe in and out. The idea is to practice mindfulness, to let any anxiety or stress about the day fade, to allow yourself to be at peace. To relax your muscles, one by one."

"And this really works for you?" I ask.

He closes his eyes, settling himself. "Sometimes."

"Do you meditate a lot?"

"Do you always talk this much?" he says, eyes still closed.

This gives me permission to look at him, in a way, to really look. To see how his spiky black lashes fan across his cheekbones, the small bow of his lips, the refined features. He's not handsome the way Shields are, with muscle and strength and vibrant energy. His beauty is quieter, calmer, like he's been carved from ice. And his eyes—now closed, but I can imagine them, sparkling like the emeralds I saw Queen Orothea wear in Estana once. The rarest gemstone, more precious than diamonds.

"Stop staring at me and close your eyes," he says.

I blink—then catch the smile on his lips.

"How did you know—"

"I guessed. Was I wrong?" he asks, his eyes still closed.

I snort and cross my arms.

He lets out a long breath, relaxing his posture. I wonder what word he's thinking of.

"Why do *you* meditate?" I ask. "Nothing bothers you."

"Someone told me once that Water Mages are still on the surface, like a lake. Or like a glacier—you can only see a small fraction of it, the rest is hidden."

"That's not really an answer," I say, and I scratch an itchy spot on my knee.

I wonder if I'm going to shed again soon. It's not fun. Tekton usually stays out of my way all week, except to help me peel off the dead bits when I whine.

"There have been two attempts on my life since I came to the school. I promise you, that bothers me."

So he's realized the javelin in my wing was about him.

"Then why come to my room? Want me to make it three?"

He cracks an eye open at that, giving me a half smile.

"Ironically, it's the one place here where I feel safe. Now shut up and meditate."

I ponder this as his breathing slows, as the muscle feathering in his jaw relaxes. I'm the one person here he can count on not to kill him—maybe because we've saved each other already. How ironic.

But what about Caius? And Silas, and the twins? He doesn't feel safe with them? I know I'm supposed to be meditating, finding some point of focus and deep breathing and all that, but I can't help but try to unravel the enigma in front of me. Why wouldn't he feel safe with his own countrymen? I mean, Caius I totally understand. I wouldn't trust that man as far as I could throw him.

But what about the others? The twins are evil bitches, fine. But Silas at least? I thought they were friends. Has being the heir made Reyn paranoid, thinking everyone's out to get him, to try to kill him so they can take his crown? Not that there *is* a crown, not anymore. And he doesn't *seem* paranoid. In fact, he's probably the most rational thinker I know.

After a while—a half hour, maybe—he sighs and opens his eyes. *He* seems more relaxed, at least. I still feel wound tight as a spring, my skin still tingling, itching for my knife.

"It takes practice. We can try again another time. Tomorrow, then," he says, and he unfolds his long limbs from my chair, collecting his satchel.

"Don't come back tomorrow," I say.

He stops, frowning. He looks … disappointed.

"All right," he says, and he turns, reaching for the doorknob.

"Wait!" I say.

Reyn pauses but doesn't turn around. He's stiffened up again, like he's waiting for some blow.

"I meant … tomorrow night I've got lessons with Tulliano. He's letting me practice my fire-breathing in his workshop. I won't be back until after midnight. But the day after, if you want …" Gods, I sound like an idiot. And what am I saying? Telling the Snake Prince to come back?

"All right," he says again. His shoulders relax, and mine do too.

He lets himself out, shutting the door softly behind him.

CHAPTER 24

"You know, I've got a theory," Athan says.

Aletheia rolls her eyes playfully. The four of us—Athan, Kora, Aletheia, and I—have formed our own little pack of sorts. Athan's a wolf shifter, but he's the only one who hasn't joined Lyssa's pack—where she's the alpha, of course. The other wolf shifters are annoyingly subservient to her, so I generally ignore them. I like our little pack better, anyway, most of the time.

"If it's the one about the squirrels, then no, I don't think they're spies for Head Mage Iraklis," Kora says, smothering a smile.

Athan points his spoon at her accusingly. "It's not. And yes, they are. This theory is about how the elements choose Mages. I know magic runs in families, but sometimes there's a new Mage from an ungifted family, right? It's got to do with hair color," he announces proudly.

I snort out a laugh. Aletheia gives Athan an encouraging smile and pats his arm.

"That's why so many Fire Mages are redheads! Look at Kora and her family," he says. "All redheads. And your friend Rafael? Redhead. It's because redheads are hotheaded. Fire likes them more."

"*I am not hotheaded!*" Kora screeches, throwing a cookie from her latest batch at him.

Athan snags it from the air and takes a big bite. His eyes go wide.

"What did you put in these?" he asks suspiciously around a mouthful of crumbs.

Kora gives him a smug smile. "I guess you'll find out," she says sweetly.

He swallows, casting a nervous glance at his groin.

"Not all Fire Mages are redheads," I say, rolling my eyes at him. "That's like saying all Water Mages have blue eyes. Aletheia doesn't. Neither do the Roallacan Mages."

"Why do they call them Black Water Witches, anyway?" Athan asks around a mouthful of oatmeal, like he's trying to wash the taste of the cookie from his mouth.

"Don't you know *anything*?" I ask.

Athan shrugs. "What? I've got muscles and my god-given good looks. I plan on claiming the smartest Mage I can to make up for the rest." He slings an arm around Aletheia, who blushes.

It's a good thing she and Kora don't have to compete, at least in their classes, or I doubt they'd remain friends—they're so smart they make the rest of us look like toddlers. Aletheia's fingertips are black with ink stains today, matching the black ribbons she's woven through her hair.

"The decaying trees in their swamps release a compound that colors the water, like tea leaves, turning it black, right, Del?" Aletheia explains.

I shrug. "I didn't pay attention to the color of the water," I say, running a fingernail over a splinter in the table.

"The Slayer of Soltaire," Athan crows. "Too busy kicking Aenon's ass, right?"

"Right," I say, dropping my spoon into my bowl, fire flaring in my veins. "It's so clever. Their swamps have black water—let's use some stupid alliteration to dehumanize the enemy so we don't feel so bad when we kill them."

The table falls silent.

"Gods, Del. I thought you hated them," Aletheia says gently.

"Yeah, we all hate them," Athan agrees.

Kora nods absently, still too absorbed in her book.

"Yeah, well, it's a lot easier to hate them when you haven't smelled their flesh burning," I say.

I get up, the bench grating loudly against the stone floor. Kora finally looks up from her book, eyes wide.

"I have to ... go punch something," I say. "See you guys later."

I hear them whispering as I leave, but I don't look back. My hands clench into fists, and my heart is pounding so fast I feel lightheaded.

My skin itches for Frostbite's touch.

Reyn comes to my room several nights a week to meditate with me. Tonight it's already late, but Reyn makes no indication that he's ready to leave my room. We finished meditating an hour ago, but he seems perfectly content to sit and read one of his books, *An Advanced Practitioner's Guide to Healing Shifters,* and I read mine, *The Care of Blades.* He reads so silently—even his page turns are silent. I shuffle and shift and flip pages back and forth while I study. Frostbite twirls in my palm, one way and then the other. I'm so worried about what might happen if I don't outscore Lyssa on this next test that I'm hardly absorbing anything from the text.

Will Vassilis kick me out? Gods, I need to get my head on straight—but what if not just Lyssa outscores me? What if I fail the test completely? Lyssa and her wolfy companions are howling somewhere in the dorms, and the hair on my arms bristles—not because I'm afraid of their teeth, but I do fear their laughter.

Reyn closes his book and bends to rummage in his worn leather satchel. It's not a very princely bag. It should have golden buckles, and jewels sewn into it. Lots of sparkly jewels.

From it, as if to prove my point, he pulls a worn reed pen and a small pot of the ash-based ink the school favors. I once saw King Leonidas use a quill that had been dipped in gold, with rubies along the spine. Gods, I still dream of that pen sometimes.

Reyn scoots the chair closer to the bed—I usually sit here, in my nest of blankets. He prefers the chair and the desk. He uncorks the ink and takes my hand in his. His skin is cool and smooth against mine, which must feel roughly calloused to him. But I don't draw away—Reyn's laughter, I've learned, is not something I need to fear. Instead, I crave it.

"What are you doing?" I ask.

He dips the reed, the point starting to fray with use, into the ink and dabs two small dots on the back of my hand, in the web between my thumb and first finger.

"Snake bite," he says.

He blows on the ink softly to dry it, looking up at me with his emerald eyes as he does it. A shiver that must be from his cool breath runs through me.

"For luck."

"I'm confused," I say.

He lets my hand go, and I hold it against my chest.

"A long time ago, Diodoros, King of Roallac, was bitten on the hand by a napiat viper."

"Doesn't sound very lucky," I say.

He snorts out a little laugh and continues. "He survived, so he's the luckiest man in Roallacan history. Without several skilled healers close by, the bite is deadly within minutes. Diodoros was able to heal himself, alone—so Roallacan students will put his snake bite marks on their hands for luck."

"Did you ever do it? Put the marks on your hand?" I ask.

He considers this.

"No. But perhaps I should have."

The silence hangs heavy between us for a moment.

"Why not just tattoo it on, then?" I ask, looking at my marks. Two small black dots on my hand—for luck? Well, I've tried stupider things.

"My body would heal it within the day," he reminds me. "As would yours. We'd need some starsteel powder to mark it permanently. I can get some, if you want."

Starsteel. An incredibly rare metal known to bind magic. Saroya used it on Wren. And Reyn's crazy queen somehow accumulated enough to build Wren a cage of it. Not to mention someone *shot me* with a starsteel-studded javelin. The *last* thing I'd ever want is starsteel permanently embedded in my skin, lucky or not.

"Del, I didn't mean—shit," he says, running a hand through his hair. He can read the emotions flickering across my face as easily as he reads that healing book. "I didn't think that through."

"I know," I say, shutting my book firmly. "It's late. I should probably get some rest before the exam tomorrow."

"Right," Reyn says. He packs up his things and hoists his satchel across his shoulder. "Good night, then."

"Good night," I say.

I walk him to the door.

After he leaves, I stand there a long moment. I can hear him, on the other side. He's not walking away. Finally he mutters something under his breath that sounds like a curse, and I hear his footsteps recede down the hall. I let out a long sigh, my eyes catching on the two dots on my hand as I lock the door. They could be flecks of dirt, or dried blood, or some freckles. Or maybe I just spilled a little ink while studying. Aletheia's fingertips are black with ink half the time. No one would even notice.

In the end, I don't wash them off until after the test the next day.

And when Philandra posts the scores the following day, mine is on top.

It's late, and I'm heading back from Tulliano's forge with a few pieces of stained glass in my pocket. I'm turning them over in my hands, thinking of how I'll attach them to my suncatcher—I think I'll wrap the purple shard with wire and use a little controlled fire-breathing to melt the bits of metal together. Or maybe I can ask Kora for help with that.

I'm so wrapped up in my daydreaming that I don't notice Sinon until he presses himself up against me, pinning me to the stone wall by the staircase. I roll my eyes at the smell of ale on his breath.

"Very funny, Sinon. Now come on. I'm tired."

"Me too," he says, tracing my jaw with one calloused finger. "Tired of waiting while you play around."

Well, fuck. There goes my good mood.

"I'm not playing. I'm just not interested," I say.

I put my hands on his arm and try to shove him, but he's too big. My heart rate picks up. *Please, Rigrasil, don't make me castrate this idiot to prove a point.* I try to glance past him—but this late, there's no one else around. *Great.*

"Why don't you come back to my room? I can think of some better uses for your smart mouth," he croons, his big body still flush against mine. "I know you're not shy," he whispers, his breath hot against my ear. "They talk, you know. The boys you've slept with."

"Oh?" I ask, batting my eyes up at him. I put one hand on my chest, in affectation of false modesty, while my other hand drops to my hip. "And what do they say?"

"That all it takes to get into your bed is a pretty face, or some pretty words," he says.

He paws at my jacket, buttons popping off as he yanks it open. When I swat his hand away, he backhands me across the face. Hard.

For a moment, I'm seeing stars. My cheek aches, and I taste coppery blood—*Fuck!* He might have broken my jaw.

"C'mon, sweetheart, don't fight me," he says.

He grabs my chin and yanks my face up to his, his meaty fingers digging into the screaming bones in my cheek. He presses his lips against mine.

With one hand, I push against him.

And with the other, I bury Frostbite in his chest.

We make quite the pair waiting in the infirmary of the Water Mage building. Me with my swollen black eye and broken cheekbone, and Sinon with my dagger still sticking out of his side. He's so thick I only hit muscle and bone—I think—but it is bleeding plenty. After he pulled back from me, howling, I landed a kick to his groin, and a knee to his chin for good measure as he went down.

The healers' assistant has hurried off to get whatever healer is on call this evening, leaving just the guard who found us—rather, the guard who heard Sinon shrieking when I stabbed him. Petyr, I think his name is. A quiet ungifted who walks the walls and dormitory halls at night waiting to catch any students sneaking about. Usually he only interrupts trysts and such—this must have provided some break in the monotony of his patrols. He should be thanking me, really.

But no, he just glares at me, silent as a grave.

The healers' assistant returns in a few moments with a tired-looking Mage trailing behind her, drawing his tan-and-blue robe over loose black sleeping clothes.

Reyn. Why does it *always* have to be him? He's wearing boots, untied in his haste. His hair is rumpled, but his gaze is already wide awake, piercing. I squirm under that emerald look. Sinon sniffs, gesturing at Frostbite in his side. Reyn looks between us, trying to piece together what happened.

"Well? Let's get on with it, snake," Sinon says.

"Ladies first," Reyn says. And he offers me his hand, like I'm a noble in his court and he's still a prince.

I take it, just to piss off Sinon, and let Reyn lead me to one of the cots in the room. He draws a curtain closed, so it's just the two of us in this little cocoon. His fingers are cool but shaking in mine.

"What did he do to you?" he asks.

I'm surprised to hear anger in the prince's voice.

"He tried to take what I didn't want to give," I say. I turn and spit a gob of blood into a basin on a side table. I think my teeth cut the inside of my cheek when Sinon hit me.

When I turn back, Reyn is studying me. His eyes drop to the ripped buttons on my jacket. I'm only wearing a thin shirt below it—it's not worth wearing heavy clothing in Tulliano's forge. The shirt is stuck tight to my chest with sweat from my work this evening. I can't imagine it's too hard to piece together exactly what happened.

"And ... did he ...?" Reyn trails off, dragging his eyes back to mine.

"Just the face, Prince," I say wryly. "I'd be much obliged if you could return me to my usual gorgeous self now."

He lets out a breath and raises his hands, cool fingertips on either side of my face. He has an unreadable expression on his face—the visage of a healer, perhaps. Distant. Cold. Unfeeling. I don't think I like it. I could use one of his smiles right about now. I'm tired, and hurting, and angry, and I don't need a numb healer. I need *Reyn*.

The thought echoes in my mind for a long moment. *What the* actual fuck, *Del? He's not your friend! He's not here to comfort you!*

A blue glow suffuses the air between us as his healing magic trickles into my face, taking away the pain. I hear a click and a nauseating crunch as the shards of my jaw realign. At least the sensation keeps the other thoughts out of my aching skull. The swelling goes down rapidly from my left eye, much quicker than my own Shield magic could manage. Plus, my own magic isn't great for broken bones. They'll heal on their own, but this way I won't end up looking like a troll.

"Thanks," I sigh, reaching up to touch my face.

Reyn doesn't draw his hands back quite fast enough, and our fingers brush for an instant.

Sinon howls from the other side of the curtain. A muscle flickers in Reyn's jaw.

"You'd better go," I say quietly. "I didn't hit any major arteries, but I might have deflated his lung."

"If you had, he couldn't be carrying on like that," Reyn says, a ghost of a smile on his lips. It's more comforting than his frozen mask, anyway.

He draws the curtain back, his mask once more firmly in place, and gestures for Sinon. I'm filling out the necessary report with Petyr when I hear Sinon squeal from behind the curtain.

"*Fuck*, snake! Couldn't you numb it or something first?" he shouts.

Reyn pulls back the curtain, an innocent look on his face. In his hands is a towel—and Frostbite, it turns out. He's using the towel to wipe Sinon's blood from the blade. He hands it back to me, hilt first. Our eyes lock, and for a moment he doesn't let go of my knife.

"Healer, did you not address his pain?" his assistant asks, brows furrowed. She rushes to Sinon and holds a roll of gauze to the hole in his chest.

"*He did not!*" Sinon howls.

"I must have forgotten," Reyn says airily, eyes still fixed on mine, like I'm a puzzle he's trying to solve.

He lets go of Frostbite.

I cradle the dagger to my chest, walking backward from the room until I'm in the hall. Reyn watches me as I go. He looks like he wants to say something—but then Sinon howls again, and he reluctantly turns back to his patient.

I head back to my room, Sinon's ongoing shouts ringing in my ears.

Commander Markos interrogates Sinon the next day. Sinon plays it off as a scuffle for dominance between two Shields—fights often break out among us, so it is a very convincing story. It's *my* fault, really, and he was the victim who was stabbed by the temperamental Dragon Girl. The teachers nod, eating up his story. He even throws in a few painful winces when he talks about where I stabbed him—I roll my eyes, but miraculously hold my tongue. I'll just end up digging myself into more trouble.

I hate that the teachers agree with him. How many times have I "fallen down the stairs" this year? It fits my history, and so no one questions him. In the end, *I* am lucky that Sinon has decided not to take the matter before Head Mage Iraklis, which could have resulted in my suspension from Shield lessons for the week. I ask for Darius, the Wind Mage, to use his magic to get Sinon to tell the truth—but I am told that magic is only for *important* matters.

I shift in the courtyard as soon as the disciplinary meeting is over, not caring that I am leaving my clothes there, and take to the sky. I blow fire into the clouds for a few hours before coming back to the ground, spent. I would have preferred to spend the afternoon pounding Sinon's smug face into the arena sand, but burning off some energy will have to do.

And the worst part of all this? The only one who believes me is the Prince of Snakes.

Not even the sting of Frostbite's touch clears my head enough to unravel that conundrum.

CHAPTER 25

"Can I ask you something?"

"You've literally never asked for permission before—what's got you tongue-tied this time?" Reyn asks. He's standing, putting his hands high over his head and leaning from one side to the other, like a tree in a storm, stretching out the kinks that an hour of meditating—and probably too little sleep—has settled into his muscles.

For a moment I watch him—shining obsidian hair long enough to tuck behind his ears now, skin like white marble, impervious to the sun's attempts to add some color to it. Black and white, like the Roallacan flag—a black snake eating its tail on a field of ivory.

"Did you like being a prince?"

He stops, then straightens, pulling the bottom of his shirt down to smooth it. He frowns as he gathers his satchel, the vials of healing salves inside clinking together.

"I imagine you have a guess," he says, shouldering the bag and turning back to face me. His features are calm, his mask firmly in place.

"I don't think you did," I say. "You hardly talk about it—life as a royal. You never try to lord it over your Roallacan friends. You *hate* it when Caius calls you Prince Reyn. I just ... don't understand why. Was it boring, eating off silver plates all the time?"

He takes a deep breath, his emerald eyes fixating on a spot somewhere on the wall behind me as he thinks.

"I never wanted to be a prince. Michail did, and that was fine with me. I only challenged him because of my ... friend. Because of Rosalyn. We were ... close," he says.

He swallows hard, then clears his throat.

"I didn't really consider the consequences, battling Michail. It was her or me, and I was stronger. I had the better chance. I knew Michail's fighting style, his weaknesses, better than anyone."

He pauses to take a deep breath, a crease forming between his brows.

"It was never about becoming the heir, though Evanthia was pleased enough. I don't think she liked Michail much. He was too impulsive. A month later, King Leonidas's envoy arrived. After that ... well, you know the rest," he says, finally looking me in the eye.

"After Evanthia died and King Leonidas was freed, he met with me and the Council of Elders. I was too young to take the crown, so technically, the council would have ruled until my eighteenth birthday," he explains. He rubs the back of his neck absently. "He's a good man, your king. Our king, I mean. He insisted I be part of the negotiations for surrender. There wasn't much to negotiate. His terms were our complete surrender, and in return he'd treat the citizens of Roallac immediately as citizens of Ocron. I helped with the transition, more of a figurehead than anything, really. I spent some time with Rafael and Remiel as they started their school in Soltaire, you know." His gaze flicks to mine. "They speak very highly of you."

I grin. I miss them. It occurs to me that when I was writing to Rafael about my fire control, he was working with Reyn at the same time. But I don't say anything, waiting for Reyn to continue.

"My role has become less and less important over the past few years. I still hold to my vow to never use my magic against another again. I told King Leonidas of this—we wrote quite extensively for a while. When he offered to let me attend this school, to officially train as a healer, I took the opportunity immediately. To just ... be a student, not a symbol of a deposed royal family, not someone for the fanatical rebels to rally behind. Not someone to be paraded around like a prize horse or something. To just ... be me. Pursue the things *I* want. It ... sounds selfish, when I say it out loud."

"It's not selfish to want something for yourself, Reyn," I say, frowning. *I would never let anyone fight for me, the way he fought in Rosalyn's place.*

"It's cowardly," he says, averting his eyes. "It's all right, if you think I'm a coward now, for abandoning my people. I am. Cowardly, and selfish. But you asked, and I ... I want to tell you the truth."

I stand and put my hands on his shoulders. It surprises the hells out of him, and he flinches before becoming still again. I wait until he looks me in the eye.

"You are *not* a coward," I say firmly.

"I took the easy way out—"

"Shut up," I say.

His mouth snaps shut, an amused smile on his lips.

"You are one of the bravest people I know," I say. "You took your friend's place against your brother, knowing how strong he was, knowing you might die, that even if you won, you'd have to endure a *lifetime* of royal duties and apparently assassination attempts. And you did that for her, not for yourself. You have helped your country for *years*, living your life for them, to make sure they were taken care of. You *still* try to help them, making sure that the Roallacan students here aren't bullied, that they're given every opportunity to have a normal life. And *gods*, Reyn, you were still a child when all that happened! Let it go! You have more than earned the right to live your own life now."

My hands are still on his shoulders. He's taller than I am, which means we're standing very close, close enough for the cool breath of his exhalation to stir the hair on my head.

"You've been practicing that speech," he accuses me with a smile.

"I have," I confirm. "What do you think?"

"I think you are ... very persuasive, Dragon Girl," he says. This time, the nickname sounds almost like a caress from his lips, his voice low and gravelly. It startles me more than if he'd stabbed me.

I drop my hands, take a step back, and wipe my tingling palms against my tunic. I recognize that tone in his voice. I've heard it from many men. I've just never heard it from *him*.

"Well," I say, at a sudden loss for words. I stare at the far wall, since I can't look him in the eye, for some reason. I focus on the chink between stones where I like to practice throwing Frostbite. "I might just be a dumb Shield, but even a rusty blade strikes true now and then."

"You're not a dumb Shield," he says, frowning. He hasn't moved.

"And you're not a coward," I reiterate, finally looking back at him.

He studies me for a moment.

"Same time tomorrow, then?" he asks. The words are his normal parting words, but his tone is different. Softer. And something inside me cracks.

I nod, no more words forming in my brain at the moment. My heart is suddenly pounding.

"Good night," he says.

He turns to leave. As he opens the door, he looks back over his shoulder, like he wants to say something else—but he changes his mind and leaves, shutting the door soundlessly behind him.

CHAPTER 26

Athan and I are picked to be sparring partners today. I try to talk him out of it—I feel the need to really pummel something today, and I would have preferred it to be Lyssa instead of him. I still suspect she was the one who trashed my room and broke my suncatcher, but I haven't been able to get her to admit it yet. Maybe a mouthful of arena sand will loosen her lips. At least Athan managed to sneak those Ignatius peppers into her gruel last night—the swears coming from her mouth as tears ran down her beet-red face were a sound I'll treasure for the rest of my life.

But instead of being paired with Lyssa, I'm paired with Athan. The idiot might look like Rigrasil incarnate, all shiny and golden in the afternoon light, but he still goes down like a ton of bricks when I kick his knees out. Thank the gods that Vassilis has decided not to let us use weapons today.

"Fuck, what's got you in such a mood today?" Athan says once he gets the air back into his lungs.

He winces as he stands, limping for a moment until his Shield magic repairs whatever damage I did to his joints. He stretches, then attacks, hoping that his little charade has distracted me, that I'll be caught off guard.

I'm not. I duck to the side, landing a swift punch to his kidneys. He swings around, one big hand aimed at my temple, but I duck again, leap back, and land a kick to his other side.

He lets his guard down to protect his side, and I land a punch to his chin.

He drops.

"Yield! Seriously, Del," Athan says, hands up in surrender. He sits up and spits out blood, then feels his jaw warily.

"That time of the month, sweetie?" Lyssa calls, from where she's pummeling Herondas.

I crack my knuckles, glaring at her.

"Shit, is she right? Not that it matters," Athan says, throwing an arm around my shoulders. "Um, you know I have sisters, so I understand how a woman's cycles can be, um ..."

I glare at him, and he backs off, hands once again raised in mock surrender.

"Athan, if you want to make it through this day with your balls still attached to your body, you'll stop right now," I say, stretching, still glaring at Lyssa.

He moves one hand protectively over his second-favorite body part.

"Noted," he says. "Shutting up."

My skin itches, like a thousand ants are writhing underneath it. I can't sit still—at my lessons this morning, I tore two quills to shreds and then bolted from the room when I couldn't take it anymore. No one came after me, which I guess I was thankful for.

But then again, no one cared if I was all right.

That night, I am still sitting up in bed around midnight, flipping Frostbite over and over in my hands. I make half a dozen small cuts to my forearms, but they don't help. Soon there are trails of dried blood down my arms, like melted wax on the side of a candle. I am ready to literally start tearing my hair out.

I eye the jar of cream that Reyn gave me. I open it and gingerly stick a finger into the oily mess. I sniff it—well, I am willing to try anything at this point. I rub it on my forearm, which smears the blood around. It helps, a little. It would help more if I was a dragon, but I can't exactly use my talons to do this. And like all the hells am I asking anyone for help.

My door creaks open. Reyn eyes me, the blood on my forearms, and the open jar of cream in my lap, taking in the scene in a moment. The scent of the minty mixture fills my room. I'm embarrassed, but I'm honestly too uncomfortable to care. I wiggle on my bed, scratching my leg absently.

"Come on," he says after a moment, and he leaves.

Wait, what?

"What about the curfew?" I call after him.

When he doesn't answer, I sigh and get up, shutting the door behind me as I leave.

He's waiting, of course, leaning on the wall across from my door, arms crossed, an unreadable expression on his face.

"When have you ever cared about the curfew?" he asks, raising an eyebrow.

I shrug.

He takes the jar of cream from me—I didn't realize it was still in my hands—and heads off down the hall.

"Where are you going with that?" I ask, chasing him.

He's not wearing his Mage robe tonight, and his all-black clothing blends nicely into the dim hall and the stairwell, like mine. His pale skin shines like the moon, though, reflecting every bit of lantern light we pass.

"We'll have to be quiet," he says, stopping so suddenly I crash into him.

My mind, unsurprisingly, goes somewhere not very appropriate. *When have you cared about what's appropriate? And what exactly is he—*

Then he's off again, darting across the courtyard, and I nearly topple. I'm usually a lot more graceful, but I'm scratching my arms too badly to care right now. *Maybe if I partially shift my talons, they can get to the itch better.* I'll claw my skin right off if it takes away the itch.

Reyn leads me to the back of the dining hall, the jar still cradled in his arms. He ducks into the shadow of the wall, pulling me to his side. I'm touching him from calf to shoulder, and I fight the urge to rub against him like a cat, to use the friction to ease my skin. I dig my fingernails into my palms instead.

"Sneak out a lot, Prince?" I ask.

He *shushes* me. Arrogant snake.

"Come on," he whispers. "The guards take a very predictable route at night."

I'm uneasy at the fact that the *Fallen Prince of Roallac* knows the precise timing of the guards, but when he dashes across the courtyard, I chase after him without a second thought.

He leads me to the *library*.

"Look," I say, stopping and holding up a hand. "It's late. I'm really not in the mood for a study session. I'm just going to go back to my room, and—"

"Scratch yourself bloody?" he asks, raising an eyebrow.

I cross my arms and glare at him.

"Come on," he says. "I promise this will help."

"The promise of a snake," I scoff.

A muscle in his jaw flickers, but he doesn't otherwise let me provoke him.

"A snake who knows a thing or two about shedding. Now come on," he says.

He turns and disappears into the library without looking to see if I'll follow.

Bastard. He knows I will.

We sneak down the aisles of books to the stairs at the back, down two floors, then over to another door on the side, partially obscured by stacks of old books. He checks to make sure we're alone and eases the door open. It's a black hallway, with a glimmer of blue-white light at the far end.

"If you lured me out here to try and kill me, Prince, I'm going to be really pissed off," I say.

He *grabs my hand* and pulls me into the space, and for reasons unknown, I let him. The door closes softly behind us, and we stand chest to chest in the dark, his cool breath whispering against my cheek.

"Shut up, and let me help you," he says.

I think I feel the ghost of a touch against my face, a fingertip tracing my jaw, but I must have imagined it.

"You just can't help it, can you?" I ask quietly.

"What?" he asks.

"Helping."

He turns to go down the hall, pulling me along behind him. "Come on, Dragon Girl."

I could stop if I wanted to, I tell myself. I could take my hand back from him, but I'll let him pretend that he's in control for the moment.

The hall is musty, rough-hewn from stone with a smooth rock floor.

"Earth Mage students made this passage ages ago," he whispers as we go. "It's one of the worst-kept secrets at the school now."

"How come I've never heard of it?" I ask. Aris mentioned some passages tunneled under the school, but I've never explored them myself.

"Maybe I'm just a better listener," Reyn says.

The blue-white light grows brighter, as bright as a moonlit night.

I shrug. He's probably right about that.

The hall ends after about two or three hundred feet and opens into a large natural cave. It's studded with blue lights, like stars, that give a glow to the area. Stalactites or stalagmites or whatever they are called rise up from the floor and dangle from the ceiling like giant teeth, but they shine and glitter like they're made of crystal. There's a series of pools here too, and it's so quiet and still I can hear us both breathing.

"It's ... beautiful," I whisper, without really meaning to. It's like the whole thing is one big geode. My inner dragon purrs, even as I start scratching my arms again.

"The Water Mages come here sometimes. The springs are infused with all kinds of minerals that are good for healing," Reyn says. Then he shoots me a sly smile. "But we're not supposed to come here at night."

"Very sneaky, Prince. I'm impressed."

"Good. Now take off your clothes."

I blink a few times, then reach for Frostbite.

He puts his hands up in surrender. "Easy, Dragon Girl. What I meant to say was 'please.'"

"You think showing me some twinkly lights is going to get you into my pants? It's *not* happening," I snarl.

"It'll stop the itch. The water, I mean," he says, gesturing to the nearest pool. It looks like it's about five feet deep, maybe less, and about as wide as the bathing pools.

"This isn't some plot to get me naked?" I ask.

In the blue light, it's hard to tell, but I'm sure there's a flush creeping up his neck.

"If I was trying to seduce you, you'd know," he says.

I ponder this for an inordinate amount of time.

"You can shift first, if you'd prefer," he says. "The main pool will be big enough for you."

I pick my way across the cavern without waiting for him. The air smells ... minerally. Rocky. Stony? Not like earth or musty or anything. It's a clean smell.

I pause at the edge of the pool, my boots just touching the water. A thought occurs to me.

"It's not going to burn me or something? Melt my skin off?"

Reyn rolls his eyes but reaches down and scoops up a double handful of the water. He brings it to his lips and drinks it, eyes locked on mine as his throat bobs. A droplet clings to the corner of his mouth.

I clear my throat, looking back out at the pool. It does look tantalizing.

"Close your eyes, then," I tell him. I'm not embarrassed about my body; I just don't want to be responsible for the inappropriate dreams he'll be having if he *does* look. I don't look back over my shoulder to see if he's closed his eyes, though. I just start undressing. If he's peeking, well, that's on him.

I wade out into the water. It's slightly cooler than the air, but not unpleasant. My skin tingles but doesn't hurt, and I realize as the water reaches my hips that the itching in my legs has greatly diminished. I laugh in relief, the sound ringing in the cavern's quiet, and sink under the water.

It feels *amazing*. I open my eyes—the water is as clear as air, the pool made of rock without any sediment or current or anything. When I break the surface for air, my hair streaming down my back, I see Reyn on the shore, watching me.

He snaps his eyes closed a moment too late.

I don't care. I have to laugh again as pure, itch-free relief floods through me.

And then I shift.

Gods, it's glorious. I used to roll in the snow back home when I shed—I don't know if it's the cool water or the minerals or whatever, but this is a hundred times better.

"Can I ... can I come in?" Reyn asks.

I crane my neck back over my shoulder and flap my wings in the water like a bird taking a bath, droplets of water flying all over the cave. Little bits of dead skin float away from me.

I can't talk in this form, but I nod.

When he starts to undress, I turn around. I tell myself it's because I want to look at the sparkling crystals under the water better. Water Mages can cast blue light, like Fire Mages cast firelight, but I've never seen it used so freely. It must have been a powerful Mage who cast this spell, I tell myself, definitely *not* thinking about Reyn undressing behind me.

I hear his clothing hit the rocky shore and feel the slight ripples as he wades into the pool with me. It's big, more a pond than a pool, but I find I'm acutely aware of his presence, probably because I'm so much bigger now.

I feel him paddle alongside me. He's a graceful swimmer—I should have expected that, being a Water Mage and all.

I do *not* expect him to reach up when he gets to my shoulder and pull a bit of dead skin off.

I snort, smoke starting to curl from my nostrils. *Gross.*

"Easy," he says, patting my shoulder. "You'll feel better once we get this all off."

And, the gods again only know why, but I let him. He works methodically, from my shoulder to my tail and then back up the other side. He has me move to the shallower water so he can get to my chest and stomach. I try to remove the gray bits with my claws, but it's not nearly as effective, and I'm afraid I might hurt him, so I just try to stay still. He's right, though. Between the water and him removing the itchy dead skin, I am feeling like myself again.

He's not completely naked, this confusing prince, but he's close enough. He's wearing a pair of black undershorts, which cling to him in the water and don't honestly hide much of him at all, though he seems unbothered by it. His tattoo glitters in the dim light, marring his otherwise lean, sculpture-perfect torso. He's so focused on his work that it gives me time to study him. He's slicked his hair back, and his lips are pulled to one side as he concentrates, the way I've learned they twist when he's healing someone.

Globs of dead skin start to float away from us, and my newly revealed scales sparkle even in the dim light of this grotto. I butt my head against his chest, nearly bowling him over.

"I see," he says, chuckling, my nose still against his chest. He reaches up to get a bit he's missed over my left eye. His other hand scratches below my chin, an absent gesture, and I arch my neck a bit so he can get to a particularly itchy spot.

Later I'll tell myself it was the gentleness of his touch—touch that can soothe and comfort, instead of hurt and cut—that made me do it.

Regardless of the reason, while he's holding my snout, scratching my eye ridge—I shift.

I don't take into account the fact that as a dragon I displace a lot more water than I do as a girl. Or that the water is deeper than I, as a rather *short* girl, can stand in. Or that fact that I don't swim that well.

The water rushes into the area I was just displacing, the resulting wave swamping me, pushing me right into a cool, lean chest, with arms that reflexively wrap around me, holding me tightly to Reyn as the water settles. He turns us around, my feet now finding purchase on a ledge of the pool.

I'm frozen. My breasts, small though they are, are pressed right up against the hard plane of his abdomen, my hands clutching his arms, holding the rest of my body flush against his. His pupils dilate, the black centers overtaking the green. His lips part as he gazes down at me, a hesitant breath escaping them—

And then he lets go, like I've burned him, and turns around, putting his back to me. I splash and nearly stumble. He shoves a hand into his wet hair as he lets loose a string of curses under his breath.

"I, um, didn't realize you were going to ..." he says, back still facing me, spinning one finger around in the air. Then he locks his hands behind his head, taking in a deep breath like he's trying to meditate.

I watch his shoulders expand with it, count the little knobs of his spine. The water's not that deep here, barely covering my waist. He wades deeper as he realizes that we can both see *exactly* how impressively I'm affecting him. *I can hate him and still be attracted to him physically, right? And him to me?*

I decide those black undershorts are my newest nemesis.

I shrug, pretending I don't feel more than slightly insulted. "People see me naked all the time. I'm a Shield."

"I'd ... rather not think about that right now," he says, still not facing me.

I shrug and head for the shore, somehow feeling hurt that he just *dropped* me. *But what did I want him to do instead?*

I keep up a grumpy tirade under my breath and grab my clothes, yanking them on despite still being soaked. I keep my back turned to the pool, and after a moment, I hear him come to the shore too.

"I'll just ... I can make my way back from here," I say, swallowing thickly.

Gods, neither of us can look at the other. *What's got me so shy all of a sudden? And what is wrong with him, that he doesn't want me? And what is wrong with* me, *that I want him to? Did I really misunderstand that tone in his voice the other night, the look in his eyes? I don't think so.*

Fuck, we're a mess.

"All right," he says, pulling his shirt over his head. "Go. And take the cream back with you. I meant to ... It doesn't matter. It should keep your skin from itching now."

Should I wait for him? Should I go? He seems like he wants me to leave, like I've ... offended him by throwing myself naked at him. Which, fine, is fair, though I didn't *mean* to literally do that.

Right?

"All right," I echo, and I clear my throat. I gather up the jar of unused ointment, and I try again. "Thanks. I feel a lot better."

He doesn't answer. I look back over my shoulder when I reach the hallway back to the library. He's still standing with his back to me, hands on his hips, looking up and out into the cave like he's looking for answers out there.

I hope he finds them.

CHAPTER 27

Days pass. Reyn avoids me—like the plague, as they say. I head to the top of the wall, wanting to catch a breath of fresh air. I turn Frostbite over in my palm. My skin itches, tingles. My breath is coming fast, and my chest feels like it wants to cave in. Reyn hasn't so much as looked at me in days, and it's got me feeling like I'm shedding all over again. *Gods, why am I letting him affect me like this?* I duck to avoid catching the attention of the wall guards, peeking up between merlons to see if they're still coming this way. After my run-in with Sinon, I've tried to be more vigilant when I am out and about at night.

A shadowed figure catches my eye, a tall, lean form creeping across the courtyard.

I hate that I know immediately who it is by the shape of him, by the glint of moonlight on his skin. I sheathe my blade again and head for the stairs. I catch up to him in moments.

"What in the *hells* are you thinking? You want to get expelled?" I shout, not caring that it's after curfew, not caring that probably the entire school can hear me. He *will* talk to me.

"Quiet!" he hisses, clamping a hand over my mouth and dragging me into the shadows of the school's outer wall.

I elbow Reyn in the sternum and bite down on his hand, nearly hard enough to draw blood.

If I'd really wanted to, I would have.

I wrench my arm from his hand. He might be bigger, but I'm a Shield—I'll always be stronger. And I'm mad. Mad from days of him avoiding me, mad after he spent so much time helping me during my shedding but now he acts like he barely knows me. Mad at myself, for shifting like I did. Just ... mad.

He swears, shaking his hand and looking at me with blazing eyes. Overhead, I can hear the guards making their rounds on the wall. All it would take is one of them looking down, and he'd be caught. Well, *we'd* be caught—but his punishment would be far worse. I'm nearly untouchable. What are they going to do? Expel me? Doubtful. But if Reyn puts so much as one toenail out of line, he'll get the whole Roallacan group sent back to their stinking swamp. Not that I care. I glare at him, raising my chin in defiance.

"What are you doing out here, anyway?" I ask.

"Clearing my head," he says.

"Sneaking around the campus at night?"

"Do you know how hard it is to get any time alone to practice here?" he asks, running a hand through his hair. "If you must know, I was hoping to get a single bath without an entire cadre following me around. You know, Water Mage things."

"A bath," I deadpan, looking at him. "You're risking expulsion for a bath?"

He nods.

A thought occurs to me then, an ugly thought, and I cannot keep it to myself.

"If you're trying to get to Lyssa's room, you're better off going through the dorms," I say, looking up at the guards patrolling. We're fairly hidden here, but not entirely, hiding behind a column. The tingle of suspense, not really fear, fills my veins. It's intoxicating. Plus, it hides the other feeling, the one that's curdling in my gut.

"What?" Reyn asks, blinking.

"I'd probably go down to the first floor between patrols, honestly, then back up to the third once you reach the staircase by the baths. If you time it right, you should be able to avoid getting caught."

"Lyssa?" he asks, one eyebrow arching.

I frown. "You know, the wolf bitch who keeps throwing herself at you?"

He mutters a swear under his breath, his hands on his narrow hips. "She's ... she's not ..." He glances up at the wall for guards.

"What? She's not *what*?" I spit. I want to hear him say it. That it's not what Lyssa made it sound like. *Why do I want to make him say it?*

Footsteps and the sound of laughter filter down from the wall, and Reyn freezes. I stomp my foot, impatient.

I didn't anticipate that he'd be stupid enough to grab my shoulder and spin me around the column to slam my back against the wall, hiding us now entirely in shadow. It nearly knocks the breath out of me.

"She's not you!" he whispers, his voice low and harsh.

I freeze. Hells, neither of us knows what to do, between his confession and the threat of being discovered breaking curfew. His chest heaves as he draws a deep breath.

She's not you.

"But ... I hate you. And you hate me," I whisper, though I don't sound all that convincing.

He lets out a low chucklc, shaking his head. He's squeezed himself into this small space with me, our bodies flush—and the way he's looking at me. Gods, something inside me *ignites*. Fire and ice, the Dragon and the Snake, the two of us complete opposites in every possible way—and yet here we are. My breath catches in my throat.

"Oh, I should hate you, Dragon Girl. But I find I very much don't."

"You idiot," I breathe. "You really should."

His emerald eyes flicker to my lips, their black centers dilated in the dark. I could push him away if I wanted to. I *should.*

"I might kiss you," he whispers.

My mind blanks, so I say the only thing I can think of.

"I might stab you."

He considers the risk for only a heartbeat or two. I swallow, the movement sticking in my throat. He knows I'll do it. The fool doesn't even check to see if I have Frostbite with me.

Then he bends down and slants his lips over mine anyway, stealing the protest from my mouth, and stunning me into silence.

He tastes cool, like ice, in a way that sends shivers down my spine. He deepens the kiss, pressing me into the darkness of the shadows of the wall, his hands firmly on my waist, while I dimly notice the footsteps overhead receding into the distance.

He is a *very* good kisser—so it should have surprised neither of us when I grab the nape of his neck, pulling him down, closer, so I can twine my tongue with his.

It shouldn't have surprised us, but it does, as our brains race to catch up to what our mouths are doing. *I knew I hadn't misread him.* Now the danger has passed, the guards moving on, there is no longer a need to hide. Our mouths and tongues clash anyway, becoming furious and desperate. The length of his body is firm and confident against me, pressing against me—and all I can think about is how to get closer, to feel more of him, more of his coolness, his calm, everywhere.

He breaks the kiss after a moment, breathless, his dark eyes a little wild. I lean up against him, wanting more, consequences be damned—but he pulls back again, a little farther this time. His eyes stray from my eyes to my lips once, twice. He runs a hand through his thick black hair, mussing the strands.

"*Fuck,*" he mutters, pushing off the wall.

He walks away from me across the courtyard, in full view of the guards of the wall, apparently not caring anymore if they see him.

I put my fingers to my lips—they feel cold, tingly. And I am *not* about to run after the Prince of Snakes, no matter how my body reacts to his, no matter how good he is with those lips. *Gods, I wonder what else he could do with ... fuck! What are you thinking, Delphine?*

"Delphine? What are you doing out this late?" Vassilis asks, rounding the side of one of the buildings.

I nearly leap out of my skin.

"Uh, just wanted to stretch my wings. You know how it is," I say, letting my dragon wings unfurl.

Usually that's all it takes to awe people into letting me get my way—reminding them I'm a dragon, one of a kind. Vassilis, however, is a little too smart for that and does *not* look convinced, so I try again.

"Just, um, feeling a little cramped inside these walls."

"I see," he says, tilting his head in a way that suggests he certainly does not believe me. At least he didn't see Reyn. *Wait, why do I care if he saw Reyn?*

"Well, you should be out with a full Shield or Mage after hours. I'll stay with you until you're done," he says.

Well, now I'll have to eat my words.

"Thanks," I say, still reeling. At least Vassilis isn't punishing me.

I crouch and leap into the air. I don't often fly like this, as a Shield with the wings of a dragon—but it is a lot of fun. I fly a few laps around the school, diving and racing, skipping along the walls and roofs. I hope I wake a few of my classmates. If I'm up late and tired tomorrow, well, everyone else will be too. I keep an eye out for Reyn too, but he's disappeared.

I land heavily in the courtyard, a few of the guards now watching me. At least if they're watching me, they're not looking for Reyn. I fold my wings back up, and they disappear into my back.

"All stretched now?" Vassilis asks, raising an eyebrow. In the dark, his pale, freckled skin looks eerie.

"Feeling much better, thanks," I say with a flippant grin, and I turn to go.

"I'll walk you back to your room," Vassilis says.

Shit.

"Uh, thanks, but I'm pretty sure I know the way."

"It's on my way," he says, leaving no room for argument.

On his way to what, exactly, he doesn't say.

"Oh," I mutter.

What else was I going to do tonight anyway? Go after Reyn and ask him what in all the hells he was thinking, kissing me? In his dreams.

Vassilis keeps his promise and walks me all the way back to my room before closing the door after me. I don't hear his boots recede until I turn the lock.

Spring changes to summer, and then the new students arrive. Makhon wins the games and claims a pretty Fire Mage. It's a fun time, I guess, and a good excuse to have a party, but there's a tension this time that wasn't there last year. At least Sinon is gone. The next time Athan and I see a Shield game, we'll be the ones fighting.

The games end, and classes resume, and life goes on.

Reyn and I fall into a kind of easy rhythm, after we both purposely avoid the other for a while. Reyn comes by a few nights a week. Neither of us mentions the kiss. At first we're incredibly awkward around each other—walking on eggshells, as Ismini would say. He acts like nothing between us has changed, though, like the kiss never happened—all right, fine. So I do the same.

We close our eyes, and we meditate—I'm trying, honestly, but I don't know that it's doing any good. I feel anxious unless I have Frostbite on my hip, but I haven't cut myself in days, if only because I know it would disappoint Reyn. Which is a weird thing to realize, that I value the opinion of my enemy. Not to mention his mouth.

I try not to think about that too much.

We also talk. Reyn tells me about his home, which isn't Soltaire, like I thought, but rather a manor house in the far, frozen north of the country. He's a Water Mage, but he's much better with ice than liquid water, probably as a result of where he's from. He makes small sculptures of dragons while I watch, complete with little feathers that look so real I expect them to move. When he's bored, or thinking hard about something, frost spirals out from his fingertips, climbing over my window in spectacular patterns.

But they always melt when he leaves.

And in turn, he asks me about Aeturnus, about being a Shield. I tell myself he *could* just be using me for information, maybe about the Temple of the God of Night's weak points or something—but he seems genuinely curious. About life with Rosie, about having a family that isn't trying to actively murder me. About whether I think my own lifespan will be as long as a real dragon's—gods, I hope not. It's ... nice. He's so curious about everything, and I find myself talking more and more, and meditating less and less.

And sure, I think about sex. A lot. And I remind myself about what Reyn said in Spit, that he wasn't someone who was casual with his bed partners.

He doesn't deserve someone like me. Reyn deserves a soft, pretty princess. Someone who understands his sculptures and his bad poetry and who isn't afraid to be seen with him. Someone who'll remind him to take a break, who'll look after him. Someone who can make him laugh again.

And though I realize that's not me, I can't bring myself to turn him away when he comes by at night.

Maybe I am a monster after all.

I still sit with Silas and the twins at meals. Reyn doesn't mention our evening activities, so I don't either, though I'm pretty certain they know *something* is going on between us.

The Winter Festival comes around again, and there are no more attempts on Reyn's life. The caravans come to the school, bringing cloth and dresses and more lace and frills than I've ever imagined could exist. Kora decides she's going to go gold this year, highlighting the light her magic makes rather than the heat and flames. Her hair is still pink, though a little less vivid with her latest batch of dye. And since she's going in gold, we decide that I'll go in silver. She helps me pick out a long, sleek dress that looks like molten metal. It's a dress for a battle goddess, and I have no problem trading one of my diamond-hard scales for it.

The night before the festival, I come back to my room after Tulliano's. We're really making progress on my fire-breathing, and I'm tired and sweaty and ready for a nap.

When I open my door, I immediately feel something is off. I can't explain it. I can sense something is out of place, that someone has been here while I've been out. I immediately grab Frostbite, looking under the bed and behind the door for someone hiding.

Then I look at my shelves to see if anything is missing.

There, displayed neatly in front of the obsidian beads and the chandelier crystal, is a small black box.

I grab it and flip it open before I think too much. It could have been a trap, some spring-loaded poison or something—but it's much, much worse.

It's a feather, intricately crafted in silver and hung sideways on a fine chain. I've never seen anything so beautiful. I immediately put the necklace on, of course, delighted with the way it catches the small amount of candlelight in my room. In the flickering light, it sparkles like a star.

It must be from Reyn. Who else? I turn the box over, but there's no note or anything. Why would he give me a gift like this? It's not like ... *Oh, gods.*

I rip the necklace off and throw it back on the shelf like it has bitten me. My heart is pounding.

I'm not the kind of girl that boys give presents to—especially not a prince. I'm the one they flirt with, sleep with, but not the one they court. And that's fine.

But now a boy has gone and given me a present, and I *don't know what to do.*

Five minutes ago, I was exhausted and ready for bed—but now?

I grab Frostbite and turn it over and over in my hands. He didn't leave a note, so I'm left to guess at his intentions.

What do I do? What does it mean?

Not even Frostbite's touch soothes my restless heart tonight.

CHAPTER 28

Kora has outdone herself again.

Her poufy golden dress is adorned with dozens—if not hundreds—of tiny crystals. Each one she's painstakingly imbued with her magic, so they all glow like miniature stars. Her hair is done up, and she's added several larger crystals to it, like a glowing crown. In the twilight air of our gray courtyard, she is the sun. The dragon in me rejoices, loving how she sparkles.

By comparison, I am plain. In the low light, my dress appears steely gray, with delicate chain accents to mimic chain mail. They won't do a thing to deter any actual attack, but the effect is nice. Kora convinces me to leave my hair down—since I've been braiding it a lot, it has a decent wave and bounce to it at least—and she adds some black lining to my eyes. I look intimidating as all hells, as fierce as I am in dragon form. I like it. My arms are bare; the marks of last night, gone. It's like it never even happened—only the feather necklace in my pocket, as heavy as lead, won't let me forget.

"For the tenth time, Kora, the food is fine," I say, tugging on her arm.

She reluctantly leaves the table. "I still can't believe you told the *Head Mage* about my ... experiments," she whispers, but she's not mad, not really.

I don't know quite why I told him—we were chatting about the games, and he said he knew how I favored Kora. "She's an excellent Fire Mage," I said, and meant it, "but she has so many talents beyond battle." This intrigued him—enough, apparently, for him to request she assist Kemp and his staff tonight with the snacks.

Athan finds us—or rather, Kora's food—and swipes a handful of cookies before actually joining us. He's wearing a fine dark blue suit that accentuates his broad shoulders, and his golden hair is slicked back.

"They're not experiments, Kor," Athan says around a mouthful of cookie. "They're *brilliant.*"

"They really are delicious," Aletheia says. She's so quiet I didn't notice her approach—but she's rarely far from Athan most of the time. She nibbles on a cookie. "And I feel warm all the way down to my toes!"

Kora blushes. Then she and Aletheia exchange a nauseating number of compliments on each other's outfit. Aletheia looks pretty too, her dress made up of layers of fog and mist, and her nails are long black talons. Her hair is done up in a hundred braids, looped and twisted together like a crown.

Our attention is drawn to Head Mage Iraklis, who stands in the center of the courtyard. He's raised a pedestal of rock to stand on, several feet above the rest of us. He does this as easily as breathing—and the earth responds to him instinctively.

"Before we begin, I wish to announce a special feature tonight," he says. Then he gestures to someone in the crowd.

People part to make way, and Reyn solemnly approaches the stone pedestal. He's wearing his usual black, but this time as a fine suit that accentuates his long, lean frame. A column of stone rises beneath his feet, so he can stand next to Iraklis.

"A special treat, from one of our very own students," Iraklis says. He puts a hand on Reyn's shoulder—Reyn doesn't flinch, but he doesn't show much emotion either. The mask he wears in public is firmly in place.

Reyn takes his hands from his pockets. I notice a fine tremor in them, the only outward sign he might be anxious—his eyes find mine, briefly, and my breath catches. Then he looks up, at some nebulous spot over my head, and his lips start to move as he whispers something.

He raises his hands, white-blue light coalescing around them—then it drifts down, like snow, down the pedestal to the courtyard, where we all stand, waiting. There's a nervous murmur among the students.

"What is he doing?"

"Is this supposed to happen?"

I glare at them until they shut up. I'm not sure what he's doing either, but I'm sure it's going to be spectacular.

Magical snow touches the cobblestones and drifts on an unseen breeze—the way it did when I saw Reyn make his sculptures, only magnified a thousandfold. Every glowing lantern in the courtyard is soon wreathed in a frosted globe, each window decorated with intricate patterns and swirls of frost. Glittering spires grow from every building, and flames made from ice glow blue in hundreds of icy candles. It's a stunning, extravagant display of ice magic, but I can barely take my eyes off Reyn.

He looks ... *happy*. Proud. His magic is still pouring from him, like ripples in a pond, each one extending still another feature of his wonderful art. His mask is forgotten—a smile even curves the edges of his mouth. I understand why—the courtyard looks like something from a dream.

And to finish it off, a sculpture of the school in miniature before us, the ring of wall only about ten feet across—complete with a dragon perched on top of the arena, her wings outstretched.

I inhale sharply, and Kora grabs my hand.

"It's ... beautiful," she gasps. "Look, he added the greenhouse and everything."

"A nice trick," Lyssa drawls, arms crossed. She's dressed in a low-cut black gown with slits nearly to her waist on either side, leaving little to the imagination. She's practically been stalking Kora all evening, which is annoying as all hells. "It's like teaching a dog to walk on its hind legs."

I think Reyn hears this last comment. His hands drop, the snowy magic immediately snuffing out, though his creations remain. His hands go back into his pockets, his shoulders hunching a little. Iraklis begins to clap, and the stone pedestals they stand on lower them both back down to the courtyard. A slow clap begins from the rest of the crowd, along with a lot more murmuring—some of it good, some of it mean.

I make sure I note each and every person who says a negative thing about Reyn, for later.

I can't stop staring at him, and when his eyes catch mine, it's like the rest of the crowd fades away.

However, a swarm of impressed students and fawning teachers soon hides him from my sight, and then Kora drags me to the opposite end of the courtyard for a drink. I down it gratefully, trying to remind myself that I'm here to end things with him, no matter how good he looks tonight. The thought makes the wine in my stomach revolt. Kora is a great distraction as she oohs and aahs over all the costumes, pointing out the most extravagant ones.

Mages in all kinds of magical finery flit around us like so many colorful butterflies. A Wind Mage wears a dress with dozens of rainbow-colored ribbons that float on her breezes. One of the male Wind Mages *is* actually floating. One of the Earth Mages is wearing a crimson gown with fall leaves fluttering about the skirts. It's a gorgeous spectacle, a chance for magic to be shown off for fun, and the mood of the crowd is infectious.

Soon enough, I am pleasantly drunk and enjoying myself more than I have in a long time. Calix and Kora eye each other longingly from across the courtyard, but they're currently not sleeping together, so Kora pretends to ignore him. Nubs, his pet squirrel, is brazenly sitting on his shoulder. He's wearing green—Calix, not the squirrel, though the squirrel does have a small leaf-shaped hat—and a flamboyant cape with blooms on it. I think it's an eyesore, but Kora is infatuated and won't stop praising it—out of his earshot, of course.

"Can I talk to you for a minute?"

I tear my eyes from the gaudy cape when I feel cool fingers against my elbow. When I turn, Reyn's emerald eyes are a scant inch from my own. My breath catches. *Well, it's now or never.*

"I'll just be a second," I tell Kora, who frowns but takes my empty glass from me and watches as Reyn takes my hand and pulls me a little way from the crowd. There are a lot of curious eyes on us, but I find I don't want to pull my hand away from his.

I blame the wine.

"Your ice—it's stunning," I say, and mean it.

A hint of red creeps up his face, and he rubs the back of his neck. We've got a little privacy, over here by the Water Mage building, partially hidden behind a column.

"Thanks," he says, with a genuine smile. It's breathtaking. "Apparently, someone told Head Mage Iraklis that I like to do ice sculptures. He thought it would be a nice touch, for the Winter Festival."

"I'm sure I have no idea what you're talking about," I say, though I can't keep a smug grin off my face.

He chuckles, and his gaze flickers to my lips.

"Tonight, you are ... devastating, Dragon Girl," he whispers, his voice deepening. "I haven't been able to take my eyes off you all evening."

Fuck.

My throat goes dry, my hand clasping the necklace in my pocket so tightly I feel it cut into my skin. I look up at him, at his emerald eyes glowing in the night, and take a deep breath as I prepare myself for what I'm about to do. His gaze moves pointedly to my neck, which is unadorned.

"There you are!" Caius calls.

Reyn takes a step back from me, his icy mask back in place, and I take my hand from my pocket, a momentary reprieve. I take a deep breath and nearly stumble, like whatever hold he has on me has temporarily broken.

"I've been looking for you."

"Is that so?" Reyn says, straightening up. He clasps his hands behind his back, a pose of easy arrogance.

"I came by your room, evening before last, to bring you some books I thought would interest you," Caius says, narrowing his eyes at Reyn. "You weren't there."

"I wasn't? Strange," Reyn says airily. "Are you sure you had the right room?"

For a moment, I glimpse the royal he must have been, rather than the student I've known. Cold. Commanding. Intimidating. For some reason, it's really turning me on—*Shit.* I have to be careful. It's no quick dalliance to this prince, apparently, and I *will not* hurt him. He deserves better, not someone who's likely to implode at any given moment. Not somebody ... broken.

I grab Frostbite's hilt—it's strapped to my thigh, like always, and its presence is simultaneously reassuring and damning.

"I'll remind you all that leaving your rooms after curfew is strictly forbidden, unless you are accompanied by a full Mage or Shield," Caius says.

He's been saying something else while my mind has been reeling, but I didn't really catch it all. I'm sure it wasn't that interesting, anyway.

Reyn raises an eyebrow. "Are you implying that I would knowingly and willfully disobey that rule?" Reyn asks.

Caius blanches. "Just ... reminding you. Both of you," he says, looking between us—and then he leaves, whirling his blue robe behind him.

Reyn lets out a long breath. I laugh, then ineffectively clamp a hand over my mouth to try to muffle it.

"You'll have to be more careful," I say, though I can't keep the laughter from my tone.

I can't say that I've gotten any better at meditating, but seeing Reyn for a little while, calm and serene in my crazy world, is like ... well, like being in the eye of the storm, instead.

"You could always come to my room," he says, giving me a half smile that makes his emerald eyes sparkle.

I huff playfully and cross my arms. "And let Caius catch me there? That's not going to happen."

"I guess we'll have to stop, then," he says, and I freeze, disappointment washing through me—before I realize he's teasing me again.

I punch his arm, and he rubs it dramatically. *Will he still come by if I return his gift?* I don't want to lose whatever we have, this tenuous friendship between us. But I don't want to let him believe we're more, not when I don't know—

"Stop what?" Kora asks, her interruption breaking the fragile silence hanging between Reyn and me. Her dress lights up the whole area in flickering golden light.

Gods, can we not get a single moment alone?

"Nothing," we say in unison, which doesn't sound at all convincing.

Kora glances between us, her arms crossed.

"Del, you have a visitor," she says. "Head Mage Iraklis asked me to find you."

She whirls around and leaves without another word.

The air feels suddenly colder. I grit my teeth, steeling myself for what I am about to do.

"Um," I say, reaching into my pocket, cleverly hidden in a seam of the dress. I pull out the necklace, the feather glittering in the dark.

Reyn swears and runs a hand through his hair.

"I think you left this, in my room," I say, and I hand it back to him.

He takes it without touching me, his fingers closing around the feather.

"You should be more careful, Prince. Things like that are ... easily broken." *So are hearts. And I don't want to damage yours.*

He nods, putting the necklace into a pocket without looking at it.

"I thought it would be safe with you," he says, watching me carefully. "I hoped ... you'd like it."

A line has been crossed, beyond that stolen kiss in the courtyard. This is more than the attraction of two bodies, and suddenly I feel like I'm falling from the sky without wings to catch me.

"I ... have to go," I say, taking a step back.

Reyn doesn't move.

Dimly I remember Kora saying I had a visitor. I have no idea who it is, but honestly, it could be Aenon himself, for all I care, if it gets me out of this awkward situation.

I back up a few more steps before turning and fleeing as fast as my stupid dress will let me. I don't care that he sees me running away—me, the Dragon Girl, running from a boy with a necklace. I'd laugh, if it didn't feel like my heart would shatter.

I run back through the courtyard. The music is still playing; people are still dancing. I push my way through them, heading blindly toward the academic building. If Iraklis said I had a visitor, well, they were probably at his office, right? I could kick myself for not asking Kora where to go. *Fuck. I could kick myself for a lot of things right now.*

I'm so focused on the thoughts racing through my head that I nearly barrel right into a tall Shield, one dressed in simple black traveling clothes instead of the finery the rest of the school is wearing.

"Whoa, little dragon," he says, putting his hands on my shoulders.

I look up, startled, into a pair of bright sky-blue eyes.

"*Aris!*" I shout, and I throw my arms around his neck. I don't know why, but I start crying, and I don't even care that everyone can see me.

"Oh," he says, freezing for a moment, then holding on to me as I sob against his shirt. He is warm and smells of horses and leather instead of cool water and mint. He smells like *home*. "Um, Wren? I'm going to need a hand here," he calls.

CHAPTER 29

"I can't *believe* you're all here! Why didn't you tell me you were coming?" I say, punching Aris again in the arm.

He fakes a wince, though I know I didn't really hurt him. He's as strong as the mountains.

"Aris wanted to surprise you," Wren says, smiling. "And frankly, I'm tired of using magic to blow all the cat hair out of the temple. A change of scenery was definitely due. You wouldn't *believe* how much they shed." She fondly pats Rosie's head.

Rosie grins proudly and nods in agreement.

Wren and Iraklis have been writing back and forth about some ideas for the school, and Aris wanted to visit, Wren tells me. Once people at the party realize that Wren and Aris are here, we're overwhelmed by nosy people. Wren and Aris are pretty famous, I guess, so Aris and I eventually have to spirit Wren and Rosie away to my room so we can actually talk. It makes my chest feel warm when Aris parts the crowd with only a growl and a glare—*no one* gets in his way.

But now, seeing my family all crowded into my tiny room is almost funny. Rosie is sitting on my lap, refusing to let go of me.

She's grown so much since I saw her last—she's almost five now, as she tells me every few minutes. She's as tall as my waist, and it's hard for me to keep her still. She fidgets this way and that, playing with the buckles on my jacket, which I've thrown over my dress, and throwing her arms around me for a hug from "Auntie Del" every few moments. Gods, I've missed her. She's adorable, with her big green eyes and short black hair, her round little face and sweet smile. I keep trying to talk to Wren and Aris, and she interrupts me with all the fun things she got to do on the way over: riding horses—she named hers Whinny—sleeping in tents, going for long runs across the plains.

"I'm so much bigger now. Want to see?" she says, and before Wren can stop her, she's shifted, her clothes sliding to the floor.

There's a fifty-pound snow leopard on my lap and a long, fluffy tail in my face. I spit out a mouthful of white-and-black fur. Rosie purrs, butting her head against my chin, and I throw my arms around her, cuddling her like a house cat. Her furry ears twitch, and her jade-green eyes practically sparkle with mischief. She jumps from my lap and stretches, showing me her long claws and her sharp teeth, both of which I make sure to properly admire.

"Rosie, it's late, honey. Why don't we go get ready for bed?" Wren says.

The little girl shifts back, smiling a little sheepishly, and awkwardly finds her way back into her clothes. I give Wren a smile of thanks as I look for the little boots that have rolled under the bed—I love Rosie with everything, but gods, it's just impossible to get a word in with her here. She's a nonstop bundle of energy.

Wren looks tired. After Soltaire, it doesn't seem to take much to wear her out, and they must have been traveling for two weeks at least to get here. She self-consciously tucks the white strands of hair back behind her ear, exposing her scarred cheek. Against her brown skin, the scars have turned dark, like streaks of black lightning. I think it looks like the most badass tattoo ever, but I don't bring it up. I know she doesn't like to be reminded.

"I'll be up in a little while. Shield stuff," Aris says, winking at me. Then he gives Rosie a kiss on her head and tells her to be good and gives Wren a kiss on the lips and whispers something I pretend not to hear, and his girls head out of my little room.

"Head Mage Iraklis has put us up in one of the double rooms for the night," he says, stretching long legs out from my chair. "Gods, it's strange being back here."

My eyes drift to my bookshelves, to where the little black box was. My chest feels suddenly tight.

"I'm sorry you missed the end of your party. The Winter Festival was always a lot of fun. Except that one time Rafael—"

"Caught fire? Yeah, the teachers still talk about it," I say. "You know how the Mages all dress up to show off their elements? One of the Wind Mages showed up naked last year—you know, 'clothed in air.'"

Aris laughs, and it's so good to see him relaxed and happy that somehow I feel tears prickling at my eyes again.

"I'm sure you're making a lot of memories here," he says. "But ... maybe not all good ones?"

I shake my head, looking down at Frostbite, which is somehow unsheathed in my hands. I can't bring myself to say anything. Aris waits a moment, then straightens.

"Hey, is Geoff still here?" he asks suddenly.

I grin. "Yeah. He likes to hunt on the top of the wall at night and get treats from the guards. Want to go find him?"

The night air is cool, the sounds of music and laughter still lingering, though it's close to midnight. The top of the wall remains my favorite place here, especially on the north side, where I can see the river and the hills stretching out to the horizon. We take our time walking the perimeter, chatting about my lessons and teachers, until we find the arthritic old orange cat curled up on an abandoned cloak.

"Hey there," Aris says, and he sits by the cat's side.

Geoff cracks open one yellow eye, then gets up and stretches languidly, as if it's purely coincidence that he's woken up. He walks over to Aris and bumps his head against Aris's hand, like it's been hours instead of years since they last saw each other.

"So," Aris says, petting a purring Geoff, "is there anything else you want to talk about?"

I bite my lip. I sit down next to him, and Geoff alternates between us, getting all the pets he wants until he's purring delightedly and covering us in orange fur.

"Boy trouble?" Aris asks. "Need me to maim someone?"

"Aris," I chide, knocking my shoulder against his. "Nothing like that. And I'm perfectly capable of maiming him myself, if I wanted to."

"Ah. Who is 'him'?" he asks, raising an eyebrow.

I swallow hard. *Oops.*

"Well," he says, "there are three topics you've been avoiding tonight. Claiming your Mage, the Roallacan Mages, and boys. If I had to bet, at least one of these got to you tonight."

I grumble a response. I forget he grew up with two sisters. Rea might be a bitch, but I bet Adriana would understand.

"More than one thing, then?" he asks.

I shrug. "Maybe."

"Want to talk about it?"

"Not really," I say. *Hey, Uncle Aris, remember that time you attacked Roallac, killed their queen, and tore their capital apart? Well, I've been spending a lot of time with the new heir, and now I kind of think he* likes *me, and I don't know what to do about it. Or even how I feel about it. Also, I cut myself when I'm anxious. I heal, so I don't see why it's a big deal, but I still can't make myself tell you about it.*

"Any of the Mages stand out to you?" he asks, changing tack.

"A few," I concede, rubbing the back of my neck. "There's a Fire Mage named Kora. She's my best friend, and she's really strong."

"And?" Aris asks.

I frown. "And? Isn't that enough? Stefan was your best friend," I remind him.

He nods, though his posture stiffens a little at the mention of his first Mage.

All right, Delphine, low blow.

"He was like my brother. Better than my brothers, actually," he says, smiling at the memories. "I was never going to pick anyone but him."

"And what about Wren? What made you pick her?" I ask.

He's told me the story a thousand times, but I want to hear it again. I need to see if there's some speck of help I can glean from it, some ember that will help me light my own fire.

"I was going to pick Mariana, or a Fire Mage named Rubita," he says.

I huff. *Mariana. Yuck.*

Geoff has decided he's done with us and trots away down the path of the wall, fluffy tail held high.

Aris drapes his arms across his knees. "But when I saw Wren here ... well, I tried to reason myself past it. She wasn't the obvious choice. No one knew her or knew what element she was going to manifest. She was ... different. But I was drawn to her. I think ... sometimes the magic in the claim has its reasons. Caelus always said it was a sentient thing, some part of Rigrasil's own spirit."

And now they're all gone, I think. Mariana. Rubita. Caelus. I flip Frostbite over in my hands.

"So ... your mind was telling you one thing, and your heart was telling you something else?" I try.

Aris nods. "That's one way to put it, I guess," he says. "Is there ... someone besides Kora you're thinking about claiming?"

I fling Frostbite into the wall across from us. It quivers, stuck into the narrow space between blocks.

"Your aim has improved," Aris says, a hint of pride in his voice.

"Practice," I murmur.

Gods, what am I even admitting to? I can't claim *Reyn*. His people don't believe in the claim. No matter how much he says he's happy to be a part of Ocron now, that kind of prejudice is practically bred into them there. I can't claim a *Roallacan Mage.* It isn't done. Even if he's a talented healer, and a good person. Even if, I tell myself quietly, he makes *me* want to be a good person, or at least a better person.

Like he'd even want to *talk* to me right now, after I refused his gift. *Gods, I'm a mess.* I push my hands into my hair with a frustrated groan.

"I didn't know I was going to claim Wren until the day of the games," Aris offers.

I look up—he's looking at me, an unreadable expression in his eyes. "I didn't know until I'd defeated my last opponent. Mariana or Wren. But when the time comes, you'll know what to do. Trust your instincts."

He wraps one long arm around my shoulders and pulls me close to him in a hug, and I let him.

CHAPTER 30

Wren, Aris, and Rosie stay for a few more days before heading north to Estana for a few months. I catch up on all the Valorius family gossip. Spyridon and his Mage, Stathis, are still in the Prasinos Mine, but Myron and his Mage—I forget her name—have moved to Raverra. Since the Valoriuses are the closest relatives of our queen, the former ruler of Raverra, they all drew straws—literally—to decide who got the monotonous job of governing that northern city. Wren said it was quite pretty, but Aris always said he preferred our mountain. Regardless, Myron drew the short straw—I assume the game was rigged, knowing the family as well as I do—and was now living there with his Mage and their two children. Rea, Aris's other, less friendly sister, placed second in her games two years ago, and she and her Mage have been stationed in the king's navy.

Aris trains with us in the arena and keeps pace with us on our runs. Next to Aris, even Athan looks like a child. Vassilis laughs and calls him old, though they're the same age, until Aris knocks him down in a sparring match within seconds. I can't suppress a smug smile—Aris is the best. And so am I, or I will be.

It's easy to regain my confidence with Aris back at my side. Even when he's correcting me or knocking me into the sand, I feel better.

Before he goes, he finds me in the arena, doing some stretches before going for another run. I run a lot these days. It calms the itching, tingling feeling a little.

I don't want to say goodbye. I don't want them to leave.

But I'm a *Shield*, not some teary-eyed little girl, so I don't say it. Instead, I ignore my feelings, like a proper Shield.

"I have something for you," Aris says. He hands me a long, thin item wrapped in a length of thick dark cloth.

I take it, confused. It's got some weight to it. When I pull back the wrapping, I see two shining gladiuses.

"For me?" I ask, nearly in a whisper.

I let the cloth fall to the ground and wield a sword in either hand. *Dimachaerus*, just like Aris. They gleam in the afternoon light, like Rigrasil himself is blessing them. I'm so overcome with emotion I can't even speak. I just start moving. They cut through the air like a dream, the leather grips perfectly suited to my small hands. The folded steel of the blades sings as I swing them, their edges razor-sharp. I've never seen anything more beautiful in my entire life.

"I asked Tulliano to make them for you. I assume you'll name them something epic," he says, unable to hide the proud smile on his face.

"I'll have to think about it," I say, grinning too.

The swords are light, honed, deadly. I've dreamed that someday Tulliano would make my weapons, as he's made the weapons of many Shields, but I haven't yet felt worthy to ask.

I carefully sheathe them into the leather harness Aris hands me. He fits it onto my back, adjusting the straps under my arms until it fits just right. I hug him carefully around the middle, trying not to let the swords on my back poke him in the eye.

"Thank you," I say into his shirt.

"Remember, trust your instincts," he says.

"I will," I promise.

There's a sound, a scuff of sand from the side of the arena. There, in the doorway, stands Reyn in his tan Mage robe, an unreadable expression on his face. He doesn't come any closer, but neither does he leave. I haven't seen him in days, and now I can't stop looking at him.

Aris glances from me to Reyn, taking in the blue hems on his robe and immediately understanding my problem. He looks between us again and lets out a soft curse, shaking his head.

"Good luck, then, on whatever you decide," he says, clapping me on the shoulder. "You're going to need it."

CHAPTER 31

"Did you know the melting point of iron is five times the temperature needed to ignite a candle? How about the temperature of a blue flame versus white, or red? Did you know that I have to be able to produce fire of any temperature and size, on command, for my final exam?" With each sentence, Kora's voice becomes faster and shriller.

"Breathe, Kora. Here, have a cookie," Athan says, offering her one from her latest batch—no magic in these ones, though, just sugar and cinnamon.

Kora's face goes crimson, clashing with her freshly redyed pink hair. "*I do not need a cookie, Athan!*"

"Kora, I'm headed to the library to study for a while," Aletheia offers, leveling a glare at Athan. "It's creepy to be alone in the lower levels. I'd appreciate your company."

"*I'm* good company," Athan grumbles, crossing his arms.

Aletheia rolls her eyes at him but gives him a small smile.

"Yes, absolutely," Kora says, slamming her book shut. She hefts it—and several others—into her arms.

"Can I give you a hand with those?" I ask, moving to take the books.

But Kora turns away so she can glare at me around the stack in her arms.

"Just ... keep Athan away from me. That'll help more than anything," Kora says.

Athan throws his hands up. "Women!" he mutters.

All three of us turn on him, and he visibly pales.

"Uh, I meant to say, women are the best. Especially you three. The best. I mean it," he says.

I punch him on the arm.

"Come on," I say. "Let's go race while they study."

We head to the stables and convince the stable hands to let us borrow two of the old chariots. Chariots are really starting to catch on in Estana as a way for the wealthy to parade themselves around the city, showing off their jewels and clothes and fine horses for all to see.

Here, though, we use them to race.

As long as Vassilis doesn't catch us. The grooms mostly turn a blind eye, especially if we offer to help clean out a few stalls for them.

Athan and I take a chariot and horse each and drive toward the arena. I can use the distraction today—I don't want to think about Reyn anymore. He hasn't so much as looked at me since the Winter Festival. He doesn't join the other Roallacan students during meals. It's almost as if he's disappeared entirely.

Not that I'm thinking about him. At all.

Usually Athan and I are pretty evenly matched as drivers, though his horse today, a high-strung new mare, looks like she's ready to unleash all the hells. She spooks at the sounds of the chariots echoing through the stone hall into the arena. Athan's chariot slides a little, the wheels grinding against the wall.

"I know they said these two needed the exercise today, but I think yours might need it more," I call.

Athan's struggling to control her—we're both adequate horsemen, him more than me, but this mare is prancing and tossing her chestnut mane like she plans to bolt.

"What do you think? First one to do two laps wins?" he asks.

We line up at our usual spot, the afternoon sun shining down on us like Rigrasil's own blessing.

"Make it three," I say, eyeing his horse—and mine, who might actually fall asleep standing up if we don't go soon.

"I don't think so," Lyssa's taunting voice calls. She emerges from the entrance, three of her cronies at her back. She crosses her arms, glaring at me. "I booked the arena for the afternoon. Ask Vassilis."

Athan yanks on his reins, trying to keep his horse from bolting. The bit is lathered in her mouth, and her ears are lying back. *Not good.*

"Give us five minutes, Lyssa, and we'll be done," Athan says.

"Is that what you say to all the girls?" Lyssa says, eliciting sniggers from the boys at her back. They're bigger than her, but it's obvious she's in charge.

"Ignore her," I tell Athan. "Let's do this."

"Ready ... go!" he shouts, and we take off.

For a moment, the pounding of the horses' hooves, the dust in the air, the rattling of the chariots—it's all there is in the world. No stupid boys with their stupid green eyes.

We finish our first lap neck and neck. Maybe I drift a little closer than necessary to where Lyssa and her boys are standing, just to see if I can run the chariot over their feet.

I shout at Athan, giving him a cocky grin as we start our second lap.

He looks behind us, and his face goes pale.

I turn—

Lyssa and her pack aren't standing at the entrance anymore.

They're chasing us.

And they've shifted into their wolf forms.

"Head back to the stables!" I yell at Athan.

Taking our galloping horses back through the stone hall of the arena to the courtyard isn't the best idea, but if his horse gets wind of the wolves ...

He yanks, hard, on the left rein to steer his mare toward the hall. It's opposite the direction the wolves are approaching from, but they're gaining on us. They're not pulling chariots, after all. Their howls echo in the arena, and the horses' ears flick back, flattening against their skulls. The chariots rumble and groan with the speed we're going, the floorboards shaking under my feet.

We're nearly at the hall. I pull back to let Athan go first—my horse is older and more used to dealing with Shields in shifted forms—but then a small white wolf streaks past me like a bolt of lightning, teeth bared, nipping at Athan's horse. Lyssa leaps, and her claws graze the mare's flank.

Not enough to draw blood, but enough for the horse to jump and buck, trying to dislodge her attacker—

And dislodging Athan and the chariot instead, smashing them both directly into the arena wall.

Athan was saved by his thick skull. His legs weren't so lucky, but the healers soon have them straightened out. He was knocked out by the impact, the crunch of the chariot—and his femurs—ringing through the school. Healers came running before we'd even gotten him untangled. Lyssa's face was white—she'd shifted back immediately, racing to Athan's side while her pack tried to calm the horse. She might hate us; she might be a mean bitch, but she isn't completely heartless. And Athan *is* a wolf, like her, even if he doesn't run with her pack.

Because I had my own horse to control, she beat me to Athan's side. When I saw the blood on her hands, stanching the flow where his bone poked through his thigh, I felt my heart freeze. *No*, I thought. *No, no, no, no, no.* I nearly vomited from fear.

But he was fine. He will be fine.

He'll have to spend the night in the Water Mage building, where the healers can monitor him, but he'll be back to practice the next day.

Thank Rigrasil for healing magic.

Of course, we tell Head Mage Iraklis and Vassilis that the horses simply spooked when Lyssa was practicing her shifting. If they are suspicious, they don't let on. At least it is a more creative story than my usual "we fell down the stairs" one. Lyssa and I have used that one several times this year already.

In the end, Head Mage Iraklis gives us all detention, and Vassilis promises us each additional workouts for a month, since we have so much extra energy to burn. It could have been worse. Much worse.

I could have lost a friend.

Reyn doesn't come to my room again—not that night, or the next, or the next. In fact, I still don't see him at all, though I look for him all day, between classes, after classes, until I think my head might swivel off. I even think about letting Herondas graze me with his practice sword so I can go to the healers, but my pride prevents me from letting him land any serious blows.

I can't stand it.

I pull Frostbite out a thousand times—and a thousand times, I put it back. I won't let Reyn ignoring me be the trigger to cutting again, not even when Athan's injury caused me so much anxiety I wanted to tear my hair out. I won't. I *won't.* I'm better than that. Reyn made me better than that.

I pace my room until my feet hurt almost as much as my chest.

I mean, I *did* reject him. I did return his gift. I didn't want to mess up this ... whatever it was between us, but I guess I did anyway. Friends? Are we friends? Were we?

We should be *enemies.*

We *are* enemies. His queen kidnapped my family and tried to destroy my country. I burned his city down and injured or maybe even killed people he knew—but even in my head, this argument falls flat.

Besides, do enemies kiss each other in the dark?

And dream about sparkling caves and moonlight skin?

Dum vivimus, vivamus.

Fuck it.

I wait until a few hours after curfew, when I'm sure that most of the guards patrolling the halls will be on the far side of the school—and then I can't wait any longer.

I leave Frostbite, sheathed, on my bed.

I slam Reyn's door open. He merely looks up from the book he's reading, sitting cross-legged on his bed. His room is neat, spare, just what I expected. No fancy adornments, no silk sheets or gold-leafed furniture. Just ... Reyn.

"Where have you *been*?" I ask, slamming his door closed again. I don't care who hears.

He closes his book, calmly marking a page with ... a feather? *A black-and-red feather?*

"I didn't think I was welcome to visit you anymore," he says. He stands, putting his hands in his pockets, leaning back against his desk.

"But ..." The pain on his face stops me in my tracks.

"You hate me, remember? You've said as much on several occasions. I just finally learned to listen." His voice is cool. Calm. Dispassionate. He pretends to be made of ice, but even the Fallen Prince can't keep his emotions entirely off his face, not this time.

And it breaks me.

I stomp over to him, frustration and anger and ... *something* boiling beneath my skin.

"I *do* hate you," I say. Then I grab his neck and bring his face down to mine before either of us can think.

And I kiss him, hard.

"I hate you so much," I hiss against his mouth.

He groans, dropping his forehead until it rests against mine.

I kiss him again, and push him back against his desk. And then his hands are on me, and mine are on him, jackets and shirts being shed, breathing frantic, pulses racing. His hands grab my waist, strong, cool fingers pulling me hard against him.

"I hate you too," he murmurs, pausing for a breath, his lips soft against my skin.

And it occurs to me that neither of us means a word of what we're saying. He plants frosty kisses against my neck, working his way down to my collarbone, worshipping my bare skin. His chest under my fingers is cool, smooth, tempting. I writhe against him, overheated and thinking too much and desperate for his cooling touch.

I push him down onto the bed. He looks amused, a rakish smile on his face. He reaches for me, guiding me on top so I'm straddling him, only a few layers of cloth left between us. We pause, breathless, for just a moment.

"How do you know I'm not here to kill you? I could stab you through the heart," I say, my voice breathless. I lay my palm against the left side of his chest, the side without the tattoo. His heartbeat is pounding.

"Go ahead," he says, his hands resting on my thighs, his emerald eyes bright and sparkling. He swallows hard. "It's already yours, *mea diva.*"

He brushes the hair gently back from my face, tucking it behind my ear. The tenderness in that touch, the look in his eyes—something I won't give a name to, not yet—it breaks down what's left of my resolve, and I give up trying to hold back.

I oversleep for the first time in two years. I wake up, panic flooding me when I realize I'm late for my morning run.

I didn't expect to wake up *in my enemy's bed* with his arms wrapped around me.

But are we even enemies anymore? And if we're not, what are *we?*

I try to breathe slowly, to slow the frantic racing of my heartbeat so he doesn't realize I've woken. His leg is threaded between mine, his chest against my back, his cool breath tickling my neck.

I piece together the night before. I've had my share of lovers, and kicked most of them out of my room afterward. Never have I gone to their quarters; never have I ceded that control.

And Reyn knew how to take control. *Gods.* I swear he was reading my mind, knowing exactly how to touch me, exactly when to move. Over, and over again, until we both practically passed out from blissful exhaustion. *Idiot. Stop thinking about it, or you'll* never *get out of this bed.*

Even with my enhanced healing, I'm deliciously sore—but I don't have time to dwell on it, or snuggle anymore. I *have* to get out of here. My pulse starts picking up, my skin tingling where he's touching it. I reach for the blanket that covers us, but his arm around my middle only tightens, his nose nuzzling into the back of my neck.

Never would have suspected that the Prince of Snakes was a cuddler.

Never would have suspected that I liked it.

Fuck it, I'm *really* late. I can't afford to sneak out, so I push off the blanket and grab my pants, but I can't find my underthings. I crouch down to look under the bed, and when I stand, I see Reyn awake, bleary-eyed, grinning as he watches me dash naked around the room.

"I'm late," I blurt out, finding my shirt and underthings beside his desk.

I get dressed in a moment and stuff my feet into my boots. My hair is a tangled mess, so I do my best to tame it back into a hasty braid as I head for the door. *Shit, I need to check on Athan, too.*

"Wait," Reyn says. His hair is rakishly askew. He's holding the blanket around his narrow hips, wearing nothing else but a satisfied grin and his snake tattoo.

"I can't," I say.

I move to push him out of my way, but my hand is shaking for some reason. He grabs it, and a trickle of his blue magic seeps into my palm. I can feel it like a cool breeze, and my heart rate settles a bit. I don't know if it's his magic or his touch, but I feel ... good.

"What did you do to me?" I ask, yanking my hand away. The cool feeling has settled into my lower belly.

"I wanted to make sure you didn't have any soreness today that might interfere with your workouts," he says, still smirking.

I roll my eyes. "Yeah, well, next time ask me first."

"Next time?" he asks, raising an eyebrow.

I huff indignantly, unable to come up with a witty response, and push past him. The sound of his laughter chases me down the hall, and I find myself smiling too as I head out into the courtyard.

The smile quickly vanishes when Vassilis assigns me an *extra* ten-mile run today for oversleeping. I love running, but this is a little absurd. I have to admit, though—to no one but myself, obviously—that Reyn's healing magic does make me feel pretty good. I feel like my feet are flying this morning, which definitely has to do with Reyn's healing magic and definitely does *not* have to do with our other extracurricular activities, which I am certainly not thinking about so much that I trip not once but three times during my run.

When I finally make it to the dining hall, covered in dirt and probably smelling like sex, sweat, and the dirt on my clothes, I'm exhausted. I grab my food and sit with Silas and the twins. Reyn is nowhere to be seen.

"Gods, I know you agreed to sit with us, but seriously, you stink," Isadora says, wrinkling her nose.

I grin at her as I shovel barley into my mouth and chug my cup of ash water.

"Where's Reyn?" I ask.

"Doing an extra session with Caius to make up for being late this morning," Eugenia says, narrowing her eyes at me. "Why were *you* so late, hmm?"

"Oh, you know, Shield stuff. Sharpening my knives, admiring my muscles, that kind of thing."

"Really? Reyn says it's because you seduced him," Eugenia says, her eyes narrowed.

I choke on my food, spewing bits across my plate. *Gods.*

"Ew," Isadora says. She looks like she might be sick.

"He didn't say that," Silas confides to me. "But … the twins maybe figured it out. He's not a very good liar."

I groan, throwing my spoon into my bowl.

"And," Silas says, as kindly as he can, "you do kind of smell."

CHAPTER 32

I have little time before curfew, but it's enough for me to take a quick trip to the baths. And Silas is right—I stink. A little soak in the hot water sounds perfect.

I'm walking to the front door, still toweling my hair dry, when I practically walk into Reyn. He has no business looking that good in his plain black clothes, the sleeves of his robe rolled up, revealing corded forearms.

"Oh," I say. I bite my lip. *"Oh"? Smooth, Dragon Girl. Very smooth.*

"Oh," he replies, a smile on the edge of his mouth. "Didn't think I'd run into you here."

"Sorry to disappoint you," I quip. "Silas informed me that my odor was offensive. Also ..." I smack his chest with my towel. "Did you really have to tell them I slept with you?"

"I didn't realize you wanted to keep it a secret, unlike your other trysts," he says, tilting his head, his mask firmly in place. "Are you ashamed, Dragon Girl? To have been seduced by the Snake Prince?"

Fuck. He holds himself as still as a statue, and with almost as much emotion.

"No," I say quickly. "And I didn't ... *you* didn't ... I came to *your* room. I seduced *you*." Heat flares up my neck. We are standing nearly nose to nose.

"I see," he says. His eyes sparkle like emeralds as he moves closer to me. "And ... will it happen again, do you think?"

"In your dreams, Reyn," I say, though there's no venom in it.

He lifts a finger, tracing the edge of my jaw. It's hard to keep glaring at him, especially when that cool finger traces the edge of my lips.

"Reyn?" he asks softly. "Not snake? Or Prince? Or Black Water Witch?"

"Well, are we still enemies?" I say. It comes out as a whisper. It feels wrong, calling him the other names now.

"It's hard to say," he admits.

He bends, fingers landing lightly on my hips. I think he's going to kiss me, but he turns, his lips now ghosting over my collarbone, the side of my neck, his cool cheek pressed to mine. I feel the tip of his nose brush my ear.

"Mmm," he murmurs, breathing in. When he speaks again, his usually smooth voice is rough, gravelly. The voice of a man losing control. "Gods, Delphine, you could bring me to my knees."

I like that image, I decide. I let out a sound of agreement that is half moan and half laugh. His fingers grip my hips tighter as his lips brush against the shell of my ear. I arch up onto my toes, pressing against him.

A blast of heat flares up against my back, a blaze of light like the sun throwing the bath hall into sharp relief. Reyn steps back from me and puts up a hand to shield his eyes. I turn around, but I already suspect what I'll find.

Kora stands with her hand on the door, furious. I guess she came to find me before curfew. I didn't expect to be caught with Reyn like this.

And I really didn't expect her to burst into flames. *How is she doing that, anyway? I didn't know she could do that!*

She grabs my arm, which doesn't hurt, though fire licks over her fingers.

"Um," I say, looking back at Reyn.

He nods, still shading his eyes from Kora's radiance.

"Good night, then," he says, an amused smile tipping the corner of his mouth.

"Good night," I say, an equally goofy smile on my face, and I let Kora haul me outside.

She manages to put out her flames in a few steps, but she's so mad that she keeps hold of my arm, lips pressed tight to avoid yelling at me in the courtyard. She doesn't say so much as a single word until we reach my room, where she opens the door, shoves me in, and stomps in behind me. She slams the door.

"Are you sleeping with *Reyn*?"

I half expect her to spontaneously combust again as she approaches me.

"Reyn, of all people? Seriously, I thought you hated him!"

"Did you just *catch fire*?"

"Yes, I did. Now answer me!" she says, stomping her foot.

I sigh. "If I did, what does it matter? I'm free to sleep with whoever I want."

"I'm not stupid, Del. Or blind. I know he comes to your room nearly every night. And I see the way you two look at each other."

I shrug and cross my arms.

"He's the *Prince of Snakes*, Del. He's probably just using you, for information, or ... or something, or to get close so he can stab you in the middle of the night once you've let your guard down."

"You don't know him," I growl. "He's not like that."

"He's a *snake*. Of course he's like that!"

"Gods, Kora, why do you care? You've never cared who I sleep with before."

"I *care* because I'm your friend, you idiot!" she says, planting hands on her hips. "And I don't want to see you hurt! Sleep with him if you must, but do *not* fall for him."

She leaves, stomping again and slamming the door, and I'm left all alone with my thoughts.

I don't know what I expect that night. How have things changed so much? I wish Reyn would come over and meditate like he used to. I could use his calm right now. And some other things.

But he doesn't come.

It's just me, and Frostbite, and the interminable night. I stare at the blade for hours, eventually hurling it point-first into a small chink between two stones in the wall. It'll nick the blade, but that's all right. At least with it stuck in the wall, I won't be tempted to draw it across my skin.

Not much.

Just a little.

Just ... maybe more than a little.

I go get my damned blade.

Just one more time, I lie to myself.

"Are you just going to ignore me now?" I ask, cornering Reyn between classes. I'm headed to history; he's off for a turn at the infirmary.

"What?" he asks, taken aback.

"I thought—" I shut up as a couple of gossipy Wind Mages pass. "I thought you'd come over last night, like before."

He *smirks*. I glare at him, my hand flying to my dagger—

"I was *tired*, Delphine. Surely you can understand why," he says. "I'm not a Shield who can go for days without sleeping. I have certain advantages being a healer, but I don't have your ... endurance."

Well. Well ... that's fair. I rub the back of my neck, which is suddenly hot and prickly.

"Oh," I say. I can't look at him. I focus instead on the King's Messengers wheeling into the top of the Wind Mage tower.

"I promised Silas I'd tutor him after curfew tonight," Reyn says softly, looking over my shoulder to where his classmates are waiting. "But ... come by tomorrow."

"I ..." I can't say it. *I want to.*

I don't have to say it.

"See you then," Reyn says.

He doesn't kiss me, doesn't try to hold me or lay any kind of claim on me like he did with that stupid necklace. His fingers just brush mine as he passes, a tingle of frost nipping at my palm—and then he's gone.

During the reign of King Mathaios, the army of Ocron swept through the Western Mountains in a campaign against the troll hordes. While poorly organized, the trolls had the advantage of size, strength, and knowledge of the terrain. Thus it was that Earth Mages, under the guidance of Head Mage Tatiana Manola, tunneled from the Prasinos Mine north and westward, linking the coast and the heart of Ocron in an unprecedented ...

Reading the battle histories of Ocron is going to literally put me to sleep. I thump my head down on the book, groaning as I realize how many more pages of this I have to get through before my next exam. Names, dates, I have a hard time remembering them all.

But landmarks? I've flown the Western Mountains for *years*. I know where the Dragon's Spine starts and how to get to the hot springs that well up from caves along the northwestern edge. I know how the air currents funnel me down through a narrow valley between the pinnacles of the Ice Crown, and if I'm not careful, they'll dash me against the rocks. I know how Alkaia's Pass is only passable at all for three weeks a year, on foot at least. Otherwise, a traveler risks being buried in an avalanche, like Tekton and I almost were once.

But do our instructors care about any of that?

Not one damn bit.

As I close my eyes, my forehead still against the book, I feel a cool breeze at my back and hear the soft rustle of a Mage's robe as Reyn sits next to me.

"It works better with your eyes open, you know," he says.

I crack one eye open to glare at him. He raises his eyebrows innocently.

"I can still stab you with my eyes closed, you know," I say.

He nods his agreement.

A lot of us have taken to studying here in the dining hall. The library is just too tight and stuffy and dark—there are books in the depths there that I doubt have seen the sky in this century. Librarians too.

Another benefit of the dining hall is that no one cares how much we talk. And between mealtimes, like now, we can all spread out or group together if we need to, with the long tables.

Plus, Kora's making cookies.

"Here," she pants, dropping a plate in front of me.

Gods, they smell *amazing*. There's a dozen of them, perfect circles of steaming sugary goodness. Still, I know better than to be the first to try one of her experiments.

"Are those *chocolate*?" Athan asks, reaching across the table for one.

"Chocolate tempers the spices I had to add to get the light charm to bind," she explains as he chomps into one.

I sit up, waiting to see Athan's reaction before I take one for myself. Beside me, Reyn's hand drifts to my thigh. As close as we're sitting, with the folds of his robe, no one behind us can tell what he's doing. As long as I keep my face still.

But I don't have Reyn's composure.

"What are these supposed to do again?" Athan asks, licking his fingers.

"Light charm, so you can see in the dark. The last batch made Calix's eyes glow for a bit, but that's all. I think the ginger is—"

Athan sneezes, and his nose lights up like he's got half a dozen candles shoved up there. We all stare in shock for a moment before cracking up—the light only lasts a second, but Athan is laughing so hard that his face is turning red. Reyn takes the distraction as an opportunity for his fingers to wander, gliding over my thigh, making little circles higher, and higher. I can feel the steady coolness of his touch through the fabric of my pants. My mind is definitely *not* on studying at the moment, and Reyn knows it. The others might think that little half smile on my face is from Athan's glowing nose, but no one else knows where Reyn's fingers are.

"Well," Kora says, wiping her face and still giggling. "Maybe I should have added the ginger *after* the chocolate ..." She keeps muttering to herself as she grabs the cookies and heads back to the kitchen, swishing her robe as she goes.

"I've had enough studying," I say, slamming my book closed.

Reyn quirks an eyebrow. "You've barely started," he says, his hand on my leg flexing gently.

Like all hells am I going to be able to concentrate on King Mathaios and his trolls now, and he knows it.

"And I've had enough. You coming?" I ask, heading for the door. He *smirks*—but a second later, he's grabbed his satchel and is following me out of the dining hall.

"*Kora, they're running away from your baking!*" Athan yells.

I hear her shout of indignation and a clamor of pots from the kitchen—but then we're out the door.

The next day dawns hot and bright. We've got time off to train and study before the games. New students are coming to the school every day—all wide-eyed and full of themselves. Shield students are shifting in the courtyard, sizing each other up, so it's a mess of people and wolves and bears and big cats. I'm surprised to see Sinon there, wearing his Shield uniform, with a hulking boy who must be his younger brother. Sinon sees me walking and a smirk stretches across his big stupid face—but then his gaze flickers to Reyn, standing beside me, and the smirk vanishes. Sinon visibly pales, flinches, and nearly runs his brother over in an effort to get away from us. His brother looks at us for a second, then takes off after Sinon.

"What's that about?" I ask, watching Sinon's retreating form. Reyn rubs the back of his neck.

"What?"

"Sinon. I buried Frostbite in his chest and he still practically leers at me. Then he looked at you and I thought he was going to faint. What did you do to him?" I ask. I look up at Reyn, who has a very unconvincing expression of innocence on his face, his eyebrows raised high. I punch him lightly on the arm.

"Technically, I didn't do anything," Reyn says, a glimmer of a smile on his lips. We continue walking toward the library—he's going to study with Silas, and I'll head on to the arena for some last-minute training.

I roll my eyes. "Liar," I accuse. We skirt a family of Fire Mages introducing their daughter to some Shields, already trying to start alliances. Overhead, the sun is hot, and sweat is already trickling down my spine. My fingers brush Reyn's, and a whisper of cool magic washes over me. I breathe a sigh of relief.

"If you're trying to distract me, it's not working," I say, though *gods* I love his icy magic. Reyn grins.

"I've got a few other tricks if you want to be distracted," he says. My face heats, but in a good way this time.

"Tell me," I say, punching him again. He laughs and throws up a hand in mock-surrender.

"Alright! Maybe I insinuated what I *could* do to him, if he ever crossed paths with you again," Reyn says, walking onward towards the library. *Gods, what did he say to Sinon to make him flinch like that?* I realize that whatever threats Reyn made against Sinon, he'd made before we were ... well, whatever we are now. And it must have been some threat, if Sinon was more scared of Reyn than me. Something in my chest feels warm and fluttery at the thought.

I don't think about it too much. I grab Reyn's hand and pull him into the Fire Mage building, which is the closest on our path. I head straight towards a small room in the back of Tulliano's forge where he keeps extra supplies, and lock the door behind us. Reyn turns and surveys the space, the dusty shelves lit by one old spelled lantern. He arches an eyebrow in question.

"What are we doing in here?" he asks. "I'm supposed to be meeting Silas, remember?"

"Shut up and take your clothes off," I say, pulling my shirt off over my head before I crush my lips to his. "This won't take long."

From the dazed expression on his face when he finally gets to the library, he doesn't mind being a little late.

I didn't expect to be practically tackled by a large messenger hawk after lunch. He's panting with exertion as he waits—not patiently, as he bites my fingers, twice—for me to take the message scroll tied onto his claws. The first few words are written hastily in smeared black ink, in handwriting I know well.

Delphine,

WHAT IN ALL THE HELLS ARE YOU THINKING?

. . .

Oh. Great.

I take the letter to Kemp's. If I'm going to have to endure what appears to be a lengthy letter of Aleka yelling at me, I'm going to need a drink.

It's early afternoon, so the tavern is basically empty. Kemp pours me a lukewarm ale in a dented metal mug, and I take it to my favorite booth in the corner. I take a big gulp, steel myself, and continue reading.

Your Mage wrote to me. Says you're in trouble.

I frown. My Mage? I guess she means Kora. And Kora wrote to Aleka? Why didn't she tell me? *Ugh.* And wait—I'm in trouble? Does she know something I don't know? She writes *your Mage* like the claim has already been made.

Kora is worried you're going to throw away your future on a Roallacan Water Mage. I shouldn't have to remind you that they don't claim Shields —but apparently, I do. Just because we're a part of the same kingdom now doesn't mean you can trust them! And the prince? Fuck, Delphine, couldn't you have chosen anyone else?

Not that it's any of my nosy aunt's business, I think with a sigh. I take another gulp of ale, but it isn't helping. I *do* want Aleka's approval. She's the captain of Estana's guard, for Rigrasil's sake. And more than that, she's my friend. My adopted aunt. Having her yell at me—even through a letter—makes my face heat, and something clench in the pit of my stomach. My fingers trail absently over Frostbite at my hip.

. . .

Look, I know there's a lot of pressure on you right now. I can't imagine what you're going through.

But when you win your games—and you will, I have no doubt about that—you'll pick Kora. She cares about you, and she's the strongest Mage in your year. She'll be a good partner.

Don't ruin what you have with Kora over some boy. I'm not saying you should stop sleeping with him—actually, yes, I am saying that, because I'm your aunt and he's a fucking SNAKE, Del! But fine, go ahead. Have your little romance.

But remember, a claim is for life.

There are so many people who care about you. We want your happiness, more than anything else in this world.

I love you, Del. Make me proud.

Aleka

"I thought you liked pretty things," Reyn says.

We're both flopped on our backs, and despite Reyn's cool nature, we're both sweaty and worn out. After reading Aleka's letter, I was so worked up I felt I might explode.

So I went and found the one place I feel safe.

Reyn pulls a sheet over us and nuzzles the side of my neck, planting a kiss there. I stretch and curl into his side, laying a palm over his chest, tracing his tattoo. It's beautifully done, art fit for a prince—but I hate what it stands for, what it means. I hate that he had no choice in getting it, and because of the starsteel shimmering in the black ink, he has no choice in getting rid of it either, unless I cut it out. It's as much a scar as any of mine.

"I do like pretty things," I say.

Here, in his room, away from the judgment and gossip of the world around us, we can forget who we are for a little bit. I'm not the Dragon Girl. And he's not the Prince of Snakes. But that necklace still sits on his bookshelf, a glittering silver temptation.

"The necklace is beautiful. I just ... didn't expect it. It felt like ... I don't know."

"What is it?" he asks. His lips whisper against the skin of my shoulder, his obsidian hair like cool silk against my neck.

I turn in his arms, looking at him. His lips are swollen, his cheeks flushed. Some of his hair is stuck down on his forehead with sweat. I brush it back. *Gods, he's so beautiful.*

"People would talk," I say softly.

He knows that my blustery, confident facade is just that—underneath, it would bother me. Like Kora's comments bothered me. I can admit that to him. I can be safe with him, as he is safe with me. What exactly that means, though, I'm still coming to terms with.

"There's more than that," he says.

I sigh—he sees right through me, as usual.

"It would be a public declaration. That I'm *yours*," I say.

He freezes, his face once more a mask. "And is that thought so distasteful to you?"

I smack his chest. "Stop that."

He frowns, the mask cracking. "Stop what?"

"Closing yourself away. I can see it on your face. I'm trying to be honest and ... and talk about *feelings* with you. It's a big deal for me. Don't turn into ice again."

He raises an eyebrow, but my assessment amuses him. He lets out a long breath, throwing one lanky arm across my chest, grabbing me, and pulling me closer. I squeak in protest, but I don't fight him.

"It's easier, being ice," he says. "I'd nearly convinced myself that I *was* made of ice when I came here. And then I met you."

"You recognized me immediately," I say, frowning up at him. "How? I always wondered."

I'm nothing special to look at. Average height. Average brown hair. Average brown eyes. Nothing that should have given me away.

He looks down at me. There is a vulnerability there that pains me. I asked for this, I tell myself—but am I ready to see behind the mask?

"When I saw you, I saw the fire in your eyes. I *knew* it was you—and I felt the first emotion that I'd let myself feel in months, maybe in years. I thought it was hate, or the desire for vengeance, thawing me out, giving me purpose again," he says, tracing circles on my back with his cool fingers. "I think now, maybe, it was something else."

I squirm, burying my face in his chest so I don't have to meet his eyes.

Maybe it was something else. Like a claim?

"People would talk," I say again, my words muffled. I think about how Aris talked about the claim between a Mage and a Shield, like it was a conscious thing, a wisp of something divine trying to bring two people together.

"Let them," he says. His voice is confident.

"I'm not sure how to do this," I admit, so softly I'm not sure he heard it. I can't bring myself to ask him what he's offering—a claim? A relationship? Because honestly both ideas scare me more than facing down an angry blue god did.

I put a hand over his heart—it's pounding too.

"We'll find our own way," he says. "You are a wild thing, Delphine Kalla. Strong. Selfless. Hopelessly noble. Know that I only want *you*, whatever of yourself you'll give me, scars and teeth and all, for as long as you'll have me. But know also that I'd shout it to the world if you'd let me."

I don't look up. I don't want him to see the dampness on my face.

"Reyn ... I can't," I manage to choke out. "I just ... I can't be with you, and claim Kora. I can't ... it's like trying to be two different people." *I can't. I don't know how. And it's not just the pressure from Kora and everyone else—I will inevitably fuck it all up, and I can't hurt you. I won't.*

For a moment, his arms around me tighten, and I hold my breath. What he wants, I can't give. I don't know how.

Then he exhales and relaxes and plants a kiss on my hair.

"Kora's set on being a battle Mage, then?" he asks.

I mumble a confirmation.

"So you'll go off to battle with her, because you don't want to let her down? You'll kill again, for her?" he asks. It's an accusation, though his tone is as gentle as possible.

"It's not just her," I say, my face still buried in his chest. "It's everyone. Aris. Aleka. Tekton. Even Commander Markos."

"You'll be miserable," Reyn predicts.

Part of me is indignant at his assessment—but most of me realizes he's right. He's given voice to my biggest fear. I look up at him, and he brushes the hair back from my face.

"How is it any different from what you were willing to do for Rosalyn?" I ask softly.

His breath hitches for a second; his hand stills. The seconds between us stretch for an eternity.

"Just let me have tonight, then," he says quietly, snuggling me closer against him, like he wants to be touching every inch of me, to memorize the way I feel in his arms. He breathes deeply, his fingers tangling in my hair. "Just one night. You can go back to hating me in the morning."

I can't speak, but I nod, my flushed face and the dampness on my cheeks pressed against the cool skin of his chest.

He holds me all night, until the sun starts to rise. His breathing eventually becomes soft and even, though the worry that usually wrinkles his forehead is still in place.

I don't sleep at all. There's an ache in my chest that has no right being there, a feeling like having the wind knocked out of me.

I sneak out of his room before he wakes, and I don't look back.

CHAPTER 33

The next night, I don't go by his room again. Or the next. Or the one after that. I avoid him in the courtyard—I don't want to see the hurt in his eyes. I don't want to acknowledge him at all. If I did, I'd have to face the feelings that I've barricaded inside my chest like a flood, and I'm not ready to do that. He doesn't come by my room either, or seek me out like he did before. It'll be time for the games soon, and I occupy my mind with studying and exercise so it doesn't wander to thoughts of moonstone skin and emerald eyes.

When I study now, I avoid the dining hall and stick to my room and the upper floors of the library, or even the arena stands.

And at night? I spend the evenings with Tulliano at the forge, reinforcing the buckles on my flight harness or sharpening the edges of all the practice swords. He's a full Mage, so I can be out with him after curfew. His work is exhausting and exacting, and it requires all my focus. It's impossible for me to think of anything except what I'm doing in the present moment—a kind of meditation of its own, I realize.

Sometimes Head Mage Iraklis stops by and chats. At first I think it is just to see Tulliano, but then I finally realize no one who's not a Shield could possibly find weapons that exciting, and that he's just using it as an excuse to check up on me.

I call him out on it, and he laughs, and from then on my evenings with Tulliano blend into walks with Iraklis through the school. Everywhere he goes, plants bent toward him, seeking his magic. I swear the stones of the courtyard even try to follow him, sending little shivers through the earth as he passes.

He trails his sun-browned hands along the lemon balm plants, still growing tall in the small field beside the greenhouse.

"We've mixed the leaves of the Century Tree with the other herbal remedies. It is more effective than the last few attempts. We'll soon rid Ocron of this plague," he says.

I nod, lost in my own thoughts.

"You should give the leaves to all the healers, then," I muse. "If they had that mixture *and* their healing magic, I bet one healer could take care of a lot more people."

"They could indeed, especially on dragonback," Iraklis agrees, a small smile on his lips.

Before I can ask him what he means, he whispers to me, conspiratorially.

"Mage Gavriil isn't going to be happy if we prune his Century Tree."

"I could always distract him for you," I offer. "Did you know he has a 'no dragons in the greenhouse' rule?"

"I do," Iraklis says, smothering a smile. "Though I also know that hasn't stopped you. How were the mushrooms, by the way? The redhats are one of my personal favorites too."

I laugh, relieved he finds my escapade funny.

"They were delicious," I say, then give him a sly smile. "I'm happy to bring you some next time, Head Mage."

He laughs, and the trees near us shake their branches along with him.

"I'm already going to give Mage Gavriil several gray hairs after I tell him about the Century Tree," he says. "Let's not raid his mushroom cave too—I fear he'd never recover."

I'm still pissed at Kora. I *know* I didn't listen to her all those times she tried to warn me away from Reyn, but to go behind my back and talk to Aleka about it? And Aleka adores her, of course. And Ismini too. She's been sending Kora special spices and herbs from her greenhouse in Estana to add to her baking.

But what if Lyssa beats me and claims Kora, like she threatens to? Everyone acts like it's all settled, like they know I'm going to win, and they know I'm going to pick Kora—the pressure is almost more than I can bear.

I don't want to think about it too much. So I run. A lot. And I train with Vassilis and anyone else who'll enter the arena with me, until I'm too tired to move.

"Can I talk to you for a minute?"

The voice yanks me out of the exertion-induced nap I was trying to take on the arena floor. It's dusk, and I'm the only one here.

Well, me and Reyn.

He materializes from the dark of a tunnel, hands shoved in his pockets, posture hunched.

"You look guilty about something," I say, pushing myself up, leaning back on my palms. Sand sprinkles down from my hair, sticks to the patch of sweat on my shirt.

"I just ... wanted to see you," he says, then winces.

"Spit it out, Prince," I say, flopping back onto the sand. "I'm too tired to play games."

Overhead, the first stars begin to sparkle, like tiny diamonds.

He comes out into the arena and lies down beside me, his hands clasped over his stomach. We watch the sky darken, watch the moon crest the edge of the arena.

"I know we haven't spoken in a while. I'm ... well, I was worried if I wasn't around, then you might start cutting again." He's looking up at the sky, his eyes carefully focusing on some point up there, avoiding looking at me.

"Believe it or not, you don't have that kind of power over me," I say. It's mean, and it's definitely not true, but I don't apologize.

He takes a deep breath. "I told Caius about you. The cutting. Well, not that it was *you* specifically. But that I was trying to help someone who cut herself, and my methods weren't enough. I ... am not enough," he says softly.

I exhale. Reyn *is* enough. I am just ... too much.

"He's a strong healer, and he's got more experience than I do. I thought he could offer some advice. He said he'd think about it ... I just ... if you hear something from Caius, that's why. It was me."

"What I do with my body is no concern of yours, Prince," I say tiredly. Not Reyn. I can't call him Reyn now. He's just ... a prince. No one to me.

"I know," he says.

I wish I could take back my words—there's a complete and utter sadness in his voice that makes me want to cry.

"But your pain ... not the cutting. I mean the pain inside ... I wish I could do more. Take *that* away. Because you *are* enough, Delphine. Without the dragon, without the rest. Just you. And I'm not saying that because I'm your healer. Because I'm your ..." He pauses, swallowing hard.

We watch wisps of cloud drift across the darkening sky.

"Well, yours, anyway," he says.

I bite my tongue and focus on the stars overhead, winking down at us. If I'm silent, I can pretend my heart doesn't feel like it's tearing itself in two.

After a while, he gets up, dusts the sand from his legs, and leaves the arena without a single glance back. Salty water trails down my cheeks, making tracks in the dirt and sand.

Kora doesn't think she can talk to me and goes to Aleka instead.

Now Reyn fucking betrays me to his teacher, a man he knows I loathe. *Fuck.* Maybe I'd better start looking into the first-year Mages, see if any of them are worth getting to know. Maybe that Wind Mage girl. I rub the water from my eyes, getting sand in them, which only pisses me off more.

None of the other Mages come close to Kora or Reyn.

What's the point of winning the games when there's no one I want to claim?

CHAPTER 34

The games are coming up fast, and I don't have time to think about anything except training, or so I tell myself. Kora's at the library every spare hour she has. If she's smug about the fact that I'm not spending time with Reyn now, she doesn't let it show. Much.

I haven't slept in days. I train every minute the sun's up—and at night, when it's curfew, I read my textbooks over and over again until my eyes are itchy and my brain is itchier.

And then I do it all again.

"There's something to be said for *rest*, Del," Kora says, like she's any better. "Hey, healer. Tell her to get some rest."

Reyn looks at me from his seat down the table in the dining hall, his face an icy mask. He says nothing, just returns to his own book.

"Look, are you so worked up because of *him*?" Kora says, pointing at Reyn with her spoon. "In a few more weeks, he'll be deployed somewhere on the east coast with the other healers and we'll be out west fighting trolls. You won't have to see him again," she says. She makes no effort to keep her voice down—but if Reyn hears, he doesn't react.

Why does that idea make my chest ache so much? What will happen if he doesn't have a Shield to tell him to take a break once in a while? He'll burn himself out in the first week.

I square my shoulders. "Just want to make sure I'm at my best for the games," I mutter. Kora nods.

"You're *the Dragon Girl.* Half of the Shields will faint the minute they step into a ring with you, and the other half you'll beat in two moves. I don't understand why you're stressed."

"Because it's *not* that easy!" I snap. "You think I *like* being the best all the time? I'm the standard everyone else aspires to—when I lose a fight, the other Shields *cheer.*"

I think of Aris coming to my games—I can't lose, not when he's watching. I can't let him down.

I think I might vomit.

Kora huffs but closes her book. She reaches one pale hand across the table and grabs mine, which are shredding a bread roll into tiny crumbs.

"Hey," she says, squeezing my hand and waiting until I look up and meet her eyes. "It's going to be fine. No matter what place you come in, I'll be waiting for you. We'll do this together, all right?"

I swallow hard, the roll like dust in my throat. A moment of panic fleets across Kora's face but is quickly replaced by her bright smile.

"Hey, you know what we need? A sauna! Let's go to the baths. I'll steam 'em up!" she says, jumping up from the table.

Her good mood is infectious—I could do a lot worse than Kora, I think.

But I wonder if she could do better than *me.*

Kora loves a good sauna. She heats the water until the vapor is so thick we can barely see. We steep in the baths until almost curfew, our skin wrinkling and stress ebbing. My hair is a frizzy mess, plastered by sweat to my neck and forehead, but I don't mind. Having these moments with Kora ... I want to memorize them, hide them away like precious treasures, to be brought out and remembered whenever I want.

We didn't think to bring a change of clothes, and after dinner there wasn't time to fetch one, so we just wrap ourselves in towels. Our bare feet leave little wet spots on the stones. We get some wolf whistles as we cross the courtyard, but only a few, and once the idiots realize who they're toying with, they shut up and scatter. Kora does her best to conceal her giggles, but she fails. She chats away about where we're going to be sent after the games—her bet is the southern part of the Western Mountains, where the troll clans are starting to amass. She makes sure to mention the Prasinos Mine and the piles of gems there, but not even the promise of more treasures for my horde can distract me tonight. I keep quiet, wringing the towel between my hands as we walk until the fabric begins to tear.

CHAPTER 35

It's the afternoon before the games. Athan, Herondas, Lyssa, the rest of the Shields, and I are at Kemp's, getting drunk. We're surrounded by Mages, though it's pretty obvious by now who's going to claim who. I'll claim Kora, though I haven't entirely forgiven her. We'll have all the time in the world to work things out after the games. And Athan will claim Aletheia. Herondas has a friend in the class below us, a Wind Mage, and he's going to make his claim now and wait an extra year for his friend to graduate. Aris nearly did that with Wren—he'd have had to wait two years, which Kora found infinitely romantic—but Wren kind of got kicked out, or "summoned to the capital," to put it nicely. It might be a stupid tradition, getting drunk the night before we all head to the arena for the last time—but it is tradition. And thanks to Shield healing, most of us won't have too much of a hangover.

Wren, Aris, and Rosie have come to see me fight. Ismini and Aleka too, and Rafael and Remiel. Rafael showed me the fireworks he's been practicing, in miniature, and set the ends of Aris's hair aflame—gods, I've missed them.

And Uncle Tekton. He came with Adriana, as quiet as usual. I haven't seen him in two years. I hugged him so hard I think I cracked his ribs.

"I'm so proud of you," he said.

"I haven't done anything yet," I responded. "The games are tomorrow."

He smiled, tucking a strand of hair back from my face.

"You've grown," he reflected. And it sounded sad.

I down the rest of my ale in a single gulp and signal Kemp for another. Our graduation ceremony tonight was a simple affair. The Mages were given their official, solid-colored robes—red for Fire Mages, blue for Water Mages, yellow for Wind Mages, and green for Earth Mages. Each robe has been imbued with some ungodly number of spells to keep its wearer safe, and dry when it rains, that kind of thing.

Shields, of course, keep it simple. Shields for Shields. Round, steel-reinforced wooden shields made by Tulliano himself. The eponymous icon of our order. Tekton clapped louder than anyone else when Shield Commander Markos gave me mine.

My uncle, of course, never got one. He was never allowed at the school.

I guess I can almost forgive Rigrasil for that, since now Tekton runs the entire school in Aeturnus.

"Delphine Kalla?" an ungifted calls from the door. I think he's one of the groundskeepers. He's grubby and looks distinctly bored.

"Who's asking?" I say, grabbing a couple of tankards from the bar, not caring who they are destined for, and handing them out to the first hands that reach for them.

"Mage Caius would like to see you," the man says. He's probably seen a dozen of these pregames celebrations over his tenure here—I wonder if he saw Aleka fight. Or Aris.

I really, *really* do not want to talk to Caius right now. I can only imagine it's about one thing. *Thanks for nothing, Reyn.*

"I'll talk to him tomorrow," I grumble, taking another drink. Ale sloshes over the edge of the tankard and onto the floor.

"The, um ..." the messenger says, sidestepping the puddle I made. "The Roallacan prince is with him too."

Fuck.

I throw back what's left of my ale, drinking it down in a few long swallows to the cheers of my classmates.

"I'll be right back," I say, wiping the foam from my lips with the back of my sleeve.

Kora watches me, her eyebrows furrowed. She's dyed her hair freshly pink, and between the pink hair and her bright red robe, she's so bright it almost hurts to look at her.

"What do they want?" she asks.

I shrug, but I don't think it's convincing. What, am I going to tell her in this crowded tavern that I cut my skin when I'm stressed out? And that I get stressed out a *lot*? And she's never noticed in two years, because I heal too quickly for her to see? And that the Snake Prince knows my deepest, most shameful secret?

"I'll be right back," I say again, my words a little slurred.

I follow the messenger from the tavern, across the dark courtyard, and into the Water Mage building.

"They're in his office," the man says, and leaves.

It really is a pretty building on the inside, with a wide-open area in the middle that has a series of tiered pools. Spelled lanterns make it an eerie place in the dark, especially with about a gallon of ale coursing through my veins.

I find Caius's office and let myself in. I figured he'd want to talk to me about my cutting at some point, but really, his timing sucks. I should be celebrating with my classmates right now.

I enter to see Caius standing in front of his desk, which is strewn with bottles and papers. His hair is slicked back like usual, but there's a predatory gleam to his eyes, at odds with his wan smile.

"Delphine, come in," he says, gesturing me toward a low chair in front of him. It's placed so that he can sit behind his desk, like a king on a throne, and talk down to whichever student has come to see him.

Reyn is standing to the side, arms crossed, his face an unreadable mask. Which is fine. I mean, he betrayed me as much as Kora did. I try not to look at him at all, instead focusing my displeasure on Caius.

"Could this really not wait until tomorrow?" I whine. "It's kind of a big day for me."

"Sit," Caius says patiently. "I promise not to take too much of your precious evening away from you."

"Fine," I grumble, though we both know it's less about the time away from my friends, who are getting drunk and probably naked with someone, and more about the fact that I don't want to talk about what I've been doing.

I sit in the chair, sinking into it, sulking. Caius just keeps that stupid bland expression on his face. He steeples his fingers together. I refuse to look at Reyn.

"Do you know why you're here?" he asks.

I roll my eyes. "Because Reyn fed you some bullshit story and you believed it?" I say.

Two spots of pale pink appear on Reyn's face, but he doesn't deny it.

"You're here," Caius says, folding his hands inside his sleeves, "because Prince Reyn was afraid that the pressure of this school ... that it is too much for you." He begins to pace the room, circling the chair I'm sitting in, like a shark circling its victim, until he's directly behind me.

The skin on the back of my neck prickles with awareness, but I'm too drunk and too upset to care much. I glare at Reyn, who glares right back at me, his emerald eyes unblinking. Too much pressure?

"Maybe it meant something else"??

Well, fuck that.

"Whatever happened to healer confidentiality? I thought you were supposed to keep my secret," I say accusingly, unable to keep ignoring him.

"The sacred bond between a healer and their patient may be

breached when the patient is in danger," Reyn says, his voice an emotionless monotone.

I snort and roll my eyes.

"The pressure you put on yourself is too much, Delphine," he says softly. "For anyone. I only wanted to see if Caius could help you, since I couldn't."

"I should have known better than to trust a snake," I spit, still glaring at him.

"Yes," Caius says, still behind me. I practically forgot he was there. "You should have."

A blinding pain bites into the back of my neck. I roar—

Or I try to.

But nothing happens. I can't shift, not even a partial shift. I raise my hand to punch Caius in the throat—

Or I try to.

But that doesn't work either. Neither do my legs. I close my eyes, trying to focus, to calm down. A freezing cold wind blasts past my face.

"What did you do to me?" I say, my voice breathy and coming fast.

My heart flutters like a bird in my chest. When I can open my eyes, tears streaming down my face—tears I can't wipe away—I see Reyn, shackles of ice around his wrists and ankles, another across his mouth. He's stuck to the wall by one of Caius's spells.

Caius laughs—the fucker *laughs*—and strolls back around my chair. My body still won't respond. I put every ounce of muscle I have into moving my fingers, my feet, *anything*.

This is worse than going gray.

"Fascinating thing, starsteel," Caius says, like we have all the time in the world. "I put a pin into your spinal cord, between your cervical vertebrae. You're paralyzed, of course, but more than that—you are unable to shift while it is embedded in your central nervous system."

"*Fuck you*," I say, and spit at him.

I can't believe this is happening—that he thinks he'll get away with this. My mind reels, trying to push past the fog of pain. Is this his idea of punishing me for something? Stealing Reyn's attention from him? When this is over, Caius and I are going to have a chat.

"We discovered this quality some years ago. Queen Evanthia kidnapped a number of Shields over the years—from raids in Ocron—and ... learned about them."

"Experimented on them, you mean." My stomach roils, like a cauldron of snakes, and I'm worried I might vomit. In my current state, that would not be fun.

"Great *learning* requires great sacrifice," he says. "I'll kill Reyn, then you. I'll tell everyone that you killed him in a fit of rage for telling your secret—and I was too late to save either of you. Prince Reyn, run through by a Shield's blade. And the sneaky little dragon, who slit her own wrists rather than face justice. It will make a stirring story, one that will stir Roallac to action, throwing off the shackles of Ocron's oppression and rising up once more!"

I think back on every interaction I've had with Caius over the past two years. The pieces fall into place like a puzzle. Who knew that Reyn and I were flying to Spit? Caius. And who knew that starsteel embedded into weapons would incapacitate me? Caius again. And who had access and knowledge to use the very rare Roallacan snake venom used to poison Reyn? *Caius.* Gods, I'm an idiot.

"Leave Reyn out of this," I snarl. "You can both say I attacked him, but let him live."

"I'm afraid I can't," Caius says.

Reyn's face is white, his arms and legs straining where he pulls against his shackles—but he can't break free, not without being able to speak. Caius is too strong.

"Prince Reyn needs to die to stir Roallac to revolution."

Why isn't my body healing? I remember the starsteel pin from the javelin—I wasn't able to heal until Reyn removed it. *I doubt even Shield magic will heal this kind of injury*, I think. Tears begin falling again, and snot runs from my nose. It's disgusting, but I can't stop it.

Caius comes over to me and bends, unsheathing Frostbite from my hip. I snarl, but I can't stop him. He starts rolling the sleeve of my right arm back; my arm might as well belong to someone else. I can't feel it. Nor can I feel it when he draws Frostbite across my inner elbow, deep, severing the big vein there, and the tendons that make my fingers work.

"I don't blame you, you know," he says as he watches my bright blood stream down my arm. "I meant what I said earlier. You are only the sword, wielded by my enemy. But you *are* a weapon, nonetheless. And you need to be ... removed."

Blood is dripping from my fingers, puddling on the floor. Caius makes another cut, farther down, much deeper than I ever went. Skin and tissue and muscle part beneath my razor-sharp blade.

"You're jealous," I say, though it comes out as a whisper.

He cocks his head to the side. "Of you? Don't flatter yourself."

"Reyn. Of Reyn," I say. "He's twice the Mage you'll ever be. Twice the man."

I lick my lips. I'm thirsty. Parched. I'm losing too much blood. And I'm cold. So, so cold. Fear, icy and sharp, clutches at my heart. I try to think, but my mind feels sluggish. I don't have Frostbite. I can't move anything at all ... except my mouth.

Well, here goes nothing.

Caius brings his face down close to mine, and I realize how stupid it is that my last thought here before I meet Rigrasil will be that I wish Caius hadn't eaten garlic for his dinner.

"My Mage is looking for me," I say, leveling a glare at Caius the best I can. "Kora. You see this necklace? She made the flame inside. She can track it. She'll come looking when I don't return."

It's a bold-faced lie, but Caius doesn't know that. I have to put my faith in Reyn. *Vires, honos, fides.*

Caius eyes Kora's pendant, hanging heavily against my chest, and snorts. The little flame inside dances, like it's taunting him. Caius—and most Black Water Witches—hate Fire Mages. And, well, basically everyone who isn't a Water Mage.

So he reaches out and grabs the pendant, intending no doubt to rip it from my neck.

When his fingers touch the crystal, it comes to life, blazing in a sudden bright flash of Kora's stored fire magic.

Caius is startled, and for a moment, his own magic flickers.

Just a moment. Less than a heartbeat.

But it's enough.

There's a crack to my left, and then ice shatters; the shackles on Reyn explode outward, shards of ice pelting the side of my body. I can't feel it, but I see them bounce off my skin just the same. *Yes!*

Reyn stands before us, hands extended and swirling with coalescing blue magic, bright stars of light, wielding more power than Aenon himself. Caius brings his hands down from shielding his eyes with a sharp word.

"*Throw,*" Caius says. Ice shoots like a spear from his hand, right toward Reyn's heart.

It shatters into harmless mist when it touches him.

"Told you," I grunt, managing to smirk at the dismay on Caius's face. *If I'm going to die here, at least let my death be memorable.*

"I *trusted* you," Reyn says, his voice breaking with emotion, like a giant wave crashing. He swallows, momentarily glancing at me. His face is a mask, except for his eyes, which burn like green embers.

"Heal her," Reyn commands, glaring at Caius. His voice is strong now, and steady. "And I'll consider sparing you."

"Put your hands down, Prince, and I'll make your death quick," Caius retorts. He reaches out—not toward Reyn but toward me, Frostbite still in his hand, ready to make a final cut on my arm.

It's not needed, really. The dark pool of blood beneath my chair is still spreading, but slower now. There's not much left. I can't feel my body, but my eyelids feel heavier by the second. My heartbeat, which has been pounding in my ears, is a slow, stumbling pulse.

I don't have much time.

And Reyn doesn't hesitate. His fingers shoot out toward Caius, then curl in on themselves, like a claw pulling something, catching a thread of something vital and yanking on it.

"*Freeze,*" he says.

The thing about magic—you need a word, usually a gesture, and intent. Sometimes two out of three is enough, or one out of three, if you're really strong.

But Reyn uses all three, magnifying his spell—and the color instantly drains from Caius's face. His body jerks stiffly, the crackle of ice audible with his movements as Reyn freezes every drop of blood in Caius's body, as crystals of ice clog his heart and his brain. His skin turns gray, frost blooming across his clothes as Reyn literally freezes Caius to death in a matter of seconds.

I hope it fucking hurts.

At least he died before me.

And at least Reyn will live.

Reyn.

He rushes to my side—the ice statue that was once Caius, forgotten.

"I'm going to pull the pin out," he says, breathless. "Stay with me."

He is so, so beautiful, his whole body glowing with blue light as he accesses his magic. There's a tug on the back of my neck, a sensation of blessed coolness spreading down my spine, but all I can think about is this beautiful idiot. I hate that he broke his vow to save me. Tears run down my cheeks, drip from my chin.

"Don't," I croak. "Get ... someone else." I won't have him burning himself out for me—and I have no doubt that in order to heal me, he's going to have to use a massive amount of magic.

"We can go back to being enemies later. Right now, there's no time," he says, blue flaring around him like a star as he calls his magic forth.

I feel pain in my bones as he urges them to replenish my blood.

Wait.

I feel pain in my bones.

I feel.

I cry out, and my fingers twitch. The cuts on my arm knit together; the bleeding stops. It hurts, but I can curl my fingers, make a fist. He goes to work again at my back, cool magic flooding down my spine, all the way to my toes as he heals the connections of my body and undoes the starsteel's damage.

I cry, wiping the tears and snot from my face with a bloodstained hand—I probably just smeared blood all over my face, but I don't care. I look up at him, relief flooding through me as I feel my body heal, as I feel *him*, his hands on me, the brush of his hair against my neck.

Reyn looks down at me, his face pale, as pale as the moon in the dark. He urges more magic down my back. I wiggle my toes, and my shoes make little ripples in the puddle of blood at my feet. My breathing slows. *It's going to be all right. I'm going to be all right.*

Then I feel a flutter, a pulse in my spine.

The blue light sputters.

I look back up at Reyn and notice the sweat forming on his forehead, the grayish hue to his skin.

It's too much. He's giving too much.

A trickle of blood drips from his nose.

He catches my gaze, holds it, as he wills his body to heal mine, as he gives *everything*.

His eyes roll back.

And he falls.

I move to catch him, but my body isn't healed completely, and I sort of just land on top of him, not really breaking either of our falls.

"Reyn?" I shout, my face muffled against the blue robe he's wearing, struggling to get my shoulder to move. "REYN!"

He doesn't respond. I can't tell if he's breathing. I can't tell ... what color he is anymore, not in the dark of this office. I try to grab his shoulders and shake him, but his head just lolls to the side, his hair trailing into the pool of my blood, smearing it like a gruesome paintbrush. His eyes are closed.

I think fast. I have one choice, really, only one way to get help. I can't even walk right now, let alone carry Reyn anywhere. And I don't have time to run to the dorms to get another healer.

I glance around the small office, the heavy gray stones forming the walls. I deliberately do *not* look at Caius.

Well, this is going to hurt, I think.

And I shift.

CHAPTER 36

"I can't believe you destroyed half of the Water Mage building!" Athan crows, thumping me hard on the shoulder. "Couldn't you have done that *before* finals?"

I grin. I'm lying propped up on a cot in the non-demolished wing of the Water Mage building, a pair of healers fluttering around me like butterflies, checking every inch of me for injury, restoring my body to its usual superior state.

And then there's Reyn. He's across from me, a pair of senior healers working on him. He can hardly take his eyes off me, nor I him. *We made it.*

When I realized I couldn't leave to get help for Reyn, I brought the help to us. I shifted, my bulk knocking out a wall of Caius's office, a hefty chunk of stone squashing his frozen carcass—not that I minded. I bellowed into the night, and the entire school came running.

Head Mage Iraklis. Ismini and Aleka. Tekton. Wren and Aris, with a sleepy Rosie held tightly in his arms. Wren had green lightning swirling around the entire courtyard, ready to take on Aenon himself—again—if needed. My whole family, running to my aid.

"It was Caius," I sobbed. "All of it."

Once it became clear that Reyn would recover, I agreed to let the healers sit me down and tend to me too. Not that there was much to do—Reyn had done most of it already, and my body was slowly taking care of the rest. I can't believe how much he was able to repair—the healers keep remarking on it too. His is a different kind of strength from Kora's, but no less remarkable.

"We need you to be at your best," one of the healers, a nice older lady, said with a wink. "We'll have you back to fighting form in time for the games. Don't you worry."

Honestly, the games are the last thing on my mind.

Aris and Tekton never leave my side. I run my fingers over Frostbite, still strapped to my hip. I look at Reyn—if such a thing were possible, I'd swear he could read my mind sometimes. He looks at my hand on Frostbite, at my uncles—and gives me a small nod. *Go ahead*, he says.

I take a deep breath and put my hand on Aris's where it rests on the cot beside me.

"Uncle Aris? Uncle Tekton?" I say, my voice as high and wobbly as that of a child on the verge of tears. "There's something I want to tell you."

"No one would blame you for skipping this year's games, you know," Lyssa says with a sniff.

"But it's going to be so much more embarrassing when I thrash you in the arena *today*," I say, stretching my arms over my head.

"What makes you think you stand a chance?" Lyssa says, looking me over with a critical eye, looking for any sign of injury that the healers might have missed, anything to give her an edge in the arena.

I give her a feral grin. "Because I'm Delphine fucking Kalla, bitch," I say, hands on my hips. "So get the hells out of my way."

Is it cheating, to have had the healers burn any trace of fatigue or soreness from my body? To make sure every nerve and muscle is working at top capacity? Probably not. I'm going to win these games, no matter what Lyssa says. My body feels good. Ready.

But my heart?

I look up at the stands. Aris, Wren, Aleka, Tekton, Ismini, Rafael, Remiel, Adriana—they're all sitting together, smiling and waving at me. My chest tightens. I cannot let them down. When I told Aris and Tekton about Frostbite, about cutting—I don't know what I'd expected, really. Aris is the person I admire most in the entire world. I didn't want to change his opinion of me, his star pupil. I can't bear to have him think of me as broken. My reputation tarnished.

They listened carefully, not saying a word, exchanging a glance or two and shifting a little uncomfortably, but they stayed quiet. And then Aris Valorius, greatest Shield of our generation, and Tekton the forsaken—they hugged me, and I cried onto their shoulders, my tears soaking into Aris's black shirt until I had no more tears left. At least the color hid the wet spots. Aris and Tekton tried to apologize.

"I was blind," Tekton said.

"And I was an asshole," Aris added. "We are so proud of you. We should never have asked you to take us east, all those years ago. You wouldn't ..." He swallowed hard, his sky-blue eyes shining.

"If you hadn't, I wouldn't be here now. Getting ready to win my games," I said, placing my hands on theirs. "I could have come to you before we got to this point. It's not that I don't trust you—I do, with my life! I just didn't want you to see me as ... weak."

Tekton profusely disputed that, arguing that I was the strongest Shield he'd ever known, and Aris actually said, "I'm sorry," and promised me he'd never let me down again.

As if they *could ever let* me *down!*

The healers pretended to ignore us, but when I peeked over Tekton's shoulder at last, I found Reyn looking back at me, a beaming smile on his face.

I shake my head—I have to concentrate, today of all days. I spy

Kora with her brothers, all redheaded Fire Mages. She gives me a smile and a wave. Something inside me cracks. I touch the little flame necklace she gave me, and it brightens—just enough for me to notice in the bright sunshine. Beside it hangs the feather pendant that Reyn gave me. Apparently, he'd been carrying it around in his pocket, and it fell out when he was healing me. I looped it around my neck as soon as my arms worked enough to do so.

Trust your instincts, Aris said.

But what if I have really, really bad instincts? What if they're broken?

Know that I only want you, whatever of yourself you'll give me, for as long as you'll have me. But know also that I'd shout it to the world if you'd let me.

I seek out Reyn. I don't see him at first, and the flutter in my heart grows stronger. I wish I'd been allowed to keep Frostbite strapped to my hip; it would have reassured me. I gave it to Aris to hold for me. He accepted it with as much reverence as if it were one of Caelus's golden gladiuses and promised to keep it safe, though I have no doubt he wanted to hurl it into the river.

We file out to the center of the arena. It's a hot day, even this early, and most of us are already sweating. We wear the traditional leather skirts and sandals of the Shields—the women also get to wear a layer of cloth and leather wrapped tight over our chests, but that's it. No armor, not for Shields. My classmates look fierce. I know I'll be forced to beat several of them in the arena today—no matter what else happens today, I *will* have my name at the top of the list for this year's class. Aris catches my eye and thumps his hand against his chest. *You are no longer a student*, he says. *You are a Shield.*

Vassilis is with us and exchanges the ceremonial phrases with Commander Markos, who is seated in the stands on a special dais, next to Head Mage Iraklis. Lukas, who could nearly be Aris's twin, is there too, at his side. I suppress a shudder when his glittering eyes fall on me. *Ugh.*

"*Vires, honos, fides,*" we chant, and we strike our fists against our chests.

On my right hand, there on the webbing between my thumb and index finger, are two small dots, made hastily in ink this morning. *Rigrasil help me. I need all the luck I can get.*

And then—it is time.

There are six red circles drawn in the sand. The rules are simple —get your opponent to yield, or throw them outside the circle. We've done this so many times in practice that I can nearly predict everyone's moves before they make them.

My first battle is against Lucius, a wolf shifter who always seemed to be the omega to Lyssa's alpha. He groans when he realizes he's paired with me.

I disarm him in three moves, and he yields with my blades pressed to his throat.

Lyssa isn't happy that I've humiliated her pack brother, but I don't really care. Today is about earning the first-place right, the right to pick a Mage first. I'm not going to waste my energy drawing out a battle I can win in moments.

"I'll pick Kora, just to fuck with you," Lyssa says, knocking her shoulder against mine, hard, as she passes.

I swallow down the torrent of expletives I want to yell, telling myself to focus. *Focus. Focus.* It becomes a kind of mantra for me today. Hells, maybe Reyn's teaching has paid off after all.

My next battle is against Herondas. I'm pretty sure he drops his swords on purpose—it's only seconds before he yields to me.

The next two, against Eleni and Iason, go nearly as quickly. I stop to pour a cup of water down my throat, and another over my head. The arena is quiet as Athan and Lyssa battle for the right to face me in the final match.

Lyssa's got a nasty scratch down her leg, but her Shield magic has already stanched the bleeding. Athan looks like the god of day incarnate, all golden, shining muscles and whirling steel. But he is getting tired. I can see it in the way his feet shuffle, the way Lyssa baits him, tiring him out. She's smart, this wolf. Athan battles with two swords, like I do, whereas she uses a sword and a round wooden shield. She makes him attack again and again, wearing out his strength against her shield.

And then she pounces. As fast as lightning, Athan is knocked flat on his back, Lyssa's sword digging into the meat of his shoulder deeper than is necessary to pin him to the ground.

"Foul!" I cry, and I'm not the only one.

But Athan yields, and she pulls the sword quickly. In a show of sportsmanship, she helps him to his feet. This has its intended effect of soothing the crowd.

Easy to get caught up in the moment, they say. *This is what she's trained for, after all. How noble of her to help her fallen foe.*

Lyssa's dark eyes glitter with contempt as she downs a mug of ash water. I am under no illusion that she'll be an easy opponent for me. Of all the Shields, she is the least predictable. Smart, always varying her style. Patient. I am all strength and offense. We'd make a good team, if we didn't hate each other's guts.

I finally spot the Roallacan Mages. They're all wearing the blue robes of full Mages now that they've graduated. I'm not sure why they're even here, given their distaste for Shields.

But I lock eyes with Reyn, who is watching me intently, seemingly oblivious to the conversations around him, as steady as a boulder in a rushing stream. He gives me the subtlest nod of his head—at least, I think he does.

I know why he's here. And it gives me strength. Enemies or not, he's here to support me.

"After I win, I'm going to choose your Fire Mage," Lyssa says again.

She stands shoulder to shoulder with me, wearing a smile and waving at a group of Shields in the stands who are probably her family, her pack. They howl in response.

This kind of posturing is typical of the games, Aris said. If she picks Kora, then I can't, nor can anyone else. Kora can reject the claim, of course, but then she'll have to wait another year for another games, for another Shield.

"You're such a bitch," I mutter, plastering a smile on my face and waving to Aris.

"Takes one to know one," she replies.

I roll my eyes but keep a pleasant expression on my face.

The groundskeepers rake the sand and redraw the red chalk circle for our battle. There are still a few others going on, to determine final ranking of the other students. Athan comes up on my other side, bumping me with his uninjured shoulder. I am pleased to see his other one, while covered in blood, appears to be healing nicely. He'll go up against Iason for the third- and fourth-place matches after I battle Lyssa. I don't want to worry about him fighting with an injury, not when Iason is winded but otherwise unhurt.

"When I said I wanted to see some girl-on-girl action, this isn't what I meant," he says, looking between me and Lyssa, and I crack a smile despite myself. He drops his voice so that only I can hear it. "Seriously, Del, look out. She won't hold back."

"Neither will I," I say. I don't bother lowering my voice.

If Lyssa hears, she gives no indication of it.

CHAPTER 37

Vassilis comes over and gives us a lecture about fighting fairly, upholding the glorious tradition of Shields, something along those lines. I pretty much ignore him and focus instead. *Focus. Focus.* The mantra brings me peace. My body is a little fatigued from the prior four fights, but uninjured. I need to be quick, end this fight before Lyssa can tire me out with her circling and feinting. We've faced each other a dozen times over the past two years—sometimes in the arena, sometimes in the predawn time before our runs, when one of us has a grudge against the other, sometimes in the dark of night, when there are no prying eyes to cry foul. If she gets the drop on me, she can beat me. She's quick, cruel, and I'd be a fool to underestimate her.

"When I win, I'll be the girl who beat the Dragon Girl. And you'll be ... no one, actually," she sneers.

I grit my teeth. *Focus.*

"Just the Black Water slut who cuts herself when she feels sad," Lyssa says, swinging her sword and stepping into the ring.

I see red. Athan grabs my elbow as I go to charge after her.

"Calm down, Del," he whispers. "It's all right."

I wrench my arm from his hand and catch myself looking into his crystal-blue eyes. What I see there troubles me—not just the reassurance of a friend but ... *pity*.

"We know," he says quietly. "Apparently, Caius told the twins, and then the twins told, well, everybody."

"Great," I say, staring at my toes. "If you want to make some stupid comment about how I'm not tough enough to be here, you can go fuck yourself."

"We're your friends, you ass. You're not alone," Athan says, giving me a punch on the arm.

I lock eyes with Reyn in the stands, still as ice, watching me. Waiting for me.

"I know," I say.

I look away from Reyn, willing the tears that have sprung to my eyes to subside. One person learned my secret, and it practically got us both killed. Well, now everyone knows. I make a vow, here and now, before Rigrasil's light, that I will *never* use Frostbite against myself again.

Then I square my shoulders and enter the ring. I haven't had time to tell Aris that I've named my swords—Umbra and Lux. Shadow and Light. Not quite as awe-inspiring as Odall's, but that's all right.

For me, they are perfect.

I draw them from the harness on my back, raising them to the sky for Rigrasil's blessing, and settle into a fighting stance.

It's a strange thing, battling with an audience watching. Shields like showing off, so it's not unusual for us to have a small group watching us practice, especially before the games. The Mages will gather and take notes as we fight—who is the fastest, who beats who in the practice battles. Alliances are formed through friendships, but that isn't always enough. There's always a Shield who wants a Mage that's already spoken for; that's why the games came along. The strongest Shield wins the right to choose.

And today it will be me.

"It's not too late to quit, you know," Lyssa says, whipping her wrist around, making her sword flash.

"Go ahead, then," I say.

The sun is brutal today, and sweat is running down my back already from my previous fights. The water I poured over my head has evaporated, leaving me prickly. I don't like heat. I'm tired, and my brain hurts from overthinking.

So I stop thinking. I just *do.*

There's a peace that's only to be found in fighting. It sounds strange, but when it's just me against an opponent, the rest of the world and all my problems fade away. Nothing matters except to defeat this one person in front of me. It's kind of terrifying, actually, how easy it is to just fall into the rhythm of it.

Lyssa paces the rim of the circle, her feet dancing along the chalk. It would be so easy to charge, to try to get her to step back, take a step out of bounds, and end this.

But that's exactly what she wants.

So I wait for her, in the middle of our ring, my swords poised. The sounds of the crowd are nothing but a hum in my ears, the buzzing of an insect.

When Lyssa senses that I'm not going to fall for her little trap, she charges.

She's as fast as a viper, dodging first one way and then another—but so am I. We are evenly matched in size and speed. Our swords clash and clang against each other, steel grating on steel as we press and jab for an advantage. We are locked in a deadly dance.

I draw first blood—a shallow scratch all the way down her dominant arm. She hisses at the pain, but her Shield magic heals it in moments. She scores me next, a jab that nearly severs the tendon in my heel, missing only by the grace of Rigrasil. An injury like that would have finished me. As it is, it sliced into a chunk of my lower calf, and I have to leap back, limping, to give my body a chance to heal.

Lyssa presses her advantage, whirling her sword in a blur of steel, hammering at me with her shield as I step back, and back, and back. I can sense I'm close to the edge of the ring, but I need to buy time. Another moment, and my leg will be strong enough to bear my entire weight again, to allow me to launch myself against her.

She whirls to my injured side, a feint, and brings her left arm up to strike from above, a scorpion's sting.

I test my leg—it'll have to do.

I drop Umbra and grab Lyssa's left wrist, ducking and yanking her over my shoulder until she flips over me, landing flat on her back on the sand, the air knocked from her lungs.

And in my right hand is Lux, poised at her throat.

She bucks, trying to swing her sword around, but I've got her arms pinned beneath my knees. It's a move Aleka taught me, and I lean on my knees, driving her elbows into the sand.

She spits at me, the movement digging the point of Lux into the hollow of her throat.

"Yield," I command. My breath is labored, sweat dripping into my eyes.

Distantly I hear a roar from the crowd, but my world is narrowed to this moment—me and Lyssa, locked together.

"Never," she says, fighting for purchase.

She manages to wiggle one arm free and grabs a handful of sand. She lobs it at my face—I turn, letting it hit my back, and lean more heavily on my blade.

A trickle of blood runs down the side of her throat.

"YIELD!"

"I'd sooner die than yield to you," she snarls.

A hand lands on my shoulder. I don't move.

"It's over, Lyssa," Vassilis says, in as gentle a tone as he can manage. "Don't make me disqualify you for poor form."

I stand, wiping the sweat from my face with the back of one arm. I bend to retrieve Umbra—Lyssa is sitting in the sand, head hanging between her knees. She's still second place—but for her, it was first or nothing. A pressure I understand. Were I in the same position, I can't say I'd have as much composure as she does now.

But I've won. As winner, my prize is first choice among the Mages. I allow myself to soak in the moment—Rigrasil's sun, beating down on my skin, blessing me.

And my family is cheering louder than the rest of the arena combined. Aris is beaming, whistling at me, while Wren rolls her eyes and tries to keep Rosie from imitating him. She fails. Rosie mostly blows raspberries, but I can see the joy and pride on her little face. Tekton's too. He's standing beside Adriana, who is jumping up and down with excitement and punching her fists into the air. Aleka gives me a nod and a smile; Ismini is chatting excitedly with Remiel, and Rafael is shooting off those miniature fireworks from his hands.

Their love overwhelms me. For so long, it was just me and Tekton. I never dreamed of having a family again. I'll do anything not to let them down.

I look at Kora, with her long pink hair, her red Fire Mage robe in place of her tan student one. Her face is pale, pinched.

I raise my sword, as is tradition.

Everyone collectively holds their breath.

And I lower it, pointing it at my choice.

CHAPTER 38

When a Mage is chosen, they're escorted to an area under the arena where the claim can be made. It's a private ceremony, between a Mage and their Shield. The Mage can refuse the claim there, if they want—it's embarrassing for the Shield, but it can be done. The Shield can then wait until everyone else picks their Mage and claim any remaining Mage, or return the following year and try again.

Please, Rigrasil, don't let me screw this up.

The tunnel to the claiming area is dark gray stone, lit only by heatless lanterns every few yards. There are banners on the walls too, a silver flame on a white background. The banner of the school, a reminder of the magic we all share through the Book of Silver. A reminder of all those who have trodden this floor before us. My heart pounds with every step I take, the sweat on my back growing cold.

I meet Kora in the hallway.

"I knew this was going to happen," she says softly. In the dim torchlight, she looks pale, tired. She pulls her red robe tightly around her.

"I know," I say, looking at my sandals, scuffing the sand that's been tracked in here. I don't know what to say to her. I should have prepared better for this. I knew we were going to end up here too. I'm a complete bitch.

She surprises me by throwing her arms around me, squeezing me so tight that she nearly knocks the air from my lungs.

I hug her back just as tight.

"I didn't get a chance to tell you earlier," I say into her shoulder. "Your necklace? It saved me. I'd be dead if not for you."

She sniffles. "I hope you know what you're doing," she says, not letting me go.

"Me too," I say, and I steel myself. "Kora ... you're still my best friend."

She pulls back then, lets me go. She wipes the back of her hand across her eyes.

"And you're mine," she says.

"What are you going to do?" I ask.

If she's down here already, it's because Lyssa chose her. I don't really know how I feel about that – Kora, claimed by *Lyssa*? I'd been praying silently to Rigrasil that Kora could forgive me, that I'd do anything he asked. If that meant seeing Lyssa with Kora, for the rest of our lives, well, so be it.

Kora's face hardens. "I'm going to choose myself for a change," she says, straightening. I give her a smile. *I don't deserve her friendship*, I think. I'll have to find a way to make it up to her.

Then she turns her back to me and walks away, head held high, leaving me alone in the dark.

I make my way down the corridor and finally enter a room only slightly wider than the hall. One where my Mage is waiting.

"You don't ever do things the easy way, do you?" Reyn asks.

He's leaning against the far wall, arms crossed, a carefully composed expression on his face.

"That would be boring," I say, and I try to smile.

I'm covered in sand and sweat, dried blood coating my leg. In short, I'm an absolute mess. And definitely the last person he should ever consider being claimed by.

And yet here we are. Remorse over what I did to Kora is curdling in my gut, though I know it was the right choice. Neither of us is meant for battle, no matter what everyone else thinks. I can only hope that someday she'll forgive me.

"People will talk," he says as I approach.

He doesn't say no, though.

Please. My heart is pounding.

"The Roallacan prince, claimed by the Dragon Girl."

"I don't want the Roallacan prince," I say. "I want the healer who saved me. I want *you*, Reyn. And if people talk, well, let them." I move closer.

"I'm not sure how to do this," he says, his mask faltering. There is worry in his emerald eyes.

I put a hand over his heart—it's pounding too.

"We'll find our own way," I say. "Together."

He puts his hand over mine, cool fingers soothing the heat in mine. A trickle of his healing magic turns my fingers blue for an instant, banishing my pain without conscious effort.

"You don't have to accept," I tell him, though my insides are twisting.

If he rejects me now, it's a shame I will never, *never* live down. But if that's what he wants ...

"This is ... just an offer," I say. "An offer to shout to the world with you."

He looks at me for a moment, eyes darting between each of my own.

"When I said I'd shout it to the world if you'd let me, I meant it," he says.

Relief surges through me.

"So ... you accept my claim?" I ask, looking up at him, holding my breath.

"I accept your claim, Delphine Kalla," he says.

Where our hands are joined, clasped over his heart, I feel a pull, a spark. A connection. An ancient, nearly unbreakable bond. I'm acutely aware of his heartbeat, and I realize that no matter how far apart we may be, I'll always, always be able to find him. Claiming Reyn feels like a cool breeze against my skin, a scent of mint and ice, a tingling in my skin.

I'll never have to feel alone again.

And neither will he.

EPILOGUE

We leave the underground chamber hand in hand. My family is waiting for us.

Tekton. Aris, holding Rosie's little hand. Wren. Aleka. Ismini. Adriana. Rafael and Remiel, who I guess finally made it official, because they're wearing matching rings now.

They all exchange somber looks, as if they're unsure how to start. Elsewhere in the courtyard, families are cheering and hugging. I don't see the other Roallacan Water Mages anywhere.

I do see Kora on the periphery, speaking animatedly to some tall redheaded Mages who must be her family. Their voices are all raised, but I can't make out their words from where I am.

Lyssa's family is literally howling. I only catch sight of Lyssa for a moment, her face red and blotchy, before she's hidden behind her pack. So Kora turned her down—Lyssa will have to wait a whole year now, and then compete in the games *again*, unless she wants to take a chance with an unclaimed Mage, of which I expect there are only three—Silas, Eugenia, and Isadora. Well, good luck to her, then. Maybe it'll mellow her out a bit.

I return my gaze to my own quiet group. At my side, Reyn's fingers squeeze mine, cool and reassuring.

"What in all the *hells* were you thinking?" a voice barks at me from across the courtyard.

I turn, already sighing. Can I not catch a break today? Do I really need to deal with him *now*?

Lukas. Great.

He storms over to us, face red and hands clenched at his sides. Behind him trails his Mage, I'm assuming, in a red robe, as well as Commander Markos, who is chatting away with Head Mage Iraklis and laughing over some shared joke.

I grip Reyn's hand tightly, but I do not back down, not even as Lukas stomps all the way up to me and leans over me, like he can intimidate me into changing my mind.

"Reyn, I'd like you to meet Lukas Valorius, Aris and Adriana's older brother," I say, in an impressive attempt at control and civility, though the words are said from behind clenched teeth.

Reyn stands tall, tall enough almost to look Lukas in the eye. He doesn't flinch. Lukas looks him up and down, and snorts.

"My pleasure, I'm sure," Reyn says, but he does not extend his hand to the man. He looks at me instead, quirking an eyebrow.

"A snake, Delphine? Really? What happened to that pretty Fire Mage?" Lukas says, his hands on his hips.

"I've decided to work with Reyn as a healer," I say, tearing my eyes away from my Mage, and my voice only cracks a little.

"Mark my words," Lukas snarls, and he has the nerve to stab me in the chest with one huge finger.

Ugh. He may look like Aris, but no one could ever confuse the two.

"You *will* be a battle Shield, no matter what stupid little daydreams you have at the moment. Head Mage Iraklis will dissolve this bond, and you *will* claim the Fire Mage."

Several things happen then, all at once.

Aleka and Aris are suddenly in between me and Lukas, and a roar like nothing I've ever heard before tears from Aleka's throat.

"*The bond between you shall be as strong as the roots of the mountains and shall never fail, even unto death*," Aleka reminds him, still snarling.

She's fucking scary, even if she is tiny. She's quoted the second law of the Shields—and not even Lukas can refute that.

"*A claim shall be unmade only at the express desires of both parties, and then only after careful consideration and approval by the Head Mage.* Which is me," Iraklis says as he approaches, an easy smile on his face. He nods to Ismini and stands beside Lukas, his pose casual, his tone light. "Does either of you desire that this claim be broken?" he asks us.

Reyn and I don't hesitate.

"No," we say at the same time. Reyn's hand tightens on mine.

Iraklis gives us a fond smile, and I swear the plants in the entire school suddenly all burst into bloom.

"Well then, I would not carefully consider it nor approve it. So that's settled. Come, Markos, and let me introduce you to young Athan," he says, steering the Commander away from us. "Oh, and congratulations on your win, Delphine. You two will make a fine team."

My chest feels warm as I watch the Head Mage walk away—I turn, and Lukas is practically purple with rage. I've humiliated him, but I find I don't really mind.

"*YOU!*" he spits, and he makes a move to grab my shirt, like he's planning to physically haul me out of here or something.

Aris steps in front of me, his right arm already swinging, and lands a blow like a hammer strike to Lukas's jaw. For a moment, Lukas is completely stunned—he doesn't fall, somehow, but he does spit out a gob of blood onto the paving stones.

"You want to quote the Law of the Shields to me?" he says, though his voice sounds thick, and a little unhinged. He jabs a thick finger into Aris's chest. "*Your fellow Shields shall be closer to you than your own flesh and blood. Any evil committed against them is made against Rigrasil himself.* Want to know what the penalty is for striking a tribune of the Ocronian army?"

"You're forgetting one thing," I say, smiling sweetly, which takes Lukas—and everyone else—aback. "Your brother isn't a Shield anymore. He was outcast, so your rules don't apply to him anymore."

"Hit him again, then!" Rafael cheers.

Aris grins and cracks his knuckles, obviously considering it.

Wren rolls her eyes, intent on keeping Rosie from running to her father's side—I guess brawling Valorius siblings are nothing new to either of them. Tekton comes up beside me, as solid as a mountain, and soon there's a wall of people all around me, standing with me. I raise my chin, blink to keep the moisture out of my eyes, and level my best glare at Lukas. Maybe I even let my fangs grow a little, and smoke curl from my nose—just to remind him what I'm capable of.

"This isn't over," Lukas says, though by now his Mage has finally come to his senses and is trying to drag his Shield away from us. "This isn't over!"

"Looks like it's over to me," Rafael says fondly, looking down at where Reyn and I are still holding hands.

Tekton breaks first. Tears are streaming down his cheeks and sparkling in his dark beard, but he doesn't care. He picks me up and twirls me around like I'm still ten.

"I've never been more proud of you," he says into my hair.

I latch on to him fiercely, hoping his tears will disguise my own. *Rigrasil, you really fucked up not giving this man a shift. He's one in a million.*

Adriana gives me a quick hug next. She's a female version of Aris, with her sky-blue eyes and obsidian-black hair. She wears it braided today, twined around two feathers—one striped brown and cream, one gleaming black and red. Hers and mine.

"We're so proud of you, both of you," she says, loud enough for the rest of the group to hear.

Rosie wriggles free of Wren's arms and leaps at me, burying her head in my stomach, which is about as high as she can reach.

"Auntie Del, tell Daddy I'm big enough for my *own* swords now," she pleads, her jade eyes round and wide, and eyeing my gladiuses with open envy.

Reyn can't quite suppress his grin—nor can I. She's ridiculously cute. She's wearing all black, like most of the other Shields—their uniform, in miniature. The effect is made a little less intimidating by the pigtails in her hair.

"Soon, little kitten," Aris says, grabbing her, squealing, under one arm and me with the other. He squeezes me tight, still proudly wearing the leather bracelet I made him all those years ago.

"So, *this* is what your instincts were telling you?" he asks me—but he's looking at Reyn, sizing him up.

Aris is terrifying. Tall, broad, strong enough to tear a mountain apart with his bare hands if he wanted to. And he's glaring at my Mage.

I surprise myself by letting out a low growl.

Aris blinks, then laughs and ruffles my hair. He hands Rosie off to Remiel, who immediately shifts his fox ears, much to her delight.

"All right, then, Del," Aris says.

And he extends his hand to Reyn.

Reyn looks between Aris and me a few times—I am definitely holding my breath—but then he takes Aris's hand in his.

Aris pulls him in tightly. It looks like a hug, but I can see Aris's mouth moving fiercely against Reyn's ear. I can't hear what he's saying, but judging by the pallor of Reyn's face—well, more paleness than usual—it isn't nice.

I smack Aris's arm, warning him to behave.

Aleka gives us terse congratulations, while Ismini gives us hugs and tells me to make sure Reyn eats more. Rafael and Remiel hug us both fiercely—they worked with Reyn in Roallac, after all, during the transition, and the three of them greet each other warmly, sharing an inside joke about some statue in the Soltaire gardens.

Wren is last. She stands out from the rest of us in her black robe. She wears a green pendant around her neck, nearly identical to the stone she gave me, with two plain metal bands flanking it to either side, one big and one small. With her scarred face and the white streak in her hair … well, if Aris is terrifying, Wren is something much, much worse.

Reyn approaches her solemnly, his hair still rakishly askew from Rafael's greeting. She looks him over, eyebrow raised. We all hold our collective breath as the Fallen Prince of Roallac and the Night Mage, the one who brought down his country, size each other up. Wren's glance shifts to mine for a moment, and the furrow between her eyebrows softens. She extends a hand to Reyn, and he takes it without hesitation, like he's afraid she's going to change her mind.

His eyes go wide, and he drops her hand like it scorched him. Wren, meanwhile, only looks vaguely puzzled.

"I didn't … I mean …" he stutters, holding his hand to his chest.

Aris is there immediately, putting himself between them.

"What did he do to you?" he asks Wren, his voice tight.

I'm at Reyn's side just as quickly, but I'm confused. It's daytime —Wren has no magic.

"I … um …" Reyn says. He takes a deep breath, glancing at the ring my family has made around him. "I'm a healer. Sometimes when I touch someone, their magic reaches back out. I just … didn't expect to feel magic when I touched you, not during the day."

Reyn looks at Wren, then pointedly at her stomach. Aris has gone as still as stone.

Wren flushes and twines her hand with Aris's.

"It's so early. I wanted to be sure before I told you," she says softly.

Aris shouts, grabbing Wren around the waist and holding her to him like he's afraid she might shatter. We all pretend not to notice the tears on his face.

Wren gives Reyn a tired smile, still trapped in Aris's arms.

"Did you … I mean, could you tell anything?" she asks.

"Only that they're healthy, and strong," Reyn says, a smile tugging at one corner of his mouth.

"*They?*" nearly everyone shouts at the same time.

"Twins," Reyn says. "Boys."

Rafael cracks up, throwing his head back and howling with laughter. Aleka joins him. Some of the color fades from Wren's face, the dark scar on her cheek showing up vividly. She mouths the word *two*, but no sound actually comes out.

But then Aris is cheering, and so is Adriana, and soon everyone is smiling and hugging and slapping Reyn on the back. Rosie is clapping and twirling, singing "I'm going to be a sister!" loudly and off-key.

"Welcome to the family," Tekton says, clapping one big hand on Reyn's shoulder.

Reyn twines his fingers with mine. He gives me a shy smile, like he's a little uncomfortable, like he can't quite trust what he's hearing.

So I pull his face down to mine and kiss him, in front of the whole world, to prove to him that he can.

THE LAW OF THE SHIELDS

- **First law**: Protect your Mage—above country, blood, and all else.
- **Second law**: The bond between you shall be as strong as the roots of the mountains and shall never fail, even unto death. A claim shall be unmade only at the express desires of both parties, and then only after careful consideration and approval by the Head Mage.
- **Third law**: Your fellow Shields shall be closer to you than your own flesh and blood. Any evil committed against them is made against Rigrasil himself.

THE GODS

- **Rigrasil**: father of the gods, and the god of day. He created the first Shield, Odall.
- **Caladrius**: the god of night, often felt to be a balance against the elemental gods. He has gifted a single person with his own magic – Verena "Wren" Harker, the Night Mage.
- **Aenon**: the god of water, patron of Water Mages
- **Helene**: the goddess of wind, patron of Wind Mages
- **Cephus**: the god of earth, patron of Earth Mages
- **Ignatius**: the god of fire, patron of Fire Mages

DEFINITIONS

1. *Mage* – a person with elemental magical powers (earth, wind, fire, and water). They undergo two years of training in one of Estana's magic schools before being claimed by a Shield, who acts as their bodyguard and partner for life.
2. *Shield* – a person gifted by Rigrasil, father of the gods, with strength, endurance, and healing beyond what an ungifted person has. They can each also shift into the form of a predatory animal. Most commonly wolves, big cats, bears, hawks, and eagles. They train for two years in one of the magic schools before competing for a chance to claim a Mage.
3. *Forsaken* – a person who should be a Shield, and is gifted with healing and strength, but does not shift into an animal. It is meant as a slur, one of the most offensive things a Shield can be called.
4. *Ungifted* – a person born without magical powers; neither a Shield nor a Mage

CHARACTERS

1. **Adriana Valorius** – a Shield. The fifth-oldest Valorius sibling. Her shifted form is a hawk. She works as a King's Messenger.
2. **Aleka Relloti** – captain of Estana's city guard. A Shield. Her shifted form is a large brown bear. Her claimed Mage is Ismini. She is the adopted aunt of Aris and Delphine.
3. **Aris Valorius** – a Shield. His shifted form is a white tiger. His claimed Mage is Wren. He trains Shield students at the Aeturnus School. At the Battle of Soltaire four years ago, he killed his friend Caelus and was outcast from the order of Shields.
4. **Dimitra Rose "Rosie" Valorius** – daughter of Wren and Aris. A Shield. Her shifted form is a snow leopard.
5. **Head Mage Iraklis** – the Head Mage of all the Estana Mages. A powerful Earth Mage. Headmaster of the School of the Silver Flame.
6. **Ismini** – a powerful Earth Mage. Her Shield is Aleka. She helped train Wren when she first discovered her powers. She is the adopted aunt of Delphine, too.

7. **King Leonidas** – ruler of Estana, and friend to Wren and Aris.
8. **Lukas Valorius** – a Shield. The second-oldest Valorius sibling. His claimed Mage is Arion, a Fire Mage. He is an assistant to Commander Markos.
9. **Myron Valorius** – a Shield. The third-oldest Valorius sibling, and governor of Raverra.
10. **Rafael** – a Fire Mage and friend of Wren and Aris's. He helped train Delphine before she started at the School of the Silver Flame. He works in Soltaire training young Mages.
11. **Rea Valorius** – a Shield. The youngest Valorius. Her shifted form is a lioness. She recently graduated the School of the Silver Flame and was assigned a position with her Mage in the King's Navy.
12. **Remiel "Remy"** – a Shield. His shifted form is a fox. He was a spy for King Leonidas before meeting and claiming Rafael. He works in Soltaire with Rafael.
13. **Shield Commander Markos Drusus** – the aging commander of Estana's Shields.
14. **Spyridon Valorius** – a Shield. Aris's oldest brother. His claimed Mage is Stathis, an Earth Mage.
15. **Tekton** – a forsaken. Delphine's uncle. He's the Head Master of the Aeturnus School.
16. **Verena "Wren" Valorius** – the Night Mage, the only Mage blessed by the god of night. She and Aris were kidnapped by the Roallac Queen, Evanthia, four years before this story takes place. Delphine helped free them – and Wren destroyed the city. Now, Wren lives in Aeturnus with her claimed Shield and partner, Aris, and their daughter, Rosie.

TRANSLATIONS

Alis volat propriis—She flies with her own wings.
Luceat lux vestra—Let your light shine.
Dum vivimus, vivamus—While we live, let us live.
Vires, honos, fides—Strength, honor, faith.
Mea diva – my goddess

Tēcum lūdere sīcut ipsa possem,
et trīstīs animī levāre cūrās!

From Catallus 2, by Gaius Valerius Catallus, translated by *Wikisource* as:
"If only I could play with you as she does,
and relieve my soul's sad torments!"

Catullus 2, by Gaius Valerius Catullus

Passer, dēliciae meae puellae,
quīcum lūdere, quem in sinū tenēre,
cui prīmum digitum dare appetentī
et ācrīs solet incitāre morsūs,
cum dēsīderiō meō nitentī
cārum nesciŏ quid lubet iocārī
et sōlāciolum suī dolōris;
crēdō ut tum gravis acquiēscat ardor.
Tēcum lūdere sīcut ipsa possem,
et trīstīs animī levāre cūrās!

1. Thomson DFS (2003). Catullus: Edited with a Textual and Interpretative Commentary (revised ed.). University of Toronto Press. ISBN 978-0-8020-8592-4.

ACKNOWLEDGMENTS

I originally intended this to be a novella. Clearly, Delphine and Reyn had other plans. Their story got away from me and ended up nearly three times longer than anticipated!

As always, thank you to my husband, who is essentially the most supportive person you could ever possibly imagine. From making me lattes to beta-reading each novel, to taking the kids to the park so I could write, to being my inspiration—to say thank you seems a poor effort compared to everything you do for me.

To my author bestie and alpha reader K. L. Hester, for your unflagging support and help. To my wonderful beta readers—Amber, Allison, Michelle, Courtney, and Alexia. Thank you for your encouragement and also for making sure the masked ball did in fact have masks. And to my reviewers — K. L. Hester, S. E. Wendel, L. B. August, and Elayna R. Gallea — a million thanks!

For the Badass Book Club, my ARC team (especially Jeanette Queen, Riniya, Brianna, and Amanda, who have been with me since the beginning!), and the readers who have read and loved these characters—you are the reason I keep writing. Thank you from the bottom of my heart.

To my editors, Ben and Leonora—I have learned so much from you over the years. I deeply appreciate the care and consideration you give to my books.

To my cover artist, Liz—I wanted something different for this book, and you exceeded my expectations. I cannot thank you enough!

For my cartographer, Sebastian—you never fail to impress me with your attention to detail and amazing artwork. Thank you for bringing their world to life—again.

About the Author

E. M. Leander lives in the American South with her husband, two children, and two fluffy cats. A life-long lover of all things literary, when she's not spending free time with family, she can be found devouring books and coffee in equal measure.

Learn more at: http://www.emleander.com

Also by E. M. Leander

"Game of Gods" trilogy

- Wren and the Tarnished Tiger
- Aris and the Obsidian Door
- The Immortal Scales

"Space Camp" series

- The View from Ganymede
- Daughters of Jupiter

www.ingramcontent.com/pod-product-compliance
Lightning Source LLC
Chambersburg PA
CBHW020247030826
48979CB00030B/2640/J
9798990466616